BALLAD

OF

NIGHTMARES

Jack Whitney

For Leighann

Thank you for being there from the start.
And thank you for reminding me to write the fucking story, no matter
how scary or dark it might seem.

Everyone has a story, and they all deserve to be heard.

Triggers

Please be advised.

Some of the issues discussed in **Ballad of Nightmares** may trigger or provoke an uncomfortableness or solicit feelings of remorse and guilt. This book might make you question your sanity. It might make you question your morals. It might make you look at death differently. After all, your main character is Death himself.

The following are potential triggers to be aware of:
Death, blood, manipulation, violence, murder, suicide, suicide stories, moments of horror, ghosts, demons, as well as brief mentions of child death, self-harm, sexual assault, and abuse.

Ballad of Nightmares also contains graphic sexual activities, including mild BDSM. No acts in this book are in any way meant as a guide to exploring sexual fantasies or to give suggestions (especially since one of these persons is Death, this is a fantasy world, and Death literally plays with the edge of life. This is not something to be taken lightly). *Do not* try these acts at home, and instead do your own research if you are curious about the world of BDSM. There are a lot of resources out there.
Please be safe, and remember aftercare.

The following are the activities to be aware of:
Blood play, mild degradation, praise, pain, bondage, breath play, spitting, fantasy mental manipulation, and mild dubcon (chasing/fighting).

With all of that being said, this book, at its core, is a romance. Please keep these triggers in mind as you read, and as always…Enjoy.

Once upon a time, there lived a shadow.
An ancient shadow of rage and sorrow.

He lived his long days in peace, using his gifts to help those in need.
He gifted reprieve. He gifted new life.
He let them see darkness and fed on their scares.
Until one day, his secret was discovered.

His shadow was trapped. His will, now theirs.
He was given a body and shed of his cares.
They called him Death. They called him Demon.
They called him Reaper.
And soon, even the kings began to fear what he could bring them.

They locked him away, calling only on him to do their deeds.
To shed blood and torture and spread darkness through the
kingdoms.
Centuries passed. Kings died. But Death remained, biding his time.
Vengeance and greed ate at his insides.

He desired his peace. He desired his mind. He desired his will.
So he built his army in secret.

He found his way out. He found his way home.
And he brought all his misfits with him.

To Shadowmyer, we wait. For revenge and blood.
But Death will atone for the things he's done.

When ravens fall, he'll meet his match.
And to his own grave, she'll lead him.

Part One

When Ravens Fall...

Chapter One

Death drowned his victim beneath a lullaby of pattering rain against the diamond-paned glass.

Lightning crashed into a great oak tree outside, and in the white light, he caught a glimpse of his shadowed wings against the jagged stone wall.

Stalking him. Taunting him. Reminding him.

Fingernails stained with blood; he washed his hands of the scarlet stick in the sink at the back of the sunroom.

Sunroom.

He wondered if it was still considered such a room as the sun had not broken through the clouds of Shadowmyer in hundreds of years.

His gaze lifted out the hazy window. Cobwebs had settled in the corners of each pane over the years. Old vines crawled up the outside like arms reaching for the sky, desperate for air and life and warmth from a golden star now shadowed from existence.

The man he'd just slain had been close to expiration. Sometimes people begged for death, and he obliged when he could. Suffering, though perhaps he did enjoy it on occasion, was not for those who had accepted their end. Those were the beings he chose to gift such a reprieve to.

Deaths of this nature kept him awake at night. To watch the brightness leave the eyes of someone who had pleaded for it. He wondered what that was like. How one could be so ready for a touch that would take them from the world and into total darkness—an abyss of beginnings and no escape.

His palms sank onto the rim of the ivory sink, knuckles whitening against the porcelain, and a heavy breath evacuated his lungs as he hung his head.

It was festival day.

Death's Day.

His day.

People would paint their bodies and parade into the old town just outside his cemetery and castle gates to celebrate the night Death saved them. The night Death conquered legions of obsidian and embers, and had salvaged this kingdom from the rest of the Myer and Moors.

He picked up the white cotton towel from the bench and began wiping his hands.

Peering over his shoulder, he watched as the shadows enveloped his victim's body as fog swirled over the tile floor. Danbri Sutton had been the man's name. He'd fallen ill to a vulgar sickness some months prior, and since diagnosis, he'd pleaded for death to take him every night.

Perhaps he'd allowed Dan to suffer a little longer than he should have.

His hands were nearly dry when the shadows receded, leaving only the blood-stained white rose petals and dying green leaves on the messy floor that had been there before he'd come to do his work.

Thunder cracked, and the glass trembled in its wake.

That was when he heard a loud purring noise from the rafters, and the noise instantly brought a smile to his lips.

"There's my girl," he said upon finding his black cat, Luna, rubbing on the wood from the jointed beams, her front feet not even touching. He shook his head as he reached up, and she practically fell into his arms. He held her and gave her head a scratch for a few minutes, letting her purr calm his heart back to normal.

Rolfe, his security detail and his friend, had black coffee ready for him in the kitchens.

"Morning, boss," Rolfe mocked upon Death's entering. But he didn't respond as he sat Luna on the table and started picking again at the dried blood under his nails. Rolfe placed the matte black mug on the table in front of his chair. Luna gave a low warning, and Rolfe, being the deathhound shifter he was, bared his teeth in response to the taunting feline, but they didn't press further.

"Didn't grab the paper before the rain started," Rolfe said after clearing his throat. He straightened and pressed one hand in his pocket before bringing his own coffee to his mouth.

"Sounds like grounds for dismissal, Roll," Death replied, lips lifting at the corner as he washed his hands again.

"I'll pack my things, Your Majesty," Rolfe bantered back.

A quiet moment passed, only the noise of the running water and sloshing of his hands beneath it sounding louder than the rain on the windows.

"Who was it?" Rolfe asked, tone more solemn this time.

Death turned and leaned his hips to the counter, leaving his hands wet as he gripped the edges at His sides. "Sutton," he replied, wisping bang falling over his left eye.

Rolfe cursed. "Damn shame," he muttered. "He was a good man."

Death pushed off the counter, bare feet brushing the cold wood floor as he stepped to the table and grasped his coffee. "He was," he agreed. "I let him suffer too long. He deserved better."

"His family might disagree."

Though the comment only made him feel a little less shitty.

"To Danbri," Rolfe said, raising his mug.

Death lifted his own in response.

The first touch of coffee on his tongue brought a sigh to his lungs. Lifting the weight of his morning off his shoulders and bringing him peace with the mere hot bean water. He'd often contemplated over the years how this small plant held the power that it did, how it calmed and surged his being in all the ways needed.

Witches.

Luna sprawled out in the middle of the table, her deep purrs sounding with the rain pelting against every window around the house.

The newspaper had a grand article in it about Death's Day, including a large photo of the castle and cemetery gates. It looked like someone had tried to break-in again to grab a photo of their King. There was a piece titled 'Will the King appear on Death's Day?' held at the bottom of the page. He skimmed over the writing, catching questions and speculations of what He looked like littering the paragraphs.

He kicked his feet up on the tabletop as he flipped to the second page.

"You should check the front lock," he told Rolfe, who was now eating cereal.

Rolfe paused mid-slurp, brow quirking. "Should I?"

Death fluttered the front page and pointed to the article with the photo of the foyer with his middle finger. Rolfe practically threw the spoon in response.

"Fuckers," he mumbled. "Knew I smelled something off the other morning. I'll change it out before the celebrations start. I was hoping to have a little fun tonight."

"With a strange being or your hand?"

"Probably both," Rolfe replied, almost making Death smile. "What about you?" Rolfe asked. "Will you be going as yourself or that shit little demon you doodle on your face every year?"

"Shit demon doodle," he replied. "You?"

"I don't need makeup to make me look scary," and the response made Death's head tilt around the paper at his friend.

Rolfe wasn't wrong. Rolfe had a rugged stature and quality about him that struck fear into most. His hair was longer on the top and he kept it swept back, buzzed on the sides with tattoos behind his ears. His handlebar mustache and neck-length beard were thick cinnamon-brown despite the darkness of the brunette hair on his head. He was always wearing snug black t-shirts, and the fabric strained against Rolfe's thick tattooed arms.

What stuck out the most about Rolfe, though, were his ice-blue eyes. They were round and wide and made him appear as though he could control one's mind if he stared for too long. Which, Rolfe had been known to do, especially in his other form.

Death knew Rolfe's co-hort, Millie, would have another plan for him. She would probably make Rolfe sit and have his makeup done after she finished doing His own 'demon doodle.'

He turned back to the paper just as Rolfe started slurping on the almond milk again. An article on autumnal season plants caught his eye at the bottom of the last page beside the advert for the farmer's market hours. He folded the newspaper in half and took another gulp of his coffee as he read.

Something thudded against the window.

Death flipped down the corner of the paper and locked eyes with Rolfe.

"On it," Rolfe said as he stood.

He turned back to the paper and continued reading, confident Rolfe would take care of whatever it was outside. And if it was an intruder or photographer, He was sure Rolfe would have a little more morning fun than he wanted to know about.

"Hey, boss, you may want to look at this," Rolfe said as he stuck his head back inside the door.

Death scowled over the paper, but upon seeing Rolfe's widened gaze, his comment stuck in his throat. "What's wrong?"

"It's the ravens."

The sentence sent his chair legs hitting the floor. He bolted up and pushed past Rolfe to the windows overlooking the gardens.

Ravens and crows littered the sky in a frenzy. Swirling and diving in the pounding rain.

One thudded into the window directly in front of him, and he jumped back. A sink befell his chest as he stared at his white roses being torn apart.

When ravens fall, he remembered from the text.

The shadowed snake tattoo around his throat tightened for the very first time, constricting his airways enough that his eyes fluttered. He craned his neck in an attempt to stretch out the feeling and pressed a hand to the glass.

"Extra patrol teams on the grounds tonight," he told Rolfe. His friend's perplexed gaze met his, and he finished with, "Someone is here."

Death didn't settle in the kitchen upon his return, only going back to fill up his coffee and take the newspaper upstairs to his study. He needed to look through his emails before his assistant, Millie, arrived.

Luna followed him.

When he reached the top of the stairs, he heard as Rolfe turned the connected speakers on throughout the home, blasting the stuffy air with the beautiful sound of heavy metal music.

His emails mainly were from Millie. He'd kept his true identity secret for centuries now, and took his meetings in the darkness of his office on video chats. As he read through her notes—which were mostly unorganized—he took a piece of paper from the printer and began folding it up into a plane.

"Hell-*ooo!*" an impatient voice echoed from the foyer over the loud music.

Millie.

He didn't bother taking his feet down from his desk as he tossed the paper airplane into the air and sent it flying in a downwards spiral over the second-floor banister.

He heard laughter come up the steps, a delightful yip carried over the stuffy air, and then Millie pressed the door open, not bothering to enter yet. He recognized the toy in her eyes that morning and wondered if she had found herself bound and kneeling at some woman's feet the night before.

Millie leaned with a stretch against the doorframe, hand sliding up the wood, blonde hair falling over her wide blue eyes and out of the long braid over her left shoulder. "You rang, master?" she mocked in a sultry whisper, knee wrapping on the frame.

He eyed her in the light bouncing off her hips and waist dip. One of his favorite parts of every morning was teasing her and hearing about her exploits from the night before after she gave him the morning updates. Millie enjoyed her time at night, and sometimes he could hear the women she held on their knees as they begged for a god to end them. But Millie would bring them back with pleasure they had only ever dreamed of. He wondered how many times a week she showed off her demon form, let her black curled horns wrap into her long blonde hair or let her tail do mischievous things.

A whispered, coiled shadow slipped across the room and tickled under her chin, making her eyes roll with the coolness of the dark breeze. She smiled, and he felt his shadow flex its tattered wings behind him in the silhouette from the firelight on his desk.

"Morning, Milliscent," he said finally, using her full name to pull her out of his spell.

Her sinister gaze dropped with an eye roll to the back of her head, and she pushed off the door. "Tease," she muttered. "You know how much I like the cold shadows."

"You're late," he said.

"Fuck of a celebration going on outside already," she told him, throwing her purse in the chair. "I had to wheelie through the front gates to get people to move." Her grin flashed. "Such beautiful screams."

He settled more in the chair, hands landing in his lap as he surveyed her. "And this is different from every other morning when you... what, exactly? Ride in calmly?" he asked, voice dripping in sarcasm.

But Millie ignored him as she stalked around to his side of the desk and scooted herself onto the top, one leg exaggeratedly crossing atop the other, exposing her upper thigh.

He reached out and toyed with the hem of her dress. "You could always stay here," he told her.

"And listen to Rolfe's snores or hear your victims screaming every night? No, thanks," she said, peering over at his computer. "Are you actually reading my emails?"

"You're late," he repeated.

Millie smiled coyly and shifted. He watched her in stillness, his shadowed wings flicking at the tips and following his even breath. Within a few seconds, she was spread eagle in front of him, and then she leaned forward, her breasts spilling from the top of her black dress as she said, "What are you going to do about it, *Daddy*?"

The umbra trickled the floor, warping and swirling over the decadent ornate rug and the legs of the grand oak desk, slowly curling up and up the dimming room. Those shadows reached her toes, her ankles, her calves—

He lunged in a snap and grabbed the back of her knee and her face simultaneously. She struggled against the bindings suddenly around her wrists, her throat. Papers flew. Her phone crashed to the floor, and she kicked, but his grip only tightened.

His increasing grasp was enough to make her words stick in her throat. He had her cheeks pinched between his fingers, nails digging into her flesh and drawing blood from both her leg and her face. Millie's knuckles whitened against the edge of the desk with every involuntary whimper as he stilled just an inch from her face. Fear and hunger flashed in her eyes, and he knew his own gaze had turned scarlet in the lightning strike—an action that he knew she would be grinning about the moment he let her go.

"Updates, *Milliscent*," he hissed in a growl that were it anyone but her, their fleeting pulse would have sent his cock twitching.

Millie swallowed, and he watched her breasts heave, her eyes flutter, as she replied, "Yes, my King," in a single breath.

The tension eased just so in his fingers, and then stroked her cheek, knuckles softly brushing over the red bruise left behind as he scanned the damage left behind.

"That's my good girl," he whispered, flicking her chin before letting her go.

Millie rocked off-balance, blinking furiously and coming back into herself as the amber lights overhead brightened once more. He stood while she took a moment to collect herself, and he didn't miss the sight of that delighted smile spreading over her lips when she sat herself in his chair to take over.

"Who needs coffee when your boss makes you bleed upon walking in the door?" she said with a wink.

His amused gaze danced back at her briefly, lips lifting, before he then focused his attention out the dingy paned window.

"If you were my type, I'd be on my knees begging you for more," she continued, moving into his chair to better access the computer. "Okay, there's a meeting today at noon. You'll need to be on the chat for this one, and I'll go uptown to be in the room. It's about exporting goods to Firemoor. Since that bitch infiltrated and cut down their king, the entire nation has been in chaos. Not to mention what's happening in the Spine. At least they are being peaceful about asking for help. Damien says they're rebuilding well."

He cursed the mention of Firemoor, the riots that were happening within it since the woman all the nations had dubbed as 'The Tower' had infiltrated their monarchies and murdered their kings. As for the Spine... they were Shadowmyer's closest neighbor. A small, elongated territory whose king had also been taken by The Tower. He had sent some supplies through to them before as one of his own demon army commanders, Damien, was so well known within its streets.

The other kingdoms were falling like flies beneath her, and he silently smiled every time he heard it happening, even with Millie condemning this woman every time her name came down the horn.

"We have another meeting at three," Millie continued. "I'll come here for that. It's with Damien. He wants to chat about upcoming plans for his legions."

"Cancel the meetings," Death said without looking away from his garden.

"But—"

"Millie." His gaze shot in her direction with a snap, and Millie nearly snarled.

"You're making a mistake..." she muttered in a sing-song voice, now typing away on the keys a little more forcefully than before.

"Damien is handling our people in the Spine fine," he said. "They just need to continue helping the people rebuild. As for Firemoor... my position hasn't changed."

"I still think you should take the meetings," she mumbled.

"Did you notice the ravens on your way up?" he asked.

"I noticed the crows dive-bombing some graves," she answered. "Why?"

When he didn't respond immediately, the noise of the tapping keys went amiss.

"Sam?"

Sam.

The name everyone knew him as. Sam, the artist.

It was never Samarius or Cain or King Arius or even Death.

Always Sam.

And he liked it that way.

"Do you remember the poem from one of the witch texts," he began, "from before the last war when the covens were on every corner. About Death."

"'*Death meets his match when ravens fall,*'" she recited incorrectly. "That old poem?" She rolled her eyes and slumped back in the chair. "You can't be serious, Sam. Do you really believe it?"

"I think we'd be stupid not to take precautions," he said.

Millie huffed out a breath and sat back up to type again. As she continued giving him updates for the day, Sam couldn't help his wandering mind. Of what exactly could be his match and why today. Why on his day.

"—but the big question is," Millie finally said as she dragged Luna into her lap from the floor. "What will the man of the hour go as for his special day?"

Sam glanced back at her. "What do you think?"

"Oh, my King," she drawled smugly, almost spinning in the chair. She picked Luna's front legs up, cuddled her against her chest, and held her so that her paws were in her hands. "I think you should go as yourself."

Sam crossed his arms, smiling at Millie as she moved one of Luna's paws in a growling gesture.

"Leave my cat," he said, though his tone was more amused than anything else.

Millie pouted. "*Ooo,* Daddy won't let us play, Loons," she mocked to the feline. She gave the cat a final kiss on her head and placed her on the desk, where the cat sprawled out, daring someone to touch her exposed stomach.

"You're really worried about this, aren't you?" Millie asked him.

"The ancient witches may not be here any longer, but their texts and prophecies are nothing to brush over. Just keep your eyes open tonight."

"Will you let me paint you in your usual?" she asked as she swung in the chair again.

"That shit demon doodle, you mean?" Rolfe grunted as he joined them, a bag of chips in his hands. He plopped in one of the grand leather armchairs by the desk and kicked his feet up. "Maybe you could paint him something better this year, Mills. Maybe a clown to match his thinking the witch tale is true."

"If you didn't believe it, why did you look so pale when you told me about the ravens this morning?" Sam drawled, to which Millie laughed.

"Watch out, Rollie, he's in a strangling mood." Millie laughed. "Something tells me Daddy Cain is looking to have his own fun tonight," she said before running her tongue along her mouth, brow arching teasingly in Sam's direction.

"Whomever it is will be disguised, if it is even a someone," Sam said, ignoring her banter.

"Or some *thing*," Rolfe added. "Don't worry, boss," he winked. "Millie and I will keep an eye out."

Laughter threatened Sam's lips, but only a crooked smile came out, and he eyed his friend through his bangs. He knew better than to think Rolfe would be paying attention to anything more than his next victim, as Millie would be too, but he didn't snap back this time.

"It's probably nothing," Millie said. "The old witches were never reliable. Now the new ones…" She sighed back in the chair as a haze took over her eyes. "They're a delightful bunch," she grinned.

"How many witches do you know in this kingdom?" Rolfe asked.

Millie seemed to count them in her head as she laid her head back. "A fair few," she finally answered. "I'm sure they'll be out hunting tonight. Would you like to meet them?"

"No," Sam answered for him.

Rolfe glared and looked like he might throw his chips in the air. "Come on, boss. Might be fun."

Sam's concerned gaze flickered to Millie. "You need to be careful of them," he said. "People know who you are. You think they won't use that to their advantage to get in here?"

"If you don't like them, maybe you shouldn't have allowed them refuge here," Millie said through a clenched smile.

Sam glared, and Millie's unbothered grin only widened.

"You're cute when you're concerned," she teased. "Don't you think, Rolfe?"

"Like a kitten." Rolfe crunched hard on his chip. "Will the claws come out tonight?" he said to Sam.

"Ooo… there's a sight I'd love to see," Millie said. "I do miss the wings. Remember when you would go as yourself to this festival just to watch people bow at your feet?"

"Those were the days," Rolfe drawled.

"Weren't they?" Mille turned to Sam. "Tell me, Samarius… When you find out who it is, or even if there is someone in your kingdom. What will you do? Will you appear to them as Death or King Arius?"

Sam stared out the window, watching the rain as it drifted to a drizzle. "Their final nightmare."

Chapter Two

The three took their motorcycles down to the festival.

They used the back entrance as they always did, ensuring no one caught them coming from the dark castle. But Millie attracted attention like no other. Swinging into old town, she popped her front wheel off the pavement, her maniacal laughter sounding over the crackling fires and conversations of the people already celebrating.

Death's Day.

Sam remembered well the day the Myers and Moors broke apart, and he shadowed this domain from the rest of the world. All he'd meant to do was bide his time in peace, let his demons roam, and report back to him when it was time to strike. In those years, he'd allowed his kingdom to flourish and grow beyond what the other nations were capable of, even Firemoor.

The *righteous* Firemoor.

Sam shook his head at the thought as they slowed their bikes down into one of the alleyways just past the great bonfire, parking outside a favorite basement speak-easy they liked to frequent.

Millie made sure to take a selfie of the three of them before they parted: Rolfe with his rocker hand gesture and tongue out, Millie holding the phone at an angle with one eye closed and making a silly, yet somehow sexy, face with her tongue also hanging out, and Sam... Sam with a rare smile that met his dark eyes, his hair falling lightly over his forehead and eye.

"Sexy as ever, boys," Millie drawled as she looked the photo over, then smiled slyly at Sam. "Boss..." She puckered her lips at him. "I think we should do this makeup more often. Really brings out your... *royal-ness*," she said with a wink.

Sam scoffed at the tease. "Pick a random Tuesday," he replied. "I'll wear the wings."

Her eyes fluttered, knees visibly weakening, like the words he'd just said had her reaching for an orgasm right there on the street. "You keep talking like that, and the witches might have to wait."

Rolfe grinned, his curling mustache hiking crookedly. "Kitty, kitty, wants to play," he bantered.

Millie's brow lifted at Rolfe. "Does the little pup want to play fetch?" she mocked. "I believe I have a tennis ball in here somewhere," she added as she began to rummage through her bag. "Oh, wait, it's just a pair of balls I took from an idiot last week."

She held up severed testicles in her palm, and Sam and Rolfe both winced.

"Come on, Mills," Rolfe grunted in disgust.

But Millie just tossed them up and down in the air, delirious grin on her face. Rolfe pushed off the bike, muttering something about wearing iron underwear from then on, and Sam chuckled as Millie blew a giant bubble in her bright pink chewing gum, which Rolfe popped with his finger.

Millie bared her teeth at Rolfe as he left them, and then she turned back to Sam, leaning on the front of his bike. "And what does his Majesty have planned for his own day?"

One glance around the square reminded Sam of how much he loved this fucking town. The people. The darkness. The nostalgia and old charm... And when a raven landed on the iron fencing behind them, Sam remembered he had a job to do that night.

"Sam?" Millie called.

He turned his attention back to her and pushed off the bike, leaning forward to give her a quick kiss on her cheek. "See you in the morning, Mills," he said solemnly as he started walking backwards. "Get into all the trouble for me."

Millie stared at him a moment, recollecting herself, then quickly blew him a kiss, saying, "You know I will," before pulling out her phone again. Sam felt his smirk growing crooked at the sight of her taking another photo, and he flipped her off with both hands. The phone flashed, and Millie smiled knowingly.

"Goodnight, Sam," he heard call after him.

Parting ways, Sam made his way over to the bar set up in the park.

To the people, he was just Sam. The charcoal artist who occasionally hosted shows in the art gallery on First. Just a simple man, though

19

some thought him one of Death's demons, relatively quiet and reserved. Men and women alike leered at him upon passing, and he let them. Most did not approach, and those that did... he didn't turn away.

There was something about his presence, though, that people didn't understand. Dangerous, and yet they were curious. Wasn't that always the case? To want what should be off-limits or forbidden. Death was one of these obscurities, and the fact that he was their hidden king made it all the more desirous to be near him.

They were all moths to his flame.

There was a bonfire stacked twelve feet tall outside the cemetery gates as there always was, but this year they'd placed a great bull's skull on the scarecrow instead of a deer skull. People were dancing around the fire. Children ran up to it with the straw dolls and placed them in the fire. After a while, the smoke thickened, and Sam played into the illusion as he usually did.

His shadows darkened the ground and wound up the spiral fire. A sign Death approved of their celebration, so the people claimed.

Uptown, they were having a grand parade and street party down main, but Sam always enjoyed the celebrations of old town better. More traditional, closer to home... the party here held a nostalgia that reminded him of why he'd shadowed this place to begin with.

Seeing his townsfolk celebrate at the sight of his darkness swirling in the fire made his chest swell. He loved the home they had made. A realm safe for people who were persecuted in other realms if found out: demons, shifters, and even some human families... over the years, more and more humans had made their way underground through the shadows to find refuge here, spending their last dimes just to find a place where they were welcome. Even witches, no matter how much he didn't trust them, had found a home in Shadowmyer.

A place for the haunted misfits, as Millie had dubbed it.

He took another hit of his smoke and sip of whiskey before heading back to the makeshift bar in the park. A glimpse of Rolfe and Millie flirting with innocents caught his eye by the oak trees. He shook his head, knowing he might have to take himself home that night as Rolfe looked like he needed a night to blow off some steam.

Sam would be hearing the girls beg for death by the morning. A different kind of begging than the kind that generally haunted his nights. This beg would result in a release far more euphoric than the darkness by Rolfe's hand.

Headlights lit up the street. His attention averted to the haze, to the illumination from the lights basking through the whirling smoke. It cast shadows upon the people with their backs turned. The children running. The couples dancing. Those throwing things into the fire.

But what emerged out of the smoke nearly sent him to his knees.

And suddenly, the ravens and crows falling made sense.

Chapter Three

She appeared in a breath of smoke.

Her long heels ticked with each calculated step. Light caught in the gleam of the intricate silver claw on her finger. She held her chin high as she stalked through the crowd, and the people unknowingly parted ways. As though she were bending them to her silent will.

He knew her.

Or at least… he knew of her.

Her name was Deianira. Deianira Bronfell.

This was the woman who had toppled the other four monarchies already, and he knew his own was next on her list.

This was *The Tower*… the name was a play on the tarot card, of course. But she'd lived up to it, to the chaos, destruction, and unsuspecting change that the card signified. He'd heard stories of her beauty and aura—how she could enter a room and command its attention. The only pictures of her had been her hair and that claw, but even those had not been released to the public. He'd only seen them through his channels underground, his spies and demons.

But nothing… *Nothing*… compared to the woman he was looking at now.

That scarlet satin dress hugged every inch of her voluptuous curves and soft figure. The high slit exposed her thick thigh with her steps. Pillowed breasts spilled over the crest of the loose scoop neckline, showcasing the flower sternum tattoo embedded between them. Her black ringlet curls cascaded down over her shoulders all the way to her elbows, a few falling and framing her face over and around her brows. Light pooled over her light brown skin, her flesh soaking it in and appearing to plan to use it as some sort of trap to ensnare unexpecting souls.

He chuckled at that. Those poor, fucking men...

It was no wonder kings had fallen at her feet so many times before. He wondered how many of them willingly offered up their throats to slit. Perhaps begged her to stomp on their neck and hold them down, as he was sure she'd pressed those heels onto someone before.

She was a siren in the moonlight.

An enchantress of desirous evils.

To fall under her spell would mean to kneel before her.

The corner of his lips twitched at the thought. He would kneel... He *knew* he would.

But she'd have to beg him first.

It was the first rule he gave himself before formulating his plan.

He didn't move as she stalked to the same bar he leaned against, and when her gaze landed on him, he didn't bother turning away.

She looked at him like he was a disease. A disease that were she to allow herself to delve in would shrivel her existence within the smoke that surrounded her. An intriguing disease he knew she was contemplating giving in to. Of whether she should allow herself to fall into his poison and consort with someone whom she assumed to be a no one.

He smiled inwardly.

She had no idea who he was.

Perfect, he thought.

Her palms pressed into the bar top, that claw scratching into the wood and leaving a mark behind. "Down, boy," she drawled to him, a smirk tugging at the corner of her lips when she looked him up and down.

His hair fell over his eyes when he smiled at the ground, and then he glanced back up to the bar, where he caught the bartender's eyes. He gave him an upwards nod and circled his finger in the air, signaling he wanted another round.

"And whatever the temptress likes," Sam added when the bartender stepped in front of them.

Her gaze wandered deliberately over him when he stood, a slight widening of her orbs as though she had not anticipated him being so tall.

"Temptress?" she repeated. "Should I be taking that as an insult or compliment?"

Sam resisted a smile, but he didn't reply. His gaze washed out to the bonfire again, and he watched the people dancing around the great blaze directly in front of his gates. He was vaguely aware of her ordering the signature vodka drink of the night when he caught a glimpse of Millie making out with one of the female cemetery groundskeepers.

Dirt was Millie's favorite poison. He'd never seen her with any of the suits from uptown, no matter how much they seemed to flirt with her.

"You know—" came the woman's voice as Sam continued to ignore her, "—most men introduce themselves after they've bought a lady a drink," she finished.

Sam took a sip of his whiskey and let it swim in his mouth a moment, eyes darting to her as she leaned against the bar.

"I don't need your name," he replied, giving her another once over. "Wicked girls like you don't get to have names."

Her lashes lifted, a playing smile on her lips. "Wicked?" She looked like she would laugh as she picked up her drink from the bar top and wrapped her lips around the straw, doe eyes lifting to his.

"Thanks for the drink," she leered before turning on her heel.

And without another word, she left him standing there.

Sam slumped onto the barstool, elbow leaned back on the wood behind him as he watched her saunter away, hips swinging in a show, impressed that she'd given him a single look and walked away like the siren he knew she was.

Son of a bitch.

The mere presence of her was more powerful than he'd thought it would be.

A smile involuntarily tugged at his mouth, sending him almost in delighted laughter, satisfied that she'd surprised even him.

He kicked back the rest of his whiskey as he watched her twirl under the hand of a random man as she walked by the bonfire, and her eyes knitted back over her shoulder in his direction.

Laughter that he'd not felt in a century threatened to leave him as a delirious challenge rose in his chest. He slammed his glass into the counter and paid the bartender for their drinks, then pushed off the stool, predator instincts kicking in like a slap to his face.

Let the games begin.

Chapter Four

My stalker wants to play…

Deianira glanced back his way over her shoulder as another man took her hand upon her passing and gave her a twirl. Her stalker continued to watch her, a smile spreading over his lips and causing his skull makeup to crease in the dimple of his right cheek. There was an air of danger in those dark brown eyes, in the way he watched her like a predator awaiting his prey. The snake tattoo wrapped around his neck moved as his throat bobbed with the swallow of his drink. She noted the tattoos on his hands then, and even through the haze, she could tell they were depictions of roses and vines stretched along his skin. His hair fell into his eye when he looked down at the ground and pushed off the stool, making her realize she'd been staring at him a little longer than perhaps she should have.

Gods, he was pretty.

And she hated him for it.

It wasn't even the typical kind of pretty.

It was the kind of pretty that one *had* to stare at. The kind of pretty that hurt the heart and skipped a breath at the first look. She glanced back at him one last time as she continued to make her way through the crowd, finding him still watching her through downcast eyes. Eyes that were meant to mark her soul and devour her flesh.

Maybe she'd have a little fun later. But for now…

For now, she had work to do.

She sipped her drink as she strode around the outsides of various groups, some huddled together and laughing, a few around great trash bins of fire. All of whom were dressed in some sort of skull makeup or mask. It was her first time venturing into the old town despite her being in Shadowmyer for three days. She'd used what money she had to get a hotel room uptown, but the celebrations in that part of the city felt... forced—more party-like. Here in the town square... that was where she knew the old magik would be.

A few men and women leered at her when she passed through the crowds, inhaling the addicting scent of the bonfires and the muddied ground. And as she reached the edge of the fenced cemetery, she took a moment to look at the castle she had come for.

Her fingers strummed over the cold iron, and she hummed her favorite lullaby about Death himself, the one she'd been taught as a child. The song, the texts said, would summon him if the ritual was performed perfectly.

It was an exaggeration of the witches. She had tried it. Multiple times. Thinking she would get out of all this work if only she could entrap him.

So now she sang it out of habit.

Tick-tock goes the clock, to watch your world fall apart.
Tick-tock, in the dark, say his name, and he'll take your heart.
Tick-tock, bend the mark.
The night goes still. The lightning barks.
He comes for blood. He comes for new.
Run, run, girl. The clock is after you.

The warmth of one great bonfire heated her left cheek as she stared into the cemetery past the great monoliths and vine-covered headstones. Paths wound through the short moss-laden dirt between the stones, creating a maze all the way up to the dark hill where Castle Corvus sat.

She paused and wrapped her hands around the twisted bars, memorizing the brushed iron beneath the pads of her thumbs, and she stared at the singular amber glow coming from the high tower.

Her claw scratched against the bar, creating little sparks.

The castle was smaller than she'd anticipated. More like a looming mansion compared to some of the other castles she'd resided in over the years. Though she supposed, with only the one person residing there and no offspring, a mansion would do just as well as a castle.

She wondered if the king was ever lonely.

King Samarius Cain.

The name rippled over kingdoms as a forbidden whisper. He was rumored to be Death, a reaper in human form that took mercy on those who begged for their ends.

Fairy tales, Ana thought.

Death was a monster who chose favorites.

And yet, she still romanticized the thought of him.

She wondered if it was true, if Samarius was Death. If he was a beautiful monster, who was just as likely to be her salvation as he was her end—not that she knew the difference on some days.

It was the first assignment she was actually nervous and slightly excited over. She had a knot in her stomach every time she thought about one day walking into his castle and meeting him. It raised her blood pressure and pushed her adrenaline.

"I haven't heard someone singing that song in years," came a woman's voice behind her.

Deianira turned, finding a shorter brunette girl with pale brown skin hidden below a purple hood staring at her. The makeup she wore was not of skulls like so many others. On her lids, the woman bore a bright green shadow and exaggerated liner that reminded her of cat eyes.

"Careful, girl," the woman said, lips splitting into a sly smile. "You sing that one too loud here, and you might find yourself beneath the boot of the reaper himself."

Deianira went to respond, to tell this woman that perhaps that was her intention, when the woman turned on her heel and walked past her to where a few had begun running around the bonfire again, hand-in-hand.

"She's exaggerating," a man said from her left.

The man was leaning against the bars a few feet away, his pale blonde hair spiked high, the sides shaved. A dark liner rimmed his eyes, contour on his cheeks to make them more pronounced. He wore a striped shirt and black jacket, along with tall platform combat boots, and the dark colors stood stark against his pale ivory skin. She met the man's bright blue eyes and nearly smiled.

"Is she?" Deianira asked. "Here I thought this the only place in this damned world where it might actually summon him."

The man chuckled but didn't reply directly to her musing. "Are you enjoying the show, love?" he asked her.

His accent wasn't of Shadowmyer. It reminded her more of the men she'd met in Ironmyer. It made her wonder if he, like her, was a transplant in this town.

She sank against the iron bars, mirroring him as she took another sip of her drink. "I am," she replied. She took in the people dancing and circling the fire. A mystical swarm of laughing bodies, all dressed up with face paints.

"You're new here," he said.

"What gave it away?" she asked, amusement in her voice.

His brow raised as he looked her over again. "I think everyone here is wondering what part of the last existence you rolled out of," he said.

"The darkest trenches imaginable," she answered. "The climb was exhausting. I think I'll take a break here."

The man smiled. "My name is Jay," he told her. "Jay Rosen. And you?"

"Ana," she replied. "Ana Smith."

Yes. Ana would do nicely here. She'd been Diana, Nita, Diane, and Ella in previous courts. But she'd always saved Ana for this one. She wasn't sure why... maybe because it was her favorite and the name some of the witches had called her in Icemyer.

"Well, Ms. Smith—" Jay pushed off the iron bars and strode toward her, "—If you find yourself in need of company, a job, or anything else, I own Rosen's Art Gallery on First. You should drop by."

"And why would I take you up on that?" she asked.

"Because, like you, I've also made that climb, and I know how hard it is to start over," he replied. "Come by the gallery. We'll have lunch. Now, if you'll excuse me—" his gaze darted out to a group of people lounging beneath one of the great oak trees in the park, "—I think I'll find a demon to play with the rest of the night."

He gave her a quick wink, and Ana followed his stare. "Demon?" she repeated.

"The only sort of person you want to spend Death's Day with, love," he said, walking backward away from her. "See you soon, Ms. Smith."

Ana watched him cross the street and be welcomed into the circle of beings with great enthusiasm. One man who was standing gave Jay a quick handshake, and Ana realized it was the beautiful stranger from the bar.

She caught his eye as Jay took a seat on the ground, unable to look away from her Stalker's mesmerizing stare. She was trapped in his dark abyss, and for a moment, she didn't mind its constriction. But another man shook her Stalker's shoulder then, breaking him out of his daze with her. Ana resisted a full smile and took another sip of her drink as she pushed off the fence, and she met his eyes once more before turning to continue walking down the sidewalk.

With every step, she felt eyes on her. But she cradled that drink to her chest and smiled at the people that passed by in celebration. A couple more men gestured to try and get her to twirl with them, which she did with enthusiasm, and every time she spun, she noticed her Stalker watching her.

Although, after a few minutes of lingering in the dance and then grabbing another drink, she seemed to lose him.

She stepped back out near the bonfire, intent on simply passing by and settling back in front of the castle, when two men came out of the circle and urged her to dance with them. Although she hadn't really intended to spend her night doing so much, the thrill of the people around her was intoxicating, and she couldn't help but give in.

Around and around they danced. People jumped in and out of the circle, some jumping so close to the fire that it licked at their skin, but they didn't seem to care or mind being burned. They laughed it off with hearty bellows. She swore she thought a small amount of people were flickering between human form and some other creature, and with a few more times of seeing it, she started to think there was some sort of hallucinogen in the smoke.

Masks and face paints shifted in her vision. The noises pulled her deeper into her own mind. Every movement around her seemed to blur. Shadows poured between her and the next person she was trying to keep up with. A dizziness took over, but she remained upright even with the world spinning. Remained in sync with those around her. She was falling deeper and deeper into the umbra's grasp. It tickled her skin and massaged her mind—

Though, with the next spin, her mind broke out of the spell.

She suddenly found herself yanked flush to a rigid body that made her breath catch.

Stalker.

Her heart stammered at the strength of him caging her against his chest. They stood steady a moment, his dark eyes pouring into hers, almost asking permission, and Ana dipped her chin just slightly.

One hand stayed wrapped around her waist, and he brought her other hand up to entwine with his. With that, he gracefully took the lead. Though, unlike the others that had spun her and had her laughing as they practically ran around the fire, her stalker slowed them to movements she hadn't danced since the balls at Firemoor's castle.

So Ana pushed her shoulders back and kept up.

Every push against him sank her further into a trance, and had it not been for the warmth of the fire near them, she would have forgotten the rest of the world. The hand on her back splayed wide, his fingers digging into her exposed flesh. And as she looked into his eyes, she felt her breaths slowing beneath his darkened stare.

"You're late," she declared.

He pushed her into a formal twirl, his vacant arm going behind his back as she spun beneath his hand, and he pulled her flush again. "Am I?" His rasp was a chill over her flesh, but she didn't let him see just how he affected her.

"I wondered if you would let me dance with these other idiots all night and simply stalk me from the edge," she continued. "Or if you would have the credence to show them all what they're truly missing."

"Not to show them what they're missing," he said as he leaned closer. Close enough, she felt his next words hit her. "To show them what you deserve."

"And what would that be?" she managed.

He spun her once and caught her back and thigh before dipping her low. Low enough that Ana let her head extend when he paused them. Long enough that she allowed him full exposure of her neck, her chest… and when he brought her upright, they were so flush that air had escaped the space between. His nose lingered against her forehead, hand on her back squeezing at her waist.

"To be worshipped like the goddess of Death that you are," he whispered against her skin.

Ana's lips lifted. "Show me to him and make it official," she whispered back.

Another twirl, and he caught her eyes when he led her into the next steps. The roaring fire muted in the background with the now echoing laughter of the people she'd mingled with just minutes before. His touch and gaze lulled her to the point that she did not have to tell her feet where to go. She was moving on air, on shadow, his hands caging her and holding her hostage to the sway of the music. And every time he spun and brought her back in, she swore they became closer. His head seemed to bend, making the heat nearly unbearable.

Their hands splayed flat against each other once, and he took his time enclosing his own around hers, tasting every second and watching their hands become one. Ana wasn't sure how that simple act made her pussy ache. Maybe it was because she could see those fingers spread wide on her stomach, on her legs, on her breasts. The images were so vivid that the next twirl caught her off guard, but she didn't stagger.

31

Warmth spread through her extremities to the depths of her stomach and between her thighs, and when he pulled her back in, Ana's breath caught.

Ana had danced with plenty of men, but she'd never felt this. She'd never felt such arousal and tension from music and movement. She was entranced by the fire, the shadows, the rise and fall of his chest against hers. His breath tickling her skin. His hair falling into hers.

"Where did you learn to dance?" he asked, breaking her out of the daze.

Ana's hand traveled from his chest to his neck as she pulled back slightly to see his eyes, her claw gently scratching his skin. "I should ask you the same, stalker," she replied.

He chuckled under his breath. "Sam," he told her. "My name."

"I think I like stalker better," she said, though it was a complete lie. She loved his name. Was prepared to plead his name. Perhaps even say it again as she killed him like she'd done so many other one-night stands.

"And yours?" he asked.

"I didn't think you wanted my name," she teased.

He smiled softly. "I decided I'd like to know the name of the woman responsible for keeping me up the rest of the night."

"Planning a party with your hand already?" she couldn't stop herself from saying.

That quiet laugh skated over her skin and rose goosebumps on her arms. "Maybe I am," he said. "Or maybe…" He leaned closer to her ear. "Maybe I'd like to know what name to pray to from beneath you."

Her lips lifted at the thought of riding his face, and her thighs tightened with the fantasy. "You can pray to whomever you want," she said. "But when you beg, you'll be begging for Ana."

Something sparked in his brown eyes then. "Ana…" He said her name as though he were trying out how it tasted, to see if it was a name he could worship or if he'd have to call her something different.

But he spun her out once, faster this time, and another man grabbed her hand and pulled her into the circle before she could protest.

Reality hit her like cold water. She broke out of her haze, remembering where she was, and even *who* she was, as her feet moved quickly with the rest of the crowd. And when she looked over her shoulder toward where Sam had released her, she found him smirking at her, hands in his pockets.

Ana needed a cold shower.

She relaxed as she joined in the rest of the people for a couple of minutes, but her eyes kept darting around the darkness in search of him, but to no avail.

He had disappeared.

And yet, she could still feel his touch on her skin. Like shadows swirling and warping over her flesh, entwining with her curls, even whispering up her exposed thigh and between them. She blamed it on her vivid imagination, the entrancement of the festival, and the lingering brand of his touch on her skin.

Dirt bikes screeched over the asphalt in the direction of the bonfire. They circled the fire, going faster and faster, swirling the smoke up as they'd done earlier in the night. Ana and a few others paused to watch the black shadows mingle with the bright white smoke and reach for the sky.

A few people let out whistles and cheers at the sight of the shadows again, and Ana clapped a couple of times when the bikes sped off into the night.

One of the men she'd been near asked if she wanted to dance again, but Ana waved him off, smiling as she gave him a nod of appreciation, and then she turned to make her way to the bar again.

She'd not moved ten steps when a hand latched onto hers. The person didn't pull her, just entwined their fingers, and her heart skipped when she found Sam simply looking sidelong at her.

The right corner of his lip quirked when she raised an expectant brow.

"Walk with me?" he asked.

She hesitated, eager to say yes in the hopes that he intended to pull her into some dark corner and fuck her sideways. But she looked toward the bar and then back to him. "You've not brought anything to bargain with," she said. "Why would I say yes?"

A quiet laugh left him, making his hair fall into his face. "Drink. Dance. I believe you're in my debt," he countered.

"On the contrary, I believe I have gifted you with my presence," she said. "Or was it not you that called me a goddess earlier?"

His eyes brightened with her tease, and she wondered if it had been a long while since he'd last played such games. "Okay, temptress," he gave in. "Another drink, and you entertain me with a walk."

Ana paused in fake consideration, unwilling to pull her eyes away from him. The fire swirled in the bottom of his pupils, enticing her with every passing breath.

"Okay."

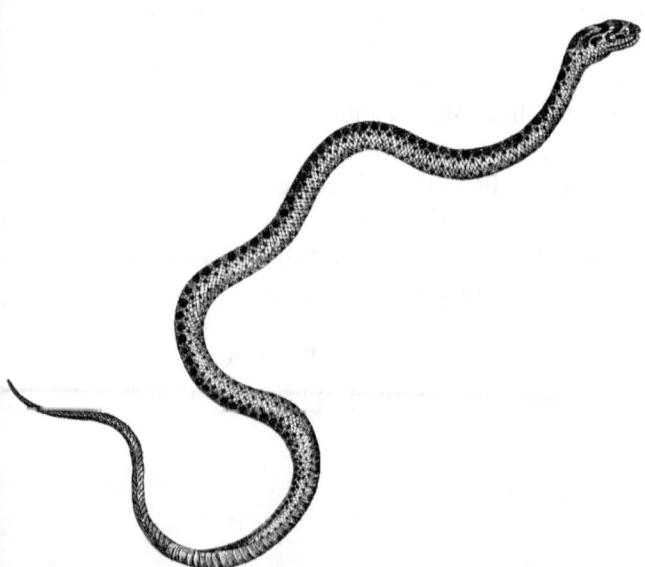

Chapter Five

Sam couldn't believe his luck.

The dance had been a last-minute thought. She'd been so fucking cute playing innocent dancing with those other men that he'd been unable to resist seeing what she would do in the presence of a formal dance.

Deianira hadn't disappointed.

Ana. He nearly laughed at the name she'd chosen to concoct from her true one. It would be easy enough to remember, at least. He'd heard of the others she'd used in previous realms. Diana. Nita. All of them seemed like a different woman. But Ana...

Ana was his to play with.

And what a wonderful game it would be.

He told himself he was enjoying it too much. Feeling her dancing against him had nearly spiraled his mind. The way she moved and pressed and matched his every step. It was cosmic and debilitating. The only reason he'd let her go was that he'd found himself sinking into her depths, becoming mesmerized by those bright green eyes, the indulgence of her hair and body.

He'd used his powers to mute some of the surrounding sounds and push a few visions into her mind, and he'd nearly forgotten to mask his face when he saw her eyes closing with a few of them.

Such perfection.

He wondered if she would also allow him a glimpse into her mind as well.

New drinks in hands, Sam led her down the sidewalk by the cemetery. A couple of his friends ran up to him, their masks on full display or face painted similar to his. Sam chuckled but didn't stop to talk to them, and the others simply skipped on about their night.

She noticed something about the smiles and soft laughs he gave the others. Barely alive laughs, like he was afraid to let amusement dance within his soul. Something seemed vacant from his being, and it intrigued her more than she already was.

"Do you not enjoy the festival?" she asked him.

Sam's head jerked so quickly in her direction that it caught her off guard. His brows and eyes narrowed like she'd said some spell and turned him to stone.

"Why would you think that?" he asked.

"Something tells me that's the first time you've danced in a long while," she said.

"Maybe I don't dance with just anyone," he replied.

"So I should feel special?"

He glanced down at her, clearly confused by the conversation, but he took another sip of his drink and simply said, "What do you do, Ana?"

Ana resisted smiling outright, loving that she'd gotten under his skin. "In this world?" she asked. "Ah… I think I'll be a curator in this one."

"What were you in the last one?"

Flashes of what was just four weeks prior poured through her: seducing higher soldiers and taking control of Firemoor's greatest weapons, then turning them on Ironmyer's great castle fortress. All while she sat safely in the forests of the Spine with a stolen computer and codes, the soldiers that had helped lying dead around her. She still remembered the murky taste of the tobacco they'd smoked and the light of the fire blazing so wild that she'd been able to see it from a hilltop clearing.

"I dabbled in home remodeling," she told him. She noted the apprehension in his gaze as she said, "And you?"

Sam pulled a smoke from his pocket after dumping his cup into a passing recycling bin, and he lit the end of it. His cheeks pulled taut with the inhale, and she watched him curiously, wondering how that light flickering over his skull makeup had twisted her stomach with desire.

"Artist," he replied, blowing out a plume of sweet-smelling smoke. "Charcoals and line-art mostly."

"Oh, it all makes sense now," she said.

"What?"

"The whole brooding, mysterious, stalker thing you have going on," she replied, and when he smiled at the ground and back to her, she swore it nearly reached his eyes. "Do you ever have shows?"

He nodded. "Down at Rosen's on occasion," he said. "Last one was a couple of years ago."

"Nothing since?"

"Nothing worth being inspired by," he answered.

Ana glanced to the castle in the distance, the fog starting to swirl over the headstones. "I think if I were an artist, I'd be inspired by this," she said, pausing at the fence. Her claw scratched the iron, and she caught Sam eyeing it as he stopped beside her.

"What about it?" he asked.

"I suppose to someone who has lived here their entire life, you wouldn't see it," she said. "But the fog here makes me think of silent thunder, how it rolls over the headstones as thunder would roll over dense air and erupt over your flesh, send your heart into a spin. I love the way the fog entwines with the moss in the mornings. And the castle… I've heard rumors of the roses and stained glass. I wonder if it would be worth breaking into the cemetery just to glimpse it."

She did a double-take at the look on his face then. He was squinting at her in confusion. Different from how he'd meant to seduce her earlier during their dance. This was admiration and curiosity, and she reveled at the newness of it.

He leaned over, his hands grasping the bars on either side of her body. Instinct had her hands ready to grab the lapels of his jacket. Her fingers stretched like an invisible barrier was suspended between them. One that had her heart stumbling over itself.

"I think tomorrow I might have something new," he said as he pushed a curl away from her cheek and rested his fingers on her jaw.

She leaned into his touch despite herself. "Calling me your muse, stalker?" she managed.

"Muse... Witch..." He stared at her with intention, his fingers delicately moving over her skin. "Siren... *Temptress*." The last word was practically a hiss, and she sucked in a breath at the press of him against her, the trap of his body on hers. Iron railings dug into her skin, and she pulled her thigh up to his waist to allow him in further.

Maybe a taste.

Maybe that was all she'd give him tonight.

Maybe she could play.

He was a delightful thing, after all.

And why shouldn't she have a little fun?

He was staring at her lips like he might kiss her at any moment, and she was inclined to let him. Her mouth opened and closed, body leaning into him, and then she bent to squeeze herself out of his grasp.

A quiet chuckle left him as she took a wide step back and bit her bottom lip, eyes dancing at him. "I think I should be getting back to my hotel," she said with a tilt of her head. "There is such a thing as too much fun for one night, you know." Her gaze danced over him, letting him see how attracted she was to him, the blow of her pupils, the leer in her straightened posture, and how she twirled her hair.

Sam did the same, his hands in his pockets as he took in the whole of her figure, and Ana made a point to arch slightly and chew on the end of her claw. A single drop of blood trickled from her tongue, and she swore Sam growled under his breath.

"Okay, wicked girl," he practically purred. "So, when can I take you out?"

Ana looked him over again, memorizing the way he looked at her, his lips, his tattoos, his hair, the skull makeup... She took in the broad shoulders straining against his leather jacket, the tattooed hands she wanted to be splayed over her flesh and squeezing her whole. And her lashes lifted to his.

"When you catch me."

His chin rose with the challenge, and he held up something she hadn't noticed in his hand.

Her phone.

Startled, Ana didn't move as the facial recognition unlocked the screen, and then Sam began typing away.

"What are you—"

He extended it back to her, Ana taking it in a snatch to see that he'd put his phone number in it.

Sam smiled that wicked smile that had her knees nearly giving out. "Whenever you're ready to run... *Ana.*"

Chapter Six

There was a deathhound lying at the bottom of the grand staircase inside Castle Corvus.

A gigantic black, shaggy-haired beast sprawled out and gnawing on what looked to be a rib bone of a deer. Its tall, pointed ears twisted to the front when Sam stepped into the foyer, and hollow icy orbs beneath the half-skeleton face met Sam's stare as Sam paused, his hands going into his pockets.

Sam's head tilted as he observed his friend. "Knew you were looking a little grim late last night, Roll," he said, seeing the beast's lungs flare beneath the patch of hair and skin missing over his ribcage. "But you know how I feel about you bringing your rotting carcasses inside."

Rolfe snarled, exposing his fangs with the low growl, and Sam didn't pass up the opportunity to growl back, baring his teeth, his own guttural purr vibrating the air, eyes a glowing scarlet with the thunder rumbling overhead.

Rolfe let out a great sneeze, his head shaking with it, and he rose to all four paws. Tufts of hair were missing over his ribs, half his face, and one of his hips, all showcasing a cagey grey skeleton and void of black beneath. Sam tossed the bag of breakfast pastries he'd gone out that morning to retrieve onto the foyer table where the grand bouquet of blood-covered white roses sat.

Rolfe's nose jutted into the air, sniffing out the wafts of the bakery scent, and Sam just smiled smugly as he pulled off his leather jacket and continued to stride forward until he was directly in front of the beast.

The tips of the deathhound's ears went as tall as Sam's shoulders.

Sam gave him a mocking pat on the head.

"Rolfie, Rolfie," he teased him, tutting his tongue. "Be a good boy and clean up the mess."

Rolfe growled again, tempting Sam to snarl back in warning, and the beast backed down. Rolfe shook his body like he was shaking off water, slowly transforming back into his human form, his skin enclosing over the exposed spots last. Sam lifted a challenging brow as Rolfe cracked his neck and ran his hands through his hair.

"Morning, boss," Rolfe grunted, eyes downcast.

Sam shoved one hand in his pocket, grabbed the bag of pastries, and started down the left hall to the kitchen. "Don't forget to mop," he called back.

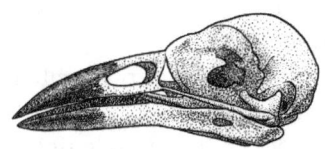

Sam's night after leaving Deianira had been busy, as it usually was. It was a surge of strength for him, to have so many under the spell of hallucinogenic drugs in an attempt to fall deep enough into the void to see Death. Sam liked to play along. He would appear to some of them as they thought Death should look: all shadows with red eyes, sometimes with his wings, sometimes in a hood and cape, scythe in his hand…

He fed on the screams and the people who pleasured themselves to that fear, and he held them at the edge until he could feel their consciousness slipping. Then he would send them back to their bodies with the rush of euphoria that only Death could give them.

Sam was already enjoying his cup of black coffee, Luna lying on the table in front of him while reading the morning news, when Rolfe finally joined them. Rolfe and Luna exchanged their morning hiss, a ritual after so many years, and the black feline went back to purring when Sam scratched her beneath her chin.

But Rolfe didn't go immediately to the counter for his own coffee. Instead, he stopped and sniffed the top of Sam's head.

Sam flinched, gaze narrowing at the grinning idiot, and then flicked his paper when Rolfe strode away.

"Glad to know one of us got a little action last night," Rolfe said gruffly as he poured coffee from the carafe into a large mug. "Who is she then?" Rolfe grinned.

Sam flicked the morning paper again, and replied, "Deianira Bronfell," in a tone so nonchalant that he waited on the demon to catch it.

Rolfe sputtered up his coffee and coughed so hard that he doubled over.

Luna flipped to her feet, back arching with a pronounced hiss, and Sam just continued reading his paper.

"Something wrong?" Sam asked.

"Deian—*fuck me*," Rolfe sputtered, grasping his chest. "Shit—*what?!*"

"The Tower of Chaos and Destruction," Sam said. "The woman who's been taking down—"

"Yeah, I know who the fuck Deianira Bronfell is," Rolfe said as he grabbed the edge of the table.

Luna jumped to the top of the double-door fridge, a low growl sounding from her.

"The fuck is she doing here?"

"I imagine she's here to take her final crown," Sam said like it was obvious.

"Wait—" Rolfe slumped into the seat beside Sam, his brows furrowing. Sam eyed the deathhound as his little mind worked, and he nearly chuckled at him putting together which female The Tower had been.

"She was the one in the red dress?" Rolfe asked.

Sam nodded. "Of course."

"Fucking minx," Rolfe drawled out. "Hope you gave her the ride of her life," he grinned.

"Patience, Roll," Sam said as he flipped the page.

"What's your plan?"

"Not really important right now," Sam muttered, eyes skimming an article on house plants. "I only have one question."

"What's that, boss?"

Sam creased the newspaper in half. "I'd like to know how she navigated the barrier."

"Could be black market traveler," Rolfe said, settling into his chair. "Rogue demon—"

"Council leak," Sam mumbled, and Rolfe stopped drinking his coffee.

The corner of the demon's mouth lifted. "Shadow visit?" he asked eagerly.

Sam drank the last bit of his coffee and pushed his chair back. "We'll wait on Milliscent to get here, granted she hasn't found herself completely indisposed by witches this morning," he said as he stood.

"Fuck the both of you," came Millie's groaning voice as she came down the darkened hall.

"Knew I smelled a tequila rat," Rolfe said.

Millie flipped him off and threw her bag into an awaiting chair. Her wild hair was matted to one side, clothes the same as the night before, her own demon doodle still smeared on her face. As she yawned, Luna meowed at her from the top of the fridge, and Millie smiled up at her.

"Morning, beautiful," she crooned to the cat as she took her in her arms and cradled her.

Sam finished pouring his second cup of coffee and leaned his hips against the counter lip. Millie just looked between them with tired, annoyed eyes as she hugged the purring feline to her face.

"What are you two plotting?" she asked.

"Ask the boss who's bed he found himself in last night," Rolfe grinned.

"Not bed," Sam said, sipping his coffee. "Just a little... light foreplay," he said with a wink.

"Ugh, not in code," Millie groaned. "Speak. One of you."

Sam tilted his head at the blonde before them, and he nudged Rolfe's elbow, sharing the silent notice of the blood still on her cheek and the extensions falling out of her hair. She was a mess, and Sam loved seeing her so disheveled.

Rolfe smirked. "I know," he grunted in response. "Guess the witches weren't so nice last night. You got a little—" Rolfe pointed to his own cheek, gesturing that she had something on her face, and as Millie frowned and started to reach for her face, Sam grabbed her wrist.

He held her stare as Luna jumped onto his shoulder from Millie's arms, and he brushed the red stain off Millie's cheek with the pad of his thumb. The smell of soil and dew and muggy water, combined with the coppery tang of the blood, filled his nostrils, and he licked it off his finger.

"Mmm..." he hummed, a smile teasing his lips. "Is that swamp?"

Millie's eyes flittered in annoyance, her mouth twisting, but Sam just smiled outright and let her go, turning his back to her.

"Deianira Bronfell," Sam said, letting the name hang in the now tense air.

"Die... what—*She's fucking here?*" Millie staggered.

Sam leaned his hips against the counter and took a long sip of his coffee. "Yes."

"But—" Her eyes widened then. "Wait... The fucking bombshell from last night?" she balked. "In the red satin dress? That curvy goddess? *That was The Tower?*"

Sam blinked slowly, chin dipping just noticeably in response.

Millie limped into the chair, staring off into nothingness. "Fuck me," she muttered under her breath. But even as she seemed to have dazed off, her eyes rolled up to Sam with a devious smirk. "She's hot. Tell me you fucked her senseless, and she's now unconscious in the dungeons."

Sam chuckled under his breath, smiling and switching his weight to cross his other leg in front of him. "So impatient," he said.

Millie and Rolfe exchanged a look. "You have a plan?" Millie asked.

Flashes of Deianira's face the night before filled Sam's mind, how she'd played so coy, teasing and tempting him with every long look and sway of her hips. An entire night that had his head spinning with everything he could do to her, everything she could do for him...

"I need you to find out if anyone on the Council knows about this," Sam said calmly.

Millie poked at the toast on Sam's plate that he'd left. "You think someone had a hand at helping her in?"

"I think The Tower is in my kingdom, and I'd like to know if any of these idiots heard rumors of her plans or if they know what she looks like," he replied.

Millie nodded. "I can make some calls," she said.

"Quietly, Mills," Sam added. "If no one knows she's here, let's keep it that way."

"What's your move, boss?" Rolfe asked.

Sam tapped his heel lightly on the floor, arms crossed over his chest. "We take this slow. I don't want to spook her. Lay low until I call." He pushed off the counter then and started down the hall, Luna trailing happily after him.

"Where are you going?" Millie called after him.

"She won't come to me immediately," he called back. "She'll bide her time. Get comfortable. Learn her surroundings. And when she's ready… she'll call."

"That didn't answer my question," Millie said.

Sam smiled as he pushed his coat on. "I'm going to watch."

Chapter Seven

Somewhere deep in the shadowed forest, miles and miles away from where Ana stood at her window taking her first sip of morning coffee, a rogue ray of sun found its way through a muddled swamp of grey clouds.

A thick fog lingered over the rolling hills of crumbling headstones and vine-wrapped monoliths in the cemetery field across the road from her. It hung heavy in the chilled air, snaking its way over the dewy grasses and between the gapes of the obsidian iron fencing. The moisture pressed onto her window and saturated the black and grey cobblestone street with its film.

And on the highest hill, far back in the distance, two arched windows of Castle Corvus radiated an amber glow.

It had been three weeks since the festival. She'd taken those three weeks to get herself settled into life here in Shadowmyer.

Ana pulled her thick looped wool cardigan tighter over her exposed arms as she took another sip of her steaming coffee, relishing its warmth on her lips and pooling in her stomach. The old hardwood floor was cold beneath her bare feet, but she didn't bother putting on more clothing than the wool shell and her scarlet silk nightdress. She didn't dare deprive herself of the luxury fabrics on her naked skin—as she was, for once, feeling its softness against her flesh without the arms of some craven trapping her in his embrace.

It was her own. Bought by her, not out of necessity to bring a man to his death. Not as a tool. But rather as something that made her feel like she had earned this.

She had earned the break that Shadowmyer gave her.

For the first time in her life, she was breathing.

In her month there, she had already decided she loved the place. It was New Age and yet, it felt vintage. Even uptown, there was a feel to it that was more home than any place she'd ever lingered. Or perhaps it was that this was her final resting place, and she was giving herself the space to enjoy a little of life before getting back to her duty.

The density of the fog across the road reminded her of smoke over the moors outside her childhood home. How the great fires had crippled their town to ashes and left the already poor with nothing more than the tattered clothes they'd been wearing—if they were even spared.

The Fire legions had collected those who were left that night, but she and her father had hidden beneath their fallen home and watched as they carted off their friends.

"Shh..." her father had told her, holding her arms as silent tears fell down her heated cheeks.

Every footstep over the crumbling board above made her wince. Trembling beneath the dust shimmering in the light of the cracks. One... two... She'd counted the steps. Memorized the silent wake between each one. The clap of their boots on the wood. The swish of the soldiers' jackets and the squeak of the rubber shoes.

"No one here," one had said.

The man didn't leave. Standing directly atop where they hid as though he could feel their presence. Ana had dared to look up through a crack, and she nearly jumped at the blue eye looking down at her.

A board cracked beneath the weight of the ashen roof, and as a light rain descended upon them, the man turned on his heel and left.

Death's demons had been busy that night.

She had often wondered if the demons that resided in Firemoor had helped the Fire legions that night, or if they had simply stood by and waited to collect.

Death himself had been nowhere to be found. No, he would not take on this job himself, not when he was supposedly held up in a castle and only coming out to play in his own realm.

Samarius Cain.

The name repeated in her head as she took another sip of her coffee and stared at the castle in the distance. Lightning lit up the sky around it at all hours of the day, almost as if Death himself had summoned it.

Perhaps the rumor of Death being the same person as this King was why she'd been obsessed with leaving this kingdom for last. Maybe that was why she'd spent years working her way into other kingdoms to learn the ropes and find the balance of what would make the royals fall.

This was the one she knew would break her, and she was ready for it.

She took another long sip of coffee and stared at the amber-lit windows, waiting to see any shadows pass by, but she never did. In her weeks of staring, she'd memorized the cars and motorcycles of the groundskeepers, and the only vehicle that went further than their warehouse was a slick black motorcycle.

She'd been told by Jay that this was the King's personal assistant, Milliscent Cambridge. Jay had told stories of her chaotic beauty and said she mingled little with the people, though she seemed to have a soft spot for the women who called themselves 'witches' down on Third Street.

Witches...

Ana had perked up when he brought up the word, but she didn't know how much these witches would be in touch with the ancient texts. She wasn't sure if they were of the same covens she had come to call family when she and her father fled to Icemyer or if they were something more. Something darker. Perhaps in the service of Death himself.

Or if they, too, looked to conquer this kingdom.

Sometimes she noticed a black fog hovering around the gates or beneath the iron fencing. Lingering. Making the hair on the back of her neck stand on end. Occasionally, she thought she was being watched. She was sure she was simply being paranoid, but... it felt like the shadows were stalking her. Dangerous and yet, inviting.

More than once, she'd considered going up to them and seeing if they had something for her.

The grey maintenance truck rumbled as it made the turn out of the gates and headed east toward the breakfast diner Ana knew one set of workers went to every morning after their shift. There were five of them on this shift. She'd gone down to the diner two days prior to listen in and get a better look.

These were the people that she would need to get to know first. She'd taken the job downstairs at the art gallery to stick close, still do what she loved but keep an eye on movements in and out, hoping perhaps she would get to know more of the people in old town. She had a feeling that these people knew more than they realized.

And then...

Then there was Sam.

She'd spotted him a few times on his motorcycle going through town, and had even seen him mingling with some of the groundskeepers on overnight shifts, and she began to wonder what he did for a living besides the art. She wouldn't deny that she'd thought about him more times than she wanted to admit, had pleasured herself with the thought of him between her thighs, hated herself for wanting him to pop into the art gallery on the off-chance she might get to see him.

Ugh.

She really hated herself for the last one. She hadn't pined after a person in years. Not since she was a teen and one of the witches had taken her under her wing to show her the pleasures and secrets that they held. She still thought about her on occasion... missed how she'd been carted around as her favored. Maybe it was that she'd liked the attention, the push and pull of punishment and assurance... How her mind and body responded to such things... She had loved her. Of course she had.

Even after she'd killed her.

A knock sounded at Ana's door.

She frowned over her shoulder, but padded her way over to it anyway and turned every lock.

The smell of pastries hit her as she opened it, finding Jay, the owner of the art gallery and now her boss, standing on the other side as he wagged the bag in her face.

"Rise and shine, love," he said with a wide smile.

Ana huffed a quiet laugh and opened the door wider. "Good morning," she said, letting him inside.

The door clicked behind him, and Jay shrugged his shoes off at the door.

She liked Jay. He was eccentric and loud, and they'd become great friends almost instantly when she'd brought her resume in the day after the festival. He'd even offered her the upstairs apartment when she'd said she had no address to put on the payment documents yet.

Jay eyed the open curtains as he sat the bag of pastries on the counter. "Admiring your view?" he asked.

Ana sipped her coffee and turned back to the view with a sigh. "The mystery is mesmerizing," she admitted. "Doesn't anyone here wonder about your king? Who he is? Why he doesn't show his face?" she asked.

Jay shrugged. "A few down at the Daily have dedicated their entire careers trying to figure it out. One, a few years ago, went a bit… crazy. She managed to get inside the castle." Jay wiggled his light brows slyly over his cup, a piece of silky blond hair falling out of the messy bun he'd tried to pull his hair into on the top. "Wasn't the same after. She kept going on and on about shadows and white roses."

Ana remembered the story she'd been told about the white roses. Cameras and reporters had been trying to get a glimpse of the king for years. Going so far as to break into his castle. But every report had said the same thing. Some parts of it were immaculate, and other looked as though they had been vacant for centuries. Cobwebs on every chandelier. Vines growing inside the walls. With polished marble floors and sleek black staircases. Grand paintings in the foyer. Updated fixtures and washrooms the size of bedrooms.

The foyer table was said to always have a bouquet of blood-stained white roses. Who's blood they used to decorate them with, no one knew.

Ana had dreamed about walking in and seeing those roses on more than one occasion.

"Have you ever offered to auction any of the old artworks inside?" she asked. "I'm sure there are a fair few. Could be worth millions. Paintings thousands of years old." She took an audible sip of her coffee, and Jay considered her.

"Yes, except the problem is getting in touch with anyone who would be capable of handling that," he said. "Not to mention, we'd never get inside."

"Oh, I'll get us inside," she smirked.

Jay laughed and shook his head. "Love, you get us inside to look at those paintings, and I'll cut you half the profits. You'll have to swoon the king's Hand first. Though maybe you…" His gaze washed over her, and she rolled her eyes at the smirk on his face. "Maybe you could. If I had those assets, I'd have won every man over already. None of this flirting nonsense," he said with a wink.

"Yes, what is the deal with the men in this place?" Ana asked. "Anyone interesting?"

"Looking to have a little fun, Ana, love?"

"Why not," she shrugged.

"Well—" Jay settled his elbows on the counter. "What's your type?"

There was only one face that came to mind. "What about Sam?"

"Ooo, direct," Jay teased. "Can't blame you. He is one of the more popular ones and also one of the king's demons," he said.

"What do you mean?"

"You can tell those that are his immortals," he continued. "They never age. There are actually quite a few. And then, of course, there are the witches."

"You've said witches to me twice now," she said. "Are they actually witches or just people who dabble in the spiritual world?"

"Actual witches," he said. "Though maybe not as powerful as the ancient ones."

"I wasn't aware Shadowmyer had such paranormally indulgent beings," Ana almost bantered, even if it confused her.

"Love, you'll find Shadowmyer houses all sorts of misfits," he said. "Half the reason why he chose to hide this place, I think."

"How long have you been here?"

"Ah... Seven years, I think," Jay answered. "Met a man that knew the way through using the ditches. Cost me all of my money. Damn shadow dealers. I barely had anything when I got here."

"What did you do?"

"I did what most people do for work when they arrive in Shadow. Groundwork in the cemetery. That's how I met Sam. And he is actually friends with the King's Hand. He's the reason I have this gallery now."

"He paid for this?"

"Sam was looking for a place to showcase some of his works. But not uptown. The Foxhole Gallery wouldn't take any of them. Said they were too dark. When I spoke with him about wanting to rent this building so I could curate some of our lower-class workers' arts... he brought it up to Milliscent. I had the building two weeks later."

Ana sipped on her coffee another moment. "So, Sam knows who the king is?"

"Not sure. I think he and Millie fuck on occasion." Jay shrugged. "They've another friend, Rolfe. Sexy bastard. You would notice them. He and Sam are usually together. I think they share an apartment in midtown. Rolfe is a demon too. He may be some sort of shifter. I'm not entirely positive on that."

"You speak of demons so causally," Ana teased.

Jay laughed. "Love, when you live in Shadowmyer, all your favorite nightmares come true."

Ana chuckled behind her coffee. "Sounds more like a fairy tale."

Jay's smile only widened. "Come on," he said, straightening. "We've got a consult in twenty-five minutes—" he paused to press his hands into the counter, giving her a full once over. "Wear something... *snug*."

Ana eyed the wink he gave her. "Oh? Is there some poor rich soul you need me to seduce?" she teased.

"Oh, no, love," he grinned. "Even better."

Ana laughed him off. "Right. I'll just wear my joggers and a crop then," she bantered as she pushed off the stool.

She glanced back at the castle in the distance as Jay exited the apartment and left her to change, her mind reeling with what her next step would be.

Sam...

Shit.

Of course, the one person she'd found worth being a distraction was the one person she might actually be able to use.

It was a dangerous and terrible idea... and it might even hurt when it came time to kill him...

But she needed more information than what Jay could tell her.

Chapter Eight

Sam was sitting on the roof of the parking garage when his phone buzzed, and he couldn't help the devious chuckle that hit his chest upon seeing the unknown number.

It had been three weeks.

Three weeks of him preparing for her.

He had Rolfe watching her at all hours of the day, finding out if she was meeting with anyone who might have any information on him. He, himself, had settled in shadows outside her new apartment in the late hours of the night and sometimes tailed her himself.

Though he still hadn't figured out her endgame. Why she was so adamant about taking all these crowns and causing an uproar. Maybe she did have a political agenda.

Or maybe she was simply greedy.

Hey, stalker, the text read.

Sam smiled at the phone. *Temptress? Finally, taking me up on dinner?*

Art consult this morning, she replied. *I'd ask you to lunch, but I think that's already covered.*

Where's your job? he asked her.

Stalker, I thought you knew already.

He smiled at her tease. *The shit gallery uptown?*

Rosen's Gallery down on First, old town.

Like it? he texted back.

So far. It's nice. Jay isn't bad to work for. He's pretty funny.

I think I'm jealous, he said, smiling at his phone.

You should be, she replied.

The three dots strummed at the bottom for a blip, appearing and reappearing like she was debating what to say next. Sam decided to reply before she had a chance to.

There's a speakeasy down the street from Rosen's, he typed. *Called the Fountain.*

Sounds nice, she said.

Have Jay show you where it is. I'll meet you there at 8pm

Three dots rippled at the bottom as she typed back. *Is this a date?* she asked.

Scared, wicked girl?

The dots disappeared altogether this time, and after a minute, he wondered if maybe she had gotten called away. He sighed and started to put away his phone, but it buzzed before he could.

I'll be there.

Chapter Nine

Ana changed clothes three times before finally deciding on high-waisted black pants and a black corset body suit that pushed her breasts up, leaving her sternum tattoo like a jewel on display, a temptation that she meant for him to lust after. She pushed her arms through the sleeves of her leather jacket and checked her outfit one more time before she left the apartment.

It amazed her when the moon showed its face at night on occasion. When clouds covered the skies all day, it was weird seeing a parting in them to allow the white light down onto the world. But it was never long. Only brief moments, and she cherished every glimpse.

When she approached the corner of the alleyway to the entrance, she nearly stopped walking at the sight of a tall man leaned against the brick building, smoke between his lips as he also stared up at the moon.

Fucking Death.

She'd seen Sam without the skull makeup a few times in the last three weeks, from across streets or from her window above the gallery, but now, seeing him up close…

Holy fucking demons was he just as sexy without the makeup.

He was wearing a thin long sleeve, V-neck black sweater, though the sleeves were pushed up, showing off the multitude of tattoos on his arms and a few peeking from beneath the vee. Rings wrapped a few of his fingers, one long necklace that dangled down to his stomach. And those fucking ripped jeans and combat boots.

Ana swallowed the dryness on her throat. "Hey, stalker," she said as she drew closer.

Sam turned to her slowly, that stray hair falling out of place over his eye when he dipped his chin and then smiled at her, the right corner of his lips hiking higher than the other side. She noticed then the slight dimple in that hollow cheek, the way shadows clung to his features despite the moonlight.

"Temptress," came his low drawl. A chill skittered her skin at the sound of his voice. His eyes skated over her in a manner that made her feel claimed and taken, as if any other man who might look at her that night would have their eyes burned for even thinking about it.

"I like this outfit," he said, gaze landing on the sheer black lace banding around her middle.

Ana's lips twisted at the way he looked at her clothes. "If you're nice, you might get to see what's beneath it," she suggested.

Sam's lips twitched again, lashes lifting to her gaze. "That's too bad," he muttered. "I've never been accused of being nice."

He pushed off the wall then, and she was grateful she'd remembered to wear her heels, so he didn't tower over her as badly. She may have only been a few inches shorter than six feet, but Sam... Sam's dominating shoulders and aura were a force that made her feel like his shadow could swallow her whole.

Which she truly hoped it did by the end of the night.

Sam squashed the lit end of his smoke and put what was left inside a case in his jacket. "Come on," he said, extending his hand. "Let's see how nice I can be."

"I hope not too nice," she said as she wrapped her hand into his, that familiar warmth settling in the pit of her stomach. "I only said you'd get to *see* what's beneath this if you're nice... I didn't say what I'd let you do if you weren't."

Sam took one slow step in her direction, shoulders rounding over her. "A nice man would take you into this bar and buy you a drink..." He slowly caressed a knuckle over the bob of her throat, sending her hair standing on end... The way he stared at her neck made her feel like he meant to own it, perhaps snap it in half.

And for a moment, she considered begging him to step on it.

"A bad man would push you against this wall and fuck your dirty little mouth until you couldn't feel your throat." His fingers wrapped around her trachea, that thumb and forefinger pressing exactly where she liked it beneath her jaw. Ana nearly smiled at the feeling of it.

Fuck, she'd missed flirting. And Sam was the most delicious treat she'd ever laid eyes on.

Her mouth sagged, chills rising on her skin. "If you mean to scare me, you'll find your hand on my throat does quite the opposite," she purred.

Sam laughed deeply, and the sin of it sent her entire body into flames. The way that laugh sounded as though it had been caged in darkness for centuries. She tried to stifle the way she needed to shift her feet and squeeze her thighs, but she swore by the way he smiled at her then that he knew precisely what that laugh had done to her.

Demon, she remembered Jay had called him...

"Wicked girl... I'm counting on it."

Amber lights hitting the brick walls and iron accents were an atmosphere she craved, and this speak-easy didn't fail to impress. Sam walked them to the bar once they were inside, and he pulled out a stool for her, though he didn't sit himself.

He waved a hand to the bartender as his eyes traveled over her again. "It was a vodka, wasn't it?" he asked.

"It was," she said as the bartender came around.

She watched him coolly order their drinks, observed the bartender smile knowingly at him. Ana glanced at her phone once, then turned it over on the counter before looking at Sam's relaxed figure.

"Why do I get the feeling everyone knows you?" Ana asked.

Sam shrugged. "Most do," he said. "Especially in old town. My friends and I frequent places like this—thank you, Lynne." The bartender presented their drinks with a nod, and Sam handed Ana hers. He paused as she wrapped her hands around the glass, watching her intently.

"To—"

"Ana!"

Jay's booming voice sounded over the music, and Ana turned her attention in time to find Jay walking up with a few friends that Ana recognized from the gallery coming in behind him.

Ana cursed her employer to the end and back. The first chance she'd taken to be alone and get to work, and of course, Jay had shown up. She knew Jay had no interest in her himself, but she wondered if his interest was in Sam, and that was why he'd shown up just minutes after she'd told Jay they would be there.

Sam exchanged a look with Ana, and she speculated if he thought she'd asked him to be there.

Jay came straight up to them, giving Ana a kiss on her cheek.

"Love, I didn't know you'd look this delicious," he teased her before turning to Sam. "Sam..."

Sam shook Jay's hand in a casual way. "How is it, Jay?" Sam asked. "I didn't realize you were back from your travels."

"Got back a couple weeks ago," Jay replied. "Thought it might be a slow season, but I'm better now that I've got this beauty in my employ," he said with a wink at Ana. "Should have seen the deal she made today for Sutton's estate pieces. They're just now getting around to divvying up his things. It's been a shit show. Danbri apparently had more worth than his family knew."

Something dark washed over Sam's eyes then as he took a long sip of his whiskey. "Shame," Sam muttered.

Two more women joined them then, one with an electric blue mohawk of curls and the other with long straight pink hair and bangs, and both women leered at Sam when they kissed his cheek and hugged him.

Ana stifled away the pang of jealousy in her stomach.

"We have a table," Jay said. "Come on. Verity is celebrating her promotion uptown at her bank."

Ana exchanged a look with Sam, who smiled at her. "Actually, Jay, I think we're going to take off," Sam said without losing her gaze.

Jay pouted, but Sam took Ana's hand. "Dinner reservations," he said, his tone of finality.

Ana said her goodbyes quickly, with Sam placing a bill on the bar top to pay for their drinks before he again excused them to Jay and his friends, and then the pair exited.

The moment they hit the outside air, Ana let out a heavy breath. "Thank fuck," Ana muttered.

Sam smirked back at her. "Didn't think you looked like you wanted to be there."

"I didn't," Ana admitted. "I was looking forward to a night teasing with my sexy stalker. Can't exactly do that in a crowd."

Sam's crooked smile lifted higher. "Where would you like to go to tease your sexy stalker?"

"Honestly?"

"Always."

"I'd rather grab drinks and go back to my apartment," she said.

"Really?" He enclosed the space between them, one hand wrapping around her waist, and Ana swallowed at the feeling of him flush against her. He leaned down like he might kiss her but paused as her hands enclosed on his shirt.

"Tell me you've been thinking about me as much as I've thought about you," he whispered.

Ana's chest heaved as she anticipated his lips on hers, hoping he would bite her and tug her roughly. "Every night," she replied breathlessly.

His hand wrapped into her hair at the nape of her neck, tugging just slightly on the roots. "What do you do when you think of me?" he rasped. "Do you imagine me pinning you somewhere? Binding you until you can't breathe or feel your limbs?"

"Yes," she admitted.

Sam released her and took a step back, chin lifting as he gazed predatorily down at her. "Good."

A simple word, but somehow... some way... it struck her to the pit of her stomach, and suddenly, her muscles were restless. Her heart began to flutter at the darkness in his eyes, wondering what he would do next, anticipating his every move.

He pulled the smoke from his pocket and lit it. "Where are you staying?"

"The apartment over Rosen's," she answered.

A long drag of smoke blew from the corner of his lips. "Ravens," he said. "For if things get... more than what you can handle."

Ana's heart skipped, and she couldn't stop her small smile as adrenaline began to surge in her veins. "Sounds like a challenge."

Sam smirked, hair falling over his eyes as he looked at her. "Run home, Ana... I want my feast waiting for me when I get there."

"Where are you going?"

"My temptress wants drinks," he said as he turned on his heel. "She gets drinks."

And Ana watched him disappear down the street before she turned toward her apartment. She didn't know why a fear had stretched into her limbs. Why making sure she got home well before he appeared at her door had her legs moving fast, her heart picking up.

But it did.

Chapter Ten

Sam pulled himself into shadows as he watched the way Ana's pace seemed to speed the closer she got to the stairway up to her apartment. He let her get a ways down... letting himself stalk in the shadows surrounding him, flipping his lighter open and close.

Sam didn't know what game she was playing, but he'd known since the moment she turned that corner that their night out wouldn't last long. She looked entirely too tempting in that fucking bodysuit. He'd wanted to push her against the wall right then, bury his face between her heaving breasts and taste that tattoo. See the fear in her eyes when he rattled and fucked her throat raw after.

But this flicker of it would do for now... He didn't intend to scare her off on the first night.

Though watching her practically run home was *delightful.*

So fucking cute.

He finished his smoke and squashed it into his palm before flicking the trash into the bin under the streetlamp, and then he made his way into the corner store nearby. He took his time, eager to have Ana impatient by the time he got back to her.

The stairs on the side of the building creaked with every slow step he took. He'd picked out wine and grabbed a tray of cheese and fruit just in case she was hungry or perhaps so exhausted after their escapades that she needed refueling.

Mortal bodies were so fragile, after all.

There were three other apartments on this block, all entrances down a narrow hall upstairs. Each apartment sat atop a particular shop. He'd once had an acquaintance that lived in the one across from the Rosen apartment, but he'd only visited once.

The hall was dark, with a window on the opposite end, amber lights cascading over the green and gold wallpaper, and beige carpeting that hadn't been updated in years. The lightbulbs flickered upon his first step onto the carpet, and Sam chuckled under his breath. And with his laugh, one bulb blew by the window. He glanced at two others, and they too blew. It would have been a beautiful scare to any unsuspecting human coming down then, with him cloaked in shadows, only appearing in faint flickers of light.

Shame it had been wasted on the vacancy. Maybe he'd play a little with Ana one day in the same way.

Her door was cracked. Sam pushed slowly but didn't go inside at first. He took in the sight of the bar to the left of the door, the grand windows on the opposite side, back of the couch to the right of the door. The room was so dimly lit that he memorized where the shadows lingered… just in case. A stereo was playing soft music, though it was nearly drowned by the thunder now rumbling outside.

Three taps on the door announced his arrival, and as he stepped inside, he noted the two wine glasses on the bar, the glass of water left half-full, her purse on the barstool, and her coat thrown across the back of one dining table chair. Sam closed the door behind him and sat the wine on the countertop and began pouring two glasses.

"Fuck, fuck, fuck, fuck—" Ana's hissing curses were drowned behind a clap of thunder, loud enough that she jumped, and when she finally noticed Sam standing in the kitchen pouring wine, she flinched to a stop.

"Fucking Death, Sam," she said, clutching her chest. "Making yourself at home?"

"The door was open," he replied. "Thought you'd left it open and bound yourself to the bed already." He picked up the glasses of wine and stepped around the counter toward her.

A quiet smile pricked her lips as he neared. "What would be the fun in that?" she asked.

He extended the wine glass to her, their fingers grazing when she took it from his hand, and he didn't look away from her bright green eyes as he took a sip of his own. The maroon liquid stained her skin with the small drop at the corner of her lips, making him wipe it away with the pad of his thumb.

Those fucking lips… that red lipstick… he wanted it smeared over her face and around his cock. Though he didn't give in to his desires all at once. He wouldn't. He wanted to give her a singular taste tonight. Wanted to watch her beg for more while she thought he was begging for her.

He could already feel her heart picking up its pace. "The fun in that would be your reward for following instructions," he replied, voice dropping. "I wanted my feast ready for me."

Ana's chin lifted. "That's cute," she said. "That you think you can just *have* this... I told you the other night what I wanted."

Catch me. Play with me.

He could practically hear her shouting it from her mind.

He smirked as he backed into the kitchen again to refill his drink. "Quite the view you have here," he said.

"And I thought you were coming up here to fuck my 'pretty little throat'," she said with a tilt of her head, her voice almost impatient. "Turns out you're more interested in the architecture and my view."

Sam chuckled quietly. He tipped one more glass and took a long drink of it, his gaze still pouring over her. He noted how far she was away from him, all the places she could run and try to get away. Maybe over the couch, to the bedroom, the bathroom.

And then he took one singular step around the counter.

"So eager, baby," he said.

Ana seemed to sense the change. She sidestepped from the window to behind the table, fingers bracing on the top.

"Are you going to run for me?" he rasped.

"Should I?"

Another laugh left him with his next advance. "Your heart seems to think so," and he could feel her pulse beginning to thunder, making his cock twitch with every galloping beat.

Her fingers scratched the tabletop, legs widening like she might jump.

"Do you know what you're going to do?" he asked.

She almost tripped on the back of a chair but steadied herself like it hadn't happened and moved oppositely him. "What?" she asked, her voice breathless.

"You're going to give me every little scream you gave the darkness when you thought of me these past few weeks."

Ana backed again, but Sam didn't stop progressing upon her.

"Those fingers sliding between your thighs... finding that delicious wet center, pinching your peaked nipples." His head tilted at her delighted, yet fearful, eyes.

Ana brought her hand up to her full breast, palming the corset over it. His tongue darted out over his lip as he eyed her.

"Show me," he said.

But Ana... to his surprise... tutted her tongue, pulling the corset down slightly and giving him a peek of her swollen nipple. "That's not the deal," she said. "You haven't caught me yet."

Sam eyed her as he reached for the hem of his shirt and pulled it over his head, and he savored the look on Ana's face when he beheld her once more.

Sam was covered in tattoos.

Nearly every inch of his trim torso, his arms, his hands... all the way to that defined vee at his hips that made her mouth water. With ravens, vines, roses, skulls, and that fucking snake around his throat and collar. His ink-covered hand stretched around the back of the chair, prompting his forearm to flex, the veins to ripple beneath the black art, and Ana's thighs tightened.

Fucking sunlight and Death, she cursed. And the way he stared at her, that hair falling so lazily over his dark eyes, his chin dipped... She wanted to trace every tattoo's edge with her tongue and hang from the necklace of his hand on her throat like she had earlier in the night, then climb his body and sit on that stupid fucking face.

She sidestepped around the table, Sam coming around the other side in her direction, his lips twisting into a dangerous smile.

"Keep running, baby," he said, stepping closer.

She bolted toward the living area, but he was on her in three strides. His arms looped around her waist and hauled her feet off the floor. She kicked, writhing and riding the adrenaline rushing through her. She managed a kick to his shin and lunged out of his arms toward the other side of the couch. Sam cursed but didn't falter. Feet slamming into the floor, he darted to the other side, blocking her.

They stood off for a split second before Ana grabbed her wine and threw it in his direction. He sputtered, and Ana ran for the counter.

Sam wiped his face and knocked over two of the barstools so she couldn't run back in that direction. Trapped, she nearly buckled against the fridge as he advanced on her.

That smile lit up the darkness as the lights flickered in the midst of the storm now picking up outside. Ana's heart thudded as he stalked toward her. He lunged, and Ana slipped down, ducking under his arms and bolting to the living area again.

She jumped over the couch, but he grabbed her in midair, his arms tightening on her body so much that she couldn't move her body. Her legs even felt trapped against him.

The windows rattled with the strike of lightning, and in that second, she yelped and shrank into him, though she wasn't sure why.

Sam's deep chuckle filled her ear, his head in the crook of her neck, his hands grasping at her full hip and soft waist. Roaming free and claiming every inch. Ana let out a quiet moan, her head sinking back onto his shoulder.

"You give in to fear like it's your home," he whispered, his fingers gripping at her breast. Her taut nipples strained behind the corset bra. She ached for him to touch her bare skin, so much so that she grabbed his hand and moved it beneath her bra. He cursed into her neck, swaying with her, his lips on her throat and trailing over her neck tattoo. The way he grabbed her flesh made her thighs squeeze, anything for that friction she so desperately needed. She could feel his length stiffening behind her, making her shift her ass and, in turn, causing him to bite her and groan.

Ana grabbed his hair, her arms curling behind his neck, her tug hard enough that he sucked in a sharp breath, and his nails dug into her breast. She whimpered audibly, hating herself for liking his push, enjoying the way he sent her blood rushing and wondering all the ways he could terrify and pleasure her—not that she thought he would truly be more than any other idiot before that had promised her all the ways they could make her scream.

Although, she really hoped she was wrong.

Whipping from his grasp, she pivoted, her hand searing across his cheek. She bolted away as he registered the sting, running toward the bedroom, but he was on her once more. He had barely taken a few more strides, and somehow her arms were pulled from her sides to behind her back, locked in his hand. His other wrapped her hair, making her head pull toward the ceiling and her body rigid. She wasn't sure how his hand had her wrists so secure, and she wondered if he was using whatever demonic powers he possessed to hold her there.

She'd heard stories of some demons manipulating shadows, the air, shifting into other creatures... The few she'd met in Icemyer had been either feral enough that they'd lost the once human part of themselves or so subdued from trying not to be the thing they'd become that they denied their demon selves. And while Sam looked human...

She was willing to push his every limit to see how far she could take him into that animalistic state.

A cold chuckle came from inside her. "Don't let it get to your head," she rasped. "I enjoy the chase."

He whipped her around, grabbed her struggling figure by the waist, and lifted her onto the table, pinning her wrists into the wood. Breathless, he hovered over her, her bent legs spread on either side of him, and for a moment, neither moved.

"I'll enjoy your screams," he hissed.

Her heart began to pound at the look in his eyes, the way they darted from her own to her lips, the way his hair fell over his lashes. His mouth twitched upward, nose nudging hers. Ana leaned forward, desperate to finally kiss him, but Sam dodged her. She caught the spark in his eyes, that devious glint that made her heart skip, and his grip tightened.

He leaned into her again, and Ana's chest sank. She wanted to taste him. She needed him to stop this game of making her wait, making her beg. She wanted his lips and his touch and his body consuming her as his eyes had been doing since they'd first met. To be devoured and drowned beneath every part of him.

She tried to kiss him again, but he pulled just out of her reach. She wriggled against his hands and wrapped her ankles behind his thighs, forcing him closer, nearly able to distinguish his length pressing between her legs behind those jeans. He was... fuck, she couldn't wait to see him freed. See that luscious cock standing at attention and awaiting her mouth around it. Filling her completely. Shit, she'd never been with a man as large as him.

Her body sang in restless abandon at the thought.

A huff of amusement left him at her eagerness, that stupid smile hiking high on the left side. His forehead pressed to hers, and for a moment, she thought she saw hesitation, and yet hunger in his eyes. Like he was holding himself back from fully giving in. Their chests rose and fell together, heavy breaths syncing. Ana was nearly trembling. Her mouth sagged, she swallowed, and this time, she didn't have to move.

Sam's lips were on hers, and Ana floated into chaos.

Chapter Eleven

Shit.

Fuck, her lips. Her taste. Her staggering heartbeat. Her soft flesh and that fight...

His entire being lit on fire as her mouth opened to him. They became a frenzy of tongues, hunger, and insatiable desire for the other. His grip on her wrists faltered, unable to stop himself from wrapping his arm around her waist and pulling her closer, her thighs squeezing around his hips, the backs of his thighs. He cupped her head in his hand, fingers entwining in her hair as she began to wrestle with his belt buckle. But he couldn't let her lips go.

She was licentious poison. Heavy gravity at the edge of a cliff that beckoned a vulnerable body. The weight of water overhead. An enticing darkness for the soul to be reborn in.

And she was all his.

Her nails scratched his stomach, making his abs flinch, and when she managed to get his buckle undone and she pressed her palm against his straining length, Sam forgot himself.

A frightening snarl left him, his teeth baring against her lips. That animal-like restriction sounded in the back of his throat, the world flashing scarlet in his eyes. It was a reflex of his true self, and he barely realized he had picked her up, thrown her onto the bed, pinned her wrists onto the mattress, and was standing over her until he heard her gasp.

Her eyes blew in fear and arousal, body stiffening beneath him. She froze there, her breath ceasing as Sam bent and leaned in closer. His nose dragged across her cheek, allowing him to inhale the perfect scent of that fear coursing through her rapid pulse. It rattled his bones and made his existence slip to the edge of whatever tiny sliver of humanity he pretended to have in him, and he held it at the precipice. A predator toying with its prey. A monster and a mouse.

So fucking sweet.

"You're going to lie back, wicked girl, and you're going to accept whatever pleasures I have for you... from tonight and until your very last breath..."

Visible goosebumps rose on her skin as his eyes met hers. A smile flinched on her lips, breath returning to her heaving lungs. "Big words, stalker," she breathed. She leaned in closer to his ear, making the hair on his neck stand as she whispered, "Make me believe it."

Sam tipped her head back, his grip tightening enough that he saw her eyes widen. "One day, this mouth is going to get you punished," he swore. His grip loosened, thumb brushing against her lips as he bent lower. "Don't stop," he whispered.

Ana's lips opened up to him and pushed around his thumb, her soft mouth taking him in, tongue dragging teasingly along the bottom. And just when he made to slip away, she bit... *hard*.

Hard enough that he felt the skin break, but he didn't move as he watched that drop trickle over his joint, and her tongue darted out to lick it up. His cock twitched behind the zipper, his instincts kicking in at the sight of what she was doing to him. As if she knew exactly what would have him lusting after her and losing control.

But he didn't have time for that.

He didn't have time to let her have that over him. At least not yet.

He would let her take that control another night. Welcome her power to take over his own curiosity. Tonight, though... tonight, he would give her that first taste of addiction.

Taking his thumb from her mouth, he wrapped her jaw instead, his lips pressing hard to hers and tasting that iron on her tongue. He needed to taste every inch of her skin, wondering if it tasted as sinful as her lips. He kissed every flower on her throat as he undid the button of her pants, his chin brushing the pillows of her heaving breasts that he was making himself wait to take in. He sat back on his knees, holding her stare as he pulled her pants off, one leg at a time, then tossed them to the ground as he admired the siren in front of him. Her full thighs, the grand rose, crown, and skull tattoo on the right one, the way her legs fell open and bent on either side of him, an invitation to that sweet fucking arousal that he was desperate for.

Ana sat up, her mouth encompassing his as she reached behind her for the tie on her corset, loosening it enough that he felt her wiggle as she stretched it down her body. He pulled back to help her slip her legs out of the bodysuit, and when she was wholly bared on that bed, his mind blanked.

His tongue wrapped her peaked nipple, her back arching as his hand delved between her thighs. Her moan sang to his soul, and his middle finger met her slick heat. He nearly cursed out loud. Nearly leapt onto her and lost his mind. Fuck, she was drenching. She jerked as he teased her clit and bit her nipple. She was arching and writhing and responding so *fucking beautifully*.

"Sam…" His name on her tongue had him aching again. He slipped one finger inside her, his thumb circling her clit, and her nails tightened on his scalp. Lower and lower he went, licking and kissing her flesh, tasting that tattoo between her breasts just as he'd promised himself he would. Until he reached the tops of her thighs, and he paused a moment to watch her eyes when he lowered.

The first kiss on her clit made the breath she had been holding exhale with a whimper. He continued tasting her, feasting on her. Alternating between slow, delicate licks and sucking those nerves into his mouth. Her back lifted off the bed, her nails scratching just enough in his hair to drive a chill over his own skin.

One finger inside her, then two… She was tighter than he'd expected, and he wondered if the pencil-dicked idiots from the other kingdoms had ever pleasured her as she deserved. He pondered if the voluptuous body he wanted to own had ever been worshiped as it should have been.

He was going to fuck her until she didn't remember anyone else, until the only memory of a cock inside her was his own.

He nearly laughed at that thought, at bringing the goddess of destruction to her absolute weakest, most vulnerable self and making her weep in pleasure for only him. *Only* him. Ever again.

Dammit, he'd missed winning like this.

His cock pressed so firmly against his pants that it hurt.

Ana writhed beneath him, her hands in his hair, and he smirked up at her when he curled his fingers inside her. She sucked in a sharp breath, a soft moan coming after, and he slowly started pumping in and out of her.

"Right there?" he said, watching her face. Ana whimpered, her head nodding, and Sam smiled before licking her clit again. "Yeah, you like it there, don't you, baby?" His tongue slowly flicked her again, and as her grip tightened in his hair, he started in on her once more. Sucking her clit into his mouth, licking her up and down. All the while, he would slowly pulse his fingers in and out, feeling her hips shift beneath him, relishing every time her grasp tightened in his hair or she cried out.

"Sam… Fuck, right there—*yes*—"

She was a mess beneath him, and he smiled at the sight of her coming undone. He felt her walls caving, saw her knuckles gripping the sheets. She threw her head back onto the pillow. Every breath that came from her sent her chest rising and falling, the whimper escaping her mouth so high-pitched that he wondered if she'd ever heard herself make such beautiful noises. Until she trembled in stillness, and the sound she cried at her end, had a curled a smile so devious on his lips he had to taste her again.

Ana sat up and pulled him from between her thighs, kissing him and tasting herself on his tongue. He let her control things for a moment. Let her twist his back onto the bed as she undid his buckle and finally freed his taut length from within. A moan left her, and he cursed when her fingers tickled the underside of his cock. She smiled against his lips, pushing that bead of liquid around the tip and stroking him slowly. Sitting up triumphant across his hips, making him admire the beauty that she was. And just as she shifted to move lower, Sam caught her by her arms.

Her eyes widened at the startle of his grasp, but he pulled her back onto his lap and sat up. Her wetness grazed his cock, his eyes fluttering at the friction.

"Tonight, you're mine to please, baby," he whispered against her lips. "And you're going to let me in."

He kissed her again, hand threading through her hair and the other squeezing her voluptuous ass. She lifted her hips, rocking against his length, and a low hiss sounded from within him.

No more fucking games.

He needed to be inside this woman. He needed to fill her and stretch her; to hear that scream come from deep within her again. He needed her begging for more from this day on.

He rolled them back again and pinned her wrists beneath his hands as he positioned himself. But even as he nudged her entrance, he knew he needed her wider to let him in. She was going to writhe and squirm in pleasure as he filled her, and he truly hoped tears fell.

Ana's hips lifted off the bed as he pushed her spread legs up, the back of one thigh on his chest, her bent leg in his hand. She closed her eyes and bit her lip, but Sam grabbed her chin.

"Look at me," he hissed. "Watch your beautiful body take me in."

He groaned and cursed, his body shuddering as he felt her relaxing for him, and he slowly pressed himself inside her. Inch by inch. His eyes never leaving hers.

Fuck, he could have buried in her for hours, and for a few moments, he considered it.

"Were you made for me, baby?" he rasped, palming her breast as he stilled at the hilt. "Did you dream of me filling you?" He leaned down and caught her lips with his as she pushed up on her elbows to meet him. And he met her eyes as he said, "Tell me how you dreamed of me."

"Screaming in pleasure and pain," she said. "In all my favorite nightmares."

The words quirked the corner of his lips. He pulled slowly out of her, nearly to his tip, and then slid back in. He watched her bite her lip, watched her eyes dart down to watch his cock disappear inside her again.

"Fuck, *Sam*," she whimpered when he slid inside her once more. "Harder."

The word was a hiss, a warning. He cocked a brow down at her. "Say it again," he said, and this time, his restraint on pushing into her waned.

"Harder," she repeated, her hips grinding into his. "Make me hurt. *Make me cry.*"

His tongue darted out over his lips, nearly smiling. She had no idea what she was asking for.

And he delighted at the thrill.

Sam didn't hesitate. He slammed into her this time, making her cry out with that noise that he then vowed he would rip from her every day from then on. He would yank it from the depths of her being. Devour it with every stroke inside her. He would bruise her thighs and leave his handprints on her ass, his teeth marks on her breasts and her stomach.

The thought of it sent him into a frenzy. He thrust harder and harder inside her, his pelvic bone slapping against her. The delicious sound of her wetness as he moved sounded over the pounding rain. She strained beneath him, and he watched her face as it hovered in the in-between of pleasure and pain. Jaw shaking, nails digging into his arms.

He yanked both her legs off the bed and held her by her ankles as he fucked her tight cunt and teased her clit with his thumb. She writhed and cried out his name, and he felt as she began to close in tighter around him. Fuck, *so tight*. She was nearly there, and he had to stifle himself from coming too quickly.

"Shit—Sam—right there. Right there—yes—"

"You're so tight, baby," he grunted, fingers digging into her thighs. "Are you coming for me, Ana?"

That fucking moan left her again, and he looked down to see her nod her head vigorously, biting her lip. Sam pushed her legs on either side of his body and grabbed her face.

"Words, wicked girl," he hissed. "I want to hear that pretty fucking voice."

"I'm coming—*Sam*—" She moaned, and Sam met her eyes as he loosened the grip on her face and brushed the tear off her cheek.

"There's my good little whore," he growled.

Ana's heart stopped. He felt it stagger in her blood. And then her entire body convulsed. *Shattered.* Like the name had triggered something in her. She screamed, her head throwing back as she squeezed the sheets.

Her insides throbbing around him stopped every thought in his head. He couldn't hold himself back. He released inside her, shooting his cum deep as he stilled fully, holding her thighs against his sides, lightning cracking outside.

And when he pulled out of her, he groaned at the sight of her juices on his cock, how pretty and swollen she was. He pumped his cock once more, and whatever was left of his release trickled out and spilled on her cunt, along with some leaking from inside her. He remained knelt between her thighs, watching that blissful state wash over her curving body.

All mine, he thought to himself.

Fuck, this would be fun.

Ana pushed up and pressed her hands to his cheeks, pulling him into a needing kiss that Sam welcomed. He pulled her body flush, arms linking around her waist as she rose to her knees, and as he sat with her straddled over him, he released her lips, and his hand brushed her cheek.

"Wicked girl..." He licked the column of her throat, her hands tightening in her hair. "Do you know how beautifully your heart stops when you come for me?" He licked the line of her collar, the top of her breast.

Her eyes fluttered as she rocked into him. "I don't," she whispered. "Show me again. Make me feel it."

Begging for the stop of heart that only Death could give her.

Sam chuckled into her skin. "So greedy," he rasped. "But not tonight. I would lick every inch of you if I didn't have to leave for work," he told her before pulling back to look at her face. "In time, baby," he swore.

Chapter Twelve

Ana's entire body was aflame with the lingering wetness of his tongue, the weight of his touch, and the devotion of his soul to hers. She wanted him inside her again, her cunt throbbing with the thought of his cock filling her. Fuck, she had never been filled like that. Never felt such adrenaline and desire coursing through her veins.

She hated him for how much she might crave him again. And so soon. Even mentioning that he wouldn't be staying the entire night had her greed riling. He was kissing her throat, squeezing and slapping her ass. She was intent on staying atop his lap until he forced her away.

"Sam..." her voice trickled as she reached between them, her fingers wrapping his length. He groaned into her neck and snatched her head back by her hair. She winced, sucking in a sharp breath as he stilled her.

"No, baby," he hissed. "I have many more nights ahead with you. More nights that I plan to make you scream loud enough that the dead rise. More nights that I want to watch this beautiful cunt swallow my dick. Maybe..." His eyes darted to the long mirror on the back of her door. "Maybe next time I'll let you watch. Doesn't that sound fun?"

Her thighs squeezed at the thought of watching him fuck her senseless, and the bubbling anticipation had her relaxing against him. "Yes," she managed.

His grip in her hair loosened, allowing her chin to fall, and he was smirking when she met his eyes.

Dangerous approval danced in those brown eyes. He cupped her cheek in a claiming manner. "Good girl," he smiled, making her chest constrict with those two words. "Will you help me find my clothes and walk me out?"

Ana nearly laughed. "Here I was hoping to see you riding away naked on that bike."

"Another time." He slapped her ass again, and Ana rose off the bed to her feet, feeling his cum leaking between her thighs. Just as she bent to pick up his pants, she saw him staring at those thighs, at her hips, at her bare ass. She resisted a smile as she fluffed her curls over to one side and bit her lip.

"What?" she asked.

Sam stood, rounding over her shoulder. "I was just thinking how I can't wait to have you sit on my face," he said with a grab of her ass.

She shifted her ass into that grab, loving how he clasped her flesh. "Last breaths," she teased.

"I fucking hope so." He leaned down and kissed her cheek hard before taking his pants from her hands.

Ana wrapped herself in a long robe and trailed to the kitchen for a drink while Sam dressed himself, and when he had everything except his coat on, she took his hand and walked him downstairs.

"I suppose you'll do for a toy," Ana said as Sam leaned back against his bike. She scratched his jaw with her nail, lips twisted in satisfaction, and she started to step away—

But her fingertips were still on his, and he yanked her back into his chest once more, kissing her hard. Tilting her backwards and grasping her ass in his hand, the roots of her hair in the other.

When he pulled back, she had to grab hold of his arms to keep her composure, and she sucked in a sharp breath at the sight of him hovering over her as he was.

"I want to watch my cum trickling down your thighs when you walk away from me," he rasped, his nose brushing her neck. "I want it dripping on the stairs back up."

"How evil," she said playfully. "Someone might slip and fall."

"Wouldn't that be a lovely thing to see?" he taunted, his head tilting as he looked at her. "Perhaps they'd get a peek at your swollen pussy while they're on their backs. Make them jealous they were not the one to make you ache."

It sounded lusciously sinister coming from his lips, and she liked the way his mind worked. So much so that her thighs throbbed at the thought of dragging him back up the stairs.

"Are you sure you don't want to stay?" she asked.

A heavy sigh left him. "Work calls," he said. He leaned back against the bike, a finger trailing delicately over her arm. "Upstairs, temptress," he said, deliberately ignoring her question. "Let me watch you walk."

She leaned forward and gave him a lingering kiss, one that she meant to burn in his mind. Ana had always had some fun while working, though never really with one singular person. But Sam... She couldn't deny how attracted she was to him, how she wanted to push him and he to push her.

She decided he would do nicely for entertainment while she did her job. She'd worked tirelessly over the years. There was nothing wrong with having this kind of fun and taking her last task easy. Maybe she'd even learn some things from him since he was one of Death's demons. Perhaps she'd offer him a place in her court once she'd bound the last king to her will. Offer him his life in exchange for his executioner skills.

Her heart sang at the thought of him on a leash.

Good girl, she heard him saying. And while she did enjoy the sound of it coming from his lips, she knew she'd enjoy taunting the good little dog he was, one day, even more.

Or perhaps she'd enjoy watching him rip his own dead heart out.

"Goodnight, Sam."

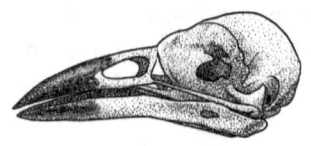

Ana's hips swayed in a show for him as she sauntered away. He stared at the edge of her bare ass slipping from beneath her robe and noted the cum sliding down her deliciously powerful thigh. It made every devious pore in his body wake again. His cum. Dripping down the thigh of the woman he would soon need to kill. Though perhaps he'd imprison her as his personal plaything.

A tremendous power to hold over those other kingdoms.

Every person left in them would want a shot at their revenge. And Death... He could use her presence to his advantage. Everything he'd promised his people... revenge, life, the entire continent. That could be his this time.

His cock twitched at the thought.

He'd have to do more work to figure it out. If her life was worth keeping alive for that, or if he should save himself the trouble and slit her throat before he had a chance to consider it. Take the other kingdoms as a savior to the people, the one to finally bring The Tower to her knees.

Decisions, decisions.

She paused at the door upon reaching it and looked back at him over her shoulder. His head tilted back, and he gave her a chin jerk. She disappeared through the open door, and he continued to stare until he saw the lights flicker off in her apartment windows.

Delirious with the amusement of his conquest, he couldn't help himself from letting his head sway back with a smile. He tossed his helmet up and down, letting that laugh emit from somewhere deep within him. A laugh he hadn't felt in years.

It felt *so good* to laugh.

Almost as good as his cock had felt buried in her.

He cracked his neck and swung his leg over the motorcycle. Body satisfied and singing in delight.

Exactly where he wanted her.

Sam threw his backpack onto the foyer table as he burst through the front entrance. The grand doors flew back with creaks and groans, cobwebs dusting the air with the toss, and Sam nearly smiled at the feeling of the old mist hitting his skin.

"Late night, boss?" Rolfe teased as he appeared from the hall.

"I want a count of every groundskeeper every morning," Sam called out as Rolfe appeared from the hall. Sam made for the stairs.

"Something wrong?" Rolfe asked after him.

"She'll start working her way through the bottom first. I want everyone on alert for anything strange," Sam replied. "Don't tell them why. Just say there is a threat from Firemoor, and we are doing our diligence."

"Are we in trouble?" Rolfe called up.

Sam paused at the top of the stairs, his night with Ana replaying in his mind, and he met Rolfe's stare.

"You have no idea."

PART TWO

...HE'LL MEET HIS MATCH

Chapter Thirteen

Ana was running.

Blood wept in her broken footprints down the marble hall. Around every corner. Down every bare step. A gunshot ricocheted off the wall to her left, and she flinched, ducking behind the next door. Her heart raced, and yet through it all, she continued to laugh. That chuckle she couldn't stop, delirious and cackling. It echoed off every wall and gave away her hide, but Ana didn't care.

The heart of the Firemoor king was still in her clenched fist. His blood still spreading wet over her chest, her gown, and her legs.

Three down.

Two to go.

Another gunshot broke the wall by the door. Ana licked her lips and let her head sag onto her neck as she steadied her breathing. She had five bullets left. Three knives. A bag of gold. And bare feet that would get her as far as she needed to go.

Back to Icemyer to plot her attack on the Iron kingdom.

"She's hiding here," she heard someone say outside the door, the sound of their clicking guns and steel-toed boots sounding loud in the air. She shook her head. Amateurs.

Ana knew this castle inside and out. Had plotted it for weeks.

She slipped back into the shadows and counted her steps. Ten paces back was a slip behind a winding staircase. She crouched down, waiting for them to make the first move.

Bullets rained through the door.

Her hands covered her ears, her head. Her body flinched with every blast. On and on, they sprayed. The marble chipped. The wood splintered. Until one of the guards stopped the supposed slaughter, and dust plumed the air.

The silence that followed made Ana's ears ring. But she'd heard this silence more times than she could count. Had learned to navigate and use it to her advantage.

She pressed her hand to the floor. Wood cracked beneath the boot of a guard. Another crack. She counted them, steadying her breath and clasping her hand around one of her knives. And with one slow exhale, Ana struck.

She rose up and yanked the hot barrel of the gun, ignoring the pain and pulling the first guard forward. He stumbled, trying to reach the trigger, but Ana spun and ripped her claw across his throat before he could fight back. Blood spewed over her. He dropped to the ground.

Ana grabbed the gun just as the second guard spotted her. She rammed the heel into his face, and he faltered over his feet. As he caught his balance, Ana pulled her knife, thrusting it into the man's face. Back and back, she pushed, until he hit the opposite wall, his head breaking on the stone. More footsteps sounded to her left. She sliced his throat and pulled her pistol, barely aiming, before letting off one round into her assailant to the side.

The bullet struck the guard's exposed neck. She ran out, the rifle at the ready to strike any others that might be around. One blocked her as she hit the threshold. He grabbed her around the waist and hauled her up into the air. The rifle fell. She pushed her pistol back into her thigh holster. Ana kicked, twisted, and squirmed. He cursed her movements and slammed her into the wall. Ana's back cracked with the thrust, but with her wince, she shook off the pain, and then she maneuvered her legs around his head and began to tighten them.

"Didn't know I'd be blessed with such foreplay today," she said as her thighs squeezed and squeezed.

The guard realized what she was doing, his face growing pale, and he hit at her legs. Stumbling, but Ana held on. She held on as he flailed and twirled them. And as he began to truly panic, her thumbs thrust into his eyes. His screech filled the hall. Other guards had stopped to watch. He clawed at her thighs, his begs and pleads and screams making Ana's insides dance.

His eyes bleeding out, Ana shifted her hands, seeing his face turning blue, and she swiftly put him out of his misery with a twist of his neck. His spine cracked, a glorious shiver ran over her skin, and as he descended to the ground, Ana jumped off and pulled her pistol from her thigh.

The guards that had stood by to watch now surrounded her. Rifles ready. Ana tensed, her eyes darting between the men.

"Pretty, pretty boys make pretty, pretty toys," she taunted, smiling at each of them. "Who wants to play?"

"Stupid witch," one muttered. "Blind her!"

Visors buckled down on their helmets. A few reached into their bags for the sun catcher weapons she knew they would pull to stun her. She wouldn't give them the satisfaction.

Ana had four bullets left. She aimed first for the grand chandelier, then the window. Glass blew out, and the light fixture fell in slow motion. Guards threw themselves to the ground. Ana bolted to the window. One guard ran into her as she flung toward the broken panes. Ana grabbed him by the lapels of his jacket and pulled him to her lips, kissing him as her knife slammed into his neck.

"Good boy," she teased, watching the shocked light leave his eyes. She pulled his jacket off as he crumbled to the floor.

The chandelier crashed, and Ana jumped out of the window.

Red banners from the celebration the night before still lined the outside. She flailed in the air but managed to grab one to slow her descent. It burned her hands, her bare feet, her thighs. She didn't let go as she fell all the way into the open skylight of a horse stable.

Bales of hay cushioned her fall and stuck into her body. She cursed the prick of it in her ass.

Well, at least she hadn't landed in the mud this time.

She grabbed a random brown piece of fabric off a pile of hay and shook the excess hay off before twisting it and pulling her hair up, covering some of it in the large bun atop her head and sliding her claw into the thick of it. A common hairstyle of the peasants who worked the markets just outside.

Something knocked over—a bucket of water—and she froze. Her eyes slid left, finding a small child watching her from behind a stall.

Ana lifted one finger to her lips, giving him a small smile, and the boy just nodded.

She grabbed a pair of overalls from the hooks on the front and slipped mud boots on her bare feet.

Sunlight greeted her as she slipped out of the barn, and no one and nothing watched her as she pushed north through the market—

The alarm on her phone went off.

Ana stirred, grumbling as she cursed the buzz.

At least the dream had only been a memory. A good memory of a day when things had actually gone right. Sometimes she still felt the warmth of kings' blood on her skin, still felt their hearts beat their last in her palm.

She remembered how scared she'd been that first time. How timid she had been to introduce herself to the Windmoor prince and play innocent, all the way into his bed. Until his father had seen them together and began making moves on her.

Her phone buzzed again, but this time it wasn't her alarm going off.

Morning beautiful, was the text on her screen.

Ana stretched, unable to stifle her smile at the welcome memory of the night before. The thorough fucking and bodily worship. She could still feel Sam's tongue between her thighs, on her neck, his cock thrusting deep within her...

She resisted the urge to touch herself at the memory and instead rose from the bed to put on a pot of coffee.

Stalker, she typed once the coffee was making. *Is that the most poetic you can be?*

I didn't know you liked poetry, he replied. *I'll have to get out my books and find the perfect one to recite when I see you later.*

Who says I want to see you later?

I think you do, he replied.

What makes you say that?

That pretty little cunt calls to me. I can practically feel you aching for more.

Ana laughed aloud and let him sit on that a few minutes while she placed a few strips of bacon on a sheet pan, then put them in the oven.

Poetry of the people, good sir. Maybe I want my mind entertained and aching before you get another chance between my thighs.

I like a challenge.

She hated herself for the twist of her lips, the eager anticipation swelling in her stomach. Her thumbs stroked the screen as she stared at it and decided to keep him guessing.

Entice me, she typed.

Done.

Ana checked on her bacon in the oven, then turned again to face the expansive windows on the opposite side of the room. In the grey light of the morning and the absence of rain, Castle Corvus stuck out beneath the fog hovering over the ground. That same window was lit up again, and she wondered if it was the King's study, or simply lit as a ploy to make people think he was actually there.

She made it a goal to find out.

"If you're interested in all the haunting things about our shadow land, maybe you should visit the witches," Jay said to her later that day. "They have a shop on Third."

"You say that as though I know exactly where it is," Ana said, brow quirking at him.

Jay's smile widened. "I'll show you," he said.

Ana reached for a plastic sleeve for the small, matted prints she was packaging. "Is it coven owned?" she asked.

"Three sisters, actually," he answered. "Though, Cordelia is normally the only one there. You met her at the festival that night."

Ana vaguely recalled the woman that had spoken to her about the song she'd sang. "What about the other two?"

Jay shrugged. "Suppose they have better things to do than run a shop." He paused in his step then and turned to look at her, a mischievous glint in his eyes. "If you're lucky, you might get a glimpse of the King's Hand."

Ana sat up. "She visits the witches?"

"Pretty sure she's fucking Cordelia," Jay answered. "Or so goes the rumor."

"Sounds like I need to meet my new best friend," Ana smiled. "If we're ever going to get those paintings from inside Corvus, that is."

Jay considered her. "You really want those paintings, don't you?"

"No one has ever seen those paintings," Ana said. "Imagine the history they could tell. The portraits of people only remembered by a rare few of the demons walking around this place. Not to mention the evolution of style over these centuries. Don't you want to see the colors and materials they were using at the start of this realm? Before this realm? Get a glimpse into the style this king loves?"

"So passionate," Jay teased her. "Fine. I'll drop you by on lunch while I grab something for us to eat at the deli."

"No deals today?" Ana asked as Jay started to walk away from her.

"Bigger day tomorrow," he said. "I'll be on a few calls until break. I expect the entire gallery to have sold by then," he bantered.

"Done," Ana called back.

Chapter Fourteen

It was afternoon when Millie decided to grace Castle Corvus with her presence.

Sam and Rolfe were in one of the grand old dining rooms, working on taking down some of the curtains on the eastern side so that the interior could glow again.

He liked rotating rooms like that, though he hadn't been in this particular one in nearly ninety years. Not since the last time he'd hosted a dinner with the council he had back then. The riots over Shadowmyer had happened a month after that gathering. Riots by witches who thought he would go along with Firemoor's desire to kill their kind. He hadn't blamed them for thinking it. With the rumors circulating and the borders feeling thinner and thinner, he knew how scared people were.

He'd declared the place safe for witches after, even though he didn't fully trust them. But it was something close to Millie's heart, and he cherished Millie's advice and friendship more than any old grudges he might have had.

Most of the witches had fled to the frigid caves of Icemyer, though.

Glittered dust hung in the air as he and Rolfe yanked down one of the sheets over the window. The ceilings in this room were nearly twenty feet up, as were the windows. Sam let the dust settle around them, inhaling its beauty while Rolfe waved it away.

Sam chuckled at him. "A little dust is good for the soul, Roll," he said.

"What about a hundred year's worth?" Rolfe grunted. "Should think that's a hazard for the lungs."

Sam looked up at the rest of the windows—six more left to uncover.

"We are a few years late on rotating this one," he muttered, hands on his hips. "Remember the cathedral in the back?"

"Forgot about that," Rolfe replied. "We should look at it next. I miss all the stained windows."

Sam recalled them. The black wings and roses. The story of the last war written in art. "You did a good job on those," he told his friend.

Rolfe waved him off. "Never doing glasswork again," he said. "That was the extent of my physical labor artistry. I'll stick to skin mutilation from now on."

"That is the worst way to describe tattoos," Sam said.

"What?" Rolfe asked, and the genuine frown on Rolfe's face made Sam shake his head.

"Nothing," Sam chuckled. He jerked his chin in the direction of the next window. "Let's get this one."

They moved their ladders over and over to each window, revealing the rest of the room in grey light as they did, and by the time they got to the last one, they heard someone shouting through the halls. The pair exchanged a quick glance before Rolfe began shouting back.

"You better've brought lunch," Rolfe called out.

They were taking down the last curtain when Millie came around the corner and slapped a bag on the grand table. She sputtered and waved her hand in front of her face as the dust crested before them.

"Fuck all," she mumbled. "Is there a reason you're rotating rooms today?"

Sam shrugged as he jumped down from the ladder and dusted off his hands. "Why not?"

Rolfe landed with a thud that shook the dust off the ground and into the air again. He went straight for the bag Millie had tossed on the table and started rummaging through it. Millie slid her arms across her chest and looked at Sam.

"You didn't feed the pup?" she asked.

"He's hit his four-hour limit," Sam replied. "You're late today," he added with a jerk of his chin. "Everything okay?"

Millie sighed but shook her head. "Nothing to worry about," she told him.

"Her girlfriend didn't call her back last night," Rolfe said through a full mouth of food.

Millie punched him in the stomach, making Rolfe sputter up his sandwich, and he growled at her, baring his teeth when she smiled.

"I'll have you know I woke up to her pretty tongue exploring all the right places this morning,"Millie countered. "What did you wake up to? Your hand cupping your balls?"

"You know he wakes up in hound form, Mills," Sam interjected. "Probably licking his balls instead."

"That was just the once," Rolfe said quickly.

"Right," Sam smirked. He noted the tiredness in Millie's eyes despite her purposeful play, and he considered her again. "Really, Mills. What's bothering you?" he asked again.

She let loose a heavier sigh this time and hugged her arms around her chest. "Damien called in the middle of the night," she said. "He's hearing reports about a possible attack on the Spine."

Damien was a demon legion commander in the Spine and Millie's closest spy. Sam trusted him as much as he trusted the two in front of him, though Damien had, on the rare occasion, blown things out of proportion.

"An attack... from Firemoor?" Sam asked.

The Spine was supposed to be the only neutral territory after the split. It divided the continent directly down the middle, meant as a space where there would be no war, no poverty. A space for trading and growing foods for the entire continent without agenda. Only equality and safety, as people continued to think Shadowmyer was full of the wretched monsters that would take your soul in your sleep. Some people feared that, though the stories grew, and the realities of Shadowmyer showed itself as the true neutral place after a few centuries.

Kings of the Spine had stayed true to the agreement for four centuries, but once the last two found themselves in power and their greed got the better of them, they began treating their citizens like Firemoor. Cleansing the poor, the supernatural, the misunderstood. Those people had worshipped Deianira's name in the street after she took the last king off the throne and took care of any offspring and wives. And those same people had taken it upon themselves to come out of hiding and help their fellow neighbors when the smoke cleared.

Perhaps that was a good enough reason for Firemoor to strike the small territory. Not to mention having that land to station troops for Ironmyer and Shadowmyer.

"Firemoor, yes," Millie said, and Sam watched her as he reached into the food bag and propped himself up on the table. He could see the apparent worry in her eyes, though he wasn't sure how to help her.

"Are you sure he's not being overly dramatic? Perhaps paranoid?"

Sam asked before chomping on a fry.

"You know he does that," Rolfe grunted.

"I'm not sure," Millie said. "This feels different. Maybe he is... But he's pretty worried."

"Why would Firemoor attack the Spine?" Rolfe asked through a full mouth of food. "What've they got Fire would want to take?"

Sam thought of the General now in charge of Firemoor, or rather had appointed himself in charge of it. General Prei. His fist curled at the thought of him.

"Probably more about power and territory," Sam said. "Prei has been getting bolder and bolder since the Fire King's death."

"Speaking of his death," Millie said, turning to Sam. "How are things with your little girlfriend?"

Sam gave her a small smile and took out his phone as he leaned forward and took a bite of the fry Millie had plucked between her fingers. "Let's find out," he said. He started to open up the phone to text her but noticed Ana had texted him only a few minutes prior.

I have an errand to run at lunch, Ana texted. *But Jay is giving me the rest of the day off.*

Sam's smile widened. *Is this your way of asking me on a day date?*

It's my way of saying you have a longer chance at engaging my mind and seeing if you deserve my pretty little cunt again.

I can already taste my victory, wicked girl, he replied. *I'll pick you up at three.*

"So. Someone got his dick wet," Millie said, brow arching at Sam.

Sam put down his phone, trying to hide the smirk on his twisting lips. "Jealous, Mills?"

"Of your dick? Maybe. It's a nice dick. I could do loads more with it than you ever could," she winked. "Funnily enough, I don't need a nice, *thick* cock to make my women scream."

"Neither do I," Sam snapped back. "Although..." He reached out to her, his fingers brushing her arm, and Millie grabbed the lip of the table, the hair visibly rising over her skin. He smiled as he let the feeling of himself sliding in and out of Ana take over, pushing that feeling into Millie, and as her bottom lip sagged, he took his hand away.

"It does feel fucking fantastic inside her," he whispered in her ear.

Millie's eyes slid to his. "So *tight*," she mused. "Tell me, Samarius. Have you been dreaming about fucking her all morning? Is that why you put poor Rollie here up to physical labor today?"

Sam took a large bite of his sandwich and shook his head. "Tried to entice him into doing another stain glass piece."

"Oh, Roll, you should," Millie said as she turned to him. "The ones in the cathedral were beautiful. We should take a walk down. I miss the place."

Sam's chin jerked toward the rummage of food. "Pack up."

As Rolfe started cleaning, Millie turned to Sam. "Another date today?" she asked.

"Thinking the art museum uptown," Sam replied. "See what history she's been taught. Last night was fun, but there's more to her than her body. She's smart enough to have woven herself into kingdoms and monarchies thought impenetrable. I want to know how she's done it."

"She's not exactly going to just tell you," Millie said.

"She will," Sam assured her.

Millie paused, her eyes dancing over him. "Why do I get the feeling you're up to something more than biding time before killing her?"

"Patience, Millie," he drawled. "I need her alive. For now."

Rolfe stopped moving, and Millie stared at him.

Sam chuckled softly at their expressions and pushed off the table. "Imagine the things she knows about these kingdoms. She's forced herself all the way to the top, something our spies have been trying to do for centuries. Sure, we have a few that have managed it, but they're forced to kill themselves off after a while, constantly working their way up and up again in different legions and parts of the realms. She clawed her way up those ladders, every time, in less than a year."

"None of our spies look like her," Millie said.

"Maybe it's time they did."

Chapter Fifteen

The bell rang over the door when Ana pressed into the witch's shop at lunch. Old smells of herbs, flowers, leather, and mist hit her, and she inhaled the familiarity. She hadn't been back to Icemyer in a few years.

A few dried flowers hung from twine on the walls. Jars of flowers and herbs lined the cabinets on the left, crystals adorning the shelves on the right. There were a few circular tables in the middle with books, journals, and other smaller objects and trinkets.

She took in the whole of the shop as she inhaled that scent again. A few other patrons looked over the flowers on the wall, one filling a few small plastic baggies. And then she noticed the woman helping this lady out.

The woman she'd met at the festival.

Cordelia, she remembered Jay calling her.

Ana picked up a leather-bound journal at the front table and thumbed through it, her eyes staying on Cordelia until the witch finally turned, and when she looked up, her gaze locking on Ana, the witch stilled.

She looked at Ana in an almost dream-like state, like Ana had walked out of another world and suddenly appeared before her. But she blinked as the lady she was helping asked a question, and then turned her attention back to the patron.

Cordelia kept an eye on Ana as she moved slowly around the shop, picking up a few trinkets with every few steps. Ana noticed Cordelia seeming to sell at a faster pace, like she were eager to get them out of the shop and only have Ana there. Ana went over to the crystals as Cordelia cashed the patrons out. She'd just picked up a rather interesting piece of tourmaline when she heard the bell over the door ring again, and she turned to see Cordelia lock the door behind her guests.

Cordelia's dark eyes hovered over Ana as she looked at her over her shoulder. Silence beckoned the space, and Ana waited on the witch to speak.

"I hoped you would find your way here," Cordelia said, her voice as smooth as reflecting sunlight rippling over water. She turned and leaned on the door, her gaze dancing over Ana. "I don't think I truly noticed your eyes when we first met," she continued. "I've never seen green eyes with such vibrance."

Ana placed the crystal back on the cabinet and relaxed against it, palms bracing the top as she ignored the witch's statement. "Lovely little shop you have here," she said with another look around the space. "I wonder if the women that just left know you sold them dried weeds from your rooftop garden mingled with the 'pure' herb you have labeled there."

Cordelia's full, purple-lined lips quirked at the corner. She wasn't wearing the bright eyeshadow today, just a little liner over her bright brown eyes, her lashes swept up, brows clean. Ana loved the dark purple shade of lipstick she was wearing, and she nearly asked her where she got it from. Until Cordelia stepped away from the door and began to chuckle under her breath.

"There are only two ways you could know the song you were singing the other night," Cordelia said. "Either you are Death in the flesh, or you were raised by the closest coven left to the ancient ones: the Icemyer shadow witches."

Ana stiffened as the woman looked her over.

"I'm inclined to believe the latter," Cordelia continued. "Beauty like you... we'd have noticed you before if you were Death."

"Seems to me no one around here notices anything about him," Ana said, picking up a jar of dried rose petals on the nearby table. "Maybe I am Death."

Another low laugh escaped the witch. "What is a girl raised by the shadow coven doing in a place like this?" she asked with a tilt of her head. "Shouldn't you be performing rituals to the old gods? Or are you one of the last followers of Hazel Carrington?"

Hazel Carrington.

Ana knew the name, though she didn't know why she knew the name. She'd never heard of an individual witch having a group of followers. Ana supposed that the woman had done something unspeakable or traitorous to her own kind.

"Do you always ask so many questions of your patrons?" Ana asked, getting bored with Cordelia's inquisition.

"None of my patrons have been as interesting as you in some time," Cordelia replied. She pushed off the door and finally started toward her. "So, tell me, girl. What brought you here?"

"I wanted to know if you were real," Ana said bluntly. "I've seen others claiming to be witches when they were nothing more than humans thinking they could worship a star and all their pitiful little dreams would come true. Not knowing the true magik was deep within and yet, all around. That magik doesn't require worship, but it does require respect."

Cordelia's smile widened. "So, you are of the shadow coven," she noted. She picked up a raven skull from the table and rubbed her thumb over it. "What I would give to see those ancient texts," she added. "You know, the demons here... some of them are quite prejudiced toward my kind. I'd be careful talking about your old friends."

"Another reason I'm here," Ana said. "I wondered what you could tell me about them. If they can be trusted."

"Trusted?" Cordelia scoffed. "Trust is a blind word. I can't tell you whom to trust, but I can offer something you might be interested in if you're feeling a bit... overwhelmed."

Ana's brow elevated at the intriguing notion. "Oh?"

Cordelia stepped toward the back of the shop and gave Ana a beckoning nod, to which Ana only hesitated a moment to follow.

"Demons in Shadowmyer are more tame than those you may have known in Icemyer," Cordelia continued. "I hear there they exist in their true forms. Feral, mostly."

Demons and reapers in Icemyer were one of two things: excruciatingly violent with no human existence left in them, or absolute lovable beings that would hug you rather than kill you. They all existed in their shifted demon forms, completely raw with power and unapologetic for their ferocity and bloodlust. These were the only demons she'd knowingly come across, though now that she knew demons and reapers in Shadowmyer existed in human-like forms...

She wondered how many she had truly met over the years. It made her question every ranking soldier she'd put her claw through and which had been responsible for cleaning up her messes in shadows of their own.

"When you were there, did you ever have to worry about being killed by any of them?" Cordelia asked.

Ana thought back to solstice nights when the feral demons were more violent than usual. She thought of how she'd been trapped in a cave by one and had to slice her way through its flesh while singing one of the texts she'd learned not a week earlier. But even that demon had managed to walk away from her assault and heal itself soon after.

The next solstice night, the witches had held a ritual around her naked body.

"And how would you kill a demon?" Ana asked, apprehensive of whatever the witch had in her backroom.

Cordelia threw back the curtain in the back and pulled a box from a shadowed compartment on the wall. Keys jangled when she fetched them off her wrist, and when she opened the dark wood box, Ana stilled.

"With this," Cordelia said.

It was a dark, silver-bladed dagger with a hilt of jagged bone. The blade curved just slightly, and on the very edge, she noted a neon green glint flickering off of it when it caught the light.

Ana recognized the glow from her time in the glacial crystal caves, from the fires the witches would sometimes burn on solstice nights.

She reached out, and Cordelia placed it in her open palms. The neon green flared with every turn, and suddenly Ana was back in the middle of that ritual. She remembered the bright green crystals placed all around her, two in her open, bleeding palms on her knees, a glittering of the crushed stones decorating her naked body and face. More of the crushed powder in two lines they had carved in the bottom of her feet, like they were merging that stone with her own blood. She had sat in the middle of that fire and felt its cold wrap over her flesh the entire night while the coven spoke in words around her. She hadn't been told what the ritual was, only that if she was to succeed in her duty, she needed to do it.

So Ana hadn't argued.

She could still smell it all around her. The sulfur and smoke that nearly made her vomit. How after, the demons hadn't fucked with her.

Ana considered the knife in her hands. It might be useful to have a backup plan should she ever have her tongue cut out, or be in a predicament that meant she couldn't use her voice. And considering she was currently dating a demon, it might not be such a bad thing to have on hand.

No matter how sexy he was.

"Where did you get this?" Ana asked.

Cordelia smiled and turned her back, heading over to another table. "Don't ask questions you cannot handle the answer to," she replied.

The coy remark sent Ana fuming. Ana lunged, her hand around the witch's throat as she shoved her into the dresser. "Sell me a knockoff, witch, and it will be your ashes scattered on this rug, not the incense," she hissed. "I was not raised by the ancient witches to be treated like some idiot girl by a new age nymph."

Cordelia raised a hand, a whisper of an energy Ana could only feel wrapping around the witch's fingers, and Ana released her like fire. She knew that wave of wrist, that feeling pulsing off Cordelia's hand. She'd felt it more times than she could count.

Cordelia smiled slyly as she gathered her wits and straightened her dress.

"You don't want it?" Cordelia asked, picking up the blade.

Ana eyed the witch, then eyed the knife. "How much?"

"For you?" Cordelia seemed to calculate her, gaze darting wholly over Ana's figure to the point that Ana resisted shifting on her feet.

"For you, I'll take one vial of your blood. Just one, and in exchange, you can have the only knife capable of killing an actual demon."

"I don't do blood deals," Ana countered.

Cordelia shrugged. "Fine." The witch started musing around the shop again in such a nonchalant way that Ana nearly threw the nearby table over. She shifted, hands stretching at her side as she resisted taking that blade and cutting this woman's throat.

"Why do you want my blood?" Ana finally asked.

"Call it mild curiosity," Cordelia said. "Besides, what is one tiny little vial of your blood compared to having this?" Her smile widened. "Tick-tock, girl. Don't let the clock catch you."

Ana considered it. She did genuinely want the knife. She hadn't known how badly she wanted it until that moment. She imagined all the times she could have used such a blade in the past. All the times she might need it in the future if she was to become Queen of the Dead.

She wondered if it might debilitate Death himself.

Ana slowly met the witch's eyes and uncurled her fist. "One vial."

And the smile that met Cordelia's eyes danced with such triumph and sadism that Ana had to swallow when the witch drew her own knife.

Chapter Sixteen

Sam picked Ana up on his bike after three in the afternoon. She was casual that day: faux leather skirt and a ripped band tee, black jacket, and tall boots. Her hair was a wild beauty of curls, and her eyes... he swore they became more of a violent green every time he saw her.

He took his helmet off and offered it to her when she approached. "Hi," he managed, giving her entire body a once over that he didn't try to hide the lust in.

Ana's lips twisted at the corner, and she bent to kiss his cheek as she took the helmet. "Stalker," she answered. "Where are you taking me?"

"I can't ruin the surprise," he replied. He jerked his chin in the direction of the helmet. "Have you ever ridden?"

"I know my way around a bike," she said, and there was something about the way she said it made him think perhaps she was very well versed in motorcycles. From what he knew about her past, it wouldn't have surprised him.

"Let's ride then, wicked girl," he told her.

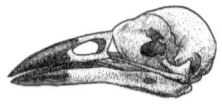

The museum was busier than Sam had anticipated it would be. Apparently, the local school had taken an after-school field trip. A few kids ran down the main entrance hall, their teacher shouting after them. He couldn't help smiling at a few, but the pair ignored them as they made their descent into the first room.

Sam inhaled the smell of the old in that room as Ana walked to one of the paintings. The old smell was one of his favorites. Antique. Dust. Leather. Paint. Perhaps that was why he left so many things as they'd been for centuries in his castle.

Sam pushed his hands in the pockets of his leather coat as he followed Ana to the first art piece on the walk, recognizing it immediately.

"Furor, 53 A.S.M.," he said. He remembered the man who had painted it. Remembered how even though it had been fifty-three years after the split of the Myers and Moors, this man had remembered what the sun looked like as a child.

"Some say he painted this from memory," he continued.

"It's beautiful," Ana said. "Amazing the detail he recalled," she added, stepping closer. "This here... the lighting over the water ripples, how the rainbow is clear. Imagine how painful this must have been for him to see so clearly."

"Why do you say that?"

Ana's eyes traveled wholly over the great canvas, a wonderment and agony stretched over her features. "The last time he'd seen the sun was at the end of a war that ended in ruin for so many. He came here for... what, exactly? Salvation?"

The question knotted Sam's stomach. "Do you think this place is a prison?" he asked.

Ana didn't look at him. "I think it's what your king thought was best at the time," she said. "But it's been centuries. Why continue hiding?"

"People are safe," he said, and he had to guard the tightness in his voice. "Maybe he wanted to make this place as strong as possible before throwing away everything the people have built."

"Or maybe he is a coward and a possessive asshole who is scared of change," she said, finally turning to him.

Sam couldn't stop his quiet huff of amusement. Of all the things he'd been called, coward wasn't one of them. Possessive asshole...

Well, he was Death, after all. He did like his things.

"So passionate," he teased. "Have you always enjoyed politics?"

They started walking to the next exhibit, and Ana sighed, a soft smile on her face. "Not really, no," she answered. "My father loved the politics. When we lived in Firemoor, he was really involved in local government and things like that."

"What were you interested in?"

"Art," she answered. "In every form. You know, there are so many talented people. The things people created from their pain and sorrow, even from the small blips of joy they could find... I fell in love with it. Art, music, poetry..." She hung her head as she kept walking, and they paused at the next painting.

Another oil painting with a more impressionistic style than the last, entitled 'Last beginnings,' by Greene, 107 A.S.M.

Ana sighed heavily as she stared up at it, her gaze softening like the painting had washed every tense bone out of her body.

"My father fell in love with the dream of a once more united Myers and Moors. I fell in love with the people who would create it."

Sam couldn't stop staring at her. He was as confused about her as he was the first night meeting her, actually more confused. The way she spoke about the beauty of the world, the people within it...

Fuck the painting. Who was the woman standing in front of him? How was this person the same one that had been so evil and seduced so many influential people on her way to power? Sent missiles flying into castles and destroyed legions of soldiers...

He wondered if maybe this was more of her act.

Ana looked twice in his direction upon finding him staring at her, and she smiled. "You have that look on your face again," she said.

"Which one?"

"The confused one," she replied.

Sam sighed a huff and shook his head. "You puzzle me," he admitted.

"Do I?" she asked, turning into him. "How so?"

Her fingers grazing the top of his pants had his abs flinching. "I'm not sure... I don't think I've met anyone who gives a damn about the people behind the art." His thumb brushed her cheek, and Ana tilted her chin back, opening up to him. "You... Are you sure you're not a witch?"

"Says the demon," she mocked.

Sam's eyes hardened on her. "Who told you that?"

"Jay likes to talk... a *lot*..." she replied. "He has quite a few stories."

Sam's arm snaked around her waist, the other still resting by her neck. Everything made sense then. Why she had actually texted him that day. The only reason she was going on dates with him.

She was using him.

Sam's body tingled at the realization.

He'd have to work harder to distract her from this.

"Does that scare you?" he asked, deciding to play along and pretend to be the demon she thought he was.

"That you're employed by Death himself?" she asked.

"Indirectly," he said. "He stays to himself, but yes."

And he waited on her to question it more.

Ana seemed to contemplate it, and Sam's thumb stroked her skin. "No," she answered. "That doesn't scare me. But you..." Her eyes swayed over him like she was taking in the whole of his soul or whatever she thought was left of one. She sucked her bottom lip behind her teeth and lifted her chin higher, granting him further access to toy with that pretty neck should he want to.

So perfectly delicate. How he could have crushed it right there and swept her up in shadows before anyone could stop him. Not that they would. Death and their king revealing himself would be more of a story to any onlookers than the ceased existence of one lonely woman who had only just appeared in their kingdom.

Her green eyes flashed up at him, head tilting slightly. "You could scare me," she finally said.

Sam shifted on his feet, their chests flush, and his tongue darted out over his lip as he fell for the lust rising between them. He reached to her neck like he might enclose his hand upon it, but he backed the grasp away to a brush of his knuckle against her jaw, and Ana's eyes fluttered.

"Tease," she muttered. "I thought you were going to grab me right here... Give all these old people a reminder of a good time."

Sam stared at the rose and flower tattoo on the side of her neck, and he resisted pressing his fingers into her skin. "They'd all have heart attacks from the excitement of that display."

"Twenty people dropping dead at the same time just from the fantasy of you choking me might be exciting," she said in a low voice.

His palm enclosed over her tattoo, and as he held her gaze, just his thumb pressed down on the nerve there, at the small indention on the side of her trachea. His fingers wrapped beneath her hair, and he stilled her, wholly at his mercy.

Her chin stretched, throat opening as he teetered forward, his bang brushing her face. "Should we find out?" he breathed.

The air around them thickened even more. Her hands wrapped his belt, and she whispered, "Yes," with a close of her eyes.

Sam's smile lifted the right corner of his lips. "I'm going to hold you like this tonight while you suck my cock until you pass out," he rasped. "And then I'm going to fuck this pretty mouth..." He leaned forward and kissed her nose, slowly releasing that tension on her.

Ana smiled. "I'll put on extra mascara," she promised. "I know how much you love seeing it run down my face."

Shit, she was good. He had a sound mind to pull her into a janitor's closet and fuck her backwards right there. But he'd toy more with guessing how wet she was in a bit. He was seemingly enjoying their date.

His crooked smirk widened as he removed his hand completely and took a step back from her. "The red lipstick, too," he said. "I didn't get to see it smeared all over that fucking face on Death's Day."

"Done," she told him.

Sam took her hand in his then, and as they started walking together to the next exhibit, the entire room seemed to let out a great exhale.

People had stopped walking and were instead gawking at the pair; one even had her phone out. Sam caught the eye of the woman standing across the way and gave her a wink, then flipped off the camera.

They stayed in the museum for over two more hours, talking about each piece and contemplating what the artist might have felt at the moment. Though Sam knew some of the artists, he had even been friends with a few. However, he kept those details to himself and speculated with her.

He couldn't remember the last time he'd simply walked around a gallery and admired Shadowmyer's past. Sure, he would visit some of the galleries on his own just to have peace. Millie was usually too busy with her work to go with him, even though she sometimes met him for lunch on the benches. And Rolfe... Rolfe wasn't really the museum type.

"I miss her," Millie said as she chewed part of her sandwich and stared at the sculpture, shoulder leaning against Sam's. "This artist, Samantha. She was fun."

"Wasn't aware you were attached to her," Sam said before taking a bite of her food.

"We had a few dates," she said.

"What are we doing here?" Rolfe grunted from the other side of Sam, leaning on his back like he and Millie were using Sam as their personal pillow between them. "What's this sitting tree thing?" he asked, pointing at the statue.

Millie and Sam huffed a laugh, and Rolfe just rolled his head over on Sam's shoulder to look at them, his eyes hazed over slightly from the mushroom tea he'd brought for the three of them. Millie snorted as Sam took another bite of her food, and then he leaned his elbows over his knees.

"Samantha was obsessed with trees," Millie said. "She thought they were connected to the soul somehow."

"Oh yeah," Rolfe said, pulling his foot onto the bench. "I remember her. Fun times."

"What did you know about Samantha?" Millie asked.

"How fucking perfect her pussy tasted," Rolfe said before blowing out his smoke to the ceiling.

"Ah, it did, didn't it?" Millie agreed.

"Excuse me, sir," someone new said as they approached their bench. "You can't smoke in here."

Sam glanced over his shoulder, a smile on his face as the security guard glared at Rolfe, and Rolfe blew a plume of smoke in the guard's face. The guard's eyes fluttered, Millie snorted, and Sam knew they were about to be kicked out.

"Yeah, we're going," Sam said as he stood. The guard looked wary, but Sam waved him off. "I've got him," he said before grabbing Rolfe's hand and hauling him up. "Never inviting you back," he bantered. "Ruined my peaceful spot."

"—Sam?"

Sam blinked back to reality as Ana squeezed his thigh, and he turned his head to find her watching him.

"You dazed off," she said.

"Sorry," he muttered. "You want to go grab some food?"

Her smile softened, and she nodded. "Yeah."

Sam took her hand, kissing her knuckles, then stood with her and headed towards the next room. There was a small cafe on the eighth floor that he liked. Great sandwiches, his favorite, a nice view of the uptown area—

Though by the way Ana was rubbing his arm and playing with his fingers, he wondered if perhaps she had a different idea for nourishment.

Ana paused in front of a marble statue on the fourth floor: a naked man, nearly eight-feet-tall with long, billowing hair, full spread wings, and a crown. Scars along his trim chest and eyes of pain.

Her fingers tenderly caressed his palm in a way that had a warmth trickling up his arm and settling in the pit of his stomach, and Sam forgot that they were staring at a depiction of Death himself.

"You know, this makes me wonder," she said, causing Sam's attention to idle on her. Her tilting head, the curl that fell over her eyes, the exposure of her throat, and the continuous toy of her teasing hand in his. He wondered how with such little touch, he was somehow unable to focus on anything else. Her lashes lifted to him, sweeping with the smile she gave him, and she seemed to laugh at his expense.

"What?" he asked.

"You're not listening to me again," she teased.

Sam smiled, turning into her. "It's your eyes," he said.

"Oh? So, I should wear sunglasses inside so that you listen to me?"

His crooked smile widened. "I listen to you." He turned his attention to the statue. "What does this statue make you wonder?" he asked.

Ana looked up at it. "It makes me wonder if Death is truly so beautiful as this statue shows he is, or—" she turned toward the one at their back, the statue of a crude demon with a forked tongue sticking out of a triangle mouth. It was taller than the first one, with bat wings and a tail, long toenails and curled feet. Sam remembered the man who had made this one as a joke one Death's Day.

"—Or if Death is as cruel and vulgar as the rest of the Myers and Moors say he is," Ana finished.

"Maybe he is all of those things," Sam answered. "And maybe his demons are the same."

She glanced up at him. "I do hope that's a promise," she said.

Sam chuckled under his breath, stepping flush to her, his hair falling over his face. "I don't make promises, wicked girl." His lips landed on hers. Soft. Fleeting. He smiled at the sight, making her lean forward like she was about to fall off-balance in his absence.

"I make vows of Death." He tugged her bottom lip between his teeth, noting a few onlookers who were staring at them. His eyes slid to one a few feet to his left, and he gave the older woman a wink that made her jump.

But Ana didn't seem to notice. She grasped the lapels of his jacket, making him look back at her. "Vow that you'll make me see stars later," she whispered.

"I'll make you see them right now."

He wasn't sure he gave two fucks about the people watching as the pair finished making their way through the statues, all the way to the elevators on the opposite side of the room. Ana made a couple of comments about a few more, though Sam didn't entirely catch her musings.

He was too focused on feeling her around his cock again.

And that smart fucking mouth... he'd fuck that too.

The line for the elevator made his lips curl. He took Ana's hand, nodding toward the stairwell door, and Ana shrugged, but followed along behind him. He'd no sooner let the door shut behind him before he was yanking her into his arms, his lips pressing greedily to hers.

Ana pulled free and slapped his cheek, making Sam growl delightedly, and upon seeing the wild glint in her eyes, his gaze snatched on the closet door behind them. Sam grabbed her wrists and yanked her flush.

"Are you going to slap me every time?" he asked through clenched teeth.

Ana fought against his grip. "That depends," she answered. "Is it going to get your cock this hard if I do?"

He nearly grinned. Fuck, she was fun.

Sam shoved her sideways, her back knocking into the closet door, and as he kissed her again, he opened the door, allowing them inside the dimly lit room. But he didn't last long on her front. He jolted and turned her into the wall as the door closed behind them. He pressed into her back, pulling a groan from her as the shelves rattled around them. Her ass ground into his hardening length. His lips were on her neck, hands bunching her skirt up at her hips. Ana's quiet moan filled the tight space, one of her hands curling around his head, the other on his left as he pushed his pelvis into her.

"Sam..." His name was a plea, a devotion.

"You feel that, baby?" he whispered, his tongue raking over the side of her neck. "Do you feel what you do to me?" His hand wrapped around to her stomach, tickling down and down, her head sinking back to his chest, and he teased over the lace underwear she wore.

He wondered if it was the black thong he'd seen peeking out of her drawer.

Fuck, she was wet, too.

"Wicked girl... How long have you been this wet for me?" he said, smiling against her. "Was it since I held this pretty fucking throat in front of everyone?"

"Don't give yourself so much credit," she ground out. "It was the naked statue on the fourth floor."

Sam whipped her around, pinning her into the wall, and Ana's lips lifted into a smile. She jerked forward like she might bite his mouth, but he grasped her tighter, and Ana chuckled under her breath. He leaned down, tongue licking hers, but he didn't kiss her yet. Every movement of her hips, her heaving breasts against his chest, had him needing her more and more.

He hovered there, his own smirk holding his lips hostage at the sight of her writhing in his grasp.

"I should really fuck some manners into that mouth," he growled.

She breathed a laugh. "I hope you do."

He finally kissed her, and when warmth bloomed in his chest, he nearly lost control.

Fucking Deianira Bronfell...

She consumed his thoughts, his heart, his every fantasy. Somehow... Somehow, he'd been on two dates with her and was already fumbling for air.

She grasped his belt, pulling the buckle free, and his fist slammed into the wall by her head when she moved her fingers over his length.

"Have you been this needing of me since I grabbed your belt?" Her mouth brushed his jaw, and Sam cursed the air.

"Yeah, baby," he told her. "That's all you."

He kissed her again, grabbing for her skirt and pushing it up to her waist. His hand trickled over her bare ass, realizing that she had worn that fucking thong, and he gripped her flesh so tightly that she moaned into his mouth. Fuck, every part of her made him wild. He loved the way he could grab her thickness and it would fill up his hands.

His thumb caught the band of her thong, and he pulled it down, nearly making her trip as she tried to pull her feet out. Sam stuffed the underwear in his pocket, and then he bent to grasp her under her ass and lift her higher on the wall. Ana gasped but held onto his shoulders. And when he slid inside her, Ana cried out while Sam cursed a little louder than he should have.

"Fuck, Ana," he groaned at the feeling her tightness surrounding him. Fucking Death, she was made for him. He couldn't get over how she felt, how he could have stayed inside her for hours and never grown tired of it—

The door rattled.

They froze, breaths holding together as they watched the shadow at the bottom of the door. But as Ana muttered a curse under her breath, Sam simply chuckled under his breath, smiling against her, and he started moving slowly in and out of her. The shadow on the other side of the door moved away, probably just one of the guests knocking into it.

"Sam…"

He clapped his hand over her mouth, their eyes meeting, and as he moved, filling her up to the hilt, he watched her chest fall jaggedly, her head tilting back.

"Shhh, wicked girl," he whispered in her ear. "You can wake the dead tonight… But right now I need you to be very… *very* quiet…" His teeth caught her, tongue licking over her pulse point, and he hiked her legs higher, pulling his hand away from her mouth.

"Let me fuck you slow," he said. "I want your legs numb when I'm finished with you."

With every push of him inside her, her mouth sagged open and she stared at the ceiling with pleasure and denial over her features. She was straining to keep herself from crying out. Her toes curled, thighs shaking and tightening around him to the point that he too began to strain at holding himself from spilling over.

"Fuck, baby," he managed breathlessly. She pulled him closer, her nails digging into his skin at denying herself, and she began to whimper. He smiled into her neck at the noise of it, and he grabbed her jaw, pushing her cheeks together in response.

"I love hearing that denial in the back of your throat," he breathed. He thrust into her hard, making a high-pitch noise leave her as her back jolted against the wall, and he threw his hand over her mouth again. "Surrender to me, temptress," he whispered, watching visible chills rise on her skin. "You surrender to me, and only me, after today." Their eyes met, and he focused on that glint of power in her dilated pupils as he finished with, "You're mine, baby."

With every thrust after, Ana seemed to limp and let herself go. She scratched his chest, neck, and forearms as she spilled over him, tears crawling down her cheeks. She was a chaotic mess of release and silence, and when he finally released inside her, he, too, couldn't stop shaking.

He only realized he was still holding his hand over her mouth when Ana's nails gently scratched his wrist, and he let her go. Heavy breaths left her as though she'd been unable to breathe for a bit, and her feet hit the ground as he slipped out of her, continuing to hold her waist. He kissed her softly, again and again, until Ana's quiet chuckle against his lips made him pull back, and his own smile lifted despite himself.

"What?" he asked.

"Nothing," she said. "I just…" She looked up at the ceiling, seeming to shake her head at herself. "I can't believe I'm about to say this. But I literally can't feel my legs, so if you could just keep holding up me a minute while the blood comes back, that would be great."

Sam actually laughed this time. He couldn't stop it from coming out. And not his usual coy laughter. This laughter met his eyes and lifted the weight off his chest, his shoulders... and for a moment, he forgot he was not supposed to be enjoying this like this. Enjoying breaking someone's heart and bringing them crumbling down, yes. But not... not *actually* laughing.

Ana stared at him, her eyes softening, and she stared at him like she couldn't discern if he were real or not. "You can laugh," she said in disbelief.

He shook his head. "That's not what that was."

"Holy Death, the brooding, dangerous asshole of a demon can laugh," she repeated, her smile wide. "I'm telling everyone. We're ruining that mysterious reputation."

"Ana—"

"It's too late, I've heard it—"

Sam kissed her before she could utter another word, and when he did, his heart fled. Both arms wrapped her waist, her hands running behind his neck, and he hugged her tight. Their laughter settled into a quiet stillness. He pulled back, his thumb brushing softly over her cheek, and soon, he couldn't move or look away from her emerald gaze.

Shit, she was beautiful.

"Can you stand yet?"

She nodded, and he let her go slowly, watching her steady herself by holding to the stool near them. When he was satisfied she was okay, he began adjusting his pants and buckling his belt. Ana shuffled her skirt down and reached for a paper towel, but Sam grabbed her wrist before she could.

"Oh, no, you're not cleaning up," he said, and Ana's brows narrowed. "You're going to walk around the rest of this museum with my cum leaking out of that pretty fucking pussy."

"So possessive," she teased.

Sam's brow heightened as he paused in buckling his belt. "Baby, you have no idea." He hovered over her and reached between her thighs, feeling the stick already threatening to spill down, and he smiled as he brought his covered thumb to her mouth, where he dragged the pad over her bottom lip. "Taste us," he said. "Tell me what you think."

Her tongue ran over her lip, and she smiled up at him. "Divine darkness," she answered.

His mouth flinched upwards. "Perfect."

Chapter Seventeen

For three weeks, Ana barely made any progress in her duty trying to find out more about the Shadowmyer king. She would wake, go to work, have lunch with Jay, and by the time she was done at the gallery, Sam was usually waiting for her out front of her apartment. For the first week, she'd found herself either on her knees or bent over some piece of furniture every afternoon. During the second and third week, they'd slowed down jumping each other every second and sometimes merely watched television together on the couch or went out for a walk.

But every night, between 2am and 3am, Sam left her bed to go to work.

And in the hours she had on her own, she would take a nap, or then roll out her notebooks on the table and open her computer.

Shadowmyer didn't have online records as the other kingdoms did. They didn't even have an active military. There were no departments for her to look through for information. Only a small council that the king allowed the people to choose every few years. But from what she could see, even their emails didn't have any valuable information in them. More than once, Ana had wanted to throw her computer out of the window. She'd hacked into the council feed once when the king had joined them for a meeting, but it was unimportant to her mission, and their elusive leader had cloaked himself in shadows.

She hadn't even been able to find any dirty little secrets on any of the council members.

So *boring*.

No affairs. No secret escorts. No pedophiles or trafficking circles.

They were absolutely clean.

The only thing she'd found of interest was the secret email of one, his last name Rogers, that had been communicating with someone Ana knew to be inside Firemoor. She thought that was interesting, but only made a note of it to continue monitoring in case her own name came up between them.

She'd not been able to tail any of them yet due to her afternoons being... occupied. But she did have a few that she followed with their phone pings. None ever went to Castle Corvus, and Ana soon realized none of them knew who their king was either.

So Ana resorted to sticking closer to the one who was actually friends with the only person allowed in that damned castle.

Not that she was complaining.

She'd tried to sneak out and follow Sam onto the cemetery grounds a few times, but she hadn't been able to see anything for the rain coming down.

It rained so much there. She wasn't used to it. Firemoor had been disgustingly hot and humid and she'd hated the way her hair reacted to it. Ironmyer was a little drier, though still felt like the stanching armpit of a deathhound. Windmoor's southern seas were breezy and dry, nearly too breezy for her liking. Icemyer was practically a cold wasteland. And The Spine... the Spine was pretty mild. Of the five territories, that was the one she'd been most comfortable in as far as weather, but their king... he'd been an old grumpy asshole that liked to watch her rather than touch her—which she hadn't complained about. Not one bit.

Ana straightened her dress as she sat outside the Hand of the King's office at SkyCor. She'd made the appointment a week earlier after chatting with Jay again about securing some of the art pieces to sell. It was her backup plan for getting into the castle if this Sam thing didn't work out.

Jay had told her she'd likely get one of the Hand's assistants or interns, but not the Hand herself.

"There's no way you're getting in to see her. She's exclusive to the King. Rather wild, honestly. You've probably seen her riding her bike up to the castle. It wakes me up every morning. She's intimidating as fuck, too. If you see her in the street, you don't talk to her," Jay had told her. *"There's a rumor that she can kill you with a wink."*

Ana rolled her eyes. "Exaggerations of witches," she replied before biting down on a crispy fry. *"I'll get in to see her."*

"I love how confident you are," he teased. *"Something tells me you've*

worked royals before."

A quiet laugh left Ana. "Royals are all the same," she said, nearly rolling her eyes. "Desperate to have the biggest cock in the room."

"Cheers to that," he agreed, holding up his drink.

"Ms. Smith?"

A girl who looked to be fresh out of high school came walking around the corner with a clipboard in her hand, her coarse curls pulled back from her face into a high ponytail, and she gave Ana a small smile.

Ana rose from her seat. "Yes?"

"The Hand will see you now."

Yes, Ana thought to herself.

She tried to hide her smile as she followed the girl down a wide, bright white hall. Modern art decorated the walls, and Ana actually found herself pausing to look for the artist names on a couple of them. The girl escorting her stopped, glancing back over her shoulder, but Ana ignored her and snapped a photo on her phone of the pieces. She sent one to Sam, an abstract line art with gold accents of a woman sitting sideways, her backside on display.

The girl cleared her throat, and Ana quickly put her phone on silent before hurrying after her.

At the end of the hall, the space darkened. A black wall lined with accents of gold light fixtures, and a few plants, met them. Long benches sat against it, plush pillows on the tops. The grand black door in the middle looked like a black hole ready to swallow her, and Ana found herself suddenly intimidated by the magnificence of the color so stark to the white and glass hallway.

Three knocks, and the girl stuck her head inside the door to announce Ana. Ana straightened her jacket and pushed her shoulders back, preparing for whomever it was on the other side. But the girl just turned and gave her a smile, and then she pushed the door open wide.

A beautiful blonde woman sat behind the desk, dressed in a pantsuit that made Ana jealous of the woman's smaller breasts. The top came down low, showcasing the long gold chain the woman had draped on her pale alabaster skin. Her hair pillowed in cascading curls over one shoulder, and she lifted her chin in Ana's direction as her assistant closed the door. Ana had to force herself not to stare, not to bow her head. This woman was undoubtedly one of the most beautiful women she'd ever seen. And when she spoke…

Ana felt her will bending.

Recognition showed in the woman's eyes, and she twisted in her chair, giving Ana her full attention as she steepled her fingers beneath her slender chin.

"You must be Jay's new curator," the woman said, her voice sultry and caressing, as if she could fuck Ana's mind without moving out of her chair.

It was that same aura she felt around Sam. Power. Assuredness. Absolution. That this woman was certainly one of Death's demons was not in question. The fact that she was also so close to the king made her all the more possessive and dangerous.

Ana could have bathed in the stench of it.

She collected herself and nodded to answer the Hand's question. "Ana Smith," she introduced herself, stepping forward.

The woman seemed to find her name amusing. "Smith... The only people using the name 'Smith' around here are running from something," she said, brown eyes trickling over her. "But I do *love* a good mystery. Tell me your official story, Ms. Smith."

Ana didn't reply directly. She'd dealt with enough people in power to know when they were trying to work her first.

"It is my understanding you have some pull with the art in Castle Corvus," Ana chose to say.

"Business first," the blonde toyed. "All right. I can appreciate someone who goes directly to the point."

"Do you have access to the art or not?" Ana asked.

The corner of the blonde's mouth quirked. "Being Hand of the King has its perks," she replied. "What's your interest?"

"Something tells me a few of these paintings haven't seen the light or a good dusting in centuries, what with the place not being open to the public and no servants or otherwise working there," Ana said. "I'd like to offer to auction some of the paintings off. Of course, we'd give the money to your King's favorite charity. It might create some good PR for him in light of everything happening in Firemoor right now. I've heard rumors of people questioning whether he will do something or remain hidden."

The woman's lips tightened. "If there's something you'd like to say about how your king handles the situation, say it."

But Ana shook her head. "I've said nothing. Only that perhaps your king should consider options for the public face."

"I wasn't aware curators had a *knack* for relations," she said, a warning in her voice.

Ana didn't say anything. She just stared, and the blonde huffed.

"Do you drink, Ms. Smith?" she asked as she stood and began grabbing her jacket from the back of her chair.

Ana pushed her bag further up on her shoulder as the blonde stalked around the desk. "I do," she replied.

"Good. I like to take my leave around now and go to the bar downstairs. The bartender is heavy-handed and quite the fuck." The blonde paused at the door and turned around to her. "You can call me Millie. Now, let's go cheers to that fucking twisted brain of yours."

Ana hated how much she liked this woman.

She'd never really had friends, unless she counted the few witches that had taught and raised her in Icemyer. Every being she'd interacted with in the last ten years had been a transaction—all business, little pleasure.

Maybe it was that need inside her for companionship that drove her to relax a little that afternoon.

Millie held up her second drink to Ana's and cheers'd her. The beautiful demon's smile was broad, and her eyes… Her eyes held such secrets. Devious secrets. Ana had looked in the mirror and seen her own eyes share that same expression a few times before. On the days when she'd slain her final enemy, on the day that she sent those missiles into the Ironmyer castle.

"To the Smiths that they find their ways through the shadows," Millie declared with a clank against Ana's drink. Ana smiled and drank a sip in agreement.

"Are there truly so many Smiths as you say?" Ana asked.

"There are, actually," Millie answered. "Lost souls that found their way here. Most of the people working the cemetery are Smiths. I've always enjoyed seeing Smith's working their way through the system to better their standings. Most get here and have so little left after paying a navigator that they start at the bottom. But the king has resources for everyone on every corner. It's one of the reasons I love this place. Everyone remembers where they came from, and no person is left behind."

"I've heard you call this place a sanctuary for people cast out of other realms," Ana said. "If he truly wanted a haven, why keep the shadow borders?"

The talk seemed to make Millie's mood weaken. "Because without them, a great number of our people would be hunted down," she answered. "How much have you been told about the people here?"

"You mean the demons and witches that live here?" Ana asked.

Millie's phone lit up, but she turned it over and shifted her full attention to Ana. "The other realms you lived in… how many demons did you meet?"

Ana thought of the ones from Icemyer, but she wasn't about to divulge that information, so she thought to Firemoor and to the Spine, where rumors of demons swept the streets and filled the air like mentioning them were poison. Newscasts blamed them for a few of the attacks on eastern Firemoor when the government army had cleansed it for fear of witches, not demons as they had been told.

"None," she answered.

"But you knew of them," Millie said. "You knew they were worse than death. And that if you were to meet one, along with a witch, you should report it immediately."

Ana stared at Millie, seeing the intensity in her eyes. "Yes," Ana said.

Millie took another long swig of her drink. "Demons cannot be killed," she said, and Ana resisted shifting at the thought of the knife that lay back at her apartment.

"They share the immortality of their maker," Millie continued. "Firemoor has been looking for a way to eliminate us since the war broke the Myers and Moors apart. But many people do not know about the prisons in the other realms. Most people don't know of the experimentation and the torture those who are caught go through every day just because of what they are." Her lashes lifted, and Ana stilled at her face.

"Samarius does not hide this place so people cannot get in. He hides this place so that the people inside are not persecuted for what they are. This place *is* a haven—"

"Why doesn't he go after his people?" Ana interjected. "If it is his own demons in these prisons, why does he allow that to go on? Why not save them? These are people he swore he could protect with their agreement to become his demons... does he not think protecting them includes saving them from these prison camps?"

"What my king does about these situations is not the business of the public," she said. "What do you think Firemoor's army would do if they saw us talking about crossing the border and taking their prisoners?" A soft chuckle came from Millie. "I don't even know why I am bothering to explain any of this to you," she said. "You're new here. Why do you care what our king does in his free time? Why can you not enjoy your new freedoms as every other person has?"

"Because maybe I have people on the outside that I want to have that freedom," Ana said. "Maybe I grew up watching all of that happen, had friends disappear and family rounded up like cattle for what they were. And maybe the only person that can save them is your king."

Ana didn't blink away from Millie for a solid moment. She waited on the demon to come back at her. To scold her for even thinking such about him. But Millie just smiled.

"Maybe the person you're searching for is the woman taking down monarchies as easily as kicking over a sandcastle," Millie said, making Ana stiffen. "I hear people worship her name in the other realms."

"Oh, they do," Ana agreed. "But she is only a mortal. Imagine what Death could do if he were to put his mind to her cause as much as he puts his mind to hiding this place."

Millie considered her, her eyes raking over Ana's entire form, and the corner of her lips lifted higher when she met her gaze again. "The paintings," she said, changing the subject. "Why do you want them?"

"I think the people immigrating into this kingdom deserve to see the true history of our world, as seen in the eyes of the people that were there, the people that are still alive and can attest to what happened," Ana answered. "Not the lies we've been taught in the others. Or is the truth another of the things your king hides?"

"Careful, girl," Millie warned.

Ana's mouth dared to flinch. "Your king and his demons are the only ones that remain alive after that war. They're the only ones that can reveal the truth, and I think revealing that starts with the art made to commemorate it. Wouldn't you like to have your story told?"

Millie's chin lifted. She chugged the last of her wine and stood, draping her coat over her arm. "I'll need a month or so to go through the collection and speak with him about any that he is willing to donate." A pause in which Millie looked at her phone and opened it up rested between them, and then the demon gave Ana a devious smile. One that held in it more secrecy than Ana had seen the entire afternoon.

"I'll be in touch, Ms. Smith."

It wasn't a moment after Millie had started walking away from her that Ana saw her put her phone to her ear. She considered following her, but figured that would be more suspicious than staying in the bar would be. But it didn't stop her from listening in on Millie's short conversation on the phone.

"Are you home?" Millie asked into the phone. There was a pause, another voice responding before she said. "I'm coming over." And with that, she hung up and pushed on the door so hard that the wall shook.

Ana resisted smiling to herself, resisted celebrating her short-lived triumph. And so, she kicked back the rest of her martini, ordered another one, and then took out a book to read.

Chapter Eighteen

Sam frowned at the call coming in on his cell, but answered quickly. "Yeah, Mills?"

"Are you home?" she asked.

He glanced across the table at Rolfe. "We are," he replied. "Just sat down to eat. You okay?"

"I'm coming over," she said.

She hung up before Sam could get another word in, and Sam stared at the screen a moment, replaying the urgent tone in her voice.

"Mills is on the way," he said, causing Rolfe to glare.

"It's fucking Tuesday," he grunted. "She doesn't usually come by at night on a Tuesday."

Sam shrugged and sipped on his beer. "Not sure." He thought that was the end of it, but Rolfe threw his napkin on the table and stood.

"What?" Sam asked.

"I don't make extra food on Tuesdays because she doesn't come," Rolfe growled as he made his way to the fridge.

Sam stared at the two trays of smoked pork and venison on the stove, but reminded himself how Rolfe liked to snack at night. Chuckling, Sam flipped open the afternoon paper he'd picked up in town.

Rolfe rummaged through the fridge and the freezer, grumbling the entire time. He finally decided on lemon pepper roasted chicken and green beans to go with the potatoes he still had going in the oven. Sam joked that he made Millie better meals than he made him, to which Rolfe glared and threw his apron onto the chair before leaving the room.

Sam laughed so loudly at his friend's tantrum that Rolfe actually came back into the room.

"The fuck was that?" Rolfe asked.

Sam settled down, realizing how boldly he'd allowed himself to let go, how good that laugh had felt, and he cleared his throat before kicking his feet back up.

"What?"

"That…" Rolfe walked back to the sheet pan of food and pushed it into the oven, his brows still narrowed as he looked Sam over. "I haven't heard you laugh like that in a century at least," he muttered. "Wouldn't have anything to do with the woman, would it?" he teased.

Sam's lips tightened into a thin line, and he flicked his paper. "Had a good day, Roll. Don't ruin it."

But Rolfe grinned. "Yeah. Right. Good day, my ass," he said. "She's already got your laugh back after three weeks of dates… What are you going to do when you fall for her?"

"She doesn't know who I am," Sam said as he flipped the page. "There's no chance of her usual seductions or games. I'm not in danger."

"That is the biggest fucking lie I have ever heard," came Millie's voice from the hall. She appeared in her usual wear for duty uptown, hair perfectly curled, makeup done, in her best black pantsuit. She threw her bag into the opposite chair from Sam and Rolfe, then stared pointedly at her king.

"You are… so fucked," she told him.

Sam eyed the way she threw her hand to her hip, how her stance radiated frustration.

"What's wrong?" he asked, creasing the newspaper.

"*What's wrong?*" Millie snorted sarcastically and shook her head. "Your fucking girlfriend showed up at SkyCor today asking about the art in Corvus," she said. "Apparently, she wants to auction some of it off. Said we could donate the money to charity for good PR, seeing as we plan to do nothing to help out the people suffering in Firemoor right now."

Rolfe choked on his drink, and Sam…

Sam smiled.

"And you said?" he asked.

"I took her out for drinks."

"Oh?" Sam's smile widened. "How did that go?"

Millie glared and stalked to the cabinets, where she took out a glass and a bottle of whiskey, poured herself a shot, then chucked it back.

"That well?" Sam teased.

Millie pushed herself to sit atop the counter. "You're fucked," she repeated. "I spoke with her over drinks for two hours, and I already feel my knees bending. You... Sam, this is a terrible idea."

"Why?"

"Because I'm worried about you," she admitted.

Sam sighed heavily and took his feet down from the table. "I'm fine, Mills," he said. "Good to know she's going straight to the top this time, though. Less of a mess to clean up."

"Samarius, this isn't funny," Millie argued.

He contemplated his demon a moment, head tilting. "You don't have to worry about me," he said, the tone a mix between a warning and a promise.

"What would you like me to tell her?" Millie asked.

"What *did* you tell her?"

"I told her I'd be in touch."

"Then say you'll schedule something at the end of next month," he said.

His phone buzzed then, and as he lifted it up to see the screen, he saw Millie cross her arms over her chest. Sam just stared at the text message on display.

I learned a new word today, Ana texted him.

Millie sat down at the table with a plate of food. She and Rolfe said something, but Sam crossed his leg over his knee and started typing back.

What's the word? he asked.

Nyctophilia, she answered.

Sam almost smiled at the word. *Are you just figuring out that you have a love of the darkness or that there is a word for it?*

I didn't know there was a word for it, she replied. *Smartass.*

Sam huffed amusedly at the message, and he sent back, X

Oh, he's too good for emojis, Ana teased him.

I like words better, he said. *Feels more meaningful.*

The three dots at the bottom of the page flickered a moment long enough that Sam took a long drink of his water, and when the message finally appeared, he hated himself for what it did to him.

"I see as much beauty in the darkness as I see horrors in light."

Sam's cock twitched at the words, at the comparison of horrors in daylight and the comfort in darkness. It attracted his mind, spoke to his heart... Had she spoken those words out loud in front of him, he might have grabbed and pulled her into a room to fuck her right then.

Who said that? he asked.

Not sure, she replied. *I read it somewhere when I was younger. It stayed with me.*

Sam's muscles suddenly ached, and he wasn't sure why. *Do you have any idea how much quotes like that turn me on?*

Oh? And he wondered if she was smiling at the phone then. *Now you have me curious what else turns you on. Is it the conversation or the darkness?*

Both.

"Mills, you have tickets to Gregg's symphony tomorrow?" he asked, interrupting whatever conversation she and Rolfe were having at the table.

"Oh, how nice of you to join us again," Millie said as she sucked on a chicken bone. Her head tilted mockingly at him, and Sam raised a brow at her.

"The horror show?" she asked. "Of course, I have a ticket for you."

"Mind adding one more?"

Millie didn't reply at first, but she considered him. "Two tickets. Usual slums, or would you like an upgrade?"

"Tiny upgrade," he said, standing up and taking his plate to the sink. "Nothing flashy."

"His Majesty doesn't want to show his consort the full extent of power?" she asked.

Sam washed the plate and placed it in the dishwasher. "You know Jay told her I was a demon?" he said, nearly laughing as he caught their amused gazes.

Millie laughed. "Poor thing, is your dick feeling smaller at being compared to us, lowly soldiers?"

Sam looked to Rolfe as he started to the hall. "She's not seen yours in a while, has she?"

"Been about a century, I think," Rolfe grinned. "Maybe she needs a refresher."

Sam flicked Millie's hair as he strode past her, winking at Rolfe, and Millie threw a bone at Rolfe, which Rolfe caught in his teeth and crunched up like a potato chip.

"Send them to my phone, Mills," he called back to her. "I'll see you both in the morning."

"Where are you going?" Millie called.

Sam's phone buzzed again, and he smiled down at the risqué photo

Ana had just sent him. He tilted his head at the position of her with her ass in the air, camera pointed back from her outstretched arm on the edge of the bed. His cock stirred at the sight of it.

Does this make it better or worse? Ana asked.

Sam circled back and bent down around Millie; the photo pulled up on his phone as he pushed the screen in front of her. Millie choked on her drink, and Sam smiled by her ear.

"Look at her, Mills," he growled in her ear. "I'm going to make her beg for me without even being in the room... do you remember how I used to do that?"

Millie swallowed, and as Sam's fingers brushed her arm, he saw her thighs squeeze with the invasion he had taken of her mind. Pushing feelings and thoughts into her with a simple touch.

He didn't always need to touch the person, though sometimes it made things a little more intimate, a little more consuming. And he enjoyed the feeling of drowning with them.

"Samarius..." Millie squeezed the table, and Sam smiled as Millie held her breath.

"Can't you see it, Mills?" he whispered in her ear. "I know you've been staring at her since the festival, imagining how perfect her cunt would taste... And it does, doesn't it? Can't you taste her? Can't you feel how tight she is? Look at how beautiful she looks when you're fucking her," he added, pushing in the memory of him fucking her in front of the mirror and making it Millie in the vision instead of himself. "Let me in, Milliscent. Taste my victory."

Millie visibly denied the vision he pushed into her, of her fucking Ana, letting Millie feel everything he had felt while fucking her, tasting her... until Millie couldn't resist any longer, and he watched as she started breathing again, nearly panting—

Sam released her fully and closed the phone.

"I fucking hate you," Millie snapped in a breathless voice.

Rolfe howled with laughter, and Sam flicked her hair again.

"Tickets, Milliscent," he said as he started down the hall again. "Maybe next time, I'll let you finish."

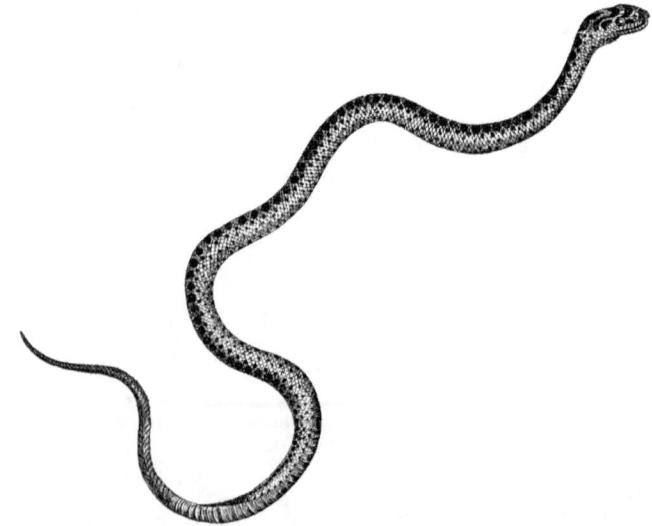

Chapter Nineteen

Ana leaned back on her pillow, staring at the three dots as she waited on Sam's message.

Fuck, baby, Sam replied. *Let me get to my room before you start with that.*

Don't want to be hot and bothered in front of your friends? she asked.

The dots rippled again, and she thought perhaps he was sending her a photo, but what he said caught her off guard.

A friend has tickets to the orchestra in midtown tomorrow, he typed. *Cinematic horror.*

Even with the abrupt change in conversation, Ana's attention perked to the idea. *That sounds amazing.*

Pick you up at six?

Perfect, she replied. *But tonight, you can stop dodging my flirting and send me a photo.*

Sam took a few minutes, and she nearly laughed as she waited for his reply, but when it did come through, she hugged the phone to her chest and grinned.

Hot, she said.

The selfie he'd sent was of him, waist up, with his shirt off, all his tattoos in full glory, holding a black cat up on its hind legs in front of his chest. She could just see the shadows around his face, his hair falling over his eyes as he looked down at the midnight cat, and the cat looked up at him.

Ana couldn't help changing her phone background to the photo. It was so irresistibly Sam. To show off his tattoos and his hands, hands she knew that he was aware drove her wild. Her eyes fluttered at the memory of how he'd held her in front of a long mirror two days before, both kneeling on the bed, with her exposed in front of him.

He'd held her from behind and teased her clit, making her watch in the mirror.

"I want you to watch the fucking look on your face when you come, baby," he'd growled in her ear. *"I want you to see how well you respond to me."*

She had seen herself. She had watched her entire body move and her thighs tighten. Had seen the sag of her mouth and how he stared at her like she was his prey. And when he'd shoved her into the mattress to yank her hair and fill her from behind, she'd watched as he pounded into her, and she cried out his name.

"What do you think, baby?" he'd asked after, *when he cradled her in his arms and held her on his lap at the edge of the bed, squeezed her ass and caressed her cheek. "Do you like the way we look together?"*

She'd genuinely looked at them then, and in that image, all she saw was power. She wasn't sure why, if maybe it was another of his demon tricks to get her to see what he wanted her to see. But she felt invincible there, in his arms, staring at each other in that mirror. His tattooed hands and body wrapped around her curves, grasping at her full flesh.

Ana had taken her phone out and captured a photo of them, to which Sam had smiled into her neck after. *"Send that one to me,"* he'd told her.

The dots on the bottom of her screen flickered again, and Ana pushed herself back to reality.

How did I know you would like a photo of my cat? Sam typed.

Lucky guess, she said. *I didn't know you were a cat man.*

She keeps me calm, he told her.

Ana smiled at the screen. *That's cute.*

And how is my kitty? he asked. *Is she wet for me?*

Ana didn't have to move her hands between her thighs to know she already was. The thought of him alone had her wet those days, and when she thought about the things he did to her… she began to throb.

The lights in her room flickered, lightning cracking outside as the rain pounded on her windows. Louder and louder, like it meant to suck out any sound she might make.

Soaking, she replied.

I wish I could taste how wet you are.

She did too. *Come over.*

Maybe I'll come over on my break.

I need you now, she told him.

Fuck, baby, he typed. *I can't tonight. I have to work soon.*

Ana slumped into the bed with a huff. *Tell me what you would do to me if you did come over.*

The three dots rippled over the bottom for a moment. *I think I would blindfold you.*

Ana stared at the screen. Shit, this was new.

I think I would tie you down, he continued. *Blind you. Headphones, too. And then I would leave you sprawled and needing on that bed. Long enough that you might begin to panic at not hearing any sounds, just the vibration of the rain pounding on your windows.*

Thunder cracked outside, making Ana jump, and her heart picked up at the next text.

Maybe for hours. Maybe for minutes. The point is… you would lose track of reality. And I would sit back and watch your breathing shorten. I would watch your nipples peak at the thrilling fear running through you.

Ana went wholly still.

Can't you see it, baby? he asked.

Shit, she could almost hear him whispering in her ear.

Your beautiful body wholly exposed and waiting, with no way of knowing if it was me or some intruder helping themselves to your flesh. You would be a feast for any demon that might walk by that door and smell your fear. Would you like that?

Ana swallowed, envisioning it, and for some reason, the warmth between her thighs began to pool.

Yes, she answered.

That pussy would glisten so nicely for us, too, he typed.

And she could practically hear the smile she was sure he had on his face with that one.

Tell me how you would end me, she nearly begged.

The dots rippled across the screen again, making Ana's breath shorten with anticipation.

With my mouth on that pretty cunt, he typed. *You would be at my mercy. Devoted to me.*

Ana's chest heaved with her heavy breaths. She pressed her hand between her thighs, finding herself soaking as she'd thought she was, and she began to slowly swirl her clit.

You would be mine to tease, he continued. *With my tongue first, then my lips. I would enjoy sucking on you while you writhed so beautifully beneath me. Restrained and bound. Wholly mine.*

Ana could suddenly see his fantasy more vividly than she'd ever even seen reality. She could feel his tongue on her clit, his silky hair on her thighs, and him devouring her. Noises seemed to mute around her. She had to put the phone down. Her eyes closed as she arched toward the ceiling, letting her fingers do the work, imagining being bound and blindfolded—or *was* she imagining it?

Her arms became heavy against her body, her right seeming to be latched between her thighs, unable to pull herself free or stop touching herself. And her left was fixated on her breast, squeezing and taunting that taut bud. Her eyes rolled back as her lights flickered again and turned completely off.

Something about the silence that filled the room made her heart jump.

Ana stilled, head lifting off the pillow to look around her.

The phone buzzed.

Are you coming for me, baby? he asked.

Thank fuck for that distraction.

Ana turned her attention away from how alarmed she'd been and tried to focus on what Sam was saying.

Call me, he texted. *I want to hear that fucking noise you make.*

She'd never reached for her earphones so quickly before.

"There's my girl," was the first thing he said when he answered.

Ana let out a heavy breath at the comfort of him on the phone. He sounded like he'd just woken up, his voice warm and throaty and seductively vibrating.

Lightning snapped right outside her window, hitting the tree. All relaxation she'd just felt hearing his voice waned, and Ana nearly fell out of bed trying to sit up.

"Are you there, Ana?" he asked when she didn't speak.

"I'm here," she said, though her voice wasn't wholly hers.

Sam chuckled quietly. "You sound breathless, baby."

"The power just went out," she said, swallowing hard as her eyes darted around.

Wind whistled by her window. The tree outside by the lamppost thrashed.

"Old building," Sam said. "I'm sure it's just the storm... nothing more *sinister*. Though there are a few reapers and shifters that live in the buildings around you."

Ana stared into the pitch black and removed one of the ear pieces so she could hear for anything. The hair on her neck prickled as she searched that darkness. She swore it felt like eyes were on her, though she couldn't see a damned thing.

"Maybe one of them heard that pretty moan of yours and decided to scare you into a little fun," Sam said in a teasing rasp. "It is… *oh-so* intriguing," he added.

"Sam," she snapped, knowing he was trying to scare her.

His soft laugh came through the earphone, and he said, "Shh…" with amusement in his tone. "Lie back and relax for me," he said. "I'll keep you safe."

Ana willed her heart to steady as she leaned back against the pillows again and closed her eyes.

"What would you do if someone did come in right now?" he asked.

"Really not helping me relax," she muttered.

"I think you'd enjoy it," he said, and Ana stared at the phone. "I think you would fight."

"I would fight," she agreed. "And I would win, too."

He laughed. "So sure of it," he said. "How would you kill a demon?"

Ana paused. She blinked into the darkness, letting the caress of the thunder humming outside move over her skin. She glanced toward the kitchen, to the knife block she knew sat on her counter in the darkness. "I have my ways."

"Hopefully never on me," he said.

"Something tells me you might like it if I came after you with a knife," she said, trying to pull her attention to anything except the noise of the wind.

"Mmm… Keep talking like that, baby," he said. "Tell me how you would kill me."

Ana smiled. "Is this what turns you on?" she asked. "Talking about how I would kill you?"

She heard him suck in a sharp breath, and then her phone buzzed. She picked it up off the pillow, finding a picture of him in her messages. A picture of his very nice cock, erect and shadowed in his tattooed hand. Her thighs squeezed at the sight of it. She could practically taste that bead of liquid on her tongue.

"I'll keep that picture for any other lonely nights you choose work over me," she said.

Sam groaned. "You're killing me, wicked girl."

And this time, it was Ana's turn to laugh. "Oh no… that's only part of how I would kill you," she teased him. "I would stroke your cock while you sucked on my nipple, let you taste me… maybe sit on your face until I forgot how to breathe, and your dick strained to be touched." She pushed her hand back between her thighs and began to touch herself as she fantasized about being on his face again, that tongue lapping her up and down.

Sam moaned. "I love the way you taste, baby," he said. "Will you let me finish you there?"

"Is that what you want?" she asked. "You want to make me come here? On your tongue?"

"Yeah, baby," he ground out. "Give me that."

Ana's whimper sounded despite herself, her eyes closing again. Heat pooled and pooled down her body to her throbbing clit.

"I would suck that clit until you beg me to stop and you ripped the headboard," Sam added.

"Sam," she moaned out, practically feeling his tongue working her, sucking her, biting her.

"You like that, baby?"

"Yes." Ana grabbed onto her own headboard, her knees bending, and once again... Her hand was latched to that rail, and her heart skipped when she couldn't move her arm.

"Ride my face," he whispered in her ear. "Soak my tongue."

"Fuck, Sam," she whimpered, that orgasm cresting with every stroke of her fingers. She tried to move her arm again, but the feeling of it being restrained only heightened her climax more. High-pitched gasps filled the air. She was almost there— "I'm—"

"Wait right there for me, baby," Sam said. "I want to feel you come around me."

"Inside me, then," she managed, straining to pull herself together. "Sam, inside me."

"Fuck, you feel so good on my cock," he said, his voice breathless. "Ride me. Just like that."

Ana's hips bucked, moving like he were in the room with her, and she could see it. She was in that fantasy with him. Moaning and at the precipice of complete surrender. Riding his cock and feeling him hit every spot inside her that made her weak. Fuck, she could feel him inside her, how he filled her up, his fingers digging into her hips.

"Shit, Sam—"

"Ana..." She could hear his hand stroking his cock, that slapping noise making her body respond and her mouth sag. She was holding herself from coming, enjoying whatever this was far too much to bring it to an end, but she didn't know how long she could wait.

"Fuck, Sam. I love how you fill me up. *Right there*," she ground out, her hips moving against her hand.

"Right there, baby," he rasped. "Grind that pussy. Take everything you need. Just like that—*Ana*—shit—wait for me—"

"I can't," she cried out. "I can't. I'm—" She let out a shrieking moan that filled her apartment, her entire body trembling at the edge of her climax.

"Ana—Fuck—Come with me." His own breathless moan toppled her over. "Fuck, Ana, I'm—"

And spill, she did.

She let herself go as she'd not done by herself before. Her mind blanked. Ana came and came, and when she thought she was done, she found her body jerking with final strokes. She could practically feel his cock twitching inside her, though they were miles apart, and she wasn't sure she cared how he was doing that. There was only the victory of his smile on her through the dark and him all around her.

When she finally calmed down, panting and continuing to moan, she heard his quiet chuckle coming over the headphones.

The mere sound of it made a chill rise on her skin.

"You're such a good little whore, baby," he said in a throaty tone.

Ana swallowed as she composed herself. "Famous last words," she said, finding her voice.

Sam's chuckle was a rasp, his breaths still heavy on the other end. "This is when you would kill me?" he asked. "With my dick still trembling inside you?"

"You'd never see it coming," she cooed.

She wondered what his face did then, if he smiled or if he thought she was crazy, or if his dick stiffened again at the fantasy.

"I can't fucking wait to see you tomorrow," he said, his voice softer, almost desperate. "All the things I want to do to you, to that sick mind of yours... *Fuck*. I guess nightmares really do come true."

The lights flickered and came back on, making Ana jump, but she sat up, her mussed hair falling over her wildly. "Six tomorrow?"

"Yeah," he said. "I have to somehow go to work now."

Ana laughed. "Maybe I'll send you something to get you through the night."

"Please," he muttered. "I'll see you tomorrow."

"Goodnight, Sam," she managed.

"Sweet nightmares, baby."

Chapter Twenty

The morning news report from Firemoor made every excited bone in Sam's body turn to dust at the sight of it. Without a true ruler, the uprisings were growing greater in the streets of their capital, regular citizens taking up arms against grand militias—who were taking orders from the general who remained at his post.

General Prei.

There was something about him that made every hair on Sam's arms rise when he saw him in front of the camera.

Sam watched the videos on a site Millie liked to frequent, one that was run by a couple of witches she was in contact with. Sam had glared disapprovingly when she'd first told him who was behind the site, but he trusted Millie, so he would trust anything she brought him —within reason.

Cryptic reports had come in from his own demons he had spying in Firemoor. Messages telling him the chaos in that territory was perfect for a strike on the Firemoor army. And as Sam sat in his chair, fingers steepled beneath his chin, he considered it.

"What are you thinking?" Millie asked as she picked the crust off her turkey and cheese sandwich and sat it on Sam's plate.

"Have you heard anything from our people in the Spine?" he asked.

Millie shook her head. "Just the same from Damien. Says he suspects something might happen, but he's not sure when. Spies in Firemoor are saying things are in shambles, so not to worry yet."

"So, you think Damien is being paranoid?" he asked.

"It's possible," she agreed. "I don't want to count him out, but at the same time... if those we have in Firemoor are saying things are too unorganized for an attack, maybe he is."

"Or they know who our spies are and are diverting them," Sam suggested, swaying his chair back and forth.

"Do you really think that is the case?"

"I think it's possible," he answered. "What about Windmoor?" Sam asked about the southernmost territory. "When did you last hear from them?"

"Haven't spoken to them in a month," she said. "No news is good news, right?"

Sam wasn't entirely sure he liked that saying, but he didn't press it. "And Ironmyer?"

"Last one stated they were still recovering from Deianira's missile strikes," she answered. "He said the people were biding their time and trying to stock up before doing anything. Sounds like maybe they're modeling it after what the Spine is doing."

Sam's eyes narrowed. "Maybe they should seize the army while their guard is down."

"And end up starving in the ditches like we were," Millie muttered. "No, they're doing the right thing. They're not strong enough to do this yet. They have a plan, at least. That's more than what we went in with."

Sam considered her, knowing the conversation was bringing up Millie's own failures from the last war. "You were outnumbered," he told her. "You didn't have the power you have now. None of you did. Not to mention, the only thing we fought with then were swords."

Millie huffed, a smile on her lips. "I like my sword," she said. "Though a bullet through the forehead does work much more efficiently."

"It does," he agreed. "But it's not our time yet."

Millie squinted at him. "You just said Ironmyer should strike while their guard is down."

"And you've made me reconsider that thought," he said. "I need to deal with our current threat before thinking about us marching across borders." He looked up at the clock then, seeing it was past noon, meaning he had a few hours to spare before picking Ana up. He turned back to the television screen once more to watch the fighting in Firemoor.

"Let them tire out," Sam said. "Our demons in their armies can't be killed. They'll be ready when we are. Firemoor can exhaust their supplies, and their soldiers. By the time we're ready to strike, they'll be so depleted, they'll fall to their knees at the very threat of what they would be up against."

Millie sighed into the chair, swiveling in it as she stared at the ceiling. "Revenge will be so sweet," she cooed. "You know what's mine," she said, looking at him.

Sam smiled. "And you know what's mine."

A silent agreement they'd made together the day he shadowed this place.

"This sounds like a lot of plotting," Rolfe said from the door.

"I knew I smelled wet dog," Millie muttered as she sat up.

Rolfe ignored her and jerked his chin in Sam's direction. "Up for a ride this afternoon, boss?"

"I have a date, remember?" Sam announced, rising from his chair.

"Boo—"

"Bullshit—"

Millie threw the stapler at him while Rolfe threw his entire sandwich—which he immediately regretted and began to scramble for the pieces off the floor.

"I can't wait to see this blow up in your face—*Rolfe!*" Millie picked her feet up off the floor as Rolfe crawled under her to retrieve his bread.

"You should've heard him last night on the phone with her," Rolfe grunted upon standing again. He grinned at Sam. "No wonder you keep going back with that fucking moan."

Sam leaned his hips on the desk, crossing his arms. "Groundskeepers numbers," he said, ignoring Rolfe's tease.

"All accounted for," Rolfe said. "Think she's given up?"

"I've been keeping her busy," Sam said, though he wasn't sure why he was shifting on his feet. "I was thinking after tonight, I'd leave her alone for a couple of days, see what she does without a distraction."

"Want me to tail her?" Rolfe asked.

Sam shook his head. "She has me for grounds information, and now Millie for a way into the castle," he said with a nod to her. "If she's any good at her job, she'll start with any journalists that have managed to get inside."

"I can make a call and have the one at St. Orphs moved," Millie said.

"Don't," Sam said. "I want to see her work." He glanced down at his buzzing phone, seeing that it was Ana sending him a photo of an art piece they'd gotten in, and he kept a blank face as he picked it up.

"I want to know all she's capable of," he said slowly. "And why no one has ever bothered to employ her rather than simply fuck her and try to contain her. I want to know why no one has taken advantage of her chaos."

"Because the other kings only think about what makes them look powerful," Millie said, annoyance in her tone. "Beautiful woman like that means maybe they know how to work their cocks. A woman unleashed means they don't have a handle on their own kingdom."

"I must be letting everything run *rampant* then," Sam said, smirking at Millie. "I wonder what they say when they see you at the forefront of this empire."

Millie grinned. "Their dicks shrivel and turn into turtle heads," she said.

Sam pushed off the desk and grabbed his coffee and phone. "Maybe we should make the Council strip next time they're on video with you in the room. I'd love to see that."

"Imagine being so intimidated by a woman's power that you chose to extinguish it," Millie added.

Sam considered it, considered the women he'd trusted over the years who had helped him. He wouldn't be who he was without them, and he certainly wouldn't be anywhere without Millie.

"Idiots," he muttered. He started to the door, and Millie stood to collect her things.

"Anything specific for us today, boss?" she called after him.

"Take the day off," he told them. "Both of you. Let me deal with The Tower."

Chapter Twenty-One

Out front when you're ready, was all Sam texted her.

My stalker can't even escort a girl from her door? she texted back.

Baby, if I go anywhere near your door, we'll never make it to the symphony.

Ana smiled at the message as she took another glance at herself in the mirror, admiring the low-cut black jumpsuit she was wearing, how it hugged her curves and the belt cinched in her waist. She grabbed her leather jacket and keys before heading out the door.

Sam was leaning against his bike out front when Ana emerged down the stairs. He looked up and let out a plume of smoke from the thin joint he was smoking, and as his eyes traveled over her, she saw the corner of his lip lift.

"This is exactly why I didn't go upstairs," he said as she drew closer.

"Why?" she asked.

Sam's eyes darted over her again, tongue darting out and wetting his bottom lip with the survey. "Because you look like a fucking goddess," he told her. "Had I gone upstairs, I would have fallen to my knees and worshipped every part of you." He slipped a hand around her waist and pulled her close. "And after last night, it's all I've been thinking about."

Ana's chin lifted, and she reached up to his face, dragging her thumb over his lip. "Me too."

He leaned down like he might kiss her, his forehead landing on hers, mouths brushing, and as she dodged his advance, he grabbed ahold of her bottom lip with his teeth instead, leaving behind a nip that made her smile swell when he pulled away. His licentious smirk met her, and he crawled over the bike, revving the engine as she slipped on behind him.

The way Sam walked was a gift to the rest of that fucking kingdom.

He walked as though he owned the place. Hands usually in the pockets of his leather jacket, his shoulders and back straight, chin held high, with confidence in every step. Somehow his presence beckoned the people around him. Whether they realized it or not, every person seemed to bow their heads slightly when he strode past. Most, she had noticed, did not even turn to look in his direction, but their subconscious knew he was there.

He radiated power and ownership. It had taken Ana an hour or so to get used to it on their first date at the gallery, but once she did... she felt like she were part of it. Like she was under that umbrella of his protection, and no one, *nothing*, would ever hurt her again.

Well, except maybe him.

A few turned their heads as they passed through the throng of people at the performing arts center. Sam held her hand and guided her through the crowd, although he always stepped into a room after her, and he never stood in front of her. He held doors for her like he were presenting a queen, smiling at her like they shared some cosmic secret about who they were and what they could do.

As though they were the most powerful people in existence, and the rest of the world should know it.

Ana loved every second of it.

Although Sam may have radiated that energy, he certainly didn't flaunt any riches he might have been hiding from her, not that she expected to be wined and dined by someone who worked at the cemetery. Ana liked that, too. She liked that he wasn't flashy and trying to buy her affections. She liked that the seats they were in were regular seats and not some box seats where she had to pretend to be a pretentious bitch and look down on the rest of the audience like peasants. She liked that she could be herself, whoever that was, with him and didn't have to put on a show.

She might have been trying to get close so she could worm her way into that castle, learn everything he knew about it, only she was also enjoying herself more than she'd ever enjoyed life.

They split the cost of their wines at the stand before heading to their seats, and Ana sighed as she sat down, unable to stop smiling all around her.

She caught Sam looking at her out of the corner of her eye. "What?" she asked.

"I didn't know you'd be this excited about an orchestra," he said, his arm sliding around the back of her chair.

"You said cinematic horror and orchestra in the same sentence," she said. "Two of my favorite things."

He considered her as he often did, looking surprised at what she'd said, and perhaps was contemplating whether she was lying. She wondered what had made him so suspicious of people that he would watch her like that.

The lights lowered then, not giving her another chance to say anything about his stare. Ana took another sip of her wine as the room began to applaud lightly with the appearance of the orchestra.

And the sounds that followed nearly made her weep.

Ana had always loved music. She'd loved how it spoke to her heart and invoked feelings in her that nothing, save for physical art, had ever made her feel. The drums, the violins, and everything in between. Every pound and strike made her heart dance. She was a part of that sound, and that sound was a part of her.

Ana found herself sitting up one song in, oblivious to whether Sam was watching her or if he was as into the music as she was. But she hugged that wine to her chest and let the screeching violins and the high-pitched flutes take her into a trance. Speeding up her heart and stopping it completely. She was happiness and rage, and her eyes filled with tears every time those emotions overwhelmed her mind and pricked her skin.

Between movements, Ana found her breath, and would finally take a sip of her wine. She once snuck a glance over to Sam, whom she found herself wholly mesmerized by for a few seconds.

And she wondered if she, too, looked as in love with the music as he did.

By the time intermission came, Ana felt like she'd run a marathon.

With the house lights came her own heavy sigh. "Fuck me," Ana muttered.

"What do you think?" Sam asked as he leaned forward.

"I think…" Ana collected herself and met his eyes. "I think if there were no other people around, I would sit in front of you and suck your cock for bringing me here."

Sam's brows lifted. "You like it that much?"

"Sam, it's… I thought I loved orchestras before, but this… the way my heart is racing right now is as if I am running from a legion of demons and Death himself. I've never…" She tried to articulate how she really felt, but she didn't have the words, so she managed two words that rarely came from her mouth.

"Thank you," she finally said.

He stared at her a moment, contemplating her words, and then he reached for her face, his thumb brushing against her cheek. "I would buy you an orchestra if it meant I could make you feel this way every day," he said softly.

A quiet huff left her. "I don't need an entire orchestra," she said. "I have you."

Sam's lips lifted, his hair falling into his eyes. "Is that what you want, baby?" he asked. "Do you want your heart racing and crashing like it's doing here? For your fear to be fed and your body to be devoured after?"

"I crave it," she said in a strained voice.

Sam held her face there a moment, their noses nearly brushing, and his eyes darted between hers as he held her stare. "A nightmare come true," he whispered. He kissed her then, engulfing and yet fleeting, and once he pulled away, he grabbed their empty glasses.

"I'll be back," he told her.

Chapter Twenty-Two

The remainder of the show continued to spiral Ana into a trance, and by the time it was over, she had wept, jumped, shivered, and nearly fell to her knees. She couldn't move when the lights came on. She hadn't even noticed that with the last movement, she'd cradled herself into Sam's body, his arm around the back of her chair, touch delicately swirling on her back as she laid her head on his shoulder. It was so domestic and ordinary that Ana nearly jumped upon realizing it.

A smile threatened Sam's lips when he looked at her. "I almost thought you'd fallen asleep until I felt your heart racing and stopping."

"I bet you loved that," Ana teased.

Sam blew out a huff of amusement and kissed her hard. "You know I did," he said. "A bit jealous of the music making you feel like that, though," he added as he stood and grabbed his coat. "I'll have to work harder."

He took her out for dinner and drinks after, and Ana swore every time she heard him actually laugh that it didn't sound real. They'd made a habit of trying to guess what other couples were talking about, if they were even talking, as some just stared at their phones the entire meal.

Conversations with him were easier than she'd ever held with anyone. Maybe it was that he actually took her sarcasm and responded with his own or made some snarky comment that had her nearly jumping him at the table. And maybe it was that he had lived so long that he was unafraid to be himself.

"I have to tell you something," Ana said when they made it back in front of her apartment.

Sam's head tilted, his hands around her waist. "What?"

Ana smiled despite herself, her lashes lifting to meet his eyes. "I really hate how much I'm enjoying you."

A quiet snort left him, and he looked over her head, then back to her. "Theres a haunted tour that goes through mid and old town on Thursday nights," he said.

"Ghosts?" She balked. "What, the demons weren't enough. We've ghosts here, too? Does this tour include a trip inside Castle Corvus's dungeon? I'm sure there are a few stories the ghosts could tell us from down there."

Sam chuckled. "Okay, temptress. So something more dangerous then."

"I like danger," she replied.

Though judging by the wicked glint he got in his eyes then, she wasn't sure she liked what she'd just agreed to.

"New moon this weekend," he said. "I have doubles tomorrow and Friday. But Saturday... Saturday, Let's do something then."

"What do you have in mind?" she asked.

But the look on his face just drew darker as he took a step back from her. "You'll love it." He leaned in and kissed her cheek, and Ana was left staring at him as he started to his bike.

"You're not coming upstairs?" she asked.

Sam swung his leg over his bike. "I don't think I will," he replied with a wink that made her shake her head. "See you Saturday. Send me something that will make me wish I'd stayed later."

And as he revved the bike and sped off, Ana stared after him. Her mind whirled with the orchestra, his every touch and smile, the kiss they'd shared, and the way he'd just promised her danger as she strode up the stairs to her apartment. The door opened, and she locked it behind her, throwing her keys onto the counter.

She pressed her hands into the granite top and closed her eyes, exhaling the last few hours and letting her head hang.

"What the fuck are you doing, Deianira?" she muttered to herself.

She thought back to the meeting she'd had with the King's Hand the day before, to the woman who was supposedly friends with Sam, and she wondered if the pair had spoken about her.

She wouldn't see him for two days.

That gave her two days to focus on other routes into the castle, maybe through another groundskeeper or one of the journalists who'd managed to get a few photos.

Maybe the one that had been driven crazy when she'd gotten inside.

Ana scrambled into her junk drawer and fetched a pad and pen, scribbling on it a reminder to search through old newspaper databases for any articles since the press was first put into production.

Time to get to work.

Chapter Twenty-Three

The symphony date still lingered in Sam's mind long after he laid down in his bed. With the close of his eyes, he replayed how her pulse had staggered, even pleasuring himself to the sound of it once. He'd never seen or felt anyone so entranced by music as he was himself. He found himself more and more intrigued by the woman he was spending so much time with. Maybe that was why he'd been glad that he'd already decided not to see her for a couple of days. He had to have a break to get his head back on straight. She consumed his thoughts more often than he dared to admit now, and he couldn't wait for the weekend when he would take her to the prison to see how she reacted to genuine fear.

Overnight was relatively quiet for Sam, except for one moment when he'd been thrown out of a nightmare he couldn't remember. He vaguely recalled a few screams and the state of his drenched sheets as the sweat beaded off his forehead and tried to calm his fleeting pulse. Luna had been in bed with him, lying by his head, and when he finally laid down again, she crawled atop his chest.

But he couldn't recall any more detail than that.

The last time he'd woken up in such a startle, the castle he'd been imprisoned in centuries earlier had been under attack, and he'd awoken to the chaos of death that he couldn't keep up with in this bodily form.

And for whatever reason, the first thing Sam did that morning was text Ana.

The most horrifying monsters are those that live within our souls, Sam typed.

He made his way to the bathroom and started brushing his teeth as he waited for her to respond. The phone buzzed just as he'd placed the brush in his mouth.

I like the monsters in my soul, Ana replied. *They tell the best jokes.*

Sam huffed at her response. *You'll have to introduce me. I love jokes.*

What about your monsters? she asked.

Sam thought about it a moment, thinking about all the things he'd seen and done in his past. *Maybe I am the monster.*

Says my stalker, she said. *Last night was amazing.*

I had no idea that you would like it so much, he replied.

I loved it, she typed. *I love how your darkness speaks to mine.*

Sam stared at the screen a moment, contemplating his next words. *So do I,* he decided on.

I know you were thinking about something Saturday, but I have an idea, Ana typed.

What's the idea?

I thought maybe we could sneak into the Corvus cemetery, she typed. *See what all the fuss is about.*

There she is, Sam thought to himself. He spat his toothpaste into the sink and gave his teeth a final brush before responding.

Corvus cemetery only looks scary from the outside. What I have planned... you'll love it. Trust me.

That's the scariest thing, she said. *I do.*

"A horrible idea, really," Sam muttered aloud.

"Talking to yourself again, Samarius?" Millie asked as she appeared in the doorway to his bath.

Sam frowned at her. "You're here early."

"Unfortunately," she mumbled. "Hurry up. I have Rolfe bringing coffee and breakfast to the office." She paused to yawn, and Sam noticed the mascara under her eyes.

"What's wrong?" he asked.

"General Prei took the Spine last night."

Sam stared at the back of her head as she walked away. "What?" He bolted after her, grabbing his robe from the back of the door as he did.

But Millie didn't stop walking as she continued to explain. "I got a call at midnight from Damien. He said the Fire armies had come across the border and started raiding like they've been doing on their edges. He said the entire line was on fire."

Sam's fist tightened in on itself. "Have you spoken with any of ours in Firemoor?"

"None," she said. "I can't find them. According to Damien, he hasn't

142

heard from them in a few days either."

The fact that he hadn't heard from any of their people in Firemoor made Sam's stomach flip.

Rolfe was already waiting for them in Sam's office, breakfast that Sam knew he wouldn't be touching on the desk. He was staring at a broadcast on the television, eyes wide and jaw clenched.

"It looks the same as it did five hundred years ago," Rolfe said upon their entering.

Sam paused to stare at the screen, and he nearly lost his balance at the sight of the fires, the rubble on the ground, and the bodies covered in dust. He cursed under his breath. This was what his dream had been about. He'd heard them in his subconscious, deep within that shadow trapped in this forsaken form.

Sam punched the desk so hard that it left a perfect imprint of his knuckles behind.

"Where is Damien?" he asked.

"Helping those he can find," Millie replied.

"Tell him to find them and get everyone home," Sam snapped, walking around to the back of his desk.

"What?" Millie asked incredulously.

"I want our people home," Sam said, finger digging into the top of the desk. "I want them home before Prei goes through those legions to cut them and see who heals. They can make it through our border shadows without a problem. I will not watch public torture."

"Sam, we have no way—"

"Get them the fuck home," he commanded in a growl that shook the room. He ran his hands through his hair as he began to pace, not looking to see if Millie was back on her phone or if Rolfe was watching him. "Prei will have Ironmyer in his grasp by the end of the year with their depleted military. Windmoor after. Bring our people home now."

"And the humans dying in the ditches trying to outrun the army?" Millie asked.

Sam met her eyes, and he knew she was remembering herself in those ditches on her final moments. He shuddered, cracking his neck, and his eyes blazed carmine.

"Do you want me to save them, Milliscent?" he asked in a low voice.

"I want Death to collect," she practically growled. "Collect for vengeance as we did—"

"I cannot save everyone—"

"You saved us," she said, her voice rising. "How are we any

different from them?"

Luna jumped on the desk then and curled herself around Sam's rigid arms, her purr sounding loud over the screams and terror on the television then. Sam took a deep breath, his eyes closing, and he picked the cat up to cradle against his chest.

"What would you have me do?" he asked calmly.

Millie shifted on her feet and took her phone out this time. "Let me talk to Damien. If there are any that he can see that edge for, that might want something after, I'll have him bring them to the neutral place. We can meet there and come back over this border with those who want an extension of this life."

"If we are caught, Prei will call it an act of war," Sam said.

"It is only helping the wounded," Millie countered.

"*It is taking souls for an army!*" Sam hissed.

Millie didn't stand down. She simply stared pointedly in his direction. "Maybe we could use a few more souls," she said. "And a declaration of war."

"Just a few weeks ago, you were adamant about not going in without a plan," he snapped.

"That was about Ironmyer," she argued. "Not us. We're prepared."

"And I told you, I'm dealing with our current threat."

"Yes, Samarius, and how is that going for you?" she practically spat, head tilting. "Have you killed her yet? I don't hear her in the dungeons screaming."

A loud snarl left Sam as he nearly lunged at Millie, teeth bared. "I don't have to explain every detail of my plans. All I have ever asked is that you trust me."

"And I do," she said. "We all do. The only thing I am saying here is that these people are close enough to us that we could do something about it. Increase our strength. Show those that will watch their loved ones cross over that we give a damn, and maybe... just maybe... when the time comes for us to declare that war, we might have a few more on our side. I'm not asking you to declare war yet. I'm asking you to recruit."

Sam sighed and looked at Rolfe.

"And you?" he asked his friend. "What would you have me do?"

Rolfe finished chewing his toast and looked back at the television. "We're all waiting on the day you give the order, boss," he said. "What's a few more in our pocket going to hurt?"

"What if we're caught? If Prei finds out I'm turning demons in his new territory to eventually fight against him?" Sam asked.

"Assume that'd be the same result as when he finds out you've been keeping The Tower safe and sound here," Rolfe said bluntly.

Triumph littered Millie's face, and Sam fully expected her to kiss Rolfe in response, but she just raised an arrogant brow in Sam's direction.

Sam cursed. "When I think we are ready for that war, I will gladly cause an uproar large enough that the southernmost isles of Windmoor hear it," he said slowly. "But it will be on my terms. Whether those terms are my offering up Deianira as bait or something different, you two will be the first to know. But right now, my concern is the demons that have been hiding in the other realms for centuries. Bring them home first." His gaze flashed between Millie and Rolfe. "Once they get here, I'll consider their reports and the humans left."

"You bring all of them home, and the dead souls won't have a new existence to go into," Millie said. "They'll have no bridge, Samarius."

A flash of lightning silhouetted Sam's wings on the wall behind him as he braced his palms on the desk once more. "And that, Milliscent, sounds like the perfect army."

Chapter Twenty-Four

Ana couldn't turn away from the broadcast on her television.

She had different streams pulled up on all her devices, the research she had been doing on Shadowmyer now amiss.

A small part of her blamed herself for the mess in the Spine right now.

But she shook it off, knowing their king had been a weakling. He'd only ever done what Firemoor did. Had decided witches were evil when Firemoor did. Had decided to get rid of impoverished people when Firemoor did, stating there was only enough food and supplies in the realm for those who could afford it. The idiot was stupid enough not to listen to his advisors and hadn't realized the ones he was murdering were the ones farming and feeding half damn continent.

He'd starved more than half of his nation in the process of trying to follow in Firemoor's footsteps, and Ana had told him that before she'd sliced his heart out.

The Spine after his death hadn't been chaos, though. People had come together and helped one another out. They'd actually begun to heal without the fear of being punished for giving their neighbor a loaf of bread.

Though Ana had believed that while they were recovering their minds and bodies, they hadn't exactly been stockpiling weapons. She kept telling herself that Firemoor would have taken over that realm regardless of whether she had interfered. At least she had been able to give them a little over a year of peace.

Back on the stream she had going on her computer, General Prei strutted in front of the old Spine capitol building, now in rubble, like he were a god.

She wished she'd taken his heart instead of their idiotic king's. He'd been a problem since she could remember, and now that he'd recouped the fire armies enough for an organized attack, she wondered how long it would be before he headed for Ironmyer.

She knew that would be next. He would gather Ironmyer and Windmoor's armies before trying to invade Shadowmyer. As for Icemyer… she wondered if he'd already infiltrated it.

Icemyer was nearly desolate, controlled by no one. It was a wasteland of forgotten power and energy. Old tales told of witches originally drawing their powers from beneath the ice and in the depths of the caves. Her father had brushed off the stories when he'd heard them from a few residents, but Ana had always known it was at least partially true.

Ana sank back onto the couch and took another sip of her wine. It might have only been lunch, but after seeing people strung up by nooses on public display for fighting back against Firemoor had driven her to an early uncorking.

Sam hadn't replied to her last message. It had been a few hours. Hours that she should have devoted to finding more information than just an article on the one girl who was said to have gotten into Castle Corvus. That poor girl was locked up in the mental wards of St Orphs, located a few miles east of midtown. She wasn't sure how she could get out there, maybe the bus to midtown and walk the rest of the way. Asking Sam to take her there would be too risky, and even asking Jay didn't feel right. As much as she liked him, including him in what she was working on didn't feel right.

Ana gulped down the rest of her wine and poured another glass before ordering lunch from the deli a few doors down. Her phone kept snagging her eye, thinking she had heard it vibrate, and she hated how distracted she was.

The storms outside had raged off and on the last few hours, a reflection of the king's mood as Jay had told her.

Ana rose from the couch and went over to stand by the window, letting her robe hang lazily over her. More lights were on in Castle Corvus today, and as she looked at the cemetery, she noticed the water from the last hour's downpouring. It rushed into the drainage ditches and sewers, taking mud and debris with it, wiping away whatever secrets the grounds could tell her about their mysterious king.

The thought of him made her jaw twitch.

A knock sounded at her door, and while Ana frowned, she

remembered she had ordered lunch. She sat her glass on the counter as she opened the door.

Jay stood on the other side.

"Jay," she said, surprised her boss had come to check on her when she'd called out that morning. "You didn't have to—"

"Had a few minutes, and when I saw Todd coming up with food, I figured it was for you," Jay said. "How are you feeling, love?"

"I'm…" She glanced over her shoulder to the glass of wine and then the streams on all her devices. "I'm not going to lie, Jay. I'm a little queasy. Assuming you've seen the news?" she asked.

He nodded, and Ana opened the door to let him in. "Another reason I came to check on you," he said as he sat her food on the counter. "I thought you'd mentioned spending some time there before crossing the border. I wanted to make sure you were okay." He kicked his shoes off and sat on her couch, Ana taking her soup out and grabbing another glass for him.

Jay took the glass and helped himself to a bit of her wine as she curled into the opposite corner. "Probably be better if I were to just turn these off," she said. "But I can't. It feels like I'm forgetting them if I do."

"Nothing you can do about it, love," he said with a sigh. "You got yourself out. I'm not saying forget about them, but unless you've got some ranking with the Council, you're not going to be able to change anything."

"Maybe I should," she said, taking a sip of her warm soup. "Figure out how to get on the Council, I mean."

Jay chuckled. "That would be something. I'd love to see that, actually. Perhaps you'd talk these shadow dealers into not charging so much for helping get through to a place of peace."

She considered it, watching Jay as he ran a hand through his blonde hair. "You used a shadow dealer to get here, didn't you?"

Jay nodded, but there was something about the look behind his eyes that made her own narrow. Enough so that she paused before taking another slurp of her soup.

"Cost a fucking fortune," he muttered. "But worth it in the end. What did you use?"

"Dealer," she replied, and a chill ran over her skin as she remembered looking at that border. The forest that hid it. To any average person, it was simply a large forest with misty fog beneath. A bit spooky to the unsuspecting, but the secrets and wards it held in it were what sometimes gave Ana nightmares those first couple of weeks.

"The voices were the worst for me," Jay muttered.

Ana nodded. "I remember the dealer giving me earmuffs to go over the noise-canceling earphones," she said. "I remember the dead deer skeletons stalking us, and how no matter how many times he told us to remain even breathed, I couldn't stop my heart from skipping when those great shadows flew overhead."

"Vultures," Jay muttered. "Somehow they're larger in that place." He looked up and met her eyes. "How many bodies did you see?"

"Three," Ana answered. "I actually thought I would see more."

Jay's eyes had hazed over. "I saw seventeen," he said. "No creatures, however. But the voices were hard not to follow."

Ana stared at the coffee table, remembering how those voices had spoken to her, pleaded for her. 'Walk with us,' they had beckoned. 'It's safe here,' another had said. Once, she'd sworn she heard her father's voice, had sworn she saw him far off in the distance.

But it was just another trick of the border.

Ana sighed against the couch after placing the rest of her food on the table. "Slow day downstairs?" she asked, eager to change the subject as she knew if she didn't, she'd be dreaming of those voices later.

"This heavy rain certainly detours the walk-ins," he said. He looked over at her and gave her a small smile as he glanced her over. "I think I'll go home. No one is coming out today, especially with the news. You should take a bath and have a long nap," he continued as he stood. He leaned over and gave her a smacking kiss on her head before heading to the door.

"See you tomorrow, love," he said. "And Ana?"

"Yeah?"

"Try to rest," he said. "Dwelling over this won't help anything. You've done what you could."

Something about that sentence made her ears perk, but even as she went to sit up, the door closed behind him, and she was left staring at the back of it, the noise of it clicking shut sounding over and over in her ears.

You're paranoid, Deianira, she told herself.

She sank herself into the couch, changed the channel on the television to a serial killer documentary, and tried to close her eyes.

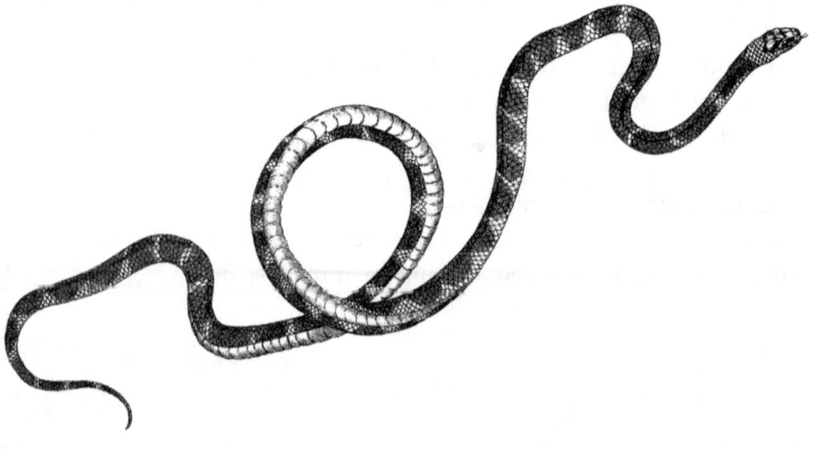

Chapter Twenty-Five

Sam stared at General Prei of Firemoor as the man walked back and forth atop a long bridge overlooking the Spine's capital. He stared at the burns on the man's face, his arm, his hands. Something struck the pit of his stomach. Something he couldn't put his finger on. It had always been like that. Ever since Firemoor began publicizing their 'cleansing' and proclaiming what they were doing as saving the world from deviants. But now that their king was dead and Prei had taken over the military, he seemed taller. More confident.

And it bothered the fuck out of Samarius.

He remember Prei once being a cowardly thing, but maybe that was because he was so new, and because the Firemoor king had been such a controlling asshat. It was like something had snapped within him after Deianira had ripped their king of his heart, and Prei had decided the world needed more correction than what Firemoor had envisioned.

It was too familiar to King Atrion's plans. So much so that it made Sam's stomach twist and churn.

And the only thing he could think of to get his mind off of it was to text Ana.

Even a white rose has a black shadow, he chose to text.

Luna was lying across the keyboard purring when his phone buzzed back.

I love white roses, she said. *They feel more dangerous. Like their innocence is hiding beneath that pure exterior.*

He thought of his garden then, the rows and rows of white roses, and he nearly suggested showing it to her.

How was your morning? he chose instead.

Not the best, she admitted. *Are you able to turn away from the disaster happening right now?* Ana had typed.

Sam sighed, but replied, *Not at all. It's tragic.*

Is your king doing anything? Ana asked. *I haven't seen any response yet.*

Sam stared at the phone and then back at the television. Millie hadn't put out any statement yet because there wasn't one to be made. He hadn't responded to Deianira's attacks except to assure people they were safe.

Another lie.

So Sam decided to see exactly what The Tower thought of all this.

If you were him, what would you do? he asked.

Those three dots strummed for a minute. Long enough that he lounged back in the chair and kicked his feet up, and Luna crawled in his lap.

I think there are a lot of dying souls looking for a few more years, and possibly a chance at revenge, she typed. *I think I would give it to them. If your king has the balls to walk across his border.*

Sam almost laughed at the last bit.

All the people in those territories that have been bombed and persecuted... should they not want revenge on the kings that took their lives simply because they are not in Death's direct line of sight? she asked.

I thought that's what the people loved Deianira Bronfell for, Sam typed. *She was their vengeance.*

A lot has happened since she took down those kings. The Spine was a growing nation after her hit. Now they've been attacked. If I were them, I'd want that revenge. No matter what it cost me.

Sam stared at the phone for a long minute, scratching the top of Luna's head. He contemplated it. Her words. Millie's words. Rolfe's. And he thought of all the things that could go wrong if he did do this. Images of all those he'd turned during the last war filled him. He remembered each of them. Remembered every voice that had begged for him and leapt on that second chance.

Come over for dinner? Ana asked, breaking him from his daze.

He wanted to. He could have used the distraction, and something about even simply sitting with her sounded relaxing. But Millie was coming over with more reports since she'd talked to Damien, and he knew he couldn't risk putting her off just to go have dinner with the person he was supposed to be breaking.

Can't tonight, he finally typed back. *Saturday, baby. I'll be so ready for you, I may not be able to hold myself back. Especially after this week.*

Poor thing. Maybe I'll send you something to hold you over until then, she said.

Please, and he nearly begged her further for the distraction, the comfort.

I'll see what I can manage.

The winky face she sent along with it almost made him smile. He picked up a stress ball from the jar on his desk and began squeezing it, and turned his attention back to the television.

"Hey, Rolfe?" Sam said into the room.

The deathhound was asleep in that form, curled up in the corner of the study. Sam had taken a photo of him earlier and sent it to Millie, but hadn't received any response. The hound huffed, but didn't wake, so Sam threw a shoe at him.

Rolfe flinched, but shook it off and transformed into his other self. "Sorry, boss," he muttered. "What's it?"

"How do you feel about helping me clear the cathedral?" Sam asked, and Rolfe's eyes narrowed at him.

"Why?"

Sam didn't reply. He was already dialing Millie's number. She answered on the first ring.

"Yes, my King?" she snapped.

"Can you come help me and Rolfe clean up the cathedral?"

"Is this an order or a favor?" she asked.

Sam hated her being mad at him. He squeezed the stress ball so tightly in his hand that the thing shredded between his fingers.

"Tell Damien and his legion to take any persons at their final edge to our border and into the forest," he said. "I'll call their souls to the cathedral here. After that, the others are to come home. But I will only do this if he brings them over the border."

"And the vultures hunting in the shadows of the forest?" she asked.

"I'll take that chance," he said. "The worst that could happen is a few go back to their bodies with only one eye."

Millie didn't speak for a moment, and when the moment grew long enough to make Sam shift in his seat, he opened his mouth to speak, but Millie cut him off.

"I expect you groveling on your knees for forgiveness when I get there," she hissed.

Chapter Twenty-Six

The front page of the newspaper was a blast of fear and terror about how the Spine was now under the control of Firemoor two mornings later. It knotted Sam's stomach enough that he pushed away his breakfast. After the two deaths he'd had to deal with overnight, he was already nauseous, and thinking about an army on his border wasn't helping.

"Who was it last night?" Rolfe asked as Sam silently drank his coffee.

Luna jumped on the table and sprawled out in the middle, ignoring Rolfe swatting at the feline's tail that had just landed—probably purposefully—in the blueberry jam on his toast. Rolfe snarled, and the cat just stretched her front legs toward Sam.

"Remember old man Taylor?" Sam said without turning away from the newspaper.

"Ah, damn. Really?" Rolfe replied.

"His son, actually," Sam continued. "Marty." Sam flipped down the paper to meet Rolfe's gaze. "Heart attack."

"Fuck," Rolfe muttered. "Find him too late?"

Sam nodded, and Rolfe slumped back in his chair. "The other was a child," Sam said softly.

Rolfe stilled, and Sam couldn't stop the line of tears in the bottom of his eyes as that memory flooded him. How he'd sat on the floor with the girl and plucked rose petals with her for a while, let her play with Luna and hug her before she began to get curious, and Sam had explained to her what was happening. The only thing the girl had asked once she understood was if Sam would check on her mother and her dog.

"Yeah," Sam whispered, pushing a blonde curl off her young face, his fingers brushing the scrape from the car accident she'd been in. "I promise. Anything for my brave girl," he told her, trying to give her a reassuring smile and hating himself that there was nothing more he could do.

It was at times like this that Sam cursed himself for who he was.

"We don't give children enough credit," Sam said as he looked at Rolfe.

Rolfe nodded in agreement, sadness taking over his entire body. "What happened?"

"Drunk driver from uptown," Sam answered.

Rolfe's eyes hardened. "You have his name?"

"He's on the list I left for you on the foyer table," Sam said.

Rolfe chewed his food slower this time, like he was taking a moment to plot out how he might take care of this new threat.

"Cathedral is all set," Rolfe said after a few minutes.

They'd spent the entire day before down the hall inside the grand room. Pulling down curtains, removing pews and sheets and anything else that might get in their way. Sam swore he had cobwebs in places he couldn't reach, no matter how many times he bathed.

"Have you talked to Millie?" Rolfe asked.

Sam shook his head. "I don't know how long it will take Damien and his people to get those to the border. Could be days."

Rolfe ran a hand through his hair, sadness in his eyes. "I remember that," he muttered.

"Three days, wasn't it?" Sam asked.

"Three days, eight hours, twenty-nine minutes under that fucking house," Rolfe sighed, speaking of the days he'd sat at the edge of his life. "Felt like my mind was hoarse from screaming out by the time you found me."

"Back then, I did it all manually," Sam muttered. "It's no excuse. I should have figured out how to call souls like I can now."

"You were angrier back then," Rolfe said.

Sam huffed, finding the statement amusing. "Angry at the world. At myself. At—" he waved a hand in the air to signal everything around him "—all of this." He met Rolfe's eyes then. "I'm sorry it took me so long."

But Rolfe waved him off. "Wouldn't change it for anything, boss," he said. "You have a date tonight?"

"Taking her to the prison," Sam answered, and Rolfe raised both brows at the statement. "Figured the ghosts could use some fun."

"You're looking to scare the fuck out of her," Rolfe said.

"I'm looking to see what Deianira does in the presence of Death," Sam said.

Rolfe's lips twitched. "Maybe I'll bring some popcorn and watch," he said. "Might be fun."

"Be my guest," Sam said. "A deathhound chasing after her could be an interesting element."

Rolfe finished chewing the last of his food and slapped his napkin on the table as he pushed back his chair. "Anything else for me today?"

There was an edge of violence in his tone, and Sam just shook his head, not daring to take away from whatever Rolfe intended.

The last he saw of his friend for the morning was Rolfe shifting into his deathhound form, and the beast gave a great howl out in the garden before setting off down the driveway.

Sam cleaned up the kitchen and put away the food Rolfe had left out before making himself another cup of coffee and heading upstairs to his office. Weekend mornings were supposed to be for relaxing, and Millie usually chose that day to sleep in instead of meeting him. Sam took the time that day to watch more of the video reports coming in from the Firemoor invasion, and he texted Ana first. After leaving her without answering the night before, he wanted to apologize.

She'd texted him twice after they'd exchanged few messages that morning, but he hadn't been able to gather the energy for flirting after they'd begun wiping out the cathedral.

Shame you can't come over. I was hoping to give you a little something before you went into work.

If you get a chance to come by at breakfast, I'll be up.

Sam stared at the phone, his thumbs going to move, but unsure of what to say. And to his great annoyance, he couldn't think of anything better than:

Hey, baby

The failure of his usual poetics made him cringe. *Hey, baby.* How fucking stupid could he sound?

Stalker, she wrote. *You're alive.*

Work was a pain. How are you feeling?

Sad, she admitted. *Tired.*

I hope not too tired for our date tonight, he said.

I'll find some strength for that, she replied.

Good. I have some things to do. Pick you up at eight. Wear something you don't mind getting filthy. Perhaps good running shoes.

You've piqued my interest, stalker, she typed. *I'll be ready.*

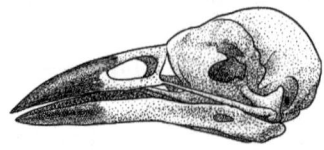

The kiss Sam met Ana with upon reaching her door was slower, more intimate than those he'd left her with the night of the symphony. He had to admit, he'd missed her presence. And when she'd opened that door, seen the tiredness beneath her eyes, he'd felt the need to hold her close and tell her he was taking care of this.

But he couldn't.

So, he'd settled on the sweeping kiss.

Her quiet moan was lethal, a swipe of a dagger to the backs of his knees as he cupped her cheek and deepened their kiss. Not in the way that would have them backing up and fucking against the wall, but in the way that said 'I missed you' or 'I needed to see you' without saying the words.

"I needed that," Ana whispered as he pulled back, her eyes opening slowly to meet his.

"As did I," he admitted softly.

Perhaps not realizing just how much the last two days had haunted them both.

His forehead met hers for a second, just another moment of breathing the other in. Sam realized what he was doing with a start, though he tried to hide it as he took a step back to look her over.

His gaze traveled over the leggings and black band tee she'd put on, the neck cut out of the shirt along with a few rips above her breasts, showing off her cleavage and sternum tattoo. With a smile, she backed out of his arms and turned off the television, then grabbed her phone and shoved it in her back pocket.

"So, where are we going?" she asked.

He was surprised by how just in the three minutes he'd been at her side, all the worries of the last two days seemed to wane to the tiniest place in the back of his mind. But he didn't answer her, and instead simply returned her smile and took her hand.

The old prison was a desolate, grown monstrosity twenty minutes outside of old town on the oceanside. Iron fencing like that around his own cemetery surrounded it, vines reaching and wrapping all around it. And the actual prison…

A large square box with as few windows as it had doors. The windows it did have had been vacated of their glass long ago, and now were nothing more than wrought iron bars. Grass and weeds had grown up through the old rocky drive, nearly confiscating the path to the doors.

"Do you know what this place is?" he asked as he moved the flashlight over the grand iron gate.

Ana's pulse had become slower since they'd parked. She hadn't spoken, but he could nearly hear her body preparing for whatever was about to happen.

"Is it a prison?" she asked.

"It was once," he said, pushing the gate open. It creaked and groaned with the swing, vines ripping away from it and bending as he lit up the jagged path inside. He was hit with his own residual power lingering there; he could smell it on every dead plant and decaying creature. His eyes fluttered with that power, the memory of everything he'd once been within that place crashing back to him.

"It was the prison of King Atrion. Where he would send the people he thought deserved to have their minds bent and their wills broken rather than a swift death."

What Sam failed to mention were the years he'd spent in this prison, carrying out sentences like some pet doing his master's bidding. He'd warped more minds there than he could remember, made a few believe they were cats, others that they were children or infants. Atrion had enjoyed the tactics and watching those people go insane before Death was to finalize the sentence.

Atrion never found out how many souls Sam had left in limbo

instead of carrying them into another existence, creating the ghostly demons he also had wandering his own cemetery, the ones—if ever he needed guards in the dungeon—that he would call upon. People had thought Death the most terrifying creature in the land…

But they hadn't met the humans that defied him.

It was the first way Death had figured out how to start an army, to start his plan for eventual retribution.

The starving, demented souls were one of the reasons he'd brought Ana there. He wanted to see her reaction to the devious ghosts he knew were up for playing tricks. Wanted to see Deianira unleash herself and show her true colors. He wanted to know if she'd truly earned the title of The Tower, or if she'd simply been lucky.

And he could sit back in the shadows and watch it all.

Living plants seemed to wilt as they walked, and Sam didn't bother relinquishing the trail of shadows that appeared in the wake of his footsteps. He wondered if Ana noticed them or was too focused on the building before her to note such small things.

"Who carried out those sentences?" Ana asked.

"Death," he answered, and her eyes lit up when he said that name. Sam squeezed her hand and smiled softly as they reached the barricaded doors.

Movement rattled the bushes behind to their left. Ana flinched slightly, but not enough that he felt the pace of her heart change.

Shame.

He'd have to do a little more.

"You remember your word?" he asked, hand resting on the handle.

Ana met his eyes. "Planning on terrifying me enough to use it?" she teased.

"Your word, Ana," he said a little more sternly.

She blinked but didn't banter back this time. "Ravens," she answered.

With a nod, Sam pushed open the doors.

The front entrance had a small foyer room before two iron-barred doors. A mouse skittered across the floor. Ana's arm hit his, making Sam smile.

"Don't let the rats take my glory, baby," he said into her ear.

A shiver rose on her flesh, and she smirked up at him. "You'll have to do much better than rats for that," she said.

The right corner of his lip flinched upward, and he let go of her hand to roll back the two iron doors. They clanked and groaned, and

Ana's eyes lit up that violent green as dust sprayed over their heads. Sam beckoned her to follow with a jerk of his head.

Silence so thick that every rustle of wind on the outside whistled and echoed off the walls. Trickles of water cascaded down several walls, the distant drips sounding in an erratic rhythm.

"How long has this place been vacant?" Ana asked.

"Who says it is?" He smiled at her over his shoulder, and she gave him a tight-lipped glare.

"Ha-ha," she drawled. "Really. How long?"

"They were all dead or released during the last war," Sam said. "Some say Death unleashed a few upon the world to distract while he shadowed this place. Other stories say he turned them all to ghosts and refused to ferry their souls into the next life."

"Fairy tales," Ana teased.

Sam's chin lifted as they continued walking. He could feel the baited breaths in the walls, feel the power practically rumbling beneath his feet. What this place had once looked like filled his mind. He knew every hall. Every cell. Remembered the names of each of them.

"They say you can still hear the screams on Death's Day," he said as he dragged his hand along the walls, the vines between the stones dying in his wake.

They took a set of winding iron stairs at the end of the hall up to the next level where the isolation rooms had been, and Ana paused at the high window that overlooked the vast grounds and the abrupt ocean cliff.

"You know, if the view looked like this, I might not have complained too much about being imprisoned here," she said as she braced her hands on the window ledge.

Sam didn't reply. He didn't join her at the window. Instead, he took her lapse in attention to settle at the back of the room and cloak himself in shadows. Anticipation filled his stomach. He hadn't seen these demons since he'd watched them die and left their bodies to rot, their souls to wander aimlessly about this place.

But they belonged to him, like the corporeal ones that he'd allowed back into their bodies. And even calling them, he knew they would have some sort of form. What that form would be, he wasn't sure.

He hadn't called on ghosts in a long time.

Sam crouched down, pressed his hand on the breaking stone floor, muttered only two words.

Wake up.

Power lurched from the depths of his bones and rumbled into the soil. The ground quaked, making Ana grab the wall and turn. Her eyes widened as she looked to every corner and then began calling his name.

"Sam?"

But Sam was too entranced by the warp of shadow now circling back into him. A chill ran down his spine as he felt those souls reach out, out, *out*. Pleading for the leashes around their necks to be cut free. His eyes lifted to Ana, cold and carmine.

Hunt.

Chapter Twenty-Seven

It had been a while since Ana had felt the stench of true death around her. But as she turned and turned, looking for Sam, she felt it rising out of every crack and inch of that fucking cell. The flashlight he'd been holding was now twisting on the ground.

And Sam…

"Sam, this isn't funny," she said, staring into the darkness.

A child's laugh sounded from a cell on her right, not too far ahead. Cackling. Echoing. Ana swallowed. She could feel an energy she hadn't caught onto when she'd first stepped inside this place. It had felt hollow upon arrival, but now…

Voices whispered in the opposite direction. Ana stepped slowly to the flashlight rolling in the middle of the floor, her gaze never leaving the other end of the hall.

A flame flickered on across the open space by another cell door. She became as still as she'd ever been and shut out every thought in her head.

She forced a laugh out as her pulse began to pick up. "Come on, Sam. I know you want to play, but you can't scare me."

Though she wasn't entirely sure of those words.

No response… at least from him.

"Sam…" She tried his name one more time, though quieter this time. She cursed the shake in her tone, her eyes darting from cell to cell. She didn't dare move that column of light from the center where she had it pointed right then.

"Who is it?" someone asked.

"Do we get to play?"

Her heart skipped, and she dared a step back.

Someone was running.

Running.

Flat-footed and uncoordinated. The steps bounced out of puddles. Echoed off the stone. The flame whooshed out with its passing. Ana's heart nearly jumped out of her chest. She dug into her fighting stance, not daring to move that light no matter the temptation—

Three fingers tickled her shoulder.

"Hello, pretty."

Ana jumped so quickly that she fell. The flashlight flew out of her hand. Those running steps hushed, but she scrambled across the ground to grab the light.

And made the mistake of pointing it down the corridor.

Bulging eyes and the broad smile of a man met her.

Ana screamed.

She bolted to the stairs again and ran down them.

A ghost—no—a ghost didn't have a form like that. That was... she didn't know what it was. Ghost. Demon. Hybrid?

Whatever it was, she knew there were more.

Her feet hit the ground floor, and just as she thought of sprinting to the exit, she heard the iron doors roll shut.

Locked.

Where the fuck was Sam?

More cages rolled shut, their bars clanking and clanking like someone were running by all of them and pulling them closed.

"Ana."

It was Sam whispering her name this time. Startling her so that she tripped over a broken stone. She fell flat to the ground, cold hands wrapping her ankles, and she screamed—*screamed*—as she was dragged backwards into the darkness. Her nails clawed the floor. She kicked. Screeched. Grabbed. Grabbed to anything and everything.

She caught a loose stone in the floor and whipped over to her back. The brick launched out of her hands and hit the being dragging her. She scrambled to her feet, only to run into some other being. Her flashlight lay in the middle of the room, flickering on and off. An arm wrapped around her shoulders.

"Pretty, pretty toy come to play," it hissed in her ear.

Ana grabbed its arm and bent, whipping the thing over her head. It slammed into the ground, and she pulled the small knife from inside her bra.

The flashlight whirled on her as she slammed that blade into the creature's throat. It was a man, or at least it had once been. A maniacal smile lit up his bleak face even with the knife in his neck. Black ooze trickled down her arm, and she kicked the creature into a heap before darting backward.

And as the rush of adrenaline caught her... As it warped and seeded itself deep within her bones, she felt her lips curling into a smile. She'd only gone a few more steps, now standing directly over the flashlight in the middle of the room—

She laughed.

She pressed her hands to her knees and she *laughed*, her head shaking as she tried and failed to contain the bit of chaos seeping out of her. She held that rush so close and let it fill her to the point that arousal peaked her core. Fuck, she had missed running. *Truly* running. Every part of her lit on fire as that familiar surge filled her body. Her head threw back as her cackle echoed and bounced, and even the water stopped dripping from the walls.

Silence, all except for Deianira's true self, filled the void of that prison, and her lungs swelled at the fear of all those demons that she now felt around her.

Ana picked up the flashlight, and this time, she pointed it everywhere.

Demons. Ghosts. Whatever they were... there were a hundred of them. Some on the ground around her, some gaping at her over the railings on the second and third floors. All with those same looks about them: decaying, demonic, maniacal. Each either grinned or gawked at the mortal woman standing before them.

"Such pretty, pretty demons," she hissed, meaning to taunt and edge them. She turned in a slow circle, her light flashing on each of them. "I know you're in there somewhere, Sam. Care to come out and play?"

She searched and searched for him, but she didn't see his face in the crowd of dying monsters around her. And when she flashed her light back on those who stood in a circle around her, she noticed they'd all stepped closer. Her lips curled into a smile, and her voice was a hiss.

"Catch me."

She clicked the flashlight off.

And she ran.

Hands swept by her. Their wind touched her hair, her skin, her legs, her now bare feet. She bolted back for the stairs, this time rising all the way to the third floor, and she didn't bother turning on that flashlight.

Flame swept on at the entrance to each cell as she reached it, and when she dared look behind her, a swarm of demons were on her tail.

And she swore across the room, on the other side of the cells, she saw Sam simply standing with his hands in his pockets watching her.

Warmth pooled into her body at the sight of him, but she didn't forget the demons so close behind her. The flames went out just as she reached the walk that wrapped over the void below, and she staggered in the middle of it.

All footsteps ceased as she grabbed the bridge railings and tried to catch her breath. Though, with the way her heart was practically flying out of her chest, she wasn't sure she could. All she could manage was another laugh.

"Scream for me."

The voice tickled her ear. Ana struck the person's leg, but they wrapped their arms around her waist. Strong arms, not the arms of whatever creatures were haunting her. She wriggled and pushed her elbows back, hitting him in the stomach. She twisted in their grasp and swept their legs out from beneath them, one foot now standing on the person's hand, the other on his throat—

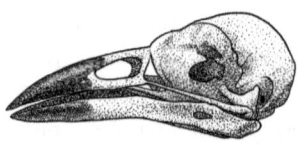

Sam nearly choked at the slam of Ana's bare foot on his neck. She pulled back her arm, ready to strike, but almost flinched when she realized it was him. Her chest heaved, hand relaxing, but she didn't move her foot.

"Having fun?" she asked breathlessly.

But Sam couldn't move. He stared up at the woman holding him down. The pure confidence in her eyes and in every move she'd just made. Standing against those deviants. He could almost see it—see *her*.

He could see her holding stabbed hearts in her hand and smeared in blood. He could see her running down corridors as guards chased and shot at her. Could see the gleam in her gaze and hear the laughter echoing off the walls as she took what was never hers and made it so.

And then another vision took over his mind.

Something greater and more devious than he'd ever seen.

Ana standing at the top of the hill at Firemoor's capitol. The world on fire at her back. Wearing thigh-high boots and a blood-stained short dress that hugged her voluptuous curves. Guns strapped in holsters on her hips, one of her thighs. A sword strapped down her back between her—

Wings.

The vision made his cock harden, and suddenly he could no longer watch that light leave her eyes, at least not in the permanent sense.

When ravens fall, he'll meet his match.

She was *his.*

Deianira Bronfell *belonged* to him.

Regardless of anything he might have begun to feel, anything he might have thought to do with her in the past. She was his to unleash upon the world and take everything he'd ever wanted—everything he'd ever promised.

And, oh… the things he could do with her.

A licentious smile split his lips, baring his white teeth. "Yours, Ms. Smith," he purred.

Her pulse raced. So fucking beautiful. So fucking fast.

Ana's head tilted, and he watched her bend to her knees, settling one on each side of his hips, and then she grabbed him by the lapels of his jacket and pulled his chest off the floor. He stayed in surrender, not daring to look away from her as she seemed to thrill at his obedience.

"Be a good little demon and open that pretty mouth for me," she said, her voice such a delicious taunt that Sam found himself obeying without a second thought.

Ana's chin lifted. He watched the corner of her lips quirk, her throat bob and her cheeks suck in slightly before she spat in his mouth.

It took everything within him not to lose control at the claim she'd just taken on him. The *blatant fucking claim.* He was rock-hard beneath her, and he knew she could feel just what that had done to him.

Ana brought him closer and licked the column of his throat. "Show me those talons," she purred in his ear. "Show me the true demon that you are and give me your darkest desires."

Fuck, he wanted to. He wanted to show her the beast she'd leered at in that museum. Wings. Claws. Eyes. Everything. But he knew if he did, it would all be over.

And he wasn't done playing yet.

So he grew those talons and pricked the shirt she was wearing, the tips digging into her flesh enough to make her mouth drop and her breath catch just slightly.

"Is this what you want, baby?" he asked as his long fingers pushed under her shirt and flicked her clothed nipple. He pulled the fabric over her head, revealing her red lingerie beneath. A claw snagged on the lace, and he ripped. Ripped. Until all that was left around her breasts were the seams. But her nipples peaked so beautifully against the chilled night air and the adrenaline coursing through her. He pricked that bud between his fingers and squeezed, watching her face the whole time as a bead of red dribbled down her skin. She sucked air between her teeth, and he captured that drip and began to suck on her. She clawed his scalp, her hips riding over his straining length, that wondrous moan echoing off the walls and the iron.

Sam felt the demons she'd run from now gathering on both sides of the bridge and down below them on the ground floor. He felt their starvation for play and release. He focused on that power as it soaked within him and he held it there. Right at the tip before it exploded out of him. The more she ground against him, the more he began to lose control.

And he would let her take him to that edge.

He would let this fucking Queen drive him to the brink of letting his existence be released. He would let her show these demons who else they should bow to.

Ana reached between them, a scuffle as she unhooked his jeans and then began to stroke him. He cursed and bit her breast hard enough to leave teeth marks behind. The pressure of her hands around his cock made him growl loud, the entire room shaking in response.

"The dead are all watching, baby," he managed once he'd collected himself, his talons now digging into her generous ass.

Her chuckle was a chill on his flesh, and the whisper... "Tell your friends to enjoy the show."

The whisper sent him snarling.

She sank onto his length and shoved him down. With her fingers wrapped into his shirt, she pushed him with every sink and rock on his dick. Her head threw back. She cried out to the ceiling, to the demons, to the very lightning striking outside. She channeled that energy into her as she writhed and screamed, and Sam...

Sam couldn't breathe.

This woman was the deadliest prayer in existence. She was mortal, and she rivaled the power thrumming through his veins and leaking out in shadows onto the floor. He was holding his release, waiting for her to find her own edge and rhythm. He could feel her walls tightening around him, her nails digging into his chest and stretching his shirt. She grabbed her hair, and he clenched her hips, settling her still as he lifted his hips and pounded inside her. Faster and faster. Her high-pitched moans singing to his power—

She came with a scream, and fog curled around them as he came after. She continued rocking on him, milking him for everything he was worth. Sam spiraled down, down, down as he kept the power at his fingertips from pulling him under.

A glint of silver caught in the next lightning strike.

Sam saw the flash, and he grabbed her wrist as she brought the small knife down toward his neck.

And the smile she gave him had him hardening for her again.

He tutted his tongue as he took the blade out of her hand and watched as her chest rose and fell with every heavy breath.

"You wicked, *wicked* girl…"

He remembered then what she'd told him on the phone that night, how she would kill him, and the fact that she'd shown him…

This was how she'd taken those kings. This was exactly how she'd ripped their hearts from their bodies. By spending their bodies and sending them begging for more of her. She'd taken that control from them and given them a grand final night.

Sam sat up as she continued to smile—no, *grin*—at him. He enclosed his hand around the knife in her fist, letting it break his skin. A quiet laugh constricted in the back of her throat, and he let that noise run over his skin and spread his own lips wide.

"My fucking *goddess*," he hissed.

The knife clattered to the bridge as their hands entwined, his blood matching hers on their palms. He wrapped his other into her hair and kissed her, unable to resist her lips after the absolute ferocity he'd just witnessed.

If this was a fraction of her true self…

Fuck, he couldn't wait to see the rest.

Chapter Twenty-Eight

Sam didn't bother caging those ghosts before they left the prison. But a few had tried to scare them again, their laughs rippling down hallways and chasing them in the darkness. Sam made a point to press his hand to the walls when they walked past and mutter a silent order for them to wait for his call. And the energy that filtered back to him was of greed and pride.

Stars greeted them as they made their way back to his bike, and when they arrived back at her apartment, Sam suggested a walk.

He was still high on the adrenaline of her, and honestly, he wasn't ready to face whatever might await him at home. She was a beautiful, yet a horrible distraction, and despite the fact that he could hear Millie's triumphant voice that she'd been right, he didn't care.

That very thought should have scared him enough to send him packing home or slicing out her heart right there in the middle of the street.

But he didn't.

"Can I tell you something?" Ana asked as they walked by the cemetery.

Sam squeezed her hand as the chilled night air wrapped around them. "Please," he said.

"I've always had this… fascination, I guess, with death," and Sam's head tilted at the words.

"How so?" he asked.

"I suppose… I suppose I've just seen so much of it. I always wondered what was there, when you're teetering on that final thread at the edge of existence. If Death is actually a person to answer the call or if he chooses those he goes to."

"He doesn't hear everyone," Sam said.

"What do you mean?" she asked.

"I mean…" His gaze skirted out to the cemetery to his left, to his home and the shadows that seemed to linger on the other side of the gates like they were waiting on his call. "The stories here. Our mythology surrounding Death. That he is a real person who hears that final call—"

"It's a big world," Ana said. "I imagine that would be tiresome. To have to take every person who dies into their new beginning."

"Not every person," he said, voice softened. "He uses his demons to take care of those in other realms. He stopped his reaching power at the borders after the last war."

"Do you hear these calls?"

Sam hesitated. "I have heard them," he finally said. "On occasion."

"What does it sound like?"

He wondered if she would understand. He wondered if the woman beside him would be accepting and helpful at someone's end. If she would help him carry them into the next life as no one else had.

Everyone else in his life had never been able to stomach it. Rolfe had helped on the rare occasion if it was a child. Millie, though… she'd stayed once, and had been so upset by the end of it that she'd told him she couldn't do that again.

"I'm sorry," Ana said then, having apparently felt the hesitation. "Sorry, I didn't think—"

"It's fine," he assured her.

"Does it say how he decides who continues and who does not?" she asked, apparently choosing to go in a different direction.

Sam shook his head slowly, feeling his eyes darken. "I think that's part of the illusion, isn't it?" he whispered. "That people have any say over when this life ends and another begins."

"Would would you do?" she asked. "If you were Death, I mean. Would you give mercy to every person who asked for that end? Or would you pick and choose who lives and who goes?"

"It's not that simple," he said, and the images of all those he'd held begging for that filled his mind. "It can't be."

"I think if I were Death… I would be tired. I would miss the sun. I would miss what it felt like to live and love," she said.

"It must be a lonely existence," he said.

"You've never met him?" she asked.

"Once," he lied. "When I was turned… but that was during the last war, and I was so far from gone that I barely remember more than the relief of that end and the breath of the new beginning."

And for some reason, the lie wrenched his stomach.

"Is there a book where all this information is written?" she asked.

He paused to meet her eyes, considering the date and what he could tell her. "There is," he said. "I can show you, soon."

"Why not today?"

He smiled, wrapping his arm around her shoulders. "Always so eager, wicked girl—"

Before Sam could kiss her, a hundred voices shouted into his head at once.

Terror struck him all the way to the bend of his knees. He staggered, hand landing on the iron rail to keep himself upright. Vomit rose in his throat. Ana's voice was a distant echo as she grabbed his arm and tried to help him. But the voices…

Voices of people from the Spine dying at his border.

"Sam—*Sam!*" Ana pleaded in front of him, her hands on his face, tapping his cheeks lightly. "Sam—what's wrong?"

His eyes rolled as he caught his breath, but he pushed the noise out. He couldn't do this right then. He couldn't shadow to his home and call them all right then. Not with Ana—

Catching his breath, he straightened and softly took Ana's hand. "It's nothing," he lied. "Maybe just something we ate. Or the adrenaline of tonight. Are you feeling okay?"

The lie was a poor one, but Ana didn't call him out on it. "Yeah, I'm okay," she said. "Do you need to lie down?"

"I should be going, actually," he said through a strained tone. His bike wasn't far away. They'd just walked across the street and down a quarter of a mile. He leaned in and kissed Ana's temple, giving her an apologetic look.

"I'll make it up to you," he promised.

But she shook her head. "It's okay," she said. "I'm used to you leaving around this time anyway."

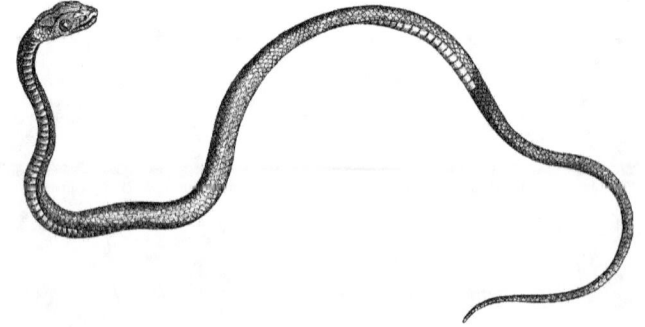

Chapter Twenty-Nine

By the time Sam made it to his castle, he'd vomited twice.

He hadn't heard so many screaming since the last war, and it had been so long that he'd forgotten how terrifying it even made him.

Rolfe was waiting for him on the steps, his hands in his pockets as lightning began to crack wildly around them. He stretched an offering of whiskey out to Sam as he met him. Sam kicked it back with one gulp.

"How did the date go?" Rolfe asked, and Sam knew it was simply to get him thinking about anything except what they were about to find inside the cathedral.

"Fantastic," Sam managed, holding his stomach a moment as another voice shouted and screeched inside his head. "Tell you about it when there aren't a hundred people shouting at us." He rubbed his temple as Rolfe poured another whiskey and slumped on the steps.

Rolfe sat with him, and together the pair simply took in a moment to look at the sky. The stars and nebulas and galaxies that stared back.

"We don't do this enough anymore," Sam said as he sipped the whiskey this time.

"That's because the last time we spent the entire night outside was the night before you shadowed this place, and I think all three of us thought that meant we'd never see the stars again," Rolfe replied.

Sam almost laughed. "I wasn't entirely sure what I was doing," he admitted.

"I don't think any of us did," Rolfe agreed. "But it was a fuck of an idea. And a shit load of people liked it."

"Who doesn't like the idea of revenge?" Sam asked, and his friend clanked his glass against his own before both took long swigs.

"Something tells me the people in that cathedral will like it too," Rolfe said.

Sam ran a hand through his hair and sighed. "Long night ahead," he said. "You don't have to help if you don't want to."

But Rolfe shrugged him off. "Wouldn't dream of missing it, boss."

Every step down the halls to the cathedral seemed to get heavier and heavier. Sam was grateful for Rolfe at his side, knowing how much his friend didn't like hearing the cries. Taking his own justice was one thing. He could fuel that behind rage and adrenaline. But helping those at their edge...

It had never been Rolfe's strong suit.

Murmurs sounded aloud as they hit the glass-covered hall connecting to the cathedral, and when Sam pushed the double doors open, he stilled on the threshold.

There were more than a hundred souls waiting for him. Some were bloodied. Some were broken. And others...

Others were so far to that edge that Sam wasn't sure he'd be able to get a response from them.

As he took a look around the room, his thoughts went to Ana, and he thought of how she would have reacted to seeing this. If she would have stood with him and helped carry those people into the next life. Or if she would have found it too hard to stick around.

Sam looked at his friend stood stiff at his side. "Are you sure you're okay here?"

Rolfe looked around again at the bodies bleeding out and choking all around them. His face was pale, sweat slowly beginning to bead on his forehead, but he clapped Sam on the shoulder. "Right behind you, boss," he swore.

Sam nodded and drew a deep breath. "We take this one at a time. Just help me keep them comfortable."

Chapter Thirty

Sam and Rolfe didn't bother washing the blood off their bodies before dawn broke the horizon.

One hundred and seventy-two souls had been given the chance at revenge, and thus turned demon in that cathedral—the cathedral with depictions of Death in the stained glass. The hardwood floor was now so covered in red that Sam was sure it was its new stain.

The pair hadn't even moved from the room after the last soul was taken, too exhausted to lift a finger.

Sam laid flat on the altar in the middle of the room and stared at the painted ceiling as the voices finally cleared his throbbing head, Rolfe leaning against it on the floor. He hadn't even transformed he was so tired.

The smell of death lingered around them, and the grand gothic doors creaked open as grey light filtered through the windows.

Millie made a grunt of disgust as she swept into the room, and Sam didn't bother sitting up or looking at her.

"If you've come to help clean—" he waved a hand, and shadows began to curl around the floor "—you're too late."

"I came to see if the bodies were far enough inside the border last night," she said. "And to make sure you didn't lie here all day. Though, I didn't expect to see Rolfe here."

"Course I'm here," Rolfe said, though his words were barely coherent.

The deathhound had held in his vomit and helped Sam as best he could the entire night. He'd kept those calm, heard their pleas, and sometimes held their hands as Sam either cut their throats to reprieve them into their next existence, or guided their dying souls into the dark abyss of an immortal, yet demonic, abyss. He talked with a few who were on the edge of making that decision, telling them what he'd gone through and how he'd made his choice, and no matter how many times Sam heard Rolfe's story, it still wove an ever-tightening thread around his heart.

Rolfe and Millie. Two who had waited and waited, held on for days just for Sam to find them because they'd heard Death was free and offering revenge. He'd met Rolfe when Rolfe was a young teen slave in the northern army. Like Millie, he had been ripped from his family as a child and sold off as a whore and servant. To bend to whatever needs of the northern Commander at the time. He'd once been beaten so poorly as a child that Sam had gone to him because he'd thought he was about to die, but Rolfe had shown resilience and told Death he would not be taken. Not yet. That young boy had refused Death, refused immortality.

So, Sam had made a vow to find him once the war broke out years later.

And he did.

"You two need showers," Millie said.

"I'm content lying here the rest of my existence," Sam muttered.

Rolfe raised two fingers. "As am I," he said.

Millie stopped on the other side of Sam and looked directly over him, brow raising. Sam resisted shoving her and finally sat up, knowing she would not give up until he was moving.

The movement was a chore, but he let his legs hang on the side of the altar and met her eyes. "We really could have used you last night," he said, his voice barely audible.

"I was dealing with our demons last night," Millie said. "I heard it, but... I had to go meet Damien."

Sam's eyes narrowed. "You went over the border?"

"No," she said, and Sam sighed in relief. "No. I met him where he was dumping bodies. He's going to call you later."

"That bad?" Sam asked.

"I think he just wants to talk to you instead of passing messages," Millie said. She looked between the two before her, obviously noting how pale and exhausted they were, and sighed heavily before saying, "Both of you smell like rotten corpses. I'll pick up some food. For now, though... can you at least make it to the bath?"

Sam exchanged a look with Rolfe, who sniffed his own underarms and gave a grunt of agreement.

"And I don't mean a hound bath, Rolfe," Millie said. "An actual bath. Please."

Rolfe pushed on the ground to stand. "I want a full lamb then."

Millie raised a lazy brow, then gave Sam an expectant glance. "And you, Your Majesty?"

Sam hopped down from the altar, his stomach churning at even the thought of food. "Whatever you want," he answered softly.

Are you okay this morning? Ana texted him later.

Sam debated how to answer. Because truthfully, he wasn't. Between what he had seen of her in the prison and the people he'd led into an immortal life that night, he was tired. And along with hearing all those humans ask for revenge, he kept thinking about Ana and how she'd faced all those things so fearlessly.

He thought about the vision he'd had while watching her. Of setting her free and letting her have everything she wanted. Of the wings and the fire and the sword at her back.

Maybe he didn't need to get rid of her.

Maybe *she* was the answer.

He'd toyed with the idea previously, before he grew to know her. But thinking about getting rid of her then seemed like the worst mistake he would ever make. It twisted his heart to think of going a day without talking to her.

What he wanted, more than anything, was to go see her and tell her about the night he'd had. He wanted to tell her what the people that he'd spoken to had said about her. How a few of them had said they wanted revenge so they could take it in her name since she had given them the will and strength to seek it.

He wanted to lie in her arms and tell her everything.

And the realization scared him so much that he turned his phone on silent, left it on the table, and walked out into his garden, Luna following behind him.

He needed time to come to terms with this new piece. To plot it out and feel confident enough in it that he could present it to his friends as the next step.

Because maybe it was time.

When ravens fall, he'll meet his match.

And to his own grave, she'll lead him.

A knot wove his stomach as he pulled a piece of old parchment from his shadows, where he'd hid it on his person since it was made. A ritual for the being the witch had told him would give him everything he truly wanted, the being that would make this prison worth it.

The Ballad.

Sam inhaled the misty fog, the moss, and the white roses all around him. Special roses that bloomed in the shade and grew the most prominent thorns he'd ever seen. He took the shears from his pocket and began cutting a few that were ready, letting the thorns prick his fingers. The blood mingled with the blood of the dead already soaked into his skin.

For two hours, he let his mind rest of all that haunted him. And by the time he walked back inside, he had an arm full of flowers for the front table and some catnip that he needed to dry out for Luna.

Ana had texted him again, just his name and a question this time, and Sam took a moment before answering back.

I'm okay, he said. *Work was tiresome.*

Was it him? she asked.

He stared at the phone briefly, biting the inside of his mouth. *A call, yes. In a different part of the realm.*

Why does he not answer all of them within his borders?

Sometimes it is too many, and his demons help.

Three dots strummed the bottom of the screen for a moment, and while he waited on her to respond, Luna jumped onto the table and began to purr and wind between his arms.

The door opened, Rolfe stepping inside, and by the look on his face, Sam knew he wouldn't have much time for flirting today.

"Damien is on the line," Rolfe said.

Sam nodded. "I'll be up in a minute."

Come over for dinner? Ana had asked.

Doubles, Sam said. *I'll call you later before I go in. Have a good day, baby. You too.*

Chapter Thirty-One

For three nights, Sam barely slept.

Even with how exhausted he'd been with the people from the Spine, he hadn't slept more than an hour or two.

The call with Damien had been brief. He'd only told him what he'd told Millie, and said he'd have more. And he wasn't exaggerating.

Damien had brought two hundred more beings over the border for him the night after the prison, but this last night had been quiet, so Sam had ended up in his garden again.

He'd lied to Ana and said he had doubles at work the last two nights. He'd needed time to recover from the Spine souls, as well as time to think about her and how things had changed. He'd even gone alone uptown to the museum to try and clear his head, see if the art could give him some sort of guidance, but all it did was remind him of her.

That morning, he'd been so bent out of shape about not seeing her that he'd broken into her apartment and fucked her over morning coffee before lying and saying he had to go back to work.

He'd brought him and Rolfe breakfast back, though because Rolfe wasn't up yet, he'd started the coffee and went out to the garden again to fertilize the roses.

A compost of bodies Rolfe had taken his own justice upon lie at the back of Sam's grand garden grounds. He grabbed a wheelbarrow and a shovel before making off for it, Luna riding in the wheelbarrow like it was her personal chariot.

Rolfe woke and brought coffee out to the garden once he'd figured out what Sam was doing. Together, they spent the morning replanting and taking new cuttings, trimming the bushes, and fertilizing the plethora of plants.

"What's wrong?" Rolfe asked him as they dumped the last pile of compost out and began to spread it. "Other than you're being tired."

"Why does something have to be wrong?" Sam asked, eager to avoid the question.

"Because you do physical labor when you can't think straight," Rolfe grunted.

Sam propped his hands on the stake of his rake, and Rolfe's mouth quirked as he realized he'd gotten under Sam's skin.

"We've been best friends five hundred years," Rolfe said. "Think I don't know when you're brooding? I'd be more worried if you were painting."

"I like painting," Sam said.

"You paint when you're sad," Rolfe said, stopping his raking. "So talk."

A heavy sigh left Sam as his gaze swept out to the far streets. "You didn't make it to the prison the other night," he said plainly.

"Had a few errands to run," Rolfe said with a shrug. "She put on a good show?"

"She put on a fuck of a show," Sam replied. And before he could stop himself, he was telling his friend everything. Every scream and laugh she'd let go. All the thoughts that had filled his head. When he was finished, all Rolfe did was shake his head and laugh.

"What are you going to do?" Rolfe asked.

Sam slumped onto the cement bench near him. "I don't know," he admitted.

"Could be a good thing to have her on our side," Rolfe said. "Sounds pretty fucking scary, and if all the rumors are true..." His brow elevated in Sam's direction, and Sam clamped his hands together.

"You would keep her?" Sam asked.

"I can't say," Rolfe said. "Might find out what exactly she wants first."

Sam had thought about that. "That might require a little more breakage," he said, meeting Rolfe's eyes.

A smile lifted into the death hound's gaze. "Keep playing, boss."

The soul is so much more breathtaking against the storm of chaos, was the quote Ana sent him that morning.

I love storms, Sam replied once he was back in his office, finally ready to face whatever reports came for him.

I was never a huge storm person until I came here, she replied. *Something about the ones in this kingdom make them irresistible. I find myself standing outside in the rain sometimes.*

One of my favorite things to do, he said. *It's the cold water on your skin and the danger of the lightning.*

The sky screams here, she said. *I love it.*

Me too.

Sam turned back to the reports on his screen, though for some reason, he couldn't stop checking his phone. Until he couldn't stop himself, and he picked up the device to text her again.

Lunch today? he asked.

Not today. I have to head uptown for an art consult and some shopping, but after… maybe you could meet me there.

Sam let that message settle with him for a moment. He had access to all of Jay's bookings, every consult, every dime spent. All because he'd helped him buy the damn place, and because… well, Millie knew her way into things she shouldn't.

Ana was lying.

It made his jaw tick.

But before he could respond, he got a text from Milliscent, and he prioritized it.

Meet me uptown at three, Millie texted him. *Restaurant at SkyCor.*

See you then, he typed back.

He pulled up Ana's messages again. *I'll meet you around five?*

Sounds great, Ana said.

What are you buying me? Sam asked.

Hm… a new jacket?

Black, he said. *Nothing flashy.*

Of course, she replied. *I'll see you this afternoon. Text me when you're close.*

Sam didn't reply, and instead, he flipped the phone to Rolfe's contact information.

"Yeah, boss?" Rolfe answered.

"You outside?" Sam asked as he walked to his window.

"Yeah."

"Find out where she's going today," Sam said, turning to grab his jacket from the counter. "I'm heading to the studio for a few hours and then uptown to see Millie."

"See you at the gallery opening tonight?" Rolfe asked.

"Yeah. Yeah, I'll see you there."

Chapter Thirty-Two

Ana stared out the windows as she took the bus to the mental hospital east of midtown. St Orphs, it was called. She hadn't asked Jay about it, only saying that she needed the rest of the day off to run a few errands. Jay didn't mind. He'd been swiping on a dating app all morning and asking her her opinion on different prospects. She'd played along, though her mood had quickly deteriorated with every word.

At least Sam had been more himself that morning. She'd been concerned that perhaps she'd scared him off at the prison, but he'd taken his break at work to come to her apartment early and fucked her on her kitchen counter with deliberate tease while the coffee made in the pot behind them. She couldn't lie... it had been a welcome wake-up call since he'd not been able to hang out with her since their last date.

She had almost begun to wonder if her slip of chaos inside the prison had made him wary, until she felt him in her bed. She'd thought him a dream. But his hands had been on her, trailing between her thighs, over her clit, and she'd opened her eyes to find him behind her, his lips on her throat.

"Sam... What are you—Fuck—" She sank into the mattress at the tease of his fingers circling over her.

"I couldn't stop thinking about you," he admitted, teeth dragging over her neck.

"How... How did you get in?" she managed as a digit tickled her entrance.

His lips quirked, and he pushed that finger inside her, making her hips buck, a moan leave her. "You think a lock is going to keep me from you?"

That should have scared her. That he'd broken into her apartment and come into her bed without telling her. He reached up and pushed a curl from her face.

"Tell me you'd rather me leave," he said softly.

Ana cursed her heart for the way it ached then. "No," she said, her lips brushing his. He pushed another finger inside her, his thumb dragging over her clit, and she tried to keep herself from falling apart when his mouth latched onto her nipple. "Are you off work?"

"I have twenty-five minutes," he replied, tongue swirling around that hardened peak.

She reached for his face and pulled him up to her. "Then you'll let me start coffee so it's ready for you when you leave."

Sam's eyes lit up, tongue darting out over his lips as he seemed to try and stifle a genuine smile. "How do you already know the key to my heart?"

She kissed him lightly. "Ass and coffee," she teased. "You're not as complicated as you think."

Ana quickly broke herself out of those thoughts as the bus lurched with its stop, unsure of why she'd actually been concerned about scaring Sam off. He was just fun, after all. Her future lay in that castle across the way, not in her apartment with some random demon she'd thought was sexy.

Even though she was no closer to figuring out anything about the king other than how his demons operated.

She hoped the journalist could tell her something. *Anything.*

A blast of cold air hit her when she entered the renovated ward. She'd half expected the place to be some old manor out of a few of her favorite books, but it was just a tall, square building with little character and grey paint coating the brick outside.

She buzzed the intercom within the antechamber, and a pleasant voice greeted her on the other side.

"Saint Orphs ward. Who are you here to see?"

"My sister," Ana said. "Rosie Brenn."

Silence rang in her ears as the woman on the other side, behind a desk that Ana could see just fifteen feet away, debated the truth of Ana's words.

"Sister?"

"Yes," Ana said into the box. "I should be in her file. We haven't spoken in a while. She and I were separated as children."

Ana had done her homework. Had seen what this girl looked like and been able to get into that hospital database. She knew Rosie had, in fact, had a sister who supposedly died at twelve, and Rose had come into Shadowmyer with their mother.

Ana could see the woman as she pushed her reading glasses up and typed away on the keyboard. Ana tapped the strap of her purse as she waited, her gaze darting down the spotless white hall to the stretch of key-locked doors.

"And your name?" the woman asked.

"Ana Smith."

Another hesitation, and then the woman spoke. "Come to the desk with your ID."

The door buzzed and opened for Ana. After giving her ID to the receptionist and seeing it verified, the woman had her wait in the chairs across the way. It was ten minutes before a nurse came to get her.

"You'll be lucky to get more than a couple of words," the nurse told Ana as they walked down the hall. "But... she's not had many visitors in some time. Maybe your being here will give her some hope."

"Who was her last visitor?" Ana asked.

"Ah." The nurse gave her a small, apologetic smile. "Afraid I can't tell you that. But I can tell you that he comes by every few months and leaves her a white rose."

The white rose.

It was part of what the article had said this woman had babbled about after her getting caught inside the castle. White roses and shadows... wings and blood. A black cat and a beastly hound with razor fangs and a body that was half bare bone.

Did Death visit this woman? Or was it simply one of the demons, perhaps a lost lover that had once given her those roses, and she'd been confused about them, imagined them inside the castle because he'd brought her a bouquet that morning.

"Does he stay long?" Ana asked.

"No more than a few minutes," the nurse answered. "She is usually asleep. The last time he was here, I'm afraid he had to leave early. She had one of her episodes."

"Episodes?"

"Nightmares," the nurse corrected. "Occasionally, she wakes up screaming."

A chill brushed over Ana's skin, and they turned the hall.

"When is the last you saw her?" the nurse asked.

"Almost twenty years," Ana said softly, allowing sadness into her voice. "Our mother and father separated us during the raids of northeastern Firemoor. Father took me west. Mother took her east."

185

"That's unfortunate," the nurse said. "To be separated like that."

"I remember..." Ana thought of the day when she'd lost her mother. How her father had cried over her body until Ana, so young at the time, had urged him up and out of the burning house. She'd never buried her mother as she'd buried her father.

"It was," were the only two words Ana pretended to manage as the nurse paused before a door.

She knocked, but didn't wait on a reply as she turned the knob, and when Ana glimpsed the woman on the bed, she nearly gasped.

This... *girl*. No older than her, once so lovely and bright-eyed as the pictures had shown online was now gaunt. Rigid. Like her mind had been swept and she was merely a hollow shell.

Rosie was staring at the ceiling, her eyes wide and mouth open like she'd just seen a ghost. She didn't flinch or acknowledge the opening door or the voices that spoke to her.

The nurse gave Ana a grim smile. "It's how she sleeps," she said solemnly. "I'll leave you two alone."

As the door closed, Ana sat her purse on the ground and sat at the girl's bedside. She took in the girl's now dulling brown skin, the untamed corkscrew curls, how lifeless her rounded eyes were, and she wondered what exactly had happened to her in that castle.

How had she come out like this? The news reports had only said she was driven insane, and she was a warning to anyone who might dare think about breaking in in the future.

"Oh, Rosie," Ana muttered aloud as she reached for her hand and gave it a squeeze. "What happened to you?"

It was a long shot, and perhaps a little ridiculous to speak aloud to someone who could very well never speak again, but Ana didn't care. She rubbed the girl's hand and began to hum a song her mother had once sung to her every night. It was a quiet, healing lullaby, and every time she felt scared of falling into that pit of never turning back, she'd sung it and reminded herself to live.

Rosie's finger twitched in her hand, making Ana stare at her unblinking eyes. She continued humming, continued that comforting sound, and again, the girl's hand twitched.

"Hey, Rosie," she said, giving her hand a squeeze. "Hey—"

Rosie sat straight up and yanked Ana out of her chair toward the bed.

Her eyes were wild, grip so tight on Ana's hand that she thought it might break. She jerked as she tried to get away, but Rosie just grabbed her other hand into hers and pulled her so close, Ana could feel her breath.

"The shadows will call you," Rosie hissed, and Ana could feel her trembling. "Don't listen to them. Don't listen to the howls or prick the roses. Don't listen to the howls or prick the roses. Don't prick the roses. Don't. Don't. *Don't*—"

But Rosie's eyes rolled and she staggered like she might fall back.

Until she spotted the white rose on her bedside table. Her eyes widened once more, and she flung herself back, kicking and throwing her sheet away. Ana bolted out of her seat—

"He's coming," Rosie hissed. "He came. He came. He's here. He's—"

An urgent knock sounded. The nurse came running in.

"Rosie—hey, calm down," she tried.

Ana took a few more steps back to the door, her heart picking up at the pure terror on Rosie's face, bleeding from her bulging eyes.

"He's coming. He's here. *He's here.*" Rosie jerked out of bed, sending the tray table crashing to the ground as she backed to the window, arms bracing against the white wall. Her head jerked in every direction and she began to shrink to the ground. "Shadows—the shadows—I said no shadows—" Her hands pushed over her face, and as the nurse tried to get to her, she shook her head. "No shadows. No dark. Only light. No shadows, no dark. No shadows—"

The nurse cut Ana a look over her shoulder as Rosie continued. "I'm sorry," the nurse said. "But you should leave." She gave her an apologetic smile. "Keep trying."

Ana nodded vigorously as she grabbed her purse, and she left out of that room more confused than she'd been before going in.

Chapter Thirty-Three

Millie was dressed in her usual business, but make it sexy, attire when Sam spotted her already sitting at a table on the high terrace restaurant inside SkyCor. She had her phone out, a glass of red wine in her hand, peering at the screen over her wide sunglasses. Sam smiled upon seeing her and shook his head, but Millie saw him before he could comment.

She took a long sip of wine and whipped her sunglasses off, lips curling upwards. "Yes, please, Sam. Dress in your usual tattered shambles even when you're meeting the Hand at the most expensive restaurant in this fucking realm," she said in a snappy voice that made Sam grin crookedly. "You couldn't even be bothered to put on your nice leather jacket?"

He leaned over and gave her a chaste kiss on the cheek, then slumped into the opposite chair. "I thought you liked this one," he said with a wink.

Millie wasn't amused. That blank face stared back at him, a slight pucker on her lips, her blue eyes taut. "Rolfe called," she said shortly.

Sam shifted just as the waiter came by to take his drink order, and when she was gone, he leaned casually back in his chair, ankle resting over his knee. "Something on your mind, Mills?"

"Your girlfriend went to St. Orphs this morning," Millie said. "To talk to the journalist that we drove insane."

Sam's jaw ticked at the information. "Reasonable place for her to go."

"Sam—"

"What, Milliscent?" he snapped, and the waitress that had just brought his drink over scurried away, muttering that she would come back later to take their food order.

Millie raised an annoyed brow as a beat of quiet passed between them, obvious she was debating how she would call him out on his plan.

"What are you doing?" she finally asked.

"Keeping an eye on her," he said.

"And fucking her senseless," Millie retorted. "Why haven't you killed her? Or at least put her in the dungeon."

"Plans change."

"For fuck's sake, Samar—" She caught herself before saying his name as loud as she nearly did, and she leaned forward so she could speak quietly, her face the picture of rage. "I want to know what's going on," she hissed. "*Now*, Samarius."

Sam let the silence settle between them, his hands clasping together in his lap. Her tone nearly had him sending shadows around her throat, and he wondered if that was why she'd asked to meet him in public. He was forced to listen to her here, unable to run away into his shadows or go to his garden to work.

"Do you ever miss the sun, Millie?" he asked, watching her expression as his voice dropped.

She contemplated it, the thin line her lips had pressed into now softening at the very mention of it. He could see that memory hazing in her eyes, feel her stiffen and weep inside.

"I do," she whispered.

"The warmth... the rejuvenation..."

"Bikinis and no umbrellas," she added.

The corner of his mouth quirked upward, but only for a blink. He shifted in his seat and sat up, making Millie rest her glass of wine on the table.

"Do you remember when I first turned you?"

Millie stared, haze drawing over her eyes. "When you deviated from Firemoor," she whispered.

"We took this realm," he said, danger in his voice. "You, me, Rolfe... The legions that we found in the gutters and trenches trying to escape the chaos. We all came here and hid this place so we could live without being forced to do things we did not agree with. Life without persecution for what we were forced to become." He settled his elbows on the table, watching that shadow of their dark past wash over her face. "What if we could have the sun again?"

And Millie's eyes widened.

"What if we could have the revenge we promised ourselves we would one day have," he asked slowly. "And what if... what if she was the key to it all."

Millie's breath visibly hitched, and with a subtle catch in her voice, she said, "Are you serious?" she asked. "You think it's time?"

"I've done a lot of thinking, barely been sleeping since the attack... And getting to know her..." Sam looked around them as he pushed forward, and then he locked eyes with Millie. "I should have realized it earlier. I should have seen her for what she truly was, not the things we'd been told. I could have saved us time if I'd asked her to become one of us instead of playing this little game, but... I needed her to love this place as we do. I needed her to see it as a home, and I needed to know how she genuinely felt about the other kingdoms. Revenge is a powerful force, but fighting for something you love is even more potent." He huffed at himself and shook his head.

"Deianira is everything that we have waited centuries for. She's already taken these kingdoms by force—something you and I have been dreaming of doing. Her very presence will march their armies into our home. Into everything we've spent years building and building, and for what? To sit back and keep to ourselves?" He paused, chin lifting, and pointed into the table as he said, "The time is *now*."

Millie leaned forward in her seat, mirroring him as her palms pressed flat. "Then bring. Her. *Home*."

Her voice was a warning, and Sam didn't blink.

"I need to know her endgame," Sam said. "I need to know what she wants."

"How do you plan on finding that out?"

Sam tapped his fingers on the table. "By breaking her."

Millie sat back in her seat and took another sip of her wine, apparently considering everything he'd just said. "Bring her to the gallery opening tonight," she said.

"Why?"

"Because I want to know if you're too far in over your head," she snapped.

Sam chuckled lightly, taking a sip of his own drink and hating how well Millie knew him. "You mean if I have the will to dangle her at the edge of the borders as bait still?" He leaned back and shook his head at the sky. "She'd welcome it."

Ana treated herself to a hair appointment and retail therapy after meeting Rosie. She couldn't get the fear in Rosie's voice out of her head. Ana wondered how exactly Death had scared Rosie so much—so much so that she slept with her eyes open, refusing to acknowledge the darkness.

And the white rose in the vase…

Ana swiped her credit card and checked her phone for the time. She was almost late meeting Sam, so she gathered her bags and made her way to the bench he'd asked her to wait for him at.

She'd spent a lot more money than she'd meant to, but for once, she had money of her own that hadn't been taken by blood, and she could wear clothes here that didn't make her feel like a peasant.

That was another reason she loved this kingdom so much more. She wasn't forced into linen dresses or ridiculously oversized cloaks. She could have her own style, feel good about herself and show off her curves without everyone calling her a whore or worse just because she had them.

A group of men and women passed by across the street, wearing dark ripped clothing and multi-colored hair. Ana waved at one of the guys, who gave her an upwards nod, a crooked smile on his lips. She uncrossed and crossed her legs, vaguely flashing a shadow of her bare cunt, then pulled her phone out to make herself busy.

She'd just pulled up one of the new social media apps Jay had told her about when she felt a hand brush her bare shoulder. And she could tell by the cold steel of the ring above his ring finger knuckle, that it was Sam.

"About time," she muttered, starting to turn to look up at him. But he wrapped his fingers around the front of her jaw, and her eyes fluttered when he held her head straight.

"Shh…" he said, his other hand moving up her other shoulder, fingers digging into her skin and massaging her collarbone.

Ana sank into the feeling of his hands on her. She loved how touches like this made her feel taken, and yet somehow, still free. As though it was a relief of safety but an encouragement to continue being herself.

"Tell me you bought that lingerie set I sent you a photo of yesterday," he said as his short nails scratched her trachea. His thumbs pressed into the back of her neck, drawing slow circles on her skin.

"That and a few more," she said, eyes closing. "I was going to show you after dinner. Though, now…" Her head rolled as she relaxed completely into his grasp. "Now, I'm thinking you can do this to my entire body first and then you can see it."

"Or I could do this to you while you're wearing it."

She groaned at the scratch of his fingers on her scalp. "Anything you want," she managed.

His hand wrapped underneath her jaw, and he tilted her head back, until she was looking directly up at him.

"Hey, stalker," she said, smiling at the perfection of him staring at her.

His lips lifted at the corner, and his fingers tightened. "Temptress," he replied. "You look freshly pampered today… Was it the new salon you found?" He picked up a curl between his fingers, twirling the fresh spiral. "Or was it the thorough fucking at sunrise?" he asked, smirking smugly down at her.

She resisted her smile widening. Every touch replayed in her mind as his fingers continued to trace her neck and play in her hair. "It was the salon," she said. "The fucking was nice, but the salon… Something about the water and a scalp massage that does things to the soul," she finished.

Sam's smile widened, his gaze washing out over the busy street. "Stand up," he told her.

She did, and Sam sucked his lip behind his teeth as she stepped around the back of the bench, his eyes darting over her. And before she could say anything, he pulled her in for a kiss. Deep, encompassing, mind-numbing… The way Sam kissed her was the way she'd only ever seen in tragic movies. At first, she'd compared it to that final kiss before the hero said goodbye before sacrificing himself for some greater good.

Though, she was sure there was nothing heroic about the man in front of her.

He was the villain waiting in the shadows for the hero to off himself, so he could take what was always his. The one the heroine had shared fevered glances with across rooms while the hero held her… Until the tension became too much, and the heroine surrendered to his claiming passion and dangerous abyss.

She sucked in a breath when he finally parted from her, still holding her neck and squeezing her waist, as his dark eyes seared through to the depths of her existence… as if he could see every breath she'd ever taken, every step in her life, all the fire and killings and everything she was.

When she blinked, and the look was replaced with a sly smirk.

"The next time some idiot makes a pass at you on the street, make sure you give him more than a wave and flash of that pretty cunt," he rasped. "I want every other person in this kingdom painstakingly jealous that they're not the one fucking you at all hours of the day."

Ana resisted the urge to smile. "You're not worried one of these other men will be as good as you and sweep me off my feet if I give them too much of an invitation?"

"There are no men like me," he swore, his eyes darkening.

And she hated the way her body responded to that.

People she'd consorted with in the past had tried to clothe her in frumpy dresses and keep her quiet. Told her never to smile at another man, not that it had ever stopped her. They'd pinned back her hair and tried to tame her spirit.

She'd enjoyed cutting their throats after, too.

Sam reached over the bench and picked up her bags, then threw them over his shoulder with a half-smile and a wink. "Not exactly sure where you wanted me to put these on the bike," he said.

"I can take the bus if you like," she said.

Sam leaned down and gave her a kiss on the cheek. "I'll make it work," he said. "How do you feel about going out?"

"Out where?" she asked.

"There's a gallery opening in midtown. A couple of friends are going and have extra tickets. Thought you might be interested."

"Wait—" Ana grabbed his hand and turned him back around. "Are you asking to introduce me to your friends?" And her stomach clenched both at the fact that he was suggesting it and who she knew his friends were.

Sam's tongue darted out over his lips as he scoffed, glancing down at the ground and then back at her. "Maybe I am," he said.

Ana stifled a laugh at the look on his face. "Oh, Sam… I wasn't aware this was long-term enough for that—"

That smile grew on his lips, reaching his eyes as he staggered in front of her, watching her laugh. He shook his head, his arm slipping around her.

"—The mysterious Sam has friends he wants his mistress to actually meet? Tell me they think they're as scary as you. They do, don't they? They—"

His lips slammed into hers, hushing her words and fleeing her heart. She could feel his smile on hers as she opened up to him, allowing his tongue to rake the top of her mouth, his hand to curl in her hair. He pulled back, holding her steady, his eyes dancing, and she softened in his embrace.

"I want them to meet the goddess I've talked about for the last few weeks," he said, his voice low. "They're very curious."

"Why do I feel as though I'll be under interrogation tonight?" she bantered.

He chuckled and kissed her forehead. "A little light foreplay, baby. I think you'll enjoy them."

Chapter Thirty-Four

As Ana changed clothes, Sam leaned against her kitchen counter. She'd felt his eyes on her the entire time, though he'd remained quiet, and had only moved when she'd come around the opening to show him the lingerie set she'd decided to wear beneath her clothes.

"Fuck, you're sexy," he'd hissed, his feet shifting, arms tightening as he resisted going any closer to her. She tugged on the bra strap, slightly exposing her full breast, and his tongue darted out over his lips, hair falling into his eyes. "*Killing* me, wicked girl."

His voice was strained, nearly unbearable, and she could see his cock pushing just slightly against his snug black jeans.

"No before dinner play?" she asked.

"With that on?" Sam shook his head. "No, baby. I've been thinking of all the ways to peel that off you, and we don't have long enough before this opening for me to do that."

Ana almost laughed. "We have an hour."

"That's not nearly long enough," and the way he said it made her entire body molten.

She blew him a kiss and went to her wardrobe to put on a dress. Not the red dress she'd worn on the festival night, but one similar. A one-shoulder, black bodycon dress that was slightly longer on the right side, along with a pair of tall heels. The exposed shoulder showcased the flowers wreathing up her arm and the side of her neck, though the hemline covered her crown and vines on her right thigh.

Sam made a noise, a restriction in the back of his throat when she came around the corner finally dressed. He gently took her chin between his fingers to tilt her head back for a kiss, swinging his jacket back over his shoulder as he did.

The show was in full stride by the time they arrived. Sam had their tickets scanned, and waiters offered them wine upon their arrival. Ana wondered why Jay hadn't offered her tickets to this party, or if perhaps it was an artist he'd tried to acquire in the past and hadn't been able to snag them.

Sam told her his friends were running late, and that one of them would probably make her entrance ridiculous and audacious when she arrived. Ana had a feeling he meant Millie, but she didn't say or mention that she'd met the Hand already.

The art was abstract, sexual, and made Ana feel like she might blush. Silhouettes and lines of women, men, and combinations of persons. White lines on black canvas, black lines on white canvas, accented by golds and silvers. Splatters that came into shape. There was nothing clean about this artist's work, but it was gorgeous, and Ana found herself staring at it.

She'd seen this art before, in the hallway of SkyCor on her way to see the Hand.

No wonder the Hand had insisted on this show.

"What do you think?" Sam asked beside her.

"I think this artist sees the body differently," she said. "Look at the lines and the body types. Skinny, curvy, muscled, or not." She turned around and looked at the rest of the room. "Everyone in this room can find a portrait and see themselves. It's beautiful."

A gruff, remarkably handsome man blundered into the room then, his words ceasing the moment he spotted Ana. His thick dark red mustache curled over his lips, long beard perfectly groomed, hair pushed back off his forehead, and his eyes... she'd never seen such piercing blue eyes.

"Forgive me for anything my friend might say," Sam muttered against his glass.

Ana frowned. "Why?"

"Just forgive me."

She met his gaze, a smile spreading at the amused concern in his eyes, and she leaned up to press a swift kiss to his mouth. "Nothing can scare me from you," she promised.

The moment Sam opened his mouth like he might say something else, the man she'd noted at the door walked directly up to them and clapped Sam on the shoulder.

"All right, enough public displays," he said, shaking Sam enough that Sam's lips twitched, and he took a step back.

"Ana, this is—"

"Rolfe Conan," Rolfe replied as he reached for Ana's hand. His mustache scratched her hand when he kissed the top of her knuckles, and Sam rolled his eyes.

"I'm glad to finally meet the so-called temptress capable of keeping this one awake and distracted at all hours of the night," Rolfe continued.

"Oh, do you work at the cemetery?" Ana asked.

"Ah... yeah. Same shifts," Rolfe answered, stuffing his hands in his pockets. "Caught him out digging in the wrong place the other night, staring at his phone a week earlier. You really got him wrapped around your finger."

Ana resisted laughing, and Sam looked like he might hit his friend. "I think we all need another drink," Sam said.

But the door opened again before Sam could make his move to signal a waiter, and this time, Ana knew the person walking in.

Millie's blonde hair was in silken waves over her left shoulder. Her black dress was long and swept over her curves, the neckline dipping down low between her petite breasts as her pantsuit had done that day.

"Always turning heads," Rolfe grunted behind his whiskey.

"It's what she does best," Sam muttered back. His hand squeezed Ana's waist as Millie saw them and started their way.

"You fools do clean up nicely once in a while," Millie said to Sam and Rolfe. "Much better than the dirt and grime I'm used to seeing you in."

"There she is," Sam said as Millie straightened. "The right hand of Death himself, Milliscent Cambridge."

"Quite the introduction, Sam," Millie said smoothly. Her gaze flickered to Ana, and those round brown eyes widened at who she was. "Well." Millie's brow lifted at the sight of Ana. "Hello again, Ms. Smith."

"Ooo, I like that," Rolfe said gruffly, smiling at Ana.

"Millie," Ana said, giving her a nod.

Sam's eyes narrowed. "You two know each other?"

"We've met," Millie said. "Your girl is quite the negotiator. Somehow talked me into letting her into Castle Corvus."

Sam's brows lifted. "How the fuck did you do that?" he asked.

Ana looked at her. "You're letting me in?"

"You won't even let us in," Rolfe argued.

But Millie just smiled at Ana. "She has a better argument than you," Millie told Rolfe. "And she's prettier."

Rolfe rubbed his beard once, giving Ana a quick glance over. "She is," he agreed.

"I didn't realize this was the woman who's had you in such a spell lately," Millie said to Sam. "It's no wonder."

Ana looked back at Sam, who was simply staring at her, a soft smile on his face, and his hand snaked to her waist again. A small touch that had her heart fluttering, and as Millie and Rolfe spoke between each other for a minute, Sam leaned down and whispered in Ana's ear.

"Any time you're ready, or if they annoy you, we leave," he told her.

Ana let out a huff of amusement. "You are truly terrified of whatever they might do, aren't you?" she asked, to which Sam's brows flickered in agreement.

Ana leaned closer. "The only person capable of chasing me anywhere is you," she said. "And I live for it."

Sam's forehead met her temple. His inhale of her scent causing Ana to close her eyes slightly, the rest of the room melting away around them.

"Ahem," came Millie's voice.

Except Sam didn't move immediately. His eyes closed tighter for the briefest of moments, his hand squeezing at her side, and then he straightened but left his arm around Ana's waist.

"Something on your mind, Mills?" Sam asked.

Millie smiled at him. "No," she answered before turning to Ana. "So, curator, what do you think of the art? He's a new find. A few of his pieces are at the uptown gallery, but these were a little too risqué for them. Colin, the owner here, was nice enough to put on his show."

"Who is the artist?" Ana asked Millie.

"He's—" Millie searched the other side of the room, and when she spotted him, she held out her elbow. "I'll introduce you. My assistant said you admired his painting outside my office."

"I love the lines," Ana said. "They're beautiful."

Millie's smile broadened. "Sam—"

Sam took a long sip of his drink as his eyes met Millie's.

"I'll be stealing Ms. Smith for a few minutes," Millie continued. "Don't worry. I'll not tell her too many embarrassing stories about you."

"None to tell," Sam said.

"Oh, but aren't there?" Millie teased with a tilt of her head.

Sam's gaze held Millie's for a moment longer than Ana knew how to consider, but she tried to ignore it as Sam looked at her instead.

"Don't believe anything she says," he said.

"That makes me want to believe *all* of it," Ana smiled.

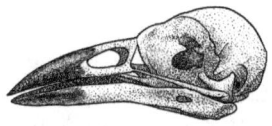

Sam watched Millie drag Ana across the room to meet the artist, and as he took another sip of his wine, Rolfe smacked him on the back again.

"How are you feeling?" he asked.

"Better than earlier," Sam replied, not looking away from Millie as she laughed with the artist and introduced Ana to him. A twinge of jealousy surged in his gut, but he just took another sip of his drink and tried to pay attention to his friend.

But, fuck, did Ana look amazing.

"How about you?" Sam forced himself to ask.

"Not bad. Today was good." Rolfe's gaze went across the room to Ana, who was now speaking with the artist by herself, as Millie was coming toward them again, and he shook his head. "She is..." He let out a low whistle.

"Yeah," Sam agreed, and for some reason, every thought of the past few days went away. It warmed his chest and sent a comfort through him that only his home had been able to do in the past.

And when she looked his way...

Thorns wrapped his chest, his heart skipping at the play of amusement she gave him as she seemingly noticed the tick in his jaw.

Shit.

Rolfe chuckled under his breath and muttered a quick 'catch you later' to Sam before leaving him to his lonesome. Sam watched Ana, watched the way the artist smiled and signaled the waiter for another drink. How he looked Ana over up and down when she spoke to someone else—

"You are... fascinated with her," Millie said, nearly making Sam jump as she joined him at the standing table. "*Too* fascinated." She propped herself against the table. "If I didn't know you, I'd say you were falling in love with her."

"It's a good thing you know me then," he growled.

Millie's smile didn't wane at his snap, and he hated her for seeing through him. Sam sighed as he ran a hand through his hair.

"Let it out," he said.

"Would it really be so terrible?" she asked. "To fall for the person who could bring us the sun."

Sam looked down at his glass again, but he refused to give Millie the satisfaction of being right.

"It would," he replied. "If I mean to use her as bait. Besides, wasn't it you who keeps telling me to kill her?"

"But you know, the more I think about it, the more I think you're right." Millie looked at Ana across the room again. "She's far too fun and delicious to kill. And that mind of hers... We could use that."

The last bit of whiskey in Sam's cup wasn't enough for the knot in his chest. "What do you want, Millie? Do you want me to tell her how I feel, how... I don't even know *if* I feel, and bring her to the castle without knowing if she feels the same?"

Millie gave him a small smile. "Sam, this woman walked into your life at that festival, and you haven't been able to get her out of your head since," Millie said. "Damn your 'reasons', whatever they might still be. You told me today that she was the key to everything. What if she was also the key to your happiness?"

Sam resisted a laugh. "Death... happy..." He shook his head. "I'm not sure I'll ever deserve a happy ending."

"And what about a happy beginning?" Millie asked. "A happy beginning with people you love in the world we fought for. That, Samarius, you deserve. No matter what powers you have and who you are." She reached up to his face, brushing his cheek with her thumb. "I like seeing you smile again," she admitted. "I like seeing you plot and giving a damn and being so passionate about this world and our future again. She did that." The soft hand on his cheek turned into a gentle slap, and he winced at it.

"Don't let her go."

Sam spotted Ana leaning against the bar, another man talking with her, angling in a flirtatious manner, so he made his way over. The man was just trying to order her another drink as Sam slipped his arm around her waist and kissed her neck in a manner so claiming, the other man stopped speaking. Ana gave Sam a sideways smile, obviously knowing what he was doing, and she watched as Sam bared his teeth at the other gentleman. The man gave Ana a nod and backed away before Sam had to say anything else.

Ana's lips twisted as Sam stepped in front of her. "Well, well… there's that jealous side I've been looking for," she said. "How many more men can I flirt with and watch you growl like that to get them to go away?"

Sam resisted a laugh as he sipped the last of his drink. "Are you ready to get out of here?"

"Did your friends leave?" she asked.

"They did," he answered.

"And?" Her brows raised expectantly, and Sam almost laughed again.

"Are you asking if they approved?" He wrapped his hand around her waist, voice dropping as he looked her over, his gaze lingering in all the places he planned on kissing, biting, and worshipping her that night. For a long while, too.

"I am curious," she said.

He bent closer, giving her a kiss on the very tip of her nose. "Yeah, baby," he said softly. "If all of these people were not so close, I'd put you on this bar top and show you just how much they approved."

Ana's smile widened. "Get me home and show me against the window instead."

Chapter Thirty-Five

For the fourth night in a row, Sam had met the light of morning outside in his rose garden. He had only seen Ana twice since the night at the gallery, both too scared and too confused to even know what to do around her, so he'd lied and said he had work commitments. He'd made time to meet her for lunch or wake her a couple of times, though... because honestly, the thought of not seeing her tore his heart into pieces.

He hadn't felt such confusion since he'd decided to deviate from Firemoor to escape his enslavement and find others willing to do the same. He'd fought with his mind then, doubted himself and all he desired, but it had been worth it.

Everything since that day had been worth it.

He hoped Ana was worth it too.

He didn't wait for Millie or Rolfe that morning before speeding off into midtown to his art studio. He liked to keep it there so he didn't have to transport his pieces from the castle, though he had a few there too. Pieces he never meant for anyone else to see.

Rolfe owned the tattoo shop down below, though he only took maybe ten appointments a year. He liked to do the line drawings himself and would tattoo extravagant pieces covering entire bodies. Sam's own tattoos had been a mixture of both his own artwork and Rolfe's, and his friend had been the one to torture him over and over with the needle.

He let his mind wander as he sat down in front of the canvas, his supplies already laid out for him from where he'd left them the week before.

His hands moved of their own accord, his music playing softly in the background. Sometimes when he drew, he allowed himself to fall so deeply into it that he would suddenly come back into reality, and he would have three drawings in front of him.

That day was no different. He needed his mind to shut down and let his body do the work. He was so consumed with thoughts and unfamiliar feelings that he could barely function. He'd even left someone dying in his sunroom for longer than he meant to the night before, and when he finally gave the woman attention, he felt horrible for the continued pain he'd put her through.

Sam needed out.

His phone buzzed after a few hours, and when the noise pulled him out of the daze, he realized it was well into the afternoon. He hadn't messaged anyone all day, though he was sure Rolfe and Millie had seen him come there, so they wouldn't have bothered him. Although he was surprised it took Ana so long to text him.

Sam finally put down the charcoal, dusted his hands off on his jeans, and then picked up his phone.

An angel yearning for chaos can fall for no other than the demon desperate for peace.

Sam smiled at the message, loving the quote she'd sent. *What if what I considered peace was someone else's chaos?* he typed back.

Sam looked up at his drawing. It had started out as a blunder of charcoal lines, but slowly, his strokes had come together to form the silhouette of a woman lying on her side, curves on full display. He hadn't exactly meant to draw her, and by the erratic lines over the page, he wasn't sure he really had.

But there she was. In the middle of what someone else would have considered a haunting interpretation of vulgarity, she came through the page.

Give me the kind of peace that makes my heart race, Ana said. *I want to be feared and scared and loved in the same breath. Do you think that's too much to ask?*

I think it sounds perfect.

Sam snapped a photo of the canvas before him as he relaxed back on the rolling stool and sent it to Ana.

Peace, he typed.

Ana sent back a heart, and said, *It's beautiful.*

It's a disaster, he said. *But I've always found beauty in things like that.*

Me too, Ana said.

Sam stared at the phone for a minute, debating what to say next. But the three dots on the bottom saved him from having to think too hard.

Haven't heard from you all day, she said.

Lost track of time when I came to the studio, he said, and it wasn't a complete lie. *How was your day?*

Long, she typed. *I miss you.*

Fuck, he hated what his heart did then. How it knotted to the point of nausea and ripped into his stomach. But—

I miss you, he replied. *I'm sorry I've had to work so much. Finally off tonight. I can pick up food on the way over if that's okay.*

I have to work late tonight. But I'm off tomorrow.

The first part was a lie, and it made his jaw twitch that she continued the ruse. But he shook his head at his aching heart and typed back.

Where do you want to go?

I was thinking of a day at home… take out and binging that new murder docuseries.

All memory of her lie left him as he read the message. *Haven't had a lazy day in weeks.*

I know, she replied. *I thought it would be a nice change. And I just wanted some time with you.*

I'd like that. Sam sighed at the phone. *I'll see you tomorrow, baby. Bright and early. I'll pick up breakfast on the way.*

I'll be waiting.

He looked at the art piece again and then switched screens to his text thread with Rolfe, but even as he started to hit the call button, he paused. His mind screamed at him. To hit the button and make sure Rolfe trailed her that night to find out where she was going and what she was up to.

But he didn't.

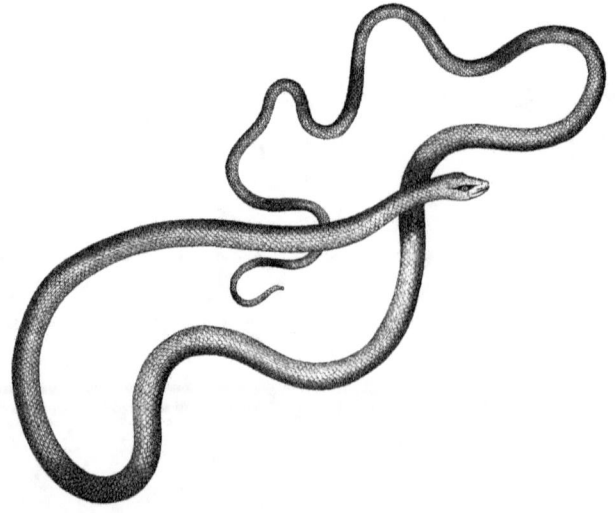

Chapter Thirty-Six

Everything Sam did was aggressive, as if he'd been starved of affection and reality. Ana wondered if she was the same. If every move she made and every kiss she placed on him felt as desperate as his.

She loved it. She loved how he made her feel like he needed her to breathe. And when he would finally slow down, he savored her. Touching every inch of her body like he meant to worship it. She memorized the moments when nothing in the world existed except her and him, lying against one another and sharing the ecstasy of a few moments of peace they'd been deprived of in the past.

Even when they weren't together, she could feel him on her skin. His touch was a branding iron to her flesh; burning and searing and blistering on her existence, leaving behind a mark that she would hold to as a reminder that she had finally felt what it was like to be loved.

As short-lived as it might be.

Every time he left in the middle of the night, the bed grew cold. It took her a long time to fall back asleep, and sometimes she would go down into the gallery instead or take a walk.

Sometimes she walked down to the cemetery and stared through the iron gates. Battling with herself on whether what she had with him was worth giving up what she'd worked her entire life for.

"Love makes you weak," her father always said. *"You are a Queen. Love has no place in your future. You will bring these tyrants to their knees, Deianira. Seduce them. Get in their heads. Win over their people. The oppressed will bow and worship you. There will be no more dividing lines between these kingdoms. The Myers and Moors will become one under your rule."*

"And Death?" she asked.

"You'll conquer him too."

Ana cried out, her hips rolling against Sam's face between her thighs as her orgasm toppled. They were on the couch, watching a horror movie. He sucked her clit into his mouth and held her thighs tighter. "Sam…" Her head threw back with the release, and she cursed to the sky, the sound of the woman's scream in the movie shrieking as Ana's orgasm caught her. Her knees twisted, and she squirmed with her release.

Sam licked her juices slowly then, letting her come down from the high with panting breaths, and when she met his eyes, he laid his cheek on her thigh and smiled up at her. Just when she thought he might say something, he pushed over her and kissed her softly. Heartachingly enough that it made her forget everything she'd just been thinking, and she wrapped her hands on his cheeks as he pulled away. His lips brushed her nose and her forehead, and then Sam stood to go to the bathroom.

She would never get over watching him walk, marveling at those tattoos, at his body, at his presence… He was art himself, and she sometimes had to pinch herself to make sure this was real.

He'd shown up that morning with breakfast, as promised, along with a list of Shadowmyer indie horror films that he insisted she needed to see. It had rained all morning, and he'd taken his time pleasuring her as she'd enjoyed the thrill of the chase on the screen.

She really did like the movies he'd suggested. The other realms she'd lived in were not nearly as into their theatrics and art as this one, and she wondered if perhaps the king himself enjoyed such things. The thought made her look out the window to the castle in the distance, to the grey illuminated manor and all the headstones and trees in front of it.

She wished her father had been with her to see this place. To see what she'd done. She wondered if he would have been proud of what she'd accomplished, or if he'd have told her she'd deviated too far from the plan by leaving so quickly after she'd killed the other kings.

And what he would have said if he'd seen her so cozy with a demon.

Ana turned her attention back to the movie, just as the killer murdered the main character's best friend. Sam sat down at the opposite end and pulled her legs into his lap, massaging her calves.

"What's it like?" she asked, watching that character die on screen.

"What?" Sam asked.

"To die," she replied.

Sam slowed his movements on her legs and glanced at her sidelong. "So macabre, wicked girl," he teased.

Ana chuckled despite herself. "We're watching horror movies. What do you expect me to ask?"

"Perhaps comment on how idiotic they make these characters," Sam said. "Really. This girl thought she could fit through a cat door. The first guy thought he could beat off a murderer with a stick."

"He had to fight back somehow," Ana argued.

"There was a shovel by the barn—"

"The barn was across the driveway."

"He literally stopped in a ditch to grab the stick when he could have made it across the street," Sam said, and Ana wondered if he was only arguing to tease her.

"It's a movie!" Ana laughed. "They have to be dramatic."

"How would you do it?" he asked.

Ana stared at him. "What? Get away from the killer?"

"Yeah," he said. "You've already told me how you would kill me. If I were your murderer, how would you go about turning the tables?"

"Thought I'd proved that when we went to the prison," she replied suggestively.

A knowing smirk rose on his lips, and she hated the seductive look he gave her through that stray hair that liked to fall over his eyes. "Foreplay, baby," he said. "You know I like watching you run."

"You like feeling my pulse race," she said pointedly.

Sam looked like he was resisting smiling outright, and his tongue darted out over his curling lips as he hung his head. "You didn't answer my question," he said.

"You could very well *be* a serial killer," she said. "Why would I reveal to you how I'd escape?"

"You think I'm a serial killer?"

"You leave at the same time every night. I've seen you with blood on your face and arm before. You're a demon. You're well-liked in the community." Ana shrugged. "It's the perfect cover-up."

"Let me get this straight," he said, shifting in his seat, arm throwing over the back of the couch in her direction. "You think I go out every night when I leave you to murder people, and yet you're perfectly fine dating me?"

It was Ana's turn to resist a smile. "Okay, we don't have to call out everything wrong with that statement, but the short answer is yes," she argued.

"Wow," Sam mocked her.

She threw a pillow at his face, and he jerked her into his lap.

Ana resisted as she laughed, but Sam was stronger, and he dragged her straddle over him. For a brief second, neither moved. There was only their heavy breaths and smiles between them. A smile Ana had thought she'd once forgotten, and yet, every time she was with him, there it was.

Chapter Thirty-Seven

Sam had never counted days or hours before.

But he counted them when he was without her.

He counted minutes.

He counted stars.

And when he was with her, he counted every breath.

He counted every smile.

He counted the stretch marks on her belly, her breasts, her thighs. Kissed them all and worshiped all that she was after. He counted the scars beneath the tattoo on her thigh that she had tried to hide from him at first. But he'd seen them while she was sleeping. He knew those scars… He knew the tattoos over them were a disguise to shadow over such a time in her life, but he didn't press making her talk about it. He hoped she would… maybe in time.

They'd fallen asleep after having lunch in the bed. He was enjoying their lazy day, enjoying just being in her company without a schedule or need to go somewhere.

In the back of his mind, though, he wished they'd been sharing this day in his own bed. In his own castle. Surrounded by the dust and roses and smells that he loved. He knew she would love them too, and maybe—

Ana stirred at his side, her nails scratching his stomach just enough to cause chills to rise over his skin. He sucked in a breath, his abs flinching, and her chuckle rattled his chest.

"Easy, baby," he groaned, hips rolling slightly.

Ana shifted and sat up, a yawn stretching her arms wide and causing a loud moan to leave her. Sam's brows elevated at the release of it, how she did not hold back and allowed herself to let go in front of him. Side to side, she cracked her neck, and he couldn't take his eyes off her sleepy figure.

He'd memorized how her body curved, how her hips dipped and her back arched. He wanted her body on canvas and displayed for the rest of the world to see.

"You're staring again," Ana teased as she rose from the bed and pulled the oversized wool cardigan over her arms.

Sam smiled slightly and looked out of the window. It was hard for the untrained eye to tell the time of day by the clouds in the sky, but Sam knew. It was an hour to sunset, which meant they'd spent more than half of the day in the bed. And as he stared out of the window to the west, he had an eager idea.

"Put some clothes on," he said, legs swinging off the bed.

Ana frowned back at him. "I thought we were having a lazy day. Where are we going?"

He buckled his black jeans and reached for his shirt on the floor. "I want to show you something."

"What is it?" she asked.

"So many questions," he bantered. "Trust me."

"I do," she admitted. "But I still should know how to dress. Should I wear a dress? Jeans? Nothing?"

He stepped flush to her, hand slithering around her back and cupping her ass in his hand as he kissed her in a teasing manner, his teeth skirting over her bottom lip and causing her to suck in a sharp breath. His forehead met hers, and he whispered,

"When's the last time you saw the sun?"

"When you laughed earlier," was her breathless response.

Sam's entire body seemed to flounder at the statement. His grip relaxed as he straightened over her. The way she looked at him then was how he'd always seen people look at each other when they were in love. An ache spread over his heart and grasped at his lungs, causing him to reach a trembling hand to her jaw, his thumb stroking her cheek.

"You shouldn't say things like that," he replied.

"Why not? It's true." She leaned forward, her lips pressing to his cheek, his jaw, his throat... making him swallow at the beautiful sight of her. And with barely another passing second, she whispered, "I don't need to see the sun as long as you're standing in front of me."

He held her there, unable to speak, barely able to breathe... paralyzed at the sudden inescapable realization that was holding his heart in its cage.

He was so fucked.

He wanted to tell her everything right then, but instead, all he could do was kiss her. Ana sucked her lip behind her teeth when she pulled back, eyes dancing up at him.

"I'll change clothes."

She stalked away then, going back to the bedroom, and it was all Sam could do to hold himself upright, to grab the lip of the counter and stare at the opposite cabinet. Mind spinning, he cursed his fleeing heartbeat for the way it had betrayed him.

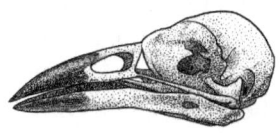

Ana laid her head between his shoulder blades and hugged her arms up his chest as they rode far out of town, all the way to the western cliffs. Confusion swept his knotted stomach, and he squeezed her hand despite himself.

The bike slowed to a cruise as they took the bend around the cliffside. He relaxed back a little, the tenseness in his shoulders eased for the first time since he could remember. He let every feeling sweep through him, and stayed present with every moment.

They rode out to the very edge of the kingdom, and he parked the bike on the grassy cliff.

Far out on the sea, a ray of sunlight poked through the grey clouds.

Sam watched as Ana stepped off the bike and went to stand at the edge. Her face was a puzzle of awe and intrigue, and he wondered what that ray of sun reminded her of.

"I didn't realize you could see the sun anywhere in Shadowmyer," she said.

"It's the only place you can see it," he replied.

Ana gazed at the sight, her face softened as she took in the sight of it. She braced herself on the guardrail, leaning over the edge, the wind brushing through her curls. That speck of light seemed to reach towards her, and Sam wondered if it was his own will breaking that caused the shift.

He'd always allowed one glimpse, far across the sea, as he knew people would yearn to see it. But he'd held tight to the rest of the clouds, the rain, the shadows… He'd held that power over the land he'd called home for so long. To protect the people until they were ready.

And as Ana stood there, as he felt himself falling further and further under her spell, he wondered how much he'd let go of already.

Ana turned toward him, her head tilting slightly. "Why did you bring me here?"

Sam pushed off the bike and walked toward her. "I remembered the way you admired that painting of the last sunset of Shadowmyer," he answered. "I thought it might bring you some comfort to see it again."

"When's the last time you saw one?" she asked. "A real sunset, I mean."

Sam ran his hand through his hair before wrapping his fingers around the railing next to her, and he hung his head. "Five-hundred, twenty-three years… seven months… thirteen days… and—" he looked down at his watch "—thirty-nine minutes."

Ana seemed to stagger as she turned toward him. "You've never left this place," she seemed to realize.

"Not since the war," he said softly.

"Sam…" Her hand squeezed on his shoulder, but Sam didn't look at her.

His mind filled with that final decision he'd made. With Millie and Rolfe at his sides. That day the rest of the world was on fire, and he'd let his power grow and grow, seen how it morphed and bent the sky and ground. He released everything that day to protect them.

"How long will we wait?" Millie asked as they watched the clouds envelop the sky.

"Not long," Sam promised her. "Enough time to heal here. We'll take it all when it's time."

Screams filled the sky, the smoke billowing and mingling with the stretch of clouds. Sam inhaled the stench of the fires, the bodies, the noise of the screams, and the bones breaking.

"When it is finally time…" Millie began, catching Sam's eyes. "I want the eastern edge."

"Why?"

"It's where my family is buried," she told him. "It's where King Atrion found me as a child and sold me to the southern army." Her neck stretched as

she looked out at the sea of fire. "My only regret in that life is that I did not get to kill him myself."

Sam considered her a long moment, a memory of the battlefield and a man evaporating into a pile of worms entering his mind, and Sam started to turn away. "Revenge, Milliscent," he said softly. "You'll get it."

The squeeze of Ana's hand on his shoulder brought him back to reality, and he reached for her fingers, giving her palm a kiss.

"What about you?" he asked.

Ana sank her head onto his shoulder, sighing. "Right before the shadow dealer took me underground," she admitted. "I remember him telling me to take one last long look at it because if I never left this place, it would be the last time I'd feel it." She shook her head. "I honestly thought it to be an exaggeration. I thought, how could it be possible to shadow and cloud an entire kingdom from the rest of the world?"

"Immense power," Sam said. "And a fuck of a reason."

Ana turned into him. "You never told me why he turned you," she said. "I mean, I know you fought in the war, but I don't know what you did before. Who you were, why you decided to live."

Sam's stomach churned to the point he thought he might vomit. "Such sad things... Why do you want to know?"

"Because it is you," she replied. "It's what made you into who you are. I want to know *you.*"

He wanted her to know him too.

Sam's gaze tore through her, and he reached up to push a stray curl from her face, his touch barely there, and yet it warmed her straight to her core.

"Are you sure you're not a witch?" he whispered.

She felt her lips curling upward as she leaned in to kiss his cheek, jaw, and neck. "That's the second time you've asked. Why would you think I am?" she asked.

His hand curled around her face, tipping her chin to look at him. "Because I am spelled beneath your touch, your presence." He paused to swallow, his eyes narrowing like he were confused. "You have bewitched me, wicked girl." His hand trailed down her skin, causing goosebumps to rise on her flesh, and she leaned into the touch. "My mind. My body. My demented soul… It's yours."

Ana had grown accustomed to men saying things they thought she might like. Trying to swoon her. To get her into their beds. Usually declarations of how beautiful she was and how lovely she would look on their arm. Sitting quietly on some throne as their newest trophy.

But there was something about the things Sam said.

Something about his words that seemed to surprise even him. As if he didn't know he meant it, but deep down he did. And something about that made his words different, made them seem real.

"Ana…" Her name was barely a whisper on his breath, but it sounded stuck to his tongue. A lingering poison destined to kill him slowly.

And what a beautiful, slow death it would be for the both of them.

"You are ridiculous," she told him.

His soft smile reached his eyes then, and he flicked her chin. "It's annoying, really. The thing you've turned me into."

"At least you've not lost your brooding touch," she said.

Sam's fingers tightened in her hair and yanked her head backwards, the minor pain making her laugh catch, her smile widen. "There's my demon," she hissed as his eyes darkened to nearly black.

Ana glanced out to the ray of sun across the horizon. The sea basked in its glow, reflection rippling across the surface as thunder rumbled somewhere in the distance, back in the direction of the city. She laid her head on his chest, her eyes closing as his arms tightened around her.

"Can we go to your place tonight?" she dared to ask.

Sam stiffened for a breath. She caught it, resisting to look up at him, and instead chose to let it be when he squeezed her side.

"Why do you want to go there?"

"I'd like to know what secrets my mystery man is holding from me."

She really did. She wanted to know why, when she peered up at him then, that he seemed to be in so much pain. Like the mere mention of him hiding anything from her broke his fucking heart.

The same face he'd made when she'd asked about his past and he'd avoided the questions.

"Soon," he promised.

So she decided on her next plea.

"Take the morning off tomorrow, then," she whispered. "Stay with me."

His jaw tightened as he looked down at her, and just when she thought he would tell her he couldn't, he said in a choked voice, "Okay."

Chapter Thirty-Eight

Ana kept waiting to feel the vacancy at her back that she usually woke up to.

But she never did.

And when grey light made its way through her large windows, Ana shifted so she could see his face, and she nearly wept at the sight.

Sam... so hauntingly beautiful. Asleep, his bangs curled over his eye and the rest mussed from their activities the night before. He stirred slightly, the noise of his quiet moan sounding over the television that they'd left on.

She pushed his hair back, and he took her hand, kissing her palm as his eyes fluttered open.

"How have I been so stupid?" he whispered as their eyes met.

"What do you mean?"

"How could I have gone this long without waking up beside you," he finished.

Ana tried not to laugh. "Oh, now you're never staying over again," she teased, rolling her eyes. "Not with cheesy words like that—*Sam!*"

He pushed up to his elbow and hovered over her, his fingers digging into her sides, grabbing her and making her laugh uncontrollably. And when he finally held her still, she pressed her hands to his cheeks, and for a moment, Ana swore she could have stayed right there all day and not cared for food or water or any other nourishment except the look in his eyes, the feeling of his touch.

"What do you want to do today?" she asked.

He pushed a curl back behind her ear. "I want to show you my art studio," he said.

"I'd love that."

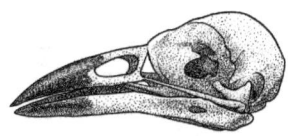

The ride to midtown was quiet. There were few people on the streets, which Sam found a little odd but didn't think much of it. He couldn't. Not as Ana's cheek rested on his back and her arms tightened around his waist. Not as he counted her breaths and became mesmerized by the mere feeling of her chest rising and falling against him.

His studio was dark and a little unorganized, he realized, when he flipped on the lights. He'd left some things uncovered when he'd last been there. He paused at the door and watched Ana walk around the room. His insides squirmed, as if he were fully exposing himself with those art pieces, including some parts of his soul that he'd buried deep.

That was one of the things he loved about drawing. They didn't have to be perfect. They could be as messy as his mind was. Art forgave him for who he was, for what he'd done. For the things he'd locked away. It showed his darkness in a way that words had failed him. It was like putting his soul to paper, letting out his inner struggles, and surrendering to the lines.

Perfect in a way he never would be.

"What is this?" she asked as she picked up a drawing.

Sam stared at the piece in her hand, the raven skull and roses… the blurred symbol that he had declared a rendition of his own mark.

His original mark was snakes, roses, thorns… but this raven skull, the soft rose, the singular snake hiding out in it… He loved it. It reminded him of the witch's text about him and thus reminded him of the one witch that had tried to save him.

He'd drawn it as a piece for a raven and roses collection that he'd done a few years back, and some people knew the symbol—including Jay. He had obsessed over it for days, scrounging ancient witch texts, until he finally found it.

"This is… this is beautiful," Ana said, her fingers stretching over the lines on the canvas. "The detail… I… Didn't you say your friend was a tattoo artist?" she asked.

217

Sam wracked his brain. He couldn't remember if he'd said that. He rarely talked about Rolfe, though maybe Jay had told her. "He is," he answered.

She looked back down at the painting, her fingers running over it, and then her lashes lifted to him. "I think I'd like this drawn on me."

He didn't know why, but the mere thought of one of his marks on her skin made his stomach drop, and his heart tighten. His body ignited to the very tips of his extremities. It was a restless ache that he couldn't figure out, and without thinking, he took his phone from his pocket and dialed Rolfe's number.

"Yeah, boss?" Rolfe answered.

"Are you busy?" Sam asked, still watching Ana pour over the drawing.

"Ah... not really. Why? Got something for me?"

"Come to the studio."

Rolfe chuckled. "Have the itch for new ink?"

"Not me," Sam replied, and his heart bled warmth when Ana's eyes met his.

"Oh... Okay. I'll be there in twenty."

As they waited for Rolfe to join them, Sam continued showing her some of his other pieces. Ana couldn't get over the detail in his madness. They were beautiful and heavy, and somehow reminded her of finding peace in never-ending darkness. Once he'd shown her nearly every piece, he escorted her down the stairs and into the empty tattoo studio.

"When does he actually do tattoos?" Ana asked as Sam began to shift a few things around.

"A few times a year," he answered. "Most of his clients do full bodywork, so sometimes he'll only take on about ten clients a year so he can focus on them. He does all of the artwork."

"And he did yours?" Ana asked.

"Every one of them," Sam said as he sat in the rolling chair and faced her.

He kicked the chair back, that soft, domineering smile that made her knees weak on his lips, hair falling into his eyes and entwining with his long lashes. Legs wide, shoulders slumped, he sat in that chair like the most confidently surrendered person she'd ever met. It was a different aura than she was getting used to with him. More dangerous.

He was full of secrets, and she was prepared to fall into his darkness to learn them.

"Sit," he said.

Ana looked at the backwards chair and the armrest he'd positioned for her, but as she started to sit down, the door opened.

"Sorry, boss, didn't—"

Rolfe blundered inside, pulling off his scarf as he did, but his words stopped upon seeing Ana standing there. A flirty smile lifted his lips beneath that full mustache. "Hello, Ms. Smith," he teased her.

She shook her head at his smirk and watched him pull off his jacket. "I told you, Rolfe. It's Ana," she insisted. "And why do you call him 'boss'?"

Sam exchanged a look with Rolfe, and both snickered under their breaths. "Inside joke," Sam said with a shrug. His chin jerked in the direction of the chair as he stood. "Sit."

Ana settled in the chair as Rolfe began to set his things up. A seriousness replaced the playful demeanor she'd seen at the gallery that night. Sam was over on the computer, cleaning up the art he'd scanned in and sizing it smaller to go on the inside of her forearm. When he'd fixed it, he came back over with a cut-out and stood behind her as he placed it on her arm.

"What do you think, baby?" he asked, his voice a soft purr in her ear, his other hand delicately touching her collar.

Ana stared at the art, at the lines that would soon be on her skin. Lines that he had drawn. Lines that would forever remind her of him, no matter which direction she chose to take her life.

That singular thought stilled her.

As though she had a choice in where her life would go after that day.

As if the last few weeks had changed her trajectory.

Her entire body pricked at the thought.

"It's perfect," she managed.

A daze took over her soul as Rolfe positioned the stencil on her arm and the buzzing noise of the needle began. She looked up at Sam standing behind Rolfe, watching every move with intensity. His eyes squinted, arms crossed over his chest. Her heart ached at the very look of him there. At the art about to mark her flesh. And when the needle finally pricked her skin, she came to a realization.

Ana had never truly been in love. Not this kind of love. Deep, unrelenting, powerful love.

But with every intimate stroke of the pen and Sam's art going onto her skin, she knew she was.

Her body was alive for the first time in her life. From the roots of her hair, to the marrow of her bones, to the knot in her stomach. She was wholly consumed with seeing Sam's smile and hearing his laugh. So consumed that the thought of giving up all she'd worked for her entire life didn't sound like such a bad idea.

Every move of his lashes as he watched the ink seep into her skin felt like a dagger on her flesh, and she wondered if this was normal.

"Should it hurt like this?" she whispered, biting back the emotion that threatened to surface.

But Sam obviously thought she meant the tattoo. A smile lifted his lips, his concentration breaking just slightly as he met her eyes, arms hugging over his chest. "It's a tender place," he said. "Relax."

Until his entire expression fell upon seeing the obvious pain in her eyes.

Sam reached down and squeezed Rolfe's shoulder, making him look up. "Ana, do you want him to stop?" he asked, and the buzzing ceased as Rolfe heard his tone.

"No," she practically begged. "No, gods no. I want you to mark my entire body."

He was silent a moment before giving Rolfe a nod, and the pen started again. Sam moved to sit straddle on the rolling bench by her, scooting so that he was directly at her side with their legs touching. He reached to her face and moved a curl before kissing her jaw.

"Should what hurt like this?" he whispered.

Her eyes flickered to Rolfe, who had his headphones in, and she realized he couldn't hear them.

"Love," she managed, feeling tears in her eyes when she looked to him. "Should my heart feel as though it will stop beating with every passing breath? Should I want to weep from tears caused by smiling too much? Should the sound of your laugh not send me into an abyss of beginnings I do not want to wake from?"

Sam looked like someone had just struck him across his face. Like his heart had stopped or he had forgotten how to breathe. He swallowed again, and her heart dropped as she thought he might get up and tell her she was crazy. Only he leaned forward and caught her lips in a devastating kiss. Like he was starving for her to say those words, needing that confirmation from her as much as she needed it from him. The kiss made a tear fall down her cheek. And when they pulled apart, breathless and heavy, their foreheads rested against the other like they were holding the sky up on their own, and only their bodies could stop the rest of their world from crumbling into chaos.

Rolfe cleared his throat, obvious that their intimacy was making her squirm while he was trying to work, and Sam smiled against her lips before straightening to look at his friend.

"Sorry, Rolfe," he said, waving him off.

Rolfe returned to his work without another word, and Sam moved behind Ana, where he sank his arms around her waist and laid his body against her back. Ana closed her eyes, feeling the full weight of him as she leaned her chest on the back of the chair and relaxed.

The vibrations singing up her arm made her eyes droop, and having Sam drawing circles on her stomach and thigh only furthered her depraved drowsiness.

His lips pressed to the back of her neck when he leaned up, chin sitting on her shoulder. And for the remainder of the time his friend tattooed her wrist, Ana felt like she might burst with the restlessness in her body that was nothing like she'd ever felt before. Euphoria swam through her—the vibrating pain of the needle, the soft kisses Sam placed on her shoulder or her neck, the way he held her and relaxed against her. She'd always enjoyed the pain of tattoos, but this one felt as if it were being marked on her soul.

And when Rolfe was finished, she stared at the raven skull and roses, the shading and the perfection of every line. It was as beautiful as he was, and her heart wept at the sight of his details.

"Rolfe—"

"Leaving, boss," Rolfe said as he stood to excuse himself. He gave Ana a quick wink before exiting the room, and Ana was left sitting in the chair and watching Sam as he leaned against the counter, hands pressed into the edge, hair falling over his face.

"Come here."

It was as if his throaty rasp held a power in it that spoke directly to her existence. A command that made her feet move despite her body not knowing it. When she was directly before him, she sank herself against his chest, and he reached for her arm to look at the tattoo. His fingers brushed against its outskirts, careful not to touch the quiet pain still in her numb skin.

"You like my art on you, baby?" he asked, lips lifting at the left corner, showing off that tiny dimple.

"I love it," she said before pulling back.

His hands wrapped beneath her jaw, and he kissed her deeply.

She didn't know how he did it. She didn't know how his kiss continued to make her heart drop, just as it had the first time he'd kissed her. How his touch made her heart flutter, and how every time his name popped up on her phone, she couldn't stifle a smile.

"Do you know what I think?" she said when she finally pulled away.

Sam's brow lifted, watching her take a step back. "What's that?"

"I think you've marked me... and now I should get to mark you."

He considered her. She could see the working in his eyes, of whether he could trust her enough for that.

"Don't worry," she added. "I won't draw a cock on your arm." She twisted the rolling chair around in his direction as a smile lifted his lips, and he finally surrendered into the chair. Ana went to turn on the equipment again, but as she did, Sam pulled her into his lap.

She let out a small yelp, hearing him laugh at her being startled, but his antics didn't stop her from her mission. She knew it was a ploy to distract her, especially as his teeth skated over her skin and he squeezed her ass.

"Sam—" A laugh left her as she reached for the pen.

"Really not funny, Ana," he said, though he continued to smile. "You could hurt yourself."

"It's fine," she teased. "What—are you scared I'll ruin this beautiful artwork of a body you have?"

"Yes—"

"Wait, wait," she laughed, hair falling over her shoulder. "Don't you trust me?" she asked upon meeting his gaze.

For a moment, he didn't blink. Like the words had triggered something in him. His mouth closed, throat bobbing, and his eyes softened dramatically. She felt him shift, and the next thing she knew, he was kissing her jaw and placing the pen in her hand.

"Gentle, temptress," he breathed.

She felt his lashes shift down, and he sighed into her hair, surrendering his head to her shoulder as he held out his left arm for her to mark.

Ana held the pen steady, making only three marks. When she was finished, she reached over to turn off the machine.

"All done," she told him.

His brows narrowed when he looked at his arm. "Did you just put a smile on my wrist?"

"I did," she said proudly.

His eyes softened from his confusion. "Why a smile?" he asked, arms hugging her tighter on his lap.

She reached for his face, thumb brushing his lip. "Because every time you smile, a piece of me falls into place, and it's like coming home," she admitted.

He looked like he was considering laughing, and she wished he would. She wanted to hear that beautiful lullaby leave his lips. But instead, his hand moved to her jaw, and he pulled her lips to his.

He pushed away the table and his hands wrapped around her back, fingers spread wide on her shoulder blades. She held his head to her chest as he kissed her skin. Her tank slipped down, nearly exposing her full breasts, and his moan vibrated her bones.

"Ana..."

Her name.

But... not her full name.

Not Deianira.

Only Ana.

It weakened her to know that he would never call her by her real name. She would never hear the word 'Deianira' come from his beautiful lips in that whispered rasp that made her wild and caused her heart to tremble.

She needed him like she needed her next breath, although if she was given a choice between the two, she was sure she would have chosen him.

She *would* choose him.

Him. Over everything she'd ever known. Everything she'd put herself through. All her promises and vows, be damned.

The realization slammed into her like cold water to the face, and Ana's heart stopped in panic.

"Ravens," she hissed urgently, her entire body staggering and splintering. "*Ravens.*"

Sam's body went wholly still. Still in the way that always caught her off guard. She swallowed, her body in a tremble as her chest ached at his touch. How she wanted him to consume her existence and burn her skin with every grace of his fingers.

And yet, she had never been more terrified in her entire life.

The way he kissed her, the way she craved his eyes on her and his laugh… how she could think of nothing more than their next moment together. He had derailed everything she'd ever worked for.

"What's wrong?" came his breathless voice.

"Doesn't this scare you?" she asked, avoiding his gaze.

"What?" He grasped her hand, giving it a squeeze, making her heart flutter at the gesture, but she continued to stare at the ground. At the singular spot she'd picked out as a comfort to her staggering soul.

"Ana, will you look at me?" Sam whispered.

She felt her jaw trembling, but she forced her head to move with the gentle tug of his finger on her chin. His dark eyes darted over her, weakening her knees even though she sat on his lap. She was sure that if she'd been standing, gravity would have evacuated beneath her limbs, and she would have become a puddle of heartbreak and fear.

"This," she finally replied. "*Us.*"

Sam's throat bobbed, and he held her gaze, his own softening slightly, and she felt his fingers tighten around her own. "Terrified," he admitted. But he leaned in, placing a kiss to the top of her shoulder and her jaw, which relaxed her body slightly as he said, "I am terrified of the things I would do to keep you," he whispered, then looked directly into her eyes. "And I am terrified that one day you'll decide I am not enough."

It was Ana's turn to stiffen. His words repeated themselves over and over in her mind, a broken record crying out to be saved. She reached to his face, her thumb grazing over his high cheek, and he moved his head to kiss her palm.

Enough.

Was this enough?

Was whatever they had… whether it was love, obsession, or something deeper… was it enough for her to give up everything she'd worked for? All the murder, the chaos, the destruction, and seductions… Everything she'd been born to do. Everything her father had taught her. Everything she'd learned in Icemyer before striking out on her own.

Was it worth it… Or was this the thing she'd been searching for all along?

Her entire body faltered as she looked over his solemn face, memorizing the lines of his cheekbones, the stern of his brows, and the dilation in his darkened eyes.

Maybe she didn't have to do all those things.

Maybe she could be *free*.

Maybe she could have this. She could have a life without pleading for death at every waking second. Maybe she could be herself as she'd never been before, fall in love and actually live.

"I'm *yours*," came her breathless whisper. "Whether the sun rises or dies, or if night encompasses us all into eternal darkness, I will be yours. Every minute. Every hour. Every moment until my dying breath, and should Death offer me a reprieve after, a choice to continue living in an eternal cycle of love and pain, I will be yours an eternity more." She paused, her thumb brushing the bottom lid of his eye where a tear had collected, and she gave him a small smile. "For as long as you'll keep me."

Sam inhaled a ragged breath, his hand curling into her hair. "I would keep you until the sun burned out, and we were driven into the chaos of a new existence," he answered. "And then I would find you in the next one."

"And after?"

"In every life," he swore.

There was a promise in his gaze that had her stomach twisting once more—a promise unlike she'd noticed in words from him before.

And Ana couldn't stop herself from falling for them.

He let go of her face and hand, reaching up to the straps of her top, and slowly beginning to pull them down, exposing her bare breasts. "Do you still want me to stop?"

She knew he would have if she'd said yes. He would have ended it right there, perhaps helped her put her clothes back on and taken her to a quiet dinner. Sat across the table and laughed with her or touched her hand while they drank wine and talked about the horrid decor or the couple staring at their phones at the next table.

But…

Ana adjusted herself on his lap, shifting up onto her knees, her cleavage pushing into his face. Sam groaned into her flesh and sucked on her nipple as she unbuckled his pants, revealing his already hardening cock. She grabbed the back of the chair behind him, hiked her skirt high, and as he captured her other puckered nipple in his mouth, she sank onto his length.

Even this time, she had to adjust herself to take him in. He filled her, his teeth dragging over her breast, fingers clutching her ass, and as she settled into a slow rock, he leaned up to press his lips to hers.

"Never stop," she whispered against his mouth.

His kiss consumed her. His fingers dug into her hips, the other hand wrapping around her throat, and he pushed into her, causing her back to arch and her eyes to stare at the ceiling as she moved her hips up and down his hard cock. Her eyes fluttered every time her ears began to feel numb and she saw stars dancing on the black above her. Her body was rolling against his. He smacked her ass hard, making her moan and whimper before cursing his name.

She was starting to writhe atop him erratically when his thumb moved between them and circled her clit, grasp on her throat intensifying simultaneously. His nails dug into her sensitive skin, breaking the flesh and causing blood to trickle into the sink of her collar.

"Let go for me, baby," he whispered. "I can feel you on that edge. Give me the rest of you. Wake the dead with my name."

The moment his fingers loosened around her, she came apart. She surrendered her body and soul to him. She surrendered her truth and everything she was. She shouted his name, and lightning cracked outside when she felt him come inside her just after. She trembled with the ecstasy, with the power of that moment as they became one. Until she couldn't hold herself upright any longer, and she limped against him.

She held around his neck, her head lying against his, his forehead on her chest. And for a moment, they simply came down from the high that was the other.

"Ana?" he whispered her name like he was questioning her existence, of whether she was still there in his arms or if it was a dream.

"Sam?"

She felt his breath tickling her flesh as he said, "Forgive me for what I will be," in a mutter against her skin.

The words confused her, to the point she pulled back to find his gaze.

"What will you be?" she asked.

"Yours," he breathed. "Forever yours."

For the remainder of the afternoon, she never even glanced at her phone or a clock. He drove her home on his bike, taking the long way, and for half of the ride, she held her hands in the air and let the wind take her. He had gripped her thigh, and she heard his laugh from beneath the helmet when he realized what she was doing.

They hardly made it into her apartment before ripping one another of clothes. Today was new. It was passion and needing and desire for more than the other's physical touch. It was a connection of their souls as she hadn't felt before. More than once, she almost slipped and said those three words that sat on the tip of her tongue, knowing it was true and that he felt it too. He kissed every part of her, took his time fucking her over and over, until they were both shaking and spent and barely able to move.

And in the afternoon, she watched him sleep. She watched the peace on his features without the furrow of his brow. So unearthly beautiful. So filled with a darkness she was sure she only knew a minuscule part of. She ran her hand through his hair as he laid in her lap, a true-crime documentary on the television and rain coming down on the wide windows.

And she wondered if she truly deserved to feel this happy after everything she'd done.

The thought knotted her stomach, but as he shifted on her lap and hugged her tighter, she cherished the full weight of his body calming her heart, and she relaxed back into the couch's grasp.

Chapter Thirty-Nine

Sam couldn't stay that night.

He'd skipped work the night before to be with her and explained he had told them he would pull a double to make up for missing it. He'd kissed her long and hard against his bike. Longer than usual, almost solidifying everything she'd felt with him in those last two days.

"I'll see you tomorrow," he said, holding her face in his hand.

"I'll text you," she said softly. "Maybe a 'good morning' selfie if I think you've earned it."

"Tease," he smiled. He reached down and picked up her wrist, then kissed the inside of it where the art was before meeting her eyes again. "Tell me why every time I look at you, it's like I'm back at that fucking festival... seeing you smile for the first time," he whispered.

"It's the absence of the rain," she said, chuckling. "First night in a week that it's clear."

Sam's smile widened. "Let me take you out tomorrow?" he asked.

"Anywhere," she answered.

He kissed her again, his tongue sweeping along hers like he were making sure she remembered who she belonged to, then he let her go, taking in her figure one more time before shaking his head and speeding off toward the cemetery.

Her body ached with all that was the last two days. Finally, spending an entire night with him wrapped around her. No getting up in the middle of the night. No disturbing the other. Just lying in his arms. His friend tattooing her. His art on her skin.

It was a brand that went straight to her depleting heart.

She took a long time in the shower, letting the steaming water run over her skin as she held her hands on the tile and stared at the swirling drain.

Everything was fucked.

It was so fucked.

All her plans. Her carefully laid out plans... They were distant dreams now. A shadow of a life that she wondered if she could forget.

He had done that. He had made her want a new life for herself.

Ana wrapped herself in jogging pants and her thickest robe before setting off down the stairs and across the street to tell the castle goodbye.

The lullaby sounded from her lips as she strode slowly down the sidewalk, the castle and cemetery to her right, the chilled air breezing through her curls. She did love the night air like this. She loved the smells of the raw, damp dirt and oak trees at her side.

She loved everything about Shadowmyer.

And she loved...

Ana shook her head as she paused at the iron bars and stared at that castle in the distance. Sam's face, his touch, his very existence poured through her. Everything they'd done, everything they'd confessed. She wanted him to know her. She wanted...

She wanted him.

Maybe she could advocate for the people she'd fought for another way. Maybe she didn't have to go through and conquer another kingdom, another man. She could express her concerns to Millie, possibly earn herself a seat on their Council. She could make change in the usual way, not the way that meant sacrificing herself.

And she could be happy.

A lump lodged in her throat.

She was *going* to be happy.

"What do you want in this life?" Sam had once asked her.

"To finally find beauty in my nightmares," she'd told him.

He hugged her tighter and laid his head on her breasts. "You are the beauty in mine," he'd whispered.

She should have known then how hard she would fall for his darkness. She should have known then how consuming he would be. But she'd never expected this.

The noise of soft footsteps scraped over the asphalt behind her, but it didn't turn her away as it muffled with the sound of a few cars driving by. She couldn't turn away from that castle. A tear rolled down her cheek when she wrapped her fist around the iron gate, and as she looked up to that bright amber window at Castle Corvus, a soft whisper came from her lips.

"No more," she declared.

A bat collided with her head.

Her face slammed into the iron bars, grip loosening. She stumbled but kept herself upright. Another blow—to her thigh this time—and Ana gathered all her strength as she kicked backward. Her foot met the groin of her attacker. He doubled over. She had just enough time to glimpse him in a black hooded raincoat before she staggered down the sidewalk. A red-gold light flickered from beneath his coat, but Ana didn't stay to figure out what it was.

Blood ran down her head as she tried to run. Her leg throbbed from the bruise, but she kept going. She heard him curse. Heard him shout. And she knew she didn't have long before he would catch up.

She bolted through the gates of the cemetery.

What felt like a wall of shadows hit her body. She stumbled over a root and grasped to a headstone to catch herself. Darkness swallowed her whole. As the pain in her head threatened to close her eyes, she blinked and pressed it out. Tried to keep herself above water and fight it.

There was a large oak tree not ten feet away. Behind it. She could get behind it. But—

She needed a weapon.

She had her claw in her hair, but that meant letting him get close to her. She needed something... *something*... this was a cemetery. There had to be—

The staff of something standing upright in the dirt caught her eye. Someone had left a shovel out.

"I know you're in here, girl," the man shouted from the gates.

Ana scraped her way across the dirt until her back hit the tree. She twisted her neck, craning to try and catch a glimpse of his shadow as he moved down the path.

He was at least another foot taller than her. A bulky man, gruff and hidden beneath that raincoat. She wracked her brain for any catch of a feature that she'd gotten when she'd turned to kick him... Nothing beneath his hood, but—

The red-golden glow she'd seen had been a Firemoor brand.

This was either a mercenary, a spy, or a soldier.

Every person in Firemoor's employ had been branded with the name of their current king on their necks. It was a tool to find demons within their ranks. Ana had often laughed about it as demons could heal themselves.

Ana waited for the man to start sniffing around that tree, waited for him to take whatever bait she could find. She crouched down, going for a thick limb, and then she tossed the limb far to her left. It thumped to the ground, diverting the man's attention. Each of his steps sounded over the mud, and Ana waited... And waited... and when he was nearly at the back of the tree, she bolted.

She ran. Ran across that path as fast as she could. Although, the man had spotted her. He lunged, fast, and grabbed her by her hair. Ana shrieked out, struggling, but the man pulled her into him.

"I've got you now," he growled.

Ana shoved her elbow back, striking him, and jerked away as he stammered. She lunged for that shovel, and when it was in her grasp, she whirled around, daring him to come closer.

"Who sent you?" she demanded.

The man held up his hands like he was giving her a chance, but she knew better than to trust it. "Easy, girl."

"You hit me over the head with a bat and have the nerve to tell me to take it easy?" Her arms flinched, stepping closer and daring him to move. "Who sent you?" she nearly shouted.

He eyed her, hesitating. "The General," he answered.

"Why me?"

The man laughed. "I watched you leap out of that fucking castle with the king's heart in your hand. You think I don't know who you are?"

"Why didn't you stop me then?"

"Bounty wasn't enticing enough," he admitted.

That laugh clawed its way out of her and surfaced in the still night. "Bounty... If I'd been paid to take those castles, you wouldn't have any qualm with it. Yet because I paid myself in blood and revenge, you condemn me."

"Condemning you is what I get paid to do," he said.

"Tell me that you have children," Ana said, and she watched the color fade from his face. "Tell me that when you don't come home, that your partner and your child will be just like I was. Poor and broken and scared. Does that not make you reconsider?"

"You act like you have any chance here," he replied.

"I don't lose," she practically growled.

Ana lunged at him. She swung, but he ducked and caught her legs. She wiped out to the ground, shovel crashing on the mud, and she scrambled for it. He caught her leg, but she kicked and reached, and kicked and reached. Until the very tips of her fingers grazed that wooden staff, nothing else in the world mattering except her survival. She had not come all this way to be taken out by some Firemoor mercenary.

Ana's fingers latched onto the wood, and she swung as hard as she could. The metal whacked into his head, and he flew backward to the ground, legs swinging out from under him.

Ana's chest heaved, her head throbbing, and she slowly made her way to her feet, made her way over him, shovel still in her hands. She stared at the groggy man beneath her, her body shaking with the panic of having an actual soldier after her again.

Rage billowed in her veins.

"I do hope you left your family with a few meals to spare," she hissed. "Because you're not coming home this time."

The shovel met his neck, and his eyes blew wide as it snapped his head off.

The cemetery fell silent around her.

Ana wiped the blood off her forehead as she looked down at the lump of a man now bleeding out at her feet.

Firemoor soldiers. Here in Shadowmyer where she thought she'd be safe, at least for a while.

Shadows began to circle her body. Ana searched over the umbra and held up her hand, letting one of them wrap her fingers like silk and water between traveling over her flesh. This was how she knew Death himself was taking this body. Because for every person she'd ever killed, she'd never felt this.

Comfort washed over her skin and settled in her stomach. Calming her thudding heart. Such a comforting euphoria that she had to blink herself out of such a daze. She could have walked into it, laid down on that wet grass and let those shadows cradle her into an abyss from which she would not return.

Ana's knees hit the dirt, and she watched. She watched that darkness take care of the blood pooling around her limbs. She watched the soldier's body fade into the fog, and all she could think of was how she would have begged for such reprieve for her father's death instead of having to bury him in the frozen waters of Icemyer... Watching his body disappear down and down, until nothing was left except the freezing ripples on the surface.

A single tear crawled down her cheek, and just as she felt her insides begin to break, she pressed that emotion back down and stared at the disappearing face of this assassin.

Firemoor.

She wondered if they actually knew she was there or if they'd just been sent to search for her. And if it was the former...

Sam's face flashed in her mind, causing her heart to ache. *Sam...* Her thumb absentmindedly brushed over the new tattoo, and she hated herself for ever thinking she could be free.

She could never have the life she had dreamt of just a few hours earlier. She would never be free of this. Someone would always want her dead. She had done too much, took too much.

Her gaze shifted over her shoulder to the dark castle, to the cemetery around her, and to the crackling thunder in the distance.

If she couldn't have that life with Sam...

Then she would have *this*.

This... *all of this*... This crown. This kingdom. This final realm. Vengeance and that final edge. The world... All of it... It was hers. She had bled and crawled and suffered her entire life for this.

Damn her heart. Damn her stupid... *fucking*... heart.

And sniffed back the rest of her tears and picked herself up off the ground, turning to look back at the castle once more time.

Her castle.

Lightning cracked high in the clouds, cascading its glow onto the grounds—

And she swore in that light, she saw a man with high tattered wings and scarlet eyes staring back at her.

Ana's heart skipped, though in the next flash, the shadow was gone. But Ana knew what she had seen. Knew Death himself was watching her, and her breaths went jagged at the thought.

There you are.

Her final conquest.

She backed away slowly in the dirt, one step after the other. The sound of her favorite lullaby hummed in her throat, a smile toying on her lips as she recalled the texts. A delirious urge snaked its way to the pit of her stomach that she hadn't felt in weeks.

Ana left the cemetery with only one thing on her mind: her crown.

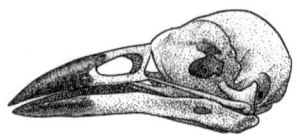

Sam took one last inhale of his smoke and then crushed it on the ground as he watched Ana walk back to the road. He couldn't tell what was on her mind. Why that last smile she shared with the darkness had his skin crawling. Why she had knelt on the ground and almost cried over this man's body. It had hurt to see it, and he hated how he'd wanted to take her into the castle right then and give her everything.

He'd watched the entire thing. Had run from his back garden steps upon hearing her scream. But he hadn't interfered.

Deianira hadn't lost her fight.

Hands in his pockets, Sam stalked back to the castle where he'd left the Firemoor soldier's final seconds suffer.

The man was choking on blood, lying on Sam's table when he went through the garden door. Sam lit another smoke and leaned back against the wall.

"Let me go," the man managed through his struggle. "Let me see that next life."

"Who sent you?" Sam asked, ignoring the man's pleas.

"No—"

Shadows snapped around the man's ankles and hauled him into the air. The man writhed, screaming, but the rings of darkness wreathed the man's body, and he dangled upside down.

Sam pushed off the wall and sat one hip on the table instead. Toying eyes traveled over the soldier's terrified face, watching every tear drop… His head tilted at the Fire mark on the man's neck.

"You're one of Prei's," Sam noted. "How did you get through my shadows?"

The man didn't answer.

Impatience fluttered through Sam's veins, and he sent shadows curling into the man's wounds. The man cried out, and Sam squashed his smoke in his palm.

"The more you deny me what I want, the longer this suffering will go on... and on... and on..." he said in a daunting whisper. "I will gladly put you back together just to watch you bleed. Over and over. Is that what you want?"

The man choked as he shook his head in a pleading manner.

"Then be a good boy and talk," Sam growled.

"There... there is a path of sunlight—"

Sam's insides grew cold.

"—on the southeastern border," the man continued. "It grows every day."

"How many have come?"

The man didn't answer, and the shadows dug deeper into his wounds. He whimpered again and shook his head. "A dozen—"

"Only a dozen?" Sam threw his head back with his laugh. "You expect me to believe that your little General found out the woman who murdered his king only sent a dozen soldiers into my mists to take her out?"

"It was a trial," the man said. "His favored assassins."

"And when none of you return with her head?"

The man swallowed, this time meeting Sam's eyes.

"The entire army."

Thunder cracked overhead, and Sam hugged his chest. "An entire army for one woman." Sam scoffed. "It sounds like your General wants more than just her head."

A gargled laugh sounded from the man as blood curdled in his throat. "He wants what is his."

And this time, Sam smiled outright. "So do I."

Chapter Forty

"You're fucked," Rolfe teased him as he slumped against the threshold of the office the next day.

Sam twisted the stem of the rose between his fingers that he'd been staring at for the last thirty minutes. "I want to tell her," he said as he met Rolfe's gaze.

Rolfe stammered, brows elevating. "Are you sure that's a good idea?"

"No," Sam admitted.

"What about when she finds out you've been playing her?"

"Maybe she doesn't have to find out," Sam said. "Maybe we can continue just being Ana and Sam."

He'd spent half the morning pacing in his room, staring at the gothic architecture and imagining Ana's face when he would soon show it to her. Maybe even the next day, and the thought began to make him nervous. Would she love his home as he did? Should he do anything to prepare? Perhaps clean the old scrolls library, the cathedral, or the ballroom.

Or did he only need to show her his true self?

Maybe he would at least give the place a minor dusting. Take down a few more of the old curtains to let the light in. Of course, he renewed the bouquet of roses on the foyer table, freshly stained with the blood of the soldier that had come for her the night before.

He wondered if she was okay that morning, but knew he couldn't even text her to ask. And even if he did ask, he'd not get an honest answer out of her.

His heart had plummeted at that thought, making him want to tell her everything at that very moment. It wrenched something in his heart that he couldn't even ask if she was okay, offer some sort of reprieve that no matter who came after her, they would deal with it together. She wasn't alone, and he would rip apart anyone who thought they could take her away.

He knew he would, and he wondered... he wondered when exactly it had come to this. When he had indeed fallen so deeply in love with her.

"Do you really think she'll no longer want your crown once she learns she's been fucking you since her first day here?" Rolfe asked.

"She'll tell me who she is once she learns who I am," Sam said. "I know she will."

"Cain..." Rolfe started forward, but Sam pushed off the table.

"Don't," Sam shook his head. "Don't tell me it could all be in my head," he added, staring down at the rose again. The image of her lying on his bed, naked with a plethora of those white roses around her, blood staining the perfect white petals filled him. He wanted her in his home, in his life. "I know—"

"Did you find out what she wants?" Rolfe asked.

Sam stared at him long enough that Rolfe let out a great sigh.

"Boss, hear me out—"

"Roll—"

"What if she chooses your crown over you?" Rolfe asked. "What if her duty means more to her?"

"I mean to give her everything she wants," Sam said. "Crown, kingdom, life, power..."

Rolfe contemplated it for a moment. "You actually love her."

But Sam didn't reply at first. He ran a hand through his hair and then over his face, letting his fingers dig into his skin. "Last night, one of the Firemoor assassins made their way through the shadows and came for her."

Rolfe perked up.

"They caught her on the streets and chased her in, presumably to kill her in one of the graves, but Ana... She was more fierce than she'd been in that prison. Her movements all calculated and controlled—"

"Had a hard-on for that, did you?" Rolfe said.

"I want her unleashed," Sam admitted. "Imagine the things we could take with her. Crowns. Kingdoms. This entire world. The whole dominion... *ours*."

Rolfe settled back against the counter. "I do miss the freedom of it."

"Remember the boiling seas?"

They shared a quiet, admired glance, and Sam sighed. "I shadowed this realm in waiting for the day it would all be ours again. With her... It's time."

Rolfe didn't speak a moment, and Sam could see his mind spinning. "You said the Firemoor soldier cornered her last night... do you think she'll come for you now that she knows they're here?"

Sam considered it. "I know she feels something for me. I think things have changed. You saw her."

"That was two days ago," Rolfe argued. "She was nearly assassinated last night. What if she decides she's done playing around and pretending she can have a regular life? What if she decides her desire is worth more than her want of life? What if she never loved you and this was all a lie because she saw you with Millie that day."

Sam's stomach knotted, his fingers curling on the banister, a mild rage suddenly latching itself onto his veins. "She can be my Queen... or she can be my bait. She doesn't have to love me for me to get what I want."

Rolfe laughed. "You would lock her up and torture her for information on the other kingdoms, try to bribe her or perhaps simply dangle her in front of the other kingdoms in the hopes that they'll give you an excuse to kill them?"

Their eyes met. "She belongs to me," Sam declared darkly. "I'll do with her whatever the fuck I please."

"Please for the love of all that is dark," came Millie's voice down the hall. "Tell me you two have seen the disaster happening on the news right now."

Sam and Rolfe frowned at each other. "Just came upstairs," Sam said. "What is it?"

Millie paused on the other side of the table, tired eyes staring at her phone as she thumbed through to a video. The noise of gunshots and screams filled the quiet room, and then she held out the phone for the pair to see.

There were three people hanging from nooses on a grand platform. Demons... *Sam's* demons... He recognized them immediately. Two were hound shifters—their paws and noses growing and turning back to normal. The other seemed to be teetering between her simple clawed form and her human-like one.

Demons that he'd left in other realms to spy for him.

"Prei found out they were working for you," Millie said softly. "He's sending a message to any demons left in his employ that think they can deviate. Publicly, now. I imagine he might start bringing people up from the prison."

Sam's hands creased the wood of the chair he leaned against. "They are my demons," he hissed. "He is sadly mistaken if he thinks that any of them are actually in his employ."

"Would you like him to do this to all of them?" Millie asked.

Sam's jaw tightened. "This is exactly why I told you to tell them to come home when the Spine was taken," he said, glaring at her. "I want them home," he said. "*All* of them."

There was a bright green sludge inside the wounds on their chests, and Sam squinted at the screen.

"What's that in their wounds?" Rolfe asked.

"There's a reason we haven't heard anything from Icemyer in a long time," Millie said as she turned off the video. "Apparently Firemoor soldiers swept one of the caves. A few witches had been working on an enchantment and substance to kill us. According to Cordelia, the others fled further north into the glaciers." She looked up at him, unyielding anger in her eyes. "No matter what lingering feelings you have about them, one fact remains the same," Millie snapped. "They are being cleansed as we were."

"And they're helping the enemy," Sam snapped.

"What choice do they have? They don't know there's another option."

"What do you want me to do, Mills?!"

Millie straightened and hugged her arms around her chest. "How are things going with your girlfriend?"

"Soon," Sam answered. "A Fire assassin tried to kill her on the street last night. He chased her onto the grounds to keep it quiet, but she killed him."

Millie's brows raised. "She killed him?"

Sam nodded and began explaining to her what happened with the soldier, but he had to let Rolfe take over midway through. The video was changing. Someone stepped up to the three demons, and one by one, the attacker cut the bottoms of their feet with a knife whose blade was tipped bright green.

"I want them taken down," Sam said as he watched his demons flinch and cry out, his voice nearly shaking. "I want them brought home."

Rolfe and Millie looked between each other, their previous conversation gone amiss. "Sam, no one will be able to get to them,"

Millie said. "You can't."

"These are beings that I swore would be safe," he hissed. "Find someone to cut them down."

"And they'll be strung up just like them," Millie snapped.

Sam stared at the video again, at the people who had trusted him now strung up for slaughter.

"I'll get them myself."

"And the prisons?" Millie asked.

Sam considered it. His demons had never had the threat of being killed. Maimed, occasionally, yes. He'd helped a few escape in years past, before they figured out how to rightly shield themselves from persecution. But now…

"I'll work on a plan to get them out, too." He rounded on her again, every part of his body tingling with keeping his true form at bay. "Tell everyone to get the fuck here. *Now*."

Behind every lovely thing that ever existed, tragedy once gave it bloom, he texted Ana later that day.

The dots strummed the bottom of the message for a moment. *The accuracy of that is terrifying.*

Sam almost smiled. *Isn't it?* he messaged back. He slumped into the armchair upstairs with a heavy sigh and typed out, *Raincheck on the fancy dinner?*

He wanted to tell her to put on a nice dress, that he would take her out on the town and show her off, but all Sam could think about were those demons strung up and being tortured.

Sure, Ana texted back. *Long day?*

Sam sighed at the question, his head leaning back against the plush chair top. *The longest… are you off soon?*

Leaving in five, she said. *Really need a shower. Manual labor moving estate pieces today.*

Jay made you move paintings?

I volunteered, she said. *It was good. I'm almost glad you changed your mind about the fancy dinner.*

Sam smiled at the phone. *Pizza okay instead?*

Sounds amazing.

Wine or beer? he asked.

The three dots rippled for a long moment. *I think it's a beer day. Something citrus?*

I'll grab something on the way over. See you soon, baby.

Okay, she replied, a kissing-face emoji with the response.

Sam was so distraught that he he didn't even remember grabbing the pizza or the beers to take to her apartment. He'd taken a long nap after his and Millie's conversation earlier, then interrogated the Fire soldier again, with Millie in the room to ask her own questions. It had ended with more blood, with fewer answers, and Sam…

Sam was tired.

The only thing that helped his deteriorating heart was the smile on Ana's face when she opened the door. He kissed her hard, wrapping his arm around her waist, nearly falling off balance with the pizza balancing on his palm.

Ana's laugh filled his ears, her smile against his lips, and she pulled him inside.

"Someone is needy today," Ana said as she took the pizza from his hand and stepped away from his grasp. He sat the beers down on the counter, leaning his elbow against it as he looked her over, his first moment of peace that entire day. She had her hair pulled up that afternoon, curled tendrils hanging out of it and around her face. He liked her like this… almost carefree.

As though she hadn't nearly died the night before.

"You have—" Ana reached up to his neck, eyes narrowed, and Sam's heart skipped. He grabbed her wrist before she could touch it, knowing it was blood on his face. Ana stared at him in confusion, and he relaxed his grip.

"Sam?"

Sam.

Never his full name. Never Samarius.

"It's nothing," he said, bringing her hand to his lips instead. "Do you mind if I use your shower?"

Ana's gaze searched him, but she leaned up on her toes and kissed his cheek, her hand settling on the other. "Yeah," she said, her voice soft. "Yeah, go ahead. I'll keep this in the oven."

Sam pulled the shirt off his head and pressed his hands into the sink once he'd closed the door behind him and turned on the shower to its hottest setting. So very unlike the sink at his home in his garden, the one he usually stared out of dusty panes to his favorite flowers. There was blood on his arm still from the morning. Scratches on his forearms from where he'd allowed the soldier the illusion that he could fight him.

The mirror steamed up as he stared at it, watching his tired face disappear beneath the opaque shadow.

He would tell her tomorrow.

He would cherish this last night of domestic life with her, with the illusion that everything around them wasn't falling apart, that there weren't assassins on their doorstep and an army threatening the borders. One last night they could simply be with each other, in total oblivious bliss. He didn't know how she would react when he told her who he was, when she found out he'd known who she was...

Sam sank to a crouch in the shower and let the splintering hot water run over his back. It blistered his skin, the wounds raising and closing, until he couldn't feel anything other than the steam on his flesh and the numbness of his heart.

The door clicked just as Sam leaned back against the wall, knees pulled into his chest.

Ana stood in the steam, her back pressed to the door as she searched through the fog for him. It reminded him of the first time he saw her. How that fog had surrounded her body as though it found a likeness in her.

"Sam..." she said as she stepped to the glass door.

Their eyes met, and Ana swallowed as she looked him over, but Sam didn't move. Not even when Ana stripped herself of her clothes and stepped into the tiled shower with him. And especially not when she sat beside him, curled her arm into his, and laid her head on his shoulder.

His throbbing heart slowed, and he actually took a deep breath.

"I used to do this all the time in Icemyer," Ana whispered. "After a long day... There was something about the hot water over my tired skin that numbed my mind."

Sam didn't mean to stiffen, but he couldn't help it. "How long were you there?" he said softly.

"A while. We fled there after we left Firemoor the first time," she said, her touch absentmindedly tracing the vine and rose tattoos on his arm. "I would hide in the shower for an hour, until my father would beat on the door and tell me I'd used all the hot water we would have had for a week. He'd make me wash the dishes in the ice water after."

Sam's lips twitched like he might smile. He laid his head against hers, inhaling the almond and rose scent of the soap she'd discovered at the apothecary a few doors down as she continued to rub his arm, finally entwining their fingers together.

Sam squeezed her hand and kissed her head before leaning his forehead against her temple and closing his eyes. He wondered if somehow the water would stop time or even push it forward so that he never had to experience the pain of seeing her broken face when she learned he had lied to her all this time.

"Was it a call from him?" Ana whispered, and he knew she meant Death.

"Something like that," he said.

"I didn't know it affected you like this," she said as she wrapped her other hand on top of their entwined fingers.

"Some days are worse than others," and it wasn't a complete lie.

Ana reached out for his other wrist and traced the small tattoo she'd given him, a quiet chuckle leaving her. "I can't believe you let me do this," she said, smile in her tone.

He sat up then and turned over her wrist to reveal her own healing tattoo. "Look at us, baby," he whispered, his wrist turned so that they were beside each other. "Look at what we are." He glanced down at her then, at the smile on her lips that didn't quite meet her eyes, and he wondered if she was thinking of the assassin from the night before.

One more night. One more night, and then... then he would show her everything.

Sam kissed her temple, her cheek, her jaw, and Ana sank into his embrace. But he didn't go any further, even though he wanted to. He would do that later after he'd laughed with her while they watched the newest episode of the comedic drama she liked, after they'd eaten and drank and his face hurt from smiling too much. He would kiss every inch of her body, take his time tasting her, fucking her, claiming her. He'd forget everything that had happened that day. He'd forget all his worries and the threats on both of them.

He'd just be with her.

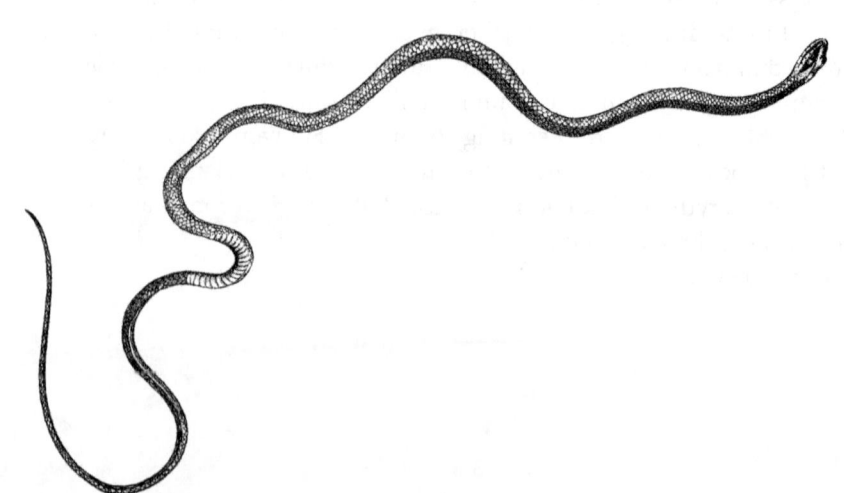

Chapter Forty-One

Ana couldn't sleep.

She tried to.

But no matter how hard she tried, she couldn't.

There was something different about that night, about the way Sam touched and kissed her, even the way he looked at her. She wondered if she had been the same. If she had kissed him as though it were her last night with him, as it felt like he was doing too.

Even after he'd taken his time devouring every inch of her. Made her explode with the deliberate tease of his tongue, raking over every part of her and making her beg. After he'd fucked her on the bed, the couch, in the shower after she'd spilled beer all over herself. Even after she'd curled up naked in fresh sheets, spent from every orgasm, and he entwined himself in the bed with her.

She couldn't close her eyes.

She'd laid on her side and stared out the window to the castle in the distance, at the singular amber glow that seemed to radiate at all hours of the day and night. And every time Sam shifted behind her, she tried to bring herself back to the present and not think about all the things she'd done to get to that exact moment.

About all the things she was about to do.

"Ana?"

"Hm?" she said, breaking free of her daze.

Sam sat up on his elbow at her side and pulled her onto her back, his thumb tracing the line of her jaw. "Tell me what you're thinking about," he asked.

She swallowed at the concern in his eyes and shook her head, sighing as she rubbed his forearm. "Just about the gallery," she lied. "I have that meeting in Castle Corvus next week with the King's Hand. Getting nervous about it."

"Take a camera," he said. "Make sure you get all the photos to sell to some greedy magazine. You'll be rich."

Ana almost smiled. Almost.

Sam's alarm buzzed then, and he groaned heavily, his forehead landing on her chest. Ana's heart skipped. Panic flooded her body.

Shit.

Shit. Shit. Shit.

She almost choked as she tried to stifle a sob.

How the fuck was she supposed to do this?

"Don't go," she said. "Stay," she whispered... *pleaded*... as her hand tightened around his arm.

Sam pushed up and kissed her nose. "You know I can't," he said, holding her face a moment longer. "I'd rather spend every day like the other day..." He leaned down, his lips landing on her collar, nibbling on her skin. "Holding you. Kissing you..."

Ana's eyes fluttered at his kisses. She didn't understand how every time he touched her, she still got butterflies in her stomach.

Not that it mattered the moment he left that bed.

His kisses moved down to the tattoo between her breasts, his tongue licking every swirled flower line, making her back arch up off the bed as her fingers wreathed in his hair. He trailed down and down, taking his time to kiss her soft stomach, leaving behind the cool wetness from his tongue.

"Sam," she moaned his name, eliciting his smile against her skin. "Don't go," she whispered again.

He straightened over her again, jaw ticked, eyes narrowing just slightly. "Why don't you want me to go?"

She looked at him one last time, her thumb brushing over his cheek, memorizing how he looked at her there, how he'd looked at her the day of the tattoo, and how he'd held her. His laugh... shit, that fucking laugh. She wished she could hear it one more time.

"I like waking up with you," she whispered.

Sam gave her a half-smile, and he kissed her lips, making her surrender to the softness of this one, his hand wrapping around her waist, tongue sweeping against hers. And even as he started to pull away, she held him tighter.

His brows lifted when he finally managed to straighten over her, and that damn smirk crooked his lips. He squeezed her ass and gave it a smack. "Hang on to that for later," he said.

"Or you could take advantage now," she argued, and she would keep arguing with him until she had no voice left if it would keep him from leaving that bed.

But Sam just smiled and ignored her.

The absence of his body nearly made her vomit. She watched him sit on the edge of the bed to stretch, then stand as he retrieved his clothes. Those tattooed arms, the ink on his back, the stupid smiley face that she'd placed on the inside of his wrist...

He went into the bathroom, and she stood to put on her white silk nightgown. Sam eyed her when he came back out and paused to kiss her once more.

"I'll see you tonight," he said, kissing her forehead. "Maybe we take care of that raincheck and go to the Roof for dinner. A friend has some connections there. And after... I have something I want to show you. Things I want to tell you."

"More surprises?" she asked.

"Something like that."

But she grabbed his hands as he went to turn and pulled him back into her. "Tell me now," she nearly begged.

Sam hesitated, his hand slowly reaching up to her cheek to push a curl back, and for a fleeting moment, she thought he might give in. His eyes burned into her, confusion sweeping those brown orbs.

"Tell me now," she repeated, her voice more hoarse than before. "Tell me everything."

His thumb brushed her cheek and lips, and she leaned into his touch, her eyes closing as she inhaled the scent of him, memorizing the feeling of his hand, the pad of his rough thumb on her flesh.

If this was her last moment with him, she would make it last as long as she could. She would hold his hand on her face, refuse to look away from the eyes she loved losing herself in. From the man she loved, and who...

Her stupid fucking heart twisted to the point she thought her knees might give out.

"Tonight," he replied again. "Tonight, I'll show you everything."

No matter how much she wondered what he meant, if he meant showing her his home, revealing any last secrets he might have, it didn't matter.

Prolonging the inevitable would hurt worse.

As if she wasn't already ripping herself apart from the inside with the decision.

The thought of all those men she'd taken hearts from filled her, and she pondered if they had felt like this when she killed them or if it had hurt them less to simply die rather than watch the world shred beneath their feet.

Sam kissed her one more time, and she held him there, gripping his shirt in her hands and savoring him. Until he finally pulled away, and he gave her chin a gentle nudge, making her lips lift despite herself.

"Tonight." His whisper was a promise, and when he released her, her entire body went numb. A hollow void filled where her heart had just been twisting. It was gone, and with it, a future she would never have.

Ana couldn't speak. Saliva stuck in her throat, and she simply gave him a nod.

Her pulse began to throb in her ears, and she looked out the window to Castle Corvus in the distance, the memory of her being attacked filling her mind. Knowing she would never be safe, she could never have a normal life, not after all she'd done.

She had to do this.

"Sam…" she said as he grabbed his coat.

"Ana, I can't stay—"

"It's not that," she cut him off, though even as the words left her, she wished she'd just had the argument and let him believe this was why she had to end things.

But it was too late.

She fumbled with her hands as he turned on her, those brows furrowing over his pained eyes.

"What's wrong?" he asked.

"I can't… I can't see you anymore," she said, forcing a firm tone.

Sam slowed, a hesitation in his movements, calculations in his next moves. But Ana stood her ground. She watched as his jaw twitched, eyes shifting to the floor.

"Is this what you've sat up thinking about for our last few hours together?" he asked in a low voice. "Is this the reason you've stared out the window and felt like a stranger beneath me? Why you were just begging me to stay?"

His words made her heart pick up, and after a few more silent moments, she realized she had yet to say anything. How could she? She didn't even know *what* to say. Why this was different from letting any other man fall at her feet and then leave. Fuck, why had she not thought this through. This was *Sam*.

This was Sam...

Her shoulders nearly caved as she struggled not to break. As she pushed away the threatening tears, the burning behind her nostrils, the weight pressing against the backs of her knees.

His eyes lifted to hers as he turned toward her, and for the briefest of moments, fear washed through her body.

And she wasn't sure why.

Lie, Ana, she told herself. *Fucking say something.*

"Speak, Ana," came his demand.

She flinched at the abrupt sharp and twisting tone of his voice, like a knife cutting the thick air. His body was so incredibly motionless that she couldn't tell if he was breathing.

But Sam continued, his blackened eyes never leaving hers, as he said, "Speak with this conviction you seem to be so sure of. Break my heart as you mean to."

Ana shifted as she finally found her voice. "This... you and me... It's over," she forced out. "I cannot see you anymore."

There was something about the abrupt turn in Sam's features that continued to chill her. He looked as if his world had just turned to dust. His hand wrapped around the top of the chair that his jacket had just been lying across, and he squeezed. Squeezed to the point that the wood seemed to melt beneath his grasp.

"Why are you doing this?" he whispered in a threatening breath.

Ana stared at him, and as her heart shattered into glass around her bare feet, she reached inside for the most painful part of herself. For the cruel and the ruthless. For the temptress, the liar, the thief.

The true Tower.

"Does it matter?" she snapped. "I do not want to see you again. Why can that not be a reason?"

"Everything..." he began, his voice still quiet. "Everything we shared the past few days, the tattoos, you saying you're mine, all of that... did it all mean *nothing*? Am I... Am I not enough for you?"

The question nauseated her just as it had the day before.

However, she didn't let it get to her, and instead, her chin lifted higher, arms curling over her chest, and every emotion—save for greed and pride—evacuated her bones.

"Did you honestly think I loved you?"

And her voice came out in such a haunting whisper that she swore Sam really did stop breathing. He stood wholly still as she continued to speak, eyes not even daring to blink.

Ana had been challenged by broken-hearted men in the past. Had seen rage wipe across their brows and end with them bleeding out on the floor.

She wondered if that was how this would end.

"What could you ever give me?" she hissed. "You're nothing, Sam. A means to an end. A good *fuck*. Nothing more."

Sam let go of the chair, eyes down casting to the floor, only Ana didn't stop.

"You have never meant any more to me than the dirt on my boots. You're a lowly demon. A groundskeeper and an artist, for fuck's sake. You could never give me the things I deserve or the life I want. You're trash, Sam. I have stepped in shit that was worth more than you."

He took one step in her direction, his shoulders rounding, and Ana side-stepped in the path of the kitchen.

"Why are you doing this?" he asked, in a calmer voice than she expected.

"Because you were right to worry yesterday if you would ever be someone I could love."

"*Liar*," he seethed, his teeth baring. "You would never have put that tattoo on your flesh had you felt nothing."

He was stalking around the opposite side of the counter, but Ana continued to sidestep. She saw the knife block from the corner of her eye where she'd hidden the cursed one, recognizing the unrelenting anger in his eyes. The rage and seething pouring from his every movement—from the twitch of his lashes to the soft clap of his boots on the floor.

"Did you think I loved it because you drew it?" A hollow laugh left her. "Look at the rest of my body. The flowers and crowns. It was just another piece of art."

"You know it wasn't," he said in a definitive voice. "I know you, Ana. I know the rest of your tattoos are there to hide a piece of your past. I know—"

"You have no idea about my past," she snapped. "This," she held up her arm "was nothing more than my loving an art piece."

"You're lying!" Sam nearly shouted. "Tell me the truth."

"Why can you not accept this?" she asked. "Deal with it Sam. We're done. I never want to see you again."

"No," he said, shaking his head. "No, this isn't... You can't—" He struggled for words, his chest now rising and falling erratically, that brief moment where he looked like he might lose control. His fists clenched and unclenched, lightning ricocheting against the window like his anger had some power over it. Talons threatened at his fingertips.

He ran those pointed claws through his hair, lashes lifting, and the devastating rage in his eyes tore through her.

"Why?" he growled.

Ana gathered herself, a wave of real anger rising in her now as frustration yanked at her core. "Because you were right," she spat. "You're not enough for me. You never were. You never have been—"

"Then why stay with me?" Sam glowered. "Why say all these things? Why continue to see me?"

A brief quip of silence pressed between them, pausing even the rain tapping on the windows, and she crossed her arms over her chest as she let her last lie fill the space.

"What can I say?" she said, her voice a threat within itself. "You're just another good fuck."

Lightning shuddered the glass, and Sam lunged around the counter.

Ana bolted toward the door. He was on her in a blink—grasping her wrists and yanking her backward. His hand wrapped around her neck before she could pull free. She was off the floor. Struggling. Windpipe crushing. One of her hands shot to his arm, the other grabbing for anything, *anything*—

Her back crashed into the wall cabinets. Her thighs jolted into the counter edge, spine hitting the handles on the doors and paralyzing her a moment. His hand was a wrench on her, tightening and tightening—squeezing to the point she began to panic. She wrestled against his grasp, feet kicking, hand slapping, lungs gasping.

He was rigid with rage. Eyes so black that she swore a scarlet seeped into them.

"You fucking *whore*—"

Ana kicked, cutting off his words, and she reached behind her with the bit of strength she could grasp. Lightheadedness began to take over, her vision hazing.

But even through the fog, she watched a silver lining glisten the bottom of his eyes, and a single tear dropped down his cheek.

"Pray, Ana," he seethed in a throaty rasp that chilled the room. "Pray, to whomever it is you pray, that your ending pleas will one day fall upon the ears of a demon other than Death himself... Because he will be deaf to you."

Ana managed to shift her neck, managed to find the handle of the cursed knife behind her in the block—

And she felt her chest rumble as laughter left her lips.

"Be sure to tell him I said 'hello.'"

PART THREE

AND TO HIS OWN GRAVE, SHE'LL LEAD HIM

Chapter Forty-Two

The knife pushed so easily into his skin that she wasn't sure she'd stabbed him until she saw his eyes widening.

Ana staggered forward as his grip on her neck faltered. He choked, stumbling back, the blade pulling from within him.

Something inside her seemed to snap at the sight of him struggling. Flashes of men who had indeed taken advantage of her, ones she had played with for sport, the kings she'd killed and the men she'd slain just to get in a royal bed... She shook with the hatred of all of it combining together.

Blood poured from his wound, and Sam couldn't speak. He tripped over the barstool and crashed to his knees, his face paling as he clutched the wound.

"Ana..."

Chest heaving, he coughed blood... Ana pushed off the top of the counter and strode in his direction. He watched with with pleading eyes, like she could somehow reverse it. But Ana was broken and tired, and the only obstacle between her and her crown was this man and her own staggering heart.

Sam grabbed her leg, pleading her name again when she paused before him. She reached a hand out, gripping his hair between her fingers, and she tugged his head up to look at her.

That beautiful fucking face.

And she hated him for it.

"Ana..."

The blade cut across his throat.

A scarlet waterfall poured over his chest. She couldn't stop shaking as she watched him die before her, just as the others had...

The others...
As if he was one of them.
As if he was...
As if he was *nothing*.
Nothing.
She couldn't breathe. Her chest heaved with his waning eyes, and suddenly her heart began to cry out.
"Sam—"
As if suddenly realizing what she'd done.
He crippled out of her grasp onto the floor, cold eyes now staring into the shadows outside. Sam—*Sam*—
She'd killed him. *Him.* Someone who she had only hours before considered giving up her entire life for. Someone who had made her feel loved and challenged and desired. Someone she'd fallen in love with and for once... *just once...* wanted to live for.
She'd ripped out his heart and throat as though he'd been one of the Firemoor soldiers.
A wail left her that she hadn't heard since her father died.
Sobbing. Crying. *Choking.*
She screamed, her grip tightening on his leather jacket like she could bring him back if she willed it so. Hoping her cries might rewind the last few minutes. Alter time to go back to when he was leaving, make herself simply kiss him goodbye instead of the cruel words she'd spoken to force herself to let him go.
She called out his name again, again, again. Staring through tear-filled eyes to his own, wishing she could see that smile in them. Remembering the way his gaze had always studied her like she was the only person in the world—like *they* were the only people in the world.
She'd killed him.
Sam was *dead*.
He had shown her the sun, and she'd shown him death.
Everything in her broke. She wailed his name over and over, sobbing onto his face as she shattered over him, her forehead to his. Screaming for him to come back to her.
You killed him.
Killed him.
Him.
An emptiness rattled her insides as she choked on a sob. Empty without him there. A void that not even the greed of her past could fill.

The same greed she'd just killed him for.

She didn't want to do this. She didn't *want* this.

Was it worth it? Was all that power worth losing him? To become mindless and numb and a shell of herself. That was what awaited her. More of *this*. More pain and sorrow and suffering, and *for what*...

The knife lying beside his body caught her eye.

Because maybe it wasn't worth it.

Nonetheless, before she could reach for it, before she could move her body and make that final decision, a black shadow curled around her trembling hands. The same shadow she'd seen the night before in the cemetery, and Ana nearly hurled onto the floor.

A flash of rage surged through her depleting body. Rage and hatred and anger for every time she'd looked for this shadow and it had never come. For all the times a lowly demon had cleaned up after her kills and never Death himself. For every time she'd begged and pleaded for that end.

The shadows curled over Sam's arms and inched across the floor.

"You..." Her voice was shaking, barely audible. Her breath wouldn't catch for the nausea in her throat. Her vision blurred behind that rage, that hatred.

"You show now... *now*... after all these fucking years... *All this time* —" She released Sam's jacket, her hands curling in on themselves. Pain pricked her palms, and she hardly realized she was breaking her own skin.

"Show your cowardice face for once," she seethed, her voice growing. "Show me, *Death*. Come out of your shadows and face me. *The things I have done for you!*" She was screaming then, throat aching, burning, and raw from everything building inside her.

"*Come for me!*" she screeched. "Show your face!" She grabbed the knife and held the point to her wrist, staring at those shadows and into the darkness surrounding her—save for the lamppost outside and the light from the TV cascading over her figure.

He was there. She knew he was. He was in her apartment.

Death watched her.

And she dared him to step forward.

"Will you show your fucking face this time?" she choked out, the tip of that knife now digging into her skin. Hyper breaths had her mind numb. She was ready. *Ready*. This was the final time she would ask for that darkness. He was here this time. He was watching. He couldn't stop her. He would finally take her.

She looked at Sam's face one last time. His *beautiful fucking face.* Remembering every time he'd held her and laughed and smiled. Every time he'd made her feel whole, like her past didn't matter. Made her feel all the things she never thought she deserved. Happiness and love and peace.

A home in his arms.

And then, she turned back to the darkness.

"Show me," she begged through screeching breaths, having to take those audible gasps, feeling her own blood seep from the cut and dribble down her shaking arm.

"Stop hiding in your shadows—"

The knife dragged further across her skin.

"—Live up to your name and *come for me! Come for me!—*"

"Stop. *Shouting.*"

It was a hiss—a *warning*, and the voice…

There, in the pitch-black corner of her room, scarlet eyes lit up the darkness. Leaning against the back wall, one hand in his pocket. Eyes cold and carmine and unblinking. The lights flickered and then went completely dark. Lightning flashed, and tattered black wings arched high behind him like a shadow waiting to be unleashed.

Broken. Burned. Hollow.

Ana nearly started shouting again. Nearly rose to her feet to demand he step forward into the light. Nearly threw herself at him—

But in the next lightning strike, Death finally showed his face, and every atom in her body went rigid. The knife clattered to the floor. Saliva stuck like sap in her throat.

Fucking…

"Sam?"

Though she wasn't even sure the name had escaped her. Breath seemed to void in her lungs. A chill shivered over her. She looked back down at the dead body, knowing her eyes had to be deceiving her.

It couldn't be…

The shadows overlapped Sam's warm corpse, his lifeless gaze still staring up at the ceiling. She turned back to the shadow in the corner, her heart hammering. The lamp near him flickered back on, and within its amber glow, it was confirmed.

Ana couldn't breathe.

Sam stood in the corner, shadows of tattered wings at his back. He shifted and pulled something from his pocket—a lighter and smoke, and he lit the end of it, cheeks pulling taut as he sucked in a long drag.

The glare in his poisonous gaze seethed through her. Pain stretched over his features as if…

"You know…" he began, his voice stiff, "I did wonder how long it would be before you carved out my heart like all the others."

Ana couldn't function.

Sam.

Sam was…

No.

But…

And suddenly, it all made sense.

Everything made *fucking* sense, and she hated that she'd not realized it sooner.

The leaving her in the middle of the night. The shadows following her. How at ease she felt in his presence. His knowledge of the realms and the witches. Why he looked so tired and pained every day. Why his laugh washed over her like the sun's warmth. And he…

Of course, he knew who she was.

A dizziness nearly made her faint. Her broken heart jumped out of her chest. Emotion clouded and twisted and wrenched every limb and muscle and bone. Teeth chattering with the tremble of her blood-covered body.

The lies. The fucking *lies*.

Everything had been a fucking lie.

He'd known who she was this entire time. Known who she was and chosen to… To what? To toy with her?

Was any of it real?

Sam.

Sam.

Sam.

The cool slither of that black fog wrapped beneath her jaw and tilted her quivering chin up just as the lights extinguished on the streets. The velvet of his shadows shifted into sharpened glass, cutting and marking her skin like he meant to pull every carmine drop from inside her. Lightning chiseled the sky, the great crack rippling over the air and making the entire town tremble. His features reflected back to her in that moment, and the silhouette on the wall flinched its torn wings.

Samarius Cain.

Death.

Chapter Forty-Three

Oh, that face.

That perfectly beautiful... terrified... *enraged* face.

Sam took his phone from his pocket and snapped a photo of it.

Deianira Bronfell. On her knees in a puddle of blood. Begging and screaming at Death to show himself to her.

Sam didn't know if he was angry or aroused.

Angry and hurt that he'd been stupid enough to think she loved him, and this was different. Angry and devastated that he'd allowed himself to fall for her. Angry, his heart shredding to the floor, that she'd killed him so easily like he meant nothing. With a cursed knife, at that. Sam could still feel the sting of the spelled blade in his abdomen, the burning on his throat.

But her pleas to Death constricted his cold heart, how she'd nearly dragged that knife across her wrists at the sight of him dead on the floor... And maybe... just maybe...

Sam pushed every thought of loving her to the back of his mind, and he watched as the realization shined in her eyes.

"It was you..." Ana rose to her feet. "This entire time... it was... *you*... it was you. It was you! It was—*YOU*—"

Ana lunged, and Sam didn't blink.

His shadows wrapped each limb as she tried to squirm out of his grasp. She opened her mouth to shout again, writhing against the bindings, but only a panicked scream left her.

Sam pushed slowly off the wall and took another draw of his smoke.

One calculated step at a time, the noise of his boots echoing off the creaking wooden floor, and her eyes never moved from him as he stalked toward her.

Closer. Closer. *Closer*.

Directly at her face, he paused and squashed his smoke in his palm.

"I'll make this easy," he said, meeting her venomous gaze. His shadows released her feet in the next strike of lightning, but still held onto her neck, and as her toes touched the ground, a broken black wing tipped her forward.

"To your knees, *Deianira*."

Thunder rumbled over the earth with her name, the very air itself quaking with the truth. Sam watched as her lip dared to twitch, as her eyes darkened with delirium. She sank slowly, one knee into the pool of blood, followed by the other.

"Something tells me you enjoy the sound of my name on your lips, Your Majesty."

The tip of his wing pushed on her back, rage coiling in his veins with the teasing tone leaving her lips.

"Lower," he said in a haunting whisper.

She bent, her arms rigid at her sides where they were being restrained. Every muscle was taut with her struggle, but Sam only pressed his hands into his pockets as he watched her kneel before him.

"*Lower*."

Her breasts pressed to her knees, her cheek nearly on the floor. He felt her tug against the bindings, her body jerking as she tried to break free, but the umbra only tightened around her skin.

Sam's head tilted at the sight of her there. Splayed in the blood she'd spilled from his own body. Her silken white night dress hiked high over her bare ass. Arms extended wide at her sides. Her cheek lying on the floor, hair a rattled mess of curls around her.

The image imprinted in his mind and burned his memory.

Sam crouched to one knee so that he could see her face. "I think this is my favorite version of you," he said, his voice haunting and throaty. "Bound in darkness and wrapped in blood. Bent over your knees... That gorgeous face on the floor..." He reached out and caught one of her curls. She flinched at the touch, jerking on the shadows, and her eyes rolled to meet his.

"Wait until you see me in your crown," came her hiss.

He bristled at her confidence, twirling that curl on his finger. "And here I was prepared to give you everything..."

Anger seeped back into her eyes. A tear jerked down her cheek. Pain flickered across her features, her lips twitching toward the floor. Every tremble in Ana's body vibrated his darkness. He felt her heart as it began thumping wildly.

"Sam…"

A shadow dove into her mouth and down her windpipe before she could say more. It threw her body back into an arch—her arms splayed wide and blood-covered chest exposed toward the sky like she were hanging by a rope from the ceiling. Ana coughed. Choked. Struggled—

Sam pulled his phone out and dialed Rolfe's number.

"Yeah, boss?" Rolfe answered gruffly.

"Have the dungeon cleaned out and call on a ghosted legion—" Sam glanced through his hair back to Ana, who was staring at him with a deadly glare that chilled even his dead heart.

"We have a guest," Sam finished.

Rolfe was quiet a moment, and Sam recognized the silent pause as Rolfe took in the hollowness of his voice.

"*Rolfe!*" Sam snapped.

"Yeah, I'm on it, boss," Rolfe said solemnly.

Sam started to hang up, but Rolfe called out for him.

"Hey, Cain—"

Sam swallowed emotion at the use of the name, knowing Rolfe would only call him that when he meant it.

"I'm sorry," Rolfe continued.

Sam's eyes flickered back to Ana. "So am I."

Chapter Forty-Four

Ana's eyes fluttered as she felt cold stone beneath her ass. A chill swept over her shoulder, and she realized someone had changed her clothes, now wearing one of her sweaters and a pair of leggings instead of the nightdress. Her throat was raw like she'd been screaming, feeling like something had been shoved inside it. And her hands... her hands were covered in dried blood.

As she looked around the dimly lit space, everything came crashing back to her in flashes of memory that throbbed in her temple.

The fight with Sam. Stabbing him. The blood spilling from him and his dying eyes—

Iron clanked with the roll of a cage, and Ana's head jerked up.

She was in a dungeon.

A filthy, cold dungeon with nothing more than a small dingy paned window high above her back. Firelight flickered from the opposite walls.

And from within the shadows, Death stared at her.

His chin was dipped, hands in his pockets. He watched her with such stillness that had she not seen his silhouette, she wouldn't have known he was there.

Ana began to shake.

"You..."

She was on her feet. Running. Jumping—her body slamming into the iron bars with a wild scream that seared her insides.

"You *BASTARD!*"

Sam winced, but he didn't move. He stared at her as she tugged and pulled and threw herself at those bars, her heart shattering onto the floor. Crashing against the iron like a stone into a window.

No amount of physical pain compared to this. Nothing would *ever* compare to this.

And the cold vacancy in his eyes only crushed her soul more.

"*You lied to me*," she seethed in a tone so gravely, saliva dripped from her trembling lips. "You're a fucking liar! Was *any* of it real?"

Rust from the bars scratched her skin as she screamed and writhed. She needed to know. She needed to know if her broken heart was valid or if she'd imagined the last month.

"You betrayed me!" she shouted. "You *manipulated* me—"

"Tell me you wouldn't have done the same had you known who I was," came his darkened words.

Ana started to retort, but she nearly choked.

Because he was right.

She hocked spit at his face, making him grimace. His eyes were shut tight, yet he didn't move.

"Fuck you," she managed in a breathless voice.

The raw stone seemed to freeze beneath her bare feet as she took a solid step back, trying to regain her composure.

"This entire time..." she breathed. "Every *day*. Every *word*. Every *touch*... You knew who I was."

Sam pulled his shirt up and wiped the spit from his face before glaring back at her. "Did you think you could come into my kingdom and I wouldn't know who you were?"

"And you chose to what, exactly?" she asked. "What was your plan here?"

"To show you how it feels to be seduced and broken as you've done to every other king," he said.

"Every other king I have been with has been nothing more than shit-eating cretins. None ever truly cared for me like they said they did. I did their kingdoms a favor by getting rid of them—"

"You caused chaos and destruction and murder—"

"Says Death himself," she seethed at the fact that he was accusing her of such things when he was... *him*. She swallowed, feeling her feet move back. "You're a coward," she whispered. "A *coward*, Sam. You're no better than them—"

"Ana, I was prepared to tell you everything," Sam blurted as he stepped to the bars.

Her heart stilled. She gawked at him, letting the words strum through her depleting body. He had to be lying. Why would he ever reveal who he was when he knew she was after his crown?

"I was prepared to *give* you everything. I was prepared to bring you here and show you why I could not stay with you every night. I—" But he ran both hands through his hair, stopping himself, and when he looked at her, she felt the world disappear beneath her feet.

Pain. Pain worse than any pain she'd ever thought she'd seen in him. This was pure agony—as though she was dying in front of him and he could do nothing to stop it.

"You chose your greed over me," he continued, voice faint and dangerous, rising and seething with the next words. "You chose to *murder* me so that you could walk away from what we had and go after a fucking *crown*—"

"What would you like me to say?" she cut him off. "Would you like me to tell you I had to do those things because I found myself falling for you? Would you like me to say that murdering you was the only way I knew how to let you go?"

"Don't try to manipulate me," he warned.

"Oh, like you manipulated me?"

Sam held her gaze a moment longer as he started descending back into the shadows once more. Ana shifted as she watched, her teeth chattering as she tried to stifle emotion in her throat. Face burning with it. She cursed her breaking heart. How moments earlier she'd felt a string of power and numbness streaking through her, but the moment he said he was going to tell her everything... the moment he admitted how she was so close to having everything she ever desired—power, duty, and love—

She was breaking.

"It hurts, doesn't it?" he said softly as he paused at the steps.

"What?"

"To fall."

Fall.

Deianira Bronfell did not fall.

She *would* not fall.

And yet, she had.

Ana gripped the iron in her hands to the point her fingers went numb. Her vision tunneled as rage poured through her.

No, this was beyond rage. This was vision black, out of body, delirious *wrath.*

"I... hate... you," she seethed, every word a heavy breath. Saliva dribbled from her lips, hair falling wildly around her face. "I... hate.... you!"

Had she been a witch, it would have been a curse. Her anger would have brought the dead back to life. She couldn't feel her body—only hatred and betrayal where her heart should have been. A numbness from the pain inflicted on her knees crashing into the ground as they never had before.

"I HATE YOU!"

I hate you.

I hate you.

I hate you.

Sobbing.

Dripping.

He paused again, and she jerked against the bars, writhing and pushing and pulling, willing her strength to break it down with her bare hands, if only she jerked hard enough. *"SAM!"*

His name shrieked from her lips before she could stop it.

"SAM!… SAM!"

It was a scream in such a blood-curdling, high pitch that the window shattered. Glass fell into her hair and cut her face. But she didn't care.

She screamed his name again and again until she couldn't feel her throat. Until she couldn't catch her breath and she choked on the vomit coming up from her stomach.

But he never came back.

I hate you.

I hate you.

I hate you.

Tears fell from her that she couldn't stop. She'd not let herself fall into such a pit since her home was destroyed; even that hadn't felt like this.

Nothing felt like this.

Audible cries left her. She couldn't hold it in. Her head hit the stone wall as she sank against it, knees pulled into her chest, blood pooling in her blistered hands from the glass that had shattered around her.

I hate you.

I hate you.

I loved you.

I love you.

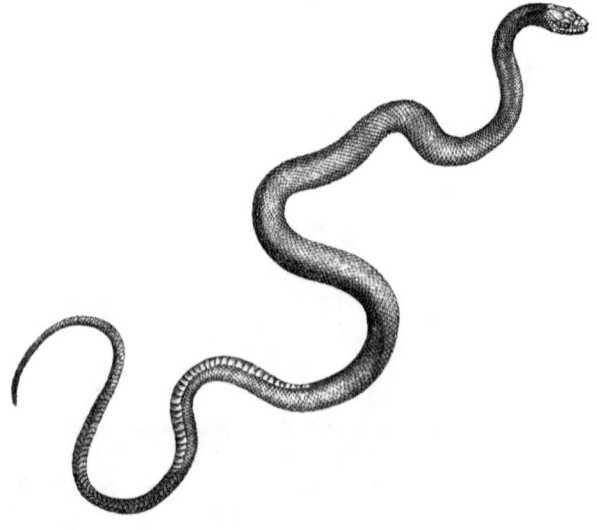

Chapter Forty-Five

Sam barely made it down the hall past the stairs.

He vomited and crippled every time he heard her scream. Every time she said she hated him. Every time she called out his name.

He couldn't help it. It sickened him what he was doing. It sickened him to know she was sitting down there cold in a cell, angry and betrayed.

They had fallen in love, and she had chosen her greed over him—at least, that's what he kept telling himself every time he started down the steps to take her in his arms and hold her in his bed. To forgive her and get on his knees to beg her forgiveness.

Cold sweat poured from his body. Even his shadows trembled with the weight of his agony.

Rolfe left with two ghost demons from the grounds to take care of the scene at Ana's apartment, and for the first time in a century, Millie stayed at the castle overnight.

Rolfe had called her the moment he got off the phone with Sam. She'd driven like a banshee all the way up to the castle steps and burst through the doors just as Sam made it to the top of the staircase from the dungeon.

"Sam—"

Millie wrapped her hands under his arms as Sam crumbled to his hands and knees, his stomach evacuating onto the floor.

"Get up, Samarius," she whispered urgently. "This is not what breaks you."

Ana screamed again, making his knees give way even though Millie held him. But she grabbed him, using her unnatural strength, and she brought his limp body to his feet, draping his arm over her shoulders.

Ana shouting his name curdled his blood. He shuddered, and Millie urged him forward.

He vomited twice more on the way to the kitchen, far enough away from the dungeons that when Millie pulled the pocket doors closed, the noise numbed behind it.

Sam collapsed into the chair and pushed his hands over his eyes as Millie made for the stove. He hadn't felt such a break since he'd had to run from the last war. Fuck, why had he done this to himself? Why had he continued going through it—trusted that she wouldn't do something drastic after the Firemoor soldier had attacked her.

He should have told her that afternoon like his instincts had told him to.

Maybe then...

"You knew it might end this way," Millie said as she sat a cup of tea in front of him.

Sam ran both hands through his hair, pushing the straight locks back, but failing to keep them out of his eyes when he dropped his chin.

"I didn't know it would hurt this much," he admitted, dipping the tea bag up and down, staring at the rippling water as it turned a muggy brown.

The scrape of the spoon in Millie's cup sounded when she dragged it over the rim. "Are you okay?"

"No," he answered without looking up.

"What's your plan?" she asked, bringing the tea to her lips. "Has it changed?"

Sam thought about it, weighed his options, and as he considered it, his insides grew cold. "Do you mean if I still intend to flaunt her in front of the legions already marching at our doors with intentions of bringing back the sun?"

Millie just raised a brow.

Sam settled his forearms on the table and wrapped his long fingers around the cup.

"Yes."

"You would watch them rip her apart just so you can strike when they are distracted?"

Same took another sip of his tea. "In theory. Yes."

"I thought you loved her."

His eyes flickered in her direction, and he shifted as his body numbed. "Make your point."

"You protect the things you love," she said.

Sam leaned slowly back in the chair, and as Luna jumped in his lap, he stroked the top of her head. He focused on Luna's bright yellow-green eyes as he spoke and scratched her beneath her chin. His chest swelled with the plan swirling in his mind, with the fantasy that had only slightly deviated since the beginning of the night.

"You're smart, Milliscent," he said. "You know the lengths I will go to to protect my things." His eyes moved to hers. "What do you think I will do to ensure that for the woman I love?"

Millie's throat bobbed with the swallow of her drink, but just as he thought she might argue with him, she said, "Death's Ballad."

The corner of his lip twitched, lashes lifting as he looked to her in confirmation, but he didn't speak.

A brief smile flickered in her eyes. "Why haven't you done it yet?"

"It's not my choice to make," he said, a little more solemnly than before.

"So you'll let her suffer in her own misery. You'll torture yourself with her screams and every manipulative word she might say... Just to hear her make that decision on her own?"

Sam reached for his tea, and just as he pressed it to his lips, he met her eyes and said, "Yes."

Chapter Forty-Six

Sam smelled the blood the moment he opened the stairwell door the following morning.

The sound of the haunting melody Ana was singing made the hair rise on his arms, and his shadows quivered. He didn't know the melody, and the way it came from her lips... The song made his awareness almost dreamlike. He wasn't sure what to expect or how she would have killed anyone whilst locked in her cage.

But...

Carnage was a nice word for the state of his dungeon.

His guards lay in puddles of their own guts and blood.

Heads ripped or smashed in.

Throats cut.

Bodies dismembered.

Like the ghosted demons had bled themselves dry or shredded their existences at the sound of the lullaby she was singing.

Sam slowed his approach as he took in the sight of Ana still in her cell.

Her hair was wild—looking as if she'd tried to pull it out, and it had settled into its own psychosis. She'd ripped her sweater and was now wearing one of his demons' embroidered trench coats.

And she was dancing with a dead man.

Her eyes lifted to his when she spun around, holding the dead man's arm out while he slumped on her body, feet dragging the ground. Her lullaby grew louder. An evil smile spread on her lips and the sinister laugh that left her imprinted in his memory.

Deianira held his gaze in ownership, enslaving him to her entrancement, and Sam's shadows flickered as they tried to break free.

This was the woman the stories spoke of. The one who had taken down kings and monarchies for a cause no one knew of.

Chaotic. Greedy. Evil.

Death's greatest match.

And yet, the most beautiful being he'd ever laid eyes on.

Even in her manic state, with the wildness and raw terror exuding from her blood-covered body, she was everything he'd ever wanted. A Queen of the darkness and a creature straight out of his favorite nightmares. She terrified him with all that she was capable of, and he wanted to kneel before her and give her what would make her invincible.

But first…

Ana let the dead body limp to the ground as Sam approached the bars, and from inside the man's body came her iron claw. Sam stopped short, freezing, realizing she'd had the thing in her possession the entire time the night before.

In her hair.

The silver decorative claw glinted in the light coming in from the high window. She tilted her head back and brought her weapon to her tongue, licking the blood from the end.

"Good morning, Samarius," she drawled, her tone sounding of a devious tease.

Sam glanced around him lazily, raising a brow at his men dropped dead on the floor. "I see you redecorated," he said. "Did you not like the look of armored demons in the corners?"

"I like the way their blood looks on the walls better," she returned. "Gives this *dreary* dungeon a pop of color."

She turned then and ran her hand across the wall, letting the blood on her skin stain the stone, and her teeth flashed at him beneath the wild hair when she looked at him over her shoulder. He opened his mouth to speak, but—

Ana lunged at the bars.

Sam flinched as she threw herself against them. The iron from her claw scratched the bar, causing sparks, and she laughed in a growling snarl that then echoed around the room with every hitch. She hung herself from her clenched fists around the rods, leaning back and exposing her neck to the ceiling.

"Samarius Cain…" she drawled, swinging on the bars. "My father used to say your name as though it held the old magik. As though saying it too loud might summon you…"

When she straightened, Sam reminded himself not to open the cage. Her delirious grin made his stomach knot, and she folded one arm over her chest, bending her other elbow and taking a piece of her hair between her fingers.

He swallowed at the memory of how he'd once pulled that hair, snapped her back, and gripped her head. How she'd arched so fucking beautifully as he struck her ass and buried his cock in her dripping pussy. He wanted to take her then, hear that laugh and see that wicked smile come from deep within her as he tamed her chaotic self…

He would devote himself to her chaos.

Soon.

"And how did you once say my name?" Sam forced himself to ask.

She held his gaze again, a daunting, restricted chuckle sounding in the back of her throat as she twirled her curl. "Oh, Samarius… I once *worshipped* your name," she teased in a pleading breath that made his weight shift. "My final conquest and crown… I have pleasured myself to your name and the thought of ripping out your heart more times than I can count."

She launched at the bars again with a great snap, jerking as she throttled against the iron, fists wrapping around them tightly. All he could see beneath her wild, frizzed curls over her face was the lift of her full lips, the streak of white teeth behind her dangerous smile.

He cursed his own twitching cock at the sight of her true self and the fantasy she told.

And then she began singing the old witch's lullaby about him in such a sinister high pitch that chills rose over his flesh, and for the first time in his life, he felt fear.

"Tick-tock… goes the clock… to watch your world fall apart… tick-tock… in the dark… say his name and—"

"Enough," Sam seethed, and the room shook in response.

Ana laughed maniacally, her head throwing back. "What's wrong, Sam? Afraid of a little magik?"

Sam stared at her smile, growing numb at the games she intended to play. It was such a difference from the Ana he'd left screaming in the cell the day before.

Two halves of the whole woman he was utterly and tragically in love with.

"Are you over your crying?" he asked coldly.

Her smile dropped, replaced with rage and fire in her eyes that he knew the words had triggered such seething inside her. Ana lunged at

272

the bars, an audible growl leaving her with the thrust of her palms against the iron.

"Over my crying..." She reared back and launched spit into his eyes. "Do you not see the dead demons around you?"

Sam wiped the spit from his eyes with a handkerchief. "Yes, tell me, my Temptress, how did you kill my demons?"

Her lips tugged at the corners, obviously excited she had mystified him. "You think my father raised me only to take kingdoms?" She chuckled softly. "He raised me in the wastelands of Icemyer after the Firemoor legions cleansed the eastern edge. I was raised by witches and demons of your own making... I know everything about you."

"You know nothing about me," Sam said coldly.

"I know you ran after this last war because you were scared. I know you hid your demons and asked them to take a vow of silence. I know how you condemned those witches and left them to—"

"Lies," he hissed.

He had to quell the shake his bones so desperately needed to let out. But he wouldn't let her see him rage. He wouldn't let her see how she affected him.

No matter how blatant the lies of her witches had been.

"Then tell me the truth," Ana challenged.

Sam considered her a long moment, unwilling to let his face show any sort of emotion, and he nearly told her everything. He nearly told her how he'd been created. How witches had trapped him in this form so long ago. He nearly told her how he'd built himself an army to one day take revenge.

But he pulled a smoke from his pocket and merely lit the end of it and allowed that first draw's fog to sit in his open mouth a moment before speaking again.

"I'm glad you're liking the accommodations enough to decorate," he taunted, his voice flat. "It's always nice when people are so accepting of their new homes."

Ana's eyes blazed. "If you think this cell will hold me—"

"I don't plan on holding you," he cut in.

"What are you talking about?"

Sam smirked at the confusion on her face. "You think I'm going to let you escape?"

"I think you'll be too busy protecting your kingdom to care what happens to me."

"You're wrong."

"And why is that?"

"Because I'm going to give you to them," he seethed. "I will dangle your pretty little body in front of those fucking kingdoms and watch them march themselves into my trap."

She laughed that laugh that made his insides curl.

"You don't know the Firemoor legions," she drawled. "He will march in here after me, and if you think he will stop at taking my head, you're wrong. I heard General Prei's plans before I killed their King. Every one of them wants your technology. They want your people. They want to know how the King of Shadowmyer has such a prosperous kingdom."

She pushed off the wall and came to stand in front of the bars again.

"I don't even have to kill you to bring your kingdom down," she teased in a sing-song voice. "All I have to do is be here. In your prison. They'll take it down for me. They'll rip each other apart trying to be the first one here, to be the person to finally kill me. Because they all want that glory. To prove their cocks are as big as their egos. And the only person that will be left standing is me." She paused at the bars, hands sliding up the iron like they once slid over his cock, fingers wrapping and tightening with the teasing gaze in her eyes.

"I will *dance* on the ashes of your kingdom while you pray at my feet."

"The only person that will be praying is you, and it will be for my scythe across your throat," he growled.

"There are a few nights I'll never forget," she snapped.

He slammed his hands against the iron bars, shadows curling on the floor. "You will beg for me, wicked girl. And not from your knees for salvation. But rather from your stomach. Your bleeding cheek will feel the floor beneath my boot—"

A sinister laugh left her. "How many times have you gotten off at that image?"

"You will *plead* for Death's mercy, Deianira."

"Stop talking about yourself in the third person, Samarius," she drawled as she turned in her circle and glared back over her shoulder. "Someone might think you're just a fairy tale."

"A nightmare."

"A *monster*."

His dark eyes traveled over her, deliberately up and down, making her shift as if she were remembering how his eyes had once devoured her existence.

"Don't look at me like that," she warned.

"Like what?"

"Like you ever loved me," she hissed.

Nausea swept over him. It spiked his forehead with a chilling sweat, and he clamped his arms around his chest as his shadows navigated over the floor to the dead bodies.

Within seconds, the bodies were gone, along with the blood, including that on Ana's shirt and body. And when it was cleaned up, he watched as she sank to the floor on the opposite side of the cage.

"Do you remember the day you took me to the sunset?" she asked, now picking at the blood beneath her nails.

But Sam couldn't let her under his skin yet. "Don't do this, Ana," he said.

"How did you make it feel so real?" she ignored him. "The day Rolfe gave me this tattoo... the day I marked you... I nearly gave up everything."

"So why didn't you?" And he knew he might be walking into a trap.

"I wasn't ready," she admitted. "I wasn't ready to give up the life I'd always been running towards just for a stupid boy."

Sam's eyes locked onto hers, feeling the pain in his heart of her admission, wary of its truth.

"You never had to," he finally said.

He backed away before she could say more, knowing any words from her might be the ones he wanted to hear.

Chapter Forty-Seven

Ana let her head sag on her neck as she held in the quietness, with only the drips of water and thunder rumbling every now and then sounding around her. She'd tried to go to sleep, but all she could see on the now clean cot was how it had been covered in blood earlier, and the thought nauseated her so that she couldn't bring herself to curl up in it.

So she'd sat on the floor, knees pulled into her chest, and stared at the ceiling.

The hollow sound of music seemed to beat against the stone walls like it were a person pounding on a door to be let free. Sometimes heavy metal, sometimes haunting classical music. The classical... the shrieking violins and organs... She hated and loved Sam all over again for playing it. It shattered her heart with the memory of the night of the symphony. And yet... every time she heard it, her entire body broke out with goosebumps.

The door up the stairs opened, and the melody blared down the stairs. Free of its cage as she only wished to be. Whomever it was started to close the door, but Ana desperately wanted to hear the music, even with the pain it caused her.

"Leave it open," she called out loudly.

The hinges creaked, but the music didn't lessen behind a wall this time, and quiet footsteps carried down the stairs.

Ana closed her eyes and tried to drown herself beneath the wailing trombones, the screeching violins, the pounding of the drums... She didn't bother looking to see if it was Millie, Rolfe, or another one of Sam's demons descending toward her. All that existed was the chill of that room and the sound carrying over her flesh.

"It's from his favorite drama," came Millie's voice. "Beautiful, really. We were there on opening night."

"That was eighty-seven years ago," Ana said. She rolled her head in Millie's direction, finding the blonde in casual street clothes as she stood on the other side of the cage, arms crossed over her chest. "People say Death was last seen publicly during the riots that night."

"It's true," Millie said. "I remember the painting that was done after. Beautiful oil on canvas. Dark colors, although she did capture the colors of the witch fires. One of them was a violent shade of green." She looked down to Ana's sitting figure. "I think you would appreciate it. I'll have to show you."

Ana didn't reply. She wasn't sure she was ever getting out of there, and if she did, why would Sam allow her to walk the halls or learn anything about his kingdom?

Millie crossed her arms over her chest after sitting in the chair.

"You knew who I was the entire time," Ana said, smiling upwards. "Why didn't you just kill me?"

Millie considered her. "I liked you too much," she admitted. "And I don't play with my King's things."

"I'm not his *thing*."

"Yes, you are," Millie countered. "The morning after you showed up was the first time I'd seen that glint of power back in his eyes. Like he was itching to use it. Back in the game…" Millie laughed softly. "You brought him back to life. He finally had a purpose again. He was no longer just meandering through the darkness."

Ana didn't reply. She stared at her hands, picking the blood from beneath her nails.

"Did you know he saved me?" Millie asked.

Ana's eyes narrowed in her direction. "What are you talking about?"

Millie let out a quiet huff, pushing her hands together as her heel began to tap. "Of course you don't," she muttered. "I imagine there is a lot you do not know about him. About the things he's done."

"Are you planning to tell me or are you just here to watch me piss myself?" Ana snapped.

Millie glared at the woman in the cage. "Sam was once employed by the Moorian King, King Atrion," she said. "He was a slave to the voices in his head and his… talents. But what Atrion didn't know was that Sam was building an army of demons to one day pull him out. When he was found out, King Atrion tried to burn Sam's wings. Not long after, war broke out with the Moors, and Sam… Sam escaped. He tried to take his revenge and failed so many times. The last thing he did before shadowing this place was to create demons from the men lying in their last breaths in ditches and promise them a free, immortal life… if only they worked for him. And we did." She sat back in the chair with a heavy sigh. "Sam found me clawing my way out of a hole I'd been forced into before the battle broke out. Men had bet on me fighting other women for entertainment. I'd killed out of survival, but at least that had been better than the servitude King Atrion sold me into. I was weak. Starving. A few dead soldiers had fallen into the pit with me. Fuck, the stench was unbearable. When Sam discovered me, he took the souls of the resting soldiers as payment, and then offered me the choice."

"How did you come to be in Atrion's grasp?" Ana asked.

"Atrion found me as a child after he'd burned my entire village. I was the only one left. I fought those soldiers, and I guess… I guess he liked my refusal to die. So, he sold me to the southern army in the hopes that they'd break me."

Ana considered the blonde demon sitting in that backwards chair, curling a strand of hair around her finger like the hair was power in itself.

"What kind of demon are you?" she decided to ask.

Something shifted behind Millie in the darkness. Ana didn't see what made the movement until she felt something twisting in her hair. She flinched, but didn't jump or move away. She knew by the coy smile on Millie's face what it was.

Her tail.

Ana watched as Millie ran her hands through her hair, and within her white-blonde locks were two curled black ram's horns. Talons elongated on her slender fingers. Her features sharpened to points, accentuating her already sharp cheekbones and perfect brows. And when she stood from the chair, Ana hated herself even more for how much she liked this woman.

Milliscent was a goddess among demons. Genuinely terrifying and intensely stunning. She had no doubt that people would fall to their feet before her if she appeared like this to their Council or the people. And standing beside Sam…

The beginnings of what nightmares were made of.

"You should stay in this form," Ana said, looking Millie up and down.

Millie turned her hand over as if studying her fingers. She looked like she might say something, but the demon just shook every part of her body like a wet dog, and she turned back into her regular self.

"If we were to all walk around in our true forms, we'd be easily targeted by any spies inside our borders," Millie said, sitting back down again. "And while we've never had to worry about being killed in the past, now..." Something clouded her eyes, but she seemed to collect herself. "Let's just say it's a good thing Samarius gave us the ability to shift."

Ana caught the hesitation in Millie's voice, but didn't press whatever had changed. "Don't people recognize you as the ones that never age?" Ana asked.

"If a spy was around long enough for that, we're not very good at our jobs," Millie said. She looked back down at her hand, at the talons that lingered. "You know, Sam and I share empath powers," she told her. "Unlike him, I have to be touching the person. Unlike him, I am unable to see visions of what they're thinking about. I can only get feelings, but like Samarius, I can make people see what I want them to see, and sometimes ease their pains." Her lips quirked upward like she was reminiscing about the past. "One of the small talents he gave me when he saved me."

"What are the others?" Ana asked.

Millie's lashes lifted, and she met Ana's eyes. The wicked glint in her gaze should have chilled Ana to her core, but it only made Ana more intrigued. "Maybe one day soon, you'll find out," Millie said.

"Why didn't you tell me about this the day we talked?" Ana asked. "You were so bent on defending him... you could have told me all of this to win me over. Make me think him more than the stories I had been told. Why didn't you?"

"Because I wasn't sure I trusted you enough to know his true self," Millie replied. "You should know how much we love him. We would all do anything for him after the things he's done for us. Even those in the camps and prisons. He gave us all a second chance." Millie leaned back in her chair and took in Ana's figure again, heel tapping on the floor.

"What do you really want, Deianira?" Millie asked. "Truly. Now that you're here and you know who he is, some of what he's done, perhaps even have fallen in love with him... You were willing to give up that love for greed once." Her head tilted, and Ana resisted arguing. "What do you want?"

"Revenge," Ana whispered without thinking.

Revenge.

Such a small word, and yet it held so much. It had slipped from her lips so easily, speaking such truth. It called to her soul and ignited her flesh. She had been built for that word. Every minute of her existence was predicated on that very concept.

"On?" Millie asked.

Ana met Millie's eyes as she went through the list of people she'd been told she should eradicate from this world. She went through the list of beings her father had once put on her. The list the witches had put on her.

"I don't mean who you have been told to seek it for," Millie said, apparently knowing where Ana's mind had wandered. "I mean you. Deianira Bronfell. The girl who once told me she'd known the people being dragged away to the camps. Been friends with those persecuted in the other realms. Who will that girl seek revenge upon?"

Ana considered it, going all the way back to the day that stoked all these flames. The day that triggered her father's desperation for her to become who she would be. She could still feel the heat on her cheeks. Hear the cracking of her home all around her.

"Firemoor," Ana answered.

Millie's smile spread, and she rose to her feet. "You'll need a crown. And an army." Her talon grazed the iron bar, creating sparks, and Ana's head tilted.

"Lucky for me, your king has both of those," she taunted.

Millie paused. "Decide how you want to acquire those things, now that it's all at your fingertips for the taking," she said. "Will you try by force again? Or will you accept the hand that's offered?"

Ana didn't get a chance to question what the demon meant before Millie disappeared up the winding steps. She sank her head back onto the wall and thought about it as the music lulled her aching mind.

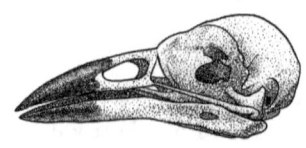

Sam stared at the live broadcast of his demons strung up in Firemoor's capital, his chair swerving back and forth, fingers steepled together. Every time he saw them, his anger heightened. Between this and the disaster happening down in his dungeon, his patience was starting to wear thin.

His phone rang, and Sam sighed at the name that popped up.

"Jay," he answered, knowing what was about to happen.

"Sam," Jay's voice seemed timid, like he was anxious about whatever was on his mind. "I was wondering if you'd seen Ana today," he continued. "She didn't show this morning. I've called her a few times. Thought maybe the two of you had run off together."

He was trying to sound light-hearted, and Sam caught the worry.

"Ah... we actually broke up last night," Sam said.

He wasn't totally lying.

"Oh," Jay replied. "Oh... I'm worried now. What if she ran away? What if something happened? Was she okay—"

"Jay, I really don't know," Sam interjected, trying not to let his tone get the best of him. "We were both upset. Things were said... if I hear from her, I'll let you know. Call me when she turns up. I'm sure she's okay."

Sam hung up the phone before he had to lie or listen to Jay's worry about Ana any longer.

His door creaked, and Millie walked in with a couple of drinks in her hands. She said nothing as she crossed to the chair by his desk and sat the glasses on the top.

"You're still watching this?" she muttered.

"How did the chat go?" he asked, unwilling to talk about why he continued to put himself through the torture.

Millie sighed into the supple armchair. "You two have a lot to talk about," she said, meeting his blank eyes.

"Like what."

"Like how she knows nothing about your past, and you know nothing about hers," she said. "And yet... you love her."

"Would you like me to argue with you and tell you all the reasons why I fell in love with her?"

"I'd like that, actually," she said, smile on her lips. "I'd love to know what Death looks for in a wife."

Sam almost smiled, his attention going back to the television. The green substance in their wounds seemed to be dwindling from its bright hue. Millie followed his gaze.

"What do you think it is?" Millie asked.

"What does your witch say it is?" he asked, glancing at her sideways.

"Ancient magik," Millie shrugged. "I didn't want to interrogate her."

"Maybe you should," Sam said, annoyance in his tone.

Millie sat up in the chair and stared at him. "Something you'd like to say?"

"You know your precious Cordelia sold Ana a dagger with the enchantment in it, don't you?" Sam blurted, growing tired of stepping around it.

"What?" Millie stiffened.

Sam lifted his shirt, revealing the still healing wound he'd received from Ana that night, then craned his neck to show her the slice across his throat.

"Ana tried to kill me with the same substance as the one in those demons' wounds in Firemoor," Sam said. "I figured it out when I could still feel the wound an hour after. Rolfe had seen her going into the shop on Third a few times." He straightened, watching Millie process it all. "You want to continue defending them now?"

"Cordelia hasn't used it on me," Millie argued.

"Maybe she hasn't felt the need to yet."

"Sam—"

"Milliscent," he snapped. "You say they do not mean us any harm, and I want to believe you. I have left them alone in this realm because I know what would be done to them in any other. But I need you to see this as I do, too."

Tears lined Millie's eyes, tears that broke his fucking heart. He sighed heavily and pressed his hands into the back of his chair.

"Just be careful," he said softly. "Please," he begged. "I have never had to fear losing you or Rolfe, but this... And with whatever lullaby they taught Ana while she was in Icemyer... I am scared," he admitted. He stared at the desk for a moment, collecting his thoughts and trying to put them into words. "Watching those demons tortured like that... I can't take seeing that happen to either of you. At least the ones Ana killed here were mere ghosts of themselves from the graveyard."

"Do you think that song will work on a thriving demon?"

"I don't know," he admitted. "But that substance... whatever magik the witches found... It hurt *me*. I could still feel it burning an hour after."

"Drain her, Samarius," Millie blurted out. "She wants revenge as we do. You have to drain her. You have to bind Ana to your existence."

Sam glanced back to the television. "Soon," he repeated.

"You—"

"The Firemoor extraction won't take long," he said, cutting her off with a glare. "We get in and out. No lingering. Rolfe will stay here to make sure Ana doesn't try anything. You and I are going in."

Millie seemed to drop her argument about Ana with this, and she crossed one leg over the other. "What's the plan?"

Sam stepped around the desk and settled on the front. "One great thing about these three being so near their ends is that I'll be able to shadow them once we're close enough. I can send them back here without ever having to step into that fucking capital."

"How close is close enough?"

His eyes met hers, jaw twisting. "We'll have to go across the border. Across the Spine and into Firemoor."

"*Fuck*," Millie said, drawing the word out as she slumped back.

But Sam just stared at her with a glitter of nostalgia in his eyes. "Days like this, I miss only being a shadow."

Millie looked like she might chuckle but thought better of it. "Don't be stupid, Samarius," she said. "Your shadow didn't have that nice dick you like getting wet so much."

Sam chuckled breathily, happy that he had eased her mood a little. "We leave at dusk tomorrow. Get some rest."

Millie shook her head. "I'll make some calls. We'll need help."

Chapter Forty-Eight

Sam sat in his office for as long as he could stand it that next day.

He stared at the television, at his demons, and fantasized about what he would have to do that night. He went through every scenario of what could go wrong, trying to make plans for every sore thought.

But he was staring at General Prei holding a news conference when he noticed something he hadn't before. Prei had a scar on his neck in the jagged shape of a star. It was so familiar, and yet, he'd never met Prei. Had never been anywhere near him. But this scar…

"You son of a bitch," Sam drawled, snapping to the edge of his seat.

It couldn't be…

He pushed to his feet and hit pause on the television, practically jumping over his desk to get closer. And when he did, when he poured over every detail on the man's face, at the starred scar on his neck, the tick of his jaw…

He knew he was right.

"I've fucking got you, you bastard," he hissed to the image.

"Got who?" came Rolfe's grunt from the door.

Sam did a double-take to his friend coming inside the office carrying a food tray. He plopped it down and raised an expectant brow to Sam when he didn't reply.

"It's nothing," Sam muttered, running his hands through his hair.

"Took your woman some food this morning," Rolfe said. "Figured you didn't want her starving."

All thought of what Sam had just figured out went away at the mention of Ana. "I don't," he sighed. "How is she today?"

"Mean," Rolfe said, to which Sam tilted his head in confusion.

"Mean?"

"Yeah," Rolfe said as if it shouldn't have surprised him. "Threw the food I made for her back in my face. Said she should have recognized the smell of pet dog when she first met me."

Sam resisted his laughter, and Rolfe glared at him.

"Sorry," Sam managed, stifling a smile. "What did you say?"

"Told her she'd look like a right pretty pet on her hands and knees when she got hungry," the hound replied.

Sam clapped his friend on the shoulder. "We need to work on your comebacks if she's to make a home here."

"Is she?" Rolfe asked.

A quiet moment filled the space as Sam thought about it. "That's up to her," he decided.

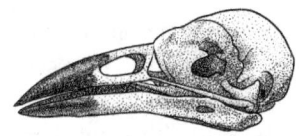

Sam waited another couple of hours before making his way down to the dungeon to see Ana. He'd brought up previous video clippings General Prei, some before the king died, and some after, and he'd compared them.

Because if he was right…

He pushed every thought of his suspicions to the back of his mind as he opened that creaking iron door and down the steps. Ana was sitting crouched in the corner on top of the cot, her forearms braced over her knees, hands clasped together. But as soon as she saw him, she stalked down that bed like a cat awaiting prey and stepped up to the bars.

"Samarius," Ana acknowledged, her hands gliding over those circular bars.

"Deianira," Sam replied. He eyed the delicate way she touched those bars, the wide way her pupils blew when he met her gaze. The tattoo on her wrist glared back at him. A constant reminder of a time when he'd thought he could avoid this part and simply bring her home instead.

A distant dream.

For a second, neither spoke. A slow trickle of water dripped down the hall, echoing off the stone, and Ana shifted her feet.

"How long are we going to do this?" she asked, her voice a little softer than he expected.

"Do what?" he asked.

"Pretend as if this isn't killing the both of us," she replied.

His jaw ticked. "I wasn't aware you were capable of feeling such hurt."

Her chest and arms slumped, and she took two steps back. "Me... Like you're any better." Her voice was low, hollow, and as she began to walk aimlessly around the cell, Sam stuffed his hands in his pockets and prepared himself for whatever hurt might come next.

"You should have taken the water Rolfe brought down," Sam said. "Although, you do look *lovely* covered in dried blood," he sneered, his head tilting.

The confident smile broke on her lips before she threw back her head to laugh. "My love... wait until you see me in a crown—Your crown, I should say. I think you'll come at the sight of it."

"Good luck finding it," he said. "I've not worn it for centuries."

"So humble," she pouted.

"How do you plan on finding it when you're locked in here?"

Ana stopped pacing long enough to give him a toothy grin that sent her pupils darkening and her chin high. "Oh, Samarius..." she said, dragging out his name in a taunting breath. "You're going to give me everything I want."

"Why?"

"Because you want me as your Queen." She stepped in front of him. "Tell me I'm wrong."

Sam stared at her a long moment. "You should be on your knees begging for forgiveness," he said.

"For breaking your heart?" She snorted. "Come now, Samarius. You —"

"Why should I trust you enough to give you that crown?" he interrupted her. "You chose your greed over me once. Why would you not do it again?"

Ana shifted again, arms crossing over her chest. "Because, unfortunately, you are Death." She shook her head, almost laughing at the ceilings, and she sank down to the ground by the bars, her knees pulled into her chest. "Every time someone said that's who you were, I thought them lying. I thought them full of fairytales and speaking of a creature that could not exist. Because how could such a monster be real?"

No matter how often he'd called himself that word, hearing it from her made his heart constrict. It hurt him to know that she thought of him as that.

Sam turned and grabbed a chair from the shadows, plopping himself in it beside her sitting on the other side of the bars.

"I never thought such a monster could be so beautiful," she whispered, and there was a pain in her breaking voice.

"Why do you think me a monster?"

An amused huff left her as she looked down at her hands, picking skin from her nail, and he watched as a tear fell down her cheek when she replied, "Because every time I begged Death to take me, I never received an answer," in a tone barely comprehensible.

Her words hit him like a dagger to the heart. He leaned over his knees toward her, nearly collapsing at the weight of what she'd just said, realizing perhaps the scars on her thighs had not been the full extent of her terror, remembering how she'd begged on her knees over his dead body...

He met her gaze, and his heart broke for her. For his Ana. For every time she'd looked at life and thought the darkness better than the next moment.

"And I *have*," she managed, voice cracking and high-pitched. "I have pleaded over and over. Every time I was told who I had to be, of the things I would have to do and endure, I got on my knees to beg and *bargain*. And when my father was taken before me, I asked Death to take me too. Because while I was free of him, I had to do the things he left for me to survive."

Saliva stuck in Sam's throat. He couldn't swallow or move. And he wanted to. He wanted to go to her and take her in his arms. He wanted to hold her and tell her she would never again feel that way. That she did not have to live that life anymore.

She could be free to love and live and be at peace.

"I have bled my body and walked off cliffs," she continued. "I have endured men's pleasures when they had no use for me except what was between my legs. I have laid beneath them and pleaded for my knife to slip after I took out their hearts, hoping that blade would come down on me instead..."

"You *are* worth living for, Ana," he finally managed.

"Not as the life I have lived," she whispered. She locked eyes with him, and his shadows circled around her, almost a comfort, if Death could give such a thing.

"You are a monster, Samarius. But…" she looked down at her wrist, rubbing the tattoo on her skin that he had put there. "But you're my beautiful monster. And I…" She pushed her hand into her hair, moving it off her face as she seemed to laugh at herself in disbelief. "I have always been in love with Death…" she whispered, meeting his gaze. "I just didn't know it was you."

Sam held her gaze.

He swallowed at the words she said and how she said them, his clammy hands rubbing together as he carefully spoke.

"When people beg for me… it's not usually a challenge as you called to me the other night," he said slowly, lashes lifting to her. "It's usually a prayer. Cathartic and euphoric. As though one tiny push over the edge will release every pain they've ever felt. And I wait it out with them. I hold them in my shadows as they teeter on that final second until they remember that life…" he gestured to the vacant air "…*all of this*… It's worth it. Because what is greater than that edge is having the strength to go on. It's fighting and defeating your own monsters, your own haunted dreams. And knowing… knowing whatever pains and struggles you might face, you can make it."

Ana wiped a tear from her cheek, sniffling back her tears. "And those that don't?"

Sam hesitated. He thought of them. Of those begging on their knees, and those he'd looked into the past of. Bearing the hurt of their lives and trying to ease some of it, if only for a moment. To the ones he'd looked at and given a choice. To the ones who had chosen to go on into a new beginning instead of an extension of this life and to live as one of his demons as both Millie and Rolfe had chosen to.

And to the ones he'd cradled in his arms and wiped their tears away as they pleaded for it all to stop.

"We fall together."

Ana watched him, and he could tell by the glisten in her eyes and the way she glanced up at the ceiling that she was shaking. Uncontrollable tears dripped down her cheeks. Like something had broken within her, and while he could hear Millie calling him an idiot in the back of his mind, he couldn't stop himself.

Sam opened the dungeon door and dropped to her side, and Ana…

Ana shattered. She crumbled into sobs, and she fell into his arms.

Death held her.

He held her as he had never held her before. He came to her as she had begged for her entire life.

"Let me fall," she whispered into his chest, her hands gripping at his shirt. He wrapped his arms tighter, chin settling on her head, his shadows curling even more as he and they enveloped her into an embrace she could not turn away from.

"Let me fall. *Let me fall*," she continued to sob.

Sam's heart broke. He pulled back and cupped her face in his hand, seeing her pleading expression's desperation and ruined rawness. She gasped on a high-pitched breath, her face so wet with tears that Sam felt himself drowning before her.

"No," he whispered. "I won't."

"*Please.*" The word was a choked breath, those green eyes so bright and sad, mascara running down her cheeks. "You should have let me go that night," she whispered. "You should have taken me for all that I had done."

He wondered if she had ever let herself go like this. If after everything she'd done and felt, she'd held it all in and simply pushed on to the next thing.

Sam swallowed and shook his head. He shook his head at the thought of life without her. At the thought of going back to the mundane routine he'd been in for centuries. At the thought of never seeing her face again or holding her in his arms.

And he swore right there that he would never return to that life.

"I won't let you go," he whispered.

She fell into his arms again, and his own tears streaked his cheeks as he rocked her in that cold cell, with no more than the purple dusk coming in from outside.

Ana calmed down after a while, but Sam didn't let her go. He held her closer, listening to her tears stop, stroking her hair and kissing her head. He wouldn't let her go. He wanted her to know he was there.

That he would hear her, he would *always* hear her.

"Why you?" Sam asked once it seemed her tears had stopped. "What made your father think you were the one to do all this? Why not someone else?"

Ana shifted in his arms. "I was an only child," she began. "My father worked in the mines after the fire legions took over northwest Firemoor. He used to come home with burns all over his body from their whips. We were poor. Starving." Her lashes lifted up to his, their eyes meeting, and she leaned her head against the wall instead of his chest. "I will not speak badly of him because he wished me a better life. He wanted more for our community and for me... He wanted revenge for all those that had been oppressed for years."

She swallowed and held a breath, and Sam let her take the time she needed to get it all out.

"I cradled that vengeance," she continued. "I stirred it and I held it. I learned everything I could from the witches and the demons, the soldiers that turned on their kings... And I climbed my way through their ranks, one kill at a time. Until the princes fell at my feet and the kings begged me to choose them in the tunnels. In secret, and in plain sight."

"What was the end game?" Sam asked. "What was to be after you'd taken me?"

Her eyes moved to his. "Power over life itself," she whispered.

Sam didn't blink away from her. "Go on," he found himself saying.

"With you..." she began, almost hesitantly. "With you, I could keep them all suffering endlessly. They would feel how we felt all those years—the people they enslaved, whipped, and marked. You... *Death*... you could hold them all at their edges and make them beg as we did. A never-ending cycle of gasping breaths and agony. Fearful of their next moments and pleading for it to end."

She stared at him a moment, and Sam let the words sink in.

"You were my last crown because I meant to use you, not kill you. You were always meant to be a thing I could control."

He thought he'd been in love with her before.

He thought he knew all there was to know.

But this...

Fuck, he nearly got down on one knee right then.

And suddenly, it was all he wanted. He had always wanted the kingdoms, but this sounded even sweeter. To watch the line of kings that had once tried to take his wings suffer endlessly. Over and over again. By his doing and hers.

"Sam."

Millie's soft tone broke the daze he'd fallen into. He forced his gaze away from the knowing look in Ana's eyes, his chin jerking to his shoulder.

"It's time to go," she said.

Sam looked to Ana, noting a question in her gaze, a silent wonder if all they'd just shared made any difference to her fate.

But he remained indifferent. Forced himself to not reveal anything on his cold expression.

His eyes looked to the floor as he stood and released her. The warmth of her vacated, her eyes watching him move, but he didn't say anything as he exited the cell.

The bell on Luna's collar jingled as she pranced down the stairs looking for him. She bounded into Millie's arms and then jumped straight to Sam's shoulders as he rolled the cage shut behind him. Sam didn't flinch when the bold cat curled her tail around his neck, her claws digging just slightly in his skin to balance herself.

Ana rose to her feet, staring at the midnight cat sitting so pointedly on Sam's shoulder, now licking her paw, and Sam paused on the other side of the bars.

"Rolfe will bring you dinner," he said plainly. "And before you get any ideas about attempting to spray the rest of this dungeon in blood, let me make one thing clear: If you touch Rolfe, Milliscent, or Luna... It won't matter how I feel about you," he warned. "You will *never* see that relief of darkness as you sit at the edge, day in and day out. Everything you just said you wanted for those kings... it will be your suffering. Not theirs."

"I wasn't aware Death had attachments," she seethed.

"No one touches the things I love."

Chapter Forty-Nine

Traffic melted behind Sam and Millie as they sped east. Past every small village on the outskirts of town, through the winding hills and the desolate shadowlands. All the way to the grand decaying forest at his borders.

Sam shut the engine of the pickup truck they'd driven off at the very edge, and he took his helmet off as he admired the expanse. Thick fog reflected from the moonlight and entwined between the great roots lifting and pulling out of the ground like the trees meant to walk. Black trees, webs on the trunks like they were diseased, though Sam knew they weren't. He knew it was the creatures inside marking their territories. Creatures that, left to the woods and the darkness and the violence of their own agressions had evolved into what most called monsters.

The border of Shadowmyer was a nightmare in itself.

Millie let out a low whistle as she stood beside him. "I forgot how haunting this place is," she said.

Quiet noises of flapping wings and shuddering growls entered Sam's ears. He lifted his hand toward the wood, extending his fingers, and when he enclosed a fist, the fog parted ways before them.

With a step back, he held open his palm to Millie. "After you," he told her.

The wood swallowed them as they entered. He left the moon uncovered to guide them through. Sam could feel the creatures lurking all around, feel their starvation and thirst for blood. Broken limbs and leaves crunched under their feet, but nothing bothered them for most of the walk.

Despite his trying to think only about the task he was about to be faced with, Sam's mind continued to wander back to that cell. To everything Ana had just confessed, to the way he'd held her breaking body in his arms.

"Do you want to explain why you were in the cage with her?" Millie asked as they stepped over roots.

"We were talking," he said, his mind going back to what Ana had revealed to him.

"Did you find out what she wants?" Millie asked.

"The same thing we want," Sam said, and Millie paused to look back at him. Their eyes met beneath the moonlight and Millie gave him a smile.

"Don't," Sam said, knowing where she was going.

"Oh, why not Samarius?" she said, voice teasing. "Cut her throat already. Bring her back as this Ballad you've always spoken of—*dreamed* of. Offer her the world."

"After this week, she may not want the world with me," he said solemnly.

"She does," Millie said. "Rolfe told me how nervous you were the other day. When you were going to tell her."

Sam ran a hand through his hair, wet dirt squeaking beneath his boot as he stepped over a large tree root. "Rolfe is full of shit."

Millie laughed. "He said you even considered dusting."

A heavy breath blew from his lips as he shook his head. "I'll neuter him when we get back," he grunted.

"I think she'd love the dust," Millie said. "But you have to let her out of the cage to see it."

"Maybe we should be focused on the insanity we're about to deal with," Sam suggested.

"This is much more fun," she argued. "I love seeing you squirm. It's how I know how much she truly means to you."

Sam picked up a pile of dirt from the ground and threw it at her.

Walking the forest expanse took most of the night. By the time they were nearly at the Spine border, they'd seen two herds of decaying deer through the mist, a couple of vultures overhead, but nothing had come out to attack them.

The sound of military trucks was how they knew they were at the border before the shadows even ended. Sam's arm crossed Millie's chest, his shadows warping their figures behind them as they approached. The pair paused, crouching at the very edge behind the last darkness before dawning sunlight poured down upon the land in lilac and grey glows.

A few men were walking around under the sporadic trees, all holding guns and looking toward the east. Some others huddled around in a circle and ate. There was one, though, that seemed to be pacing along the border, looking to the west unlike the others.

A tall man with dark brown hair pulled up into a bun atop his head. A thin brown beard covered his slim jaw. The sunrise seemed to purr over his golden-brown skin as he held the rifle at the ready.

Millie rose to her feet before Sam could stop her and whistled.

The man's head jerked in their direction, then he took another look around at the other men before he whistled back.

Sam hadn't seen this demon in person for two centuries, though he'd seen him on video just weeks before.

Damien.

Millie emerged from the shadows before Sam, carefully looking around upon stepping into the light. Damien's smile lit up his face, and he pulled Millie into a hug the moment she reached him.

"I was beginning to wonder if something went wrong," Damien said. "I expected you an hour ago."

Millie glanced back to Sam. "Had a late start last night," she said with a wink.

Damien met Sam with an outstretched hand, and Sam pulled him into a hug. Two claps on the back, and Sam gave him a stern nod.

"We don't have much time," Damien said. "You'll have to move in sunlight, boss."

Sam's eyes narrowed, but Damien said before Sam could question it, "Prei tipped off the armies to look for any blip of clouds or storm not forecasted," he explained.

"How are we getting across?" Sam asked.

Damien gave an upwards nod behind them, and the roar of a muffled engine sounded. Millie's grin spread wide as she popped a large bubble of her gum.

"Your chariot, Your Majesty," she mocked at the sight of the hauling dump truck.

The brakes ached when it came to a stop, the doors opening to reveal two men Sam vaguely remembered stepping out of it.

"Inconspicuous," Damien explained. "Sorry about the dirt."

Sam just chuckled under his breath. "Millie's always complaining about the state of my jackets," he said. "I imagine it'll take more of a toll on her than me. Imagine the immaculate Hand of the King getting dirty in the back of a dump truck," he teased her. "I'll make sure to take a photo for Rolfe. He'll enjoy seeing you covered in mud."

Three more demons came up behind them then, weapons in their arms. Millie's smile widened as she began strapping herself in, but Sam shook his head when he was offered the gear.

"What is the update on where our men are?" Sam asked Damien.

"Prei has them in the middle of an open field," Damien said. "Every time I step over the border, I can hear them amid all the others. Our people in Firemoor haven't been able to do their jobs as well as they'd like the past few months for fear of being caught. Tate, Trey, and Nolan were helping the injured when they were found out."

"Do we know what the green substance is?"

Damien shook his head, his sage eyes darkening. "This is the first we've seen it. Seems like it's the first time they've used it publicly. As far as what they've been doing in the prisons, I'm not sure. Who knows how long they've had it."

Sam's jaw ticked, his mind going to Ana, to the witch Millie was having an affair with, and then to the knife Ana had tried to kill him with. He's seen that green glint on the blade when she'd pulled it from his body.

"We can get you to the border," Damien continued as he loaded his own body with weapons. "There's a four-mile stretch that hasn't been occupied for a few days. I've my own men making a path for us, stationed at every checkpoint. No one has been able to get to those three. And the livestream hasn't moved since they were strung up. " Damien paused and considered Sam a long moment as Sam just stared ahead. "How exactly are you planning to get us out?" Damien asked.

"Just get me there," Sam said, plan formulating in his mind. "I'll take care of the rest."

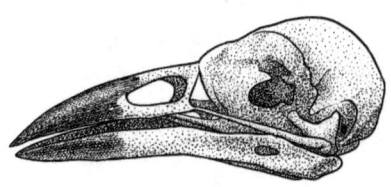

Riding through the Spine was seamless. Damien knew every guard at every stop, and they'd given Millie and Sam uniforms to blend in. There was a barrage of trucks, not just their own, that they could get in line with.

Sam couldn't stop staring out the windows.

Farms that had once been plentiful were dried up; rows and rows of army camps and barricades settled on them. The few crops that were left looked like they'd been ripped of all nutrients, like somehow, Firemoor had stripped all rain from the realm. And although Sam knew it wasn't true, he had the urge to pour thunderstorms over every mile.

The stretch Damien had told them about was easy enough to get to. They veered off from the rest of the barrage about a mile from the last checkpoint and rode down to a small farm that sat on the fencing.

"Place is deserted," Damien explained as he cut the engine, dust flying around the truck when they stopped. "I found the family about a month ago, starving. Helped them over the border into Shadowmyer so they wouldn't die. They gave me the place in exchange and told me if we ever needed a place to hide, the cellar below the last barn went under the fencing."

"It crosses?" Millie asked as she hopped out of the truck.

Damien nodded. He looked to Sam. "Think you can pull them from there?"

As Sam took in the small farm, sunlight baked on Sam's exposed skin. His eyes landed on the silver barn in the distance. "This will be different from those you left at the Spine border," Sam said. "I won't just be pulling their souls. Because they are one of us, I'll have to pull their full bodies here." He looked between Damien and Millie. "Prei will know I'm here when they disappear from the platform." His gaze lifted to the sky. "This place could use a little rain, and we could use a getaway."

"He can pinpoint where it starts," Damien warned.

"It's a chance I'm willing to take," Sam said as the wind began to pick up around them. "By the time they figure it out, we'll be halfway across the Spine, and both realms will be sopping in more mud than they've seen since the last time I was here."

"This could all be a trap," Millie muttered.

"I'm sure it is," Sam said.

"Samarius…"

"I'm not leaving without them," Sam snapped.

Millie watched Sam, her blonde hair billowing around her face.

"What happens when we get back to the border?"

"Anyone that follows us into that forest will feel the full weight of those shadows upon them," Sam said. "Open season for the starving monsters."

Damien considered the plan. "I can't help you back across the Spine."

Sam knew it would come to this, that Damien wouldn't be willing to risk exposure just yet, not when he loved this place and its people so much. Sam gave him a nod. "Millie can drive."

A smile curled on her lips. "Thunderous rain. Raging puddles. Dying demons. And you're letting me drive a big truck through all of it... Sounds like a party. Let's get started."

Chapter Fifty

The cellar was damp, dingy, and full of spiders. Millie joined Sam while Damien waited in the open air, keeping an eye on their surroundings. The border wasn't marked underground, but Sam felt it when he stepped over. He felt the dread of humans dying in secret, the terror of those at their last breaths miles away.

Even Millie grabbed her stomach and the wall as it filled her too.

"Please tell me this will be quick," she said in a strained voice.

But Sam crossed his legs beneath him and sat on the ground without responding. Quiet voices whispered in his ears as he pushed those shadows out, snaking over the grounds and mingling with the damp air.

Sam listened.

The faces of the suffering entered his mind, the pleas and the aches of their dying bodies. Just a few at first as his power wretched over Firemoor.

Five centuries. Five centuries since his power had touched this land. The ground practically buckled beneath it, the little bits of plants left withered everywhere it touched—a plague upon the realm.

Death came stalking.

Outside, clouds began to darken overhead, the temperature dropping with every swirl of the wind wreathing over the barren and broken world. Thunder rumbled as it had not in so many years.

And far, far away, as the clouds stretched their terror and encompassed the sky, as people began to whisper in fear and joy of what might have come, one man stopped his pacing on broken capital building steps.

A siren blazed somewhere in the far distance.

"Sam, hurry," Millie said at his back, and he heard the sound of her ammunition locking into place.

Sam sank further into his mind, the darkness reaching further and further along the roads, between the trees. A quiet roar of thunder skirted over the air as Sam began to lose his patience.

Where are you, he muttered to the expanse. *I've come for you. Tell me where you are.*

A jagged, wheezing and shallow gasp, filled his ears, and then he heard the woman.

Death, the woman, Tate, whispered. *Please.*

"I can see you on here," Millie's voice sounded out. "Your shadows. You have to get rid of the feed."

She must have pulled it up on her phone. Sam turned in his vision, sending his power out over that field. He looked back to Tate, and then felt the other two stirring.

I've got you, Sam promised them.

Damien shouted down the shaft to them, though Sam didn't hear what he said. He ignored the reality to focus on his demons, to get them out as he'd promised.

And just as his shadows swirled the bottom of the platform, lightning struck every tree surrounding the field.

"It's gone," Millie said. "Sam, hurry. They're—"

Sam pulled himself out of the daze as his shadows swarmed those demons, willing their corporeal bodies to his side as he'd done so many before. He snapped back to reality with a heave, his eyes clearing of scarlet, and he jumped to his feet.

Millie was behind him, her gun pointed up the tunnel, now in her horned demon form.

"Two minutes," Sam said, noting the timing it would take his shadows to bring those demons to him. He felt Millie's heartbeat beginning to pick up. "How long for us?"

"I think you may have underestimated the General," she muttered, not looking away from the target line. "Five minutes max."

Gunshots ricocheted outside.

"Maybe three," Millie corrected.

"Think they remember what rain feels like?" Sam said as his own shadows began to swarm behind him. Thunder cracked outside as Sam let go of the tether on the bursting clouds, and rain…

So much rain.

It pelted down in plops as big as his fist, as though he were slamming the earth in rage with every drop. Damien appeared again at the top of the tunnel, and he came running inside, his hand over his head, when lightning struck the tree outside.

"We have to go!" he shouted.

Sam looked back to the space he'd summoned his demons, watching as Tate formed. When she was fully transformed before them, she gasped, her eyes opening wide in fear. Sam didn't have time to explain, didn't have time to say anything as she began to panic and question and pant at being out of the chains.

"Take her!" Sam said fast. "Millie cover him. I'll get Trey and Nolan."

Damien and Millie didn't argue. Damien scooped Tate into his arms and Millie followed him up and out of the tunnel just as a surge of water came draining down into the cellar. The pair disappeared, Sam turning and waiting on his shadows to bring the other two.

"Come on, come on," he muttered, cursing the slowness he had succumbed to. Two gunshots sounded, muffled by the rain. Trey gasped as he emerged from the darkness, and Sam pressed his hands to the demon's shoulders to try and calm him down. But Trey winced with the panic and movement, falling back to the now dampening ground.

"Samarius—"

"I got you," Sam promised. "We're going home. We're just—"

"SAM!" Millie shouted down. "Sam, we have to go now!"

Nolan began to emerge. Sam held one of Trey's wounds as his friend showed himself, and when Nolan finally appeared, Millie was down the tunnel again.

"Tanks," she panted. "Two on the horizon."

"Let's get them up," he grunted, his arms under Trey. "I'll take care of it."

Damien met them halfway down and took Trey from Sam's grasp. He and Millie ran, carrying the demons to the truck where they loaded them up. And Sam…

Sam climbed the ladder on the side of the truck as Millie climbed into the driver's seat. Damien caught his arm.

"This is where I leave you," Damien shouted over the rain. "I'll hold them—"

"I can handle this. Get to the woods," Sam interjected. "You take care of these people and get home as soon as possible." He reached out and clapped Damien's hand. "Thank you."

Damien squeezed Sam's hand back, and he gave him a nod. "I'll be home in a week," he swore.

Without another word, Damien bolted through the pouring rain toward the forest where Sam knew the demon had an escape plan. Sam ensured Damien's escape with more rain and his own diversion. He hit the top of the truck twice as he climbed atop the cab, and Millie's laugh sounded as she put the truck in drive.

Sam had forgotten how chaotic a driver Millie was, but he didn't have time to think about it as the rains parted and he spotted the two tanks she'd told him about.

Millie swerved hard left, directing them out of the way and allowing Sam to focus in on the tanks as they lined in behind them. He pressed his hands to the ground, crouching to one knee, and he sent shadows swarming across the air in their direction.

The first tank flew backwards, stalling upright, the second running into it. An explosion ripped through the air, fire mixing with the pelting rain screaming over the air.

Sam stared at the explosion a moment before swinging into the cab through the open window. Millie let out a shrill holler as he shook the rain out of his hair, and then she blew the horn twice in celebration.

Flash flooding poured over the roads, melting away poorly fencing at every checkpoint. A few soldiers ran out to meet them with guns, apparently having heard Death was in the realm. But Sam washed them out with the wind and the rain. The clouds were so thick that darkness came early. And by the time they reached the western border of the Spine, it was sunset.

Five of Damien's men met them. Sam let the rain up as they cut the engine. Sam climbed out in a hurry, going to the back of the truck to check on the three they'd brought back.

But just as he did, gunshots ran out.

A gargled scream cut the air, followed by the growls of demons shifting into their more dangerous forms. Sam didn't move as his demons began their prowl.

Heads ripped, bodies shredded. The shifters leapt on their assailants and let go of every restraint they'd ever given themselves. Millie and one other woman, a fawn shifter, crouched behind a fallen tree, rifles going off as they plucked men off one by one.

Sam crawled up the ladder and laid on the top, eager to get a view of how large the legion was that had come upon them, when a familiar deathhound wretched a man's head from his body and then jumped on the truck to join Sam.

Rolfe shifted into himself, lying down at Sam's side to watch the carnage, wincing with almost every blow from the rifles so close to them.

"What are you doing here?" Sam asked. "You're supposed to be—"

"Heard it on the radios that Death had shown himself in Firemoor," Rolfe said. "Prei called to every legion to converge and hunt you down for harboring traitors."

Sam flinched at the noise of the grenade Millie had just thrown. "He's going to shit himself when he learns we have Deianira then."

Rolfe's grin widened beneath that curling mustache. "Can't wait," he grinned. "I got the truck as close as I could get it in the forest. Had to beat off a few bloodthirsty deer."

Sam took one more glance around. "I think they've got this. Let's get them loaded."

Rolfe nodded, and the pair got to work.

They ducked bullets as they dove into the back of the truck and took the injured demons out. Sam hauled Tate into his arms. She stirred, though her arms just limped in her lap. His border called to them as they pushed over it, the fog wrapping around their skin like it was welcoming them home. He laid Tate in the back of the truck and went back for Nolan as Rolfe laid Trey down at Tate's side.

Millie was on her last edge of patience when Sam made it to the back of the dump truck again. He saw her throw her empty gun aside and pulled her daggers from the straps on her thighs. Her teeth bared, and she went charging into the masses.

Sam didn't get to see much more of her except a whoosh of blood, of ripping throats and her dodging gunshots. He and Rolfe kept moving, stepping over his men healing and gathering their wits on the ground before running back into the battle.

He jumped into the back of the truck as Tate's chest rose into the air, her body convulsing slightly. He held her a moment to calm her down, promising he would have her healing soon—

A scream rang out that chilled him to his bones.

A scream that he never wanted to hear again.

A scream that put him back in the trenches five hundred years earlier.

Sam laid Tate back down and stood just in time to see Millie crash to her knees. A glint of green caught Sam's eyes, and his heart fell.

"Millie!"

Sam bolted out of the truck and out of the forest. He ran straight into the battle, watching the man standing over Millie as she held her side, blood pouring from the deep wound on her body. Pain stretched her features. Agony in her gritted teeth.

Sam's vision went red. He shifted, his talons and teeth exposed, and he launched across the field. Slashing and breaking. He sent shadows to snap the necks of every soldier with a gun pointed his way. He ripped the flesh of any person thinking they could run. Blood sprayed the ground, the trees, the air. Soldiers turned to mist beneath the pressure of his wrath.

Death stood in the middle of a scene he hadn't seen since the last war and caught his breath. Silence rang over the air as the rain faltered, and a sunset began to appear on the horizon. And all around him, laid the shredded bodies of a Firemoor legion that would never see the bridge into a new existence.

Their souls could rot in the unknown, and he would own them.

And the man that had cut Millie... Sam caught him by the throat, snapped his neck, but—

He didn't kill him.

No, there was a special place for this man. A very special place where he would enjoy watching the red stain his floor, hearing those screams through the air.

So, Sam kept this one.

When Sam finally calmed down enough to be himself, Rolfe was over Millie, helping her to her feet. He ran in their direction, the other demons gathering their wits and groaning as they got to their feet.

So much blood covered Millie, and inside the wound.

"Shit," Sam muttered upon seeing that same emerald green hue that was in the injuries of the others. He grabbed Millie's face, lifting her chin, his heart breaking at the sight of the tears in her eyes.

"I'll fix this," Sam swore.

Millie winced, cursing that she could barely walk, and she held onto Rolfe as they moved toward the border. "I'm fine. I'll be fine," she grunted.

All Sam could do was watch Rolfe help her across the shadows and into the truck on the other side.

Sam went through and thanked every demon recovering on that field, telling them to make their way into Shadowmyer as soon as possible. That they would be hunted if they stayed in the Spine much longer, and each of them nodded in return.

On his way to the border, Sam grabbed the collar of another Firemoor soldier still sputtering out on the ground, holding onto his last breath. He dragged him and the one who had hurt Millie across the shadows.

When he reached the truck, Sam stared at his demons in the back, the green ooze spilling out of them, and then to Millie, sitting up in the passenger seat but wincing every time she touched her side.

It was one thing for Prei's armies to touch and prey on demons Sam hadn't spoken with in centuries, to the ones he cared for but was not close to.

But Millie...

Touching Millie was an act of war. Touching Millie was grounds for the slowest execution he could imagine. Touching Millie...

Rage billowed from the very marrow of his bones, and as he looked back to that border, he had to remind himself not to raise the wandering dead right then.

"Boss?" Rolfe called out from the cab of the truck.

Sam wrenched his gaze from the border back to the truck, and then to the two Firemoor soldiers he'd dragged through those shadows for questioning.

"I'll send our people back to the castle," he said, his shadows swarming their bodies. "I can drive. Run home ahead of us and see if you can get them stable. Millie and I will be right behind with our new friends."

Chapter Fifty-One

For two days, Ana had nearly driven herself mad counting the same bricks, watching the same shadows on the walls. A black cat had come down to see her earlier in the day. It had sat with her a while, comforted her with a purr, and then disappeared without another glance.

Ana had just surrendered herself to sleep when she heard footsteps on the stairs. She barely moved, thinking it was Rolfe just coming to sneak her another blanket or food. But when she heard a key in the lock and the cage door roll back, she lifted her head just so off the stone floor—

Only to be met with Sam's affirmative stature staring down at her.

She nearly bolted upright at the sight of him, his shirt covered in blood, stains on his face and neck... his eyes were almost black as he stared at her through the unruly strands of hair on his forehead, his chin dipped.

"Sam—"

"Come with me," he said, the softness of his voice not matching the danger that exuded from him at that moment.

"Where... where are we going?" Ana asked, hesitantly rising to her feet.

"I want to show you something."

He turned without another word, leaving the door open. For one brief second, Ana considered bolting to the other end of the dark hall to see if there was another exit. But a shadow wrapped her wrist and tugged her forward, and Ana didn't try to stray away.

Those same shadows kept her in check as she padded up the stairs behind him into a long dimly lit hall. The artwork on the walls and the dingy burgundy runner caught her eyes with every forced step.

Her first look inside Castle Corvus.

It had a casualness that was different from the castles she was used to. Others were grand, brightly lit and audacious, with great statues and polished floors. They had rooms that did not look as though they were ever meant to be used.

But Castle Corvus was…

Comfy.

It looked as though it hadn't been dusted in centuries, which she wondered if perhaps it hadn't. It was only two people living at the castle, after all. No servants of any kind, only groundskeepers for the cemetery.

Ana paused at one of the paintings, a newer one, or so it seemed since the dust had barely settled on it. An oil on canvas, darker colors, though it depicted a building on fire in what looked like old town… there were specs of bright green littering the entire work, and Ana realized it was the painting Millie had wanted to show her.

"Deianira."

Sam's voice cut the stiff hall, and Ana was shoved forward once more.

They passed more open doors, the old smell of leather and mahogany and dust hitting her with every step.

Nevertheless, they stopped as they approached an open door, where the noise of two people arguing sounded out into the hall. Sam paused, his hand on the doorframe, and Ana stayed confined in the shadows behind him.

Millie sat on what looked like an elegant dining table that presumably hadn't been used in years due to the number of cobwebs on the paintings, the sconces, and the most massive fireplace she'd ever laid eyes on. Compared to the rest of what she'd seen, this room had the most light coming in due to the enormous windows on the opposite side. She had a long gash on her side, and her insides were a glowing green. Rolfe stood in front of Millie with gauze, forceps, alcohol, and the rest of an old first aid kit sprawled on the table.

"Fuck all, Roll," Millie snapped when he tried to force open the wound to clean it. "You're the worse nurse."

"I could strap you down if you'd prefer," Rolfe growled.

"I would—"

"Enough foreplay," Sam cut between them. "Roll, get that shit out of her body. If you can't, call her fucking witch."

The way Sam spoke told Ana it had been one fuck up of a day. She saw a glimpse of the hurt in Millie's gaze as Millie and Sam caught one another's eyes, and she heard Sam sigh heavily.

"I'm sorry," he said in a breathy voice, and Ana squinted at the pain on his face. "Just get it out. Quickly." He took one step back and hung his head, regretting his last snap, and then Ana felt as he reached for her hand.

Almost like her touch could calm him down.

Ana didn't let go.

The shadows relaxed on her arms and swirled around them the rest of the way, through two more halls and then down a set of spiral steps.

The coppery smell of blood mixing with soil and decaying leaves hit her as Sam pushed the door open and let her walk in first.

Three bodies were strung upside down from the rafters at the back of the darkened room.

Ana couldn't stop her gasp as she followed behind Sam into what looked to be a sunroom, great dirty paned windows lining the wall. The light of the moon trickled in from the outside and cascaded over the tremendous wooden table in the middle, the porcelain tub sink at the opposite end, and the dirty tiled floor.

Dirt, leaves, and dried flowers littered the ground. Sam made no move to the three bodies, and instead, made for the one lying against the wall on the opposite side.

Ana continued to stare at the ones strung up. Their clothes had been shredded, slashes along their bodies like some great animal had mauled them. Groans left their slightly conscious bodies, the rafters creaking every time the ropes they held from shifted.

"Who are they?" Ana asked without turning away.

"People who thought me a fairy tale."

He was staring at her from a crouched position beside the man on the floor when she jerked in his direction. She noticed the way Sam looked at that man there, so unlike the disdain he held when he glared at the others, and she wondered why this one was different.

Sam looked at the man again, and she heard him whisper, "Almost there, Darion," as the man drew a jagged breath. He rose back to his feet, pushing past her to the sink.

"What is this?" she managed.

Water rushed over his hands, a solid white bar of soap foamed with every scrub on his skin as he washed them. "My job."

Ana looked to him, to the haunted man before her that took on this pain alone every night, then turned to the man on the floor.

"What happened to him?" she asked.

Sam turned off the water, using a white towel to dry his hands as he straightened. "Car accident," he answered.

"And you bring them here... how?" she asked.

"Not all," he shook his head. "It depends on the being. Darion, here, is still in the hospital in midtown. This is what the darkness will take to the graveyard here. His soul."

"You show him mercy because he has asked for his end?"

Sam nodded slowly as he reached for the lighter in his pocket and lit the joint. "Mercy would have been taking him the moment that truck struck his car," he said gruffly. "Mercy would have been not allowing his family to see him as he takes his final breaths."

"I think you're wrong," she said. "I think allowing his family to speak with him a last time is a mercy they did not know they asked for."

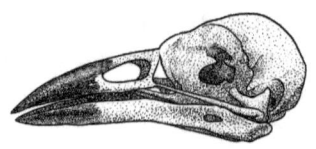

Ana crouched down in front of the man who was slowly relinquishing his last breaths. The rattle constricted the back of his throat, and he jerked every now and then. Sam usually took this moment to ask the victim if they'd prefer their end, or if they wanted to take it on their own. Either way, they would see darkness by the end of the night.

He'd just lit his smoke when he heard it.

Ana was singing.

And not the song she'd sang days before in the dungeons. This was a melody that made his heart weep. A voice so soothing and evenly pitched—

Sam had to throw the joint into the sink.

She was holding the man's hand, and he was squeezing her fingers back, eyes open and watching her. Sam stepped over the tile to the man's other side, and Ana moved behind the man as if she knew Sam's process. Her song continued as she held on, easing Darion's breaths with her voice.

And when Sam crouched down and Darion saw him, a small smile lifted his lips.

"Hey, Darion," Sam whispered, pulling his knife from his pocket.

"Sam," Darion breathed, voice sounding almost in relief. "I knew it was you."

Sam almost smiled. "You were always smarter than your brothers."

"Were..." Darion repeated. "Will you look... after my family?" he forced out.

Sam's knife tickled at Darion's skin, and he brushed his thumb against the man's cheek. "Every day," he promised. "Are you ready?"

Darion squeezed Ana's hand. "I am," came his breath.

Sam met Ana's gaze. "You may want to move," he told her.

"I'm not going anywhere," she swore.

The declaration made his chest swell, but he turned his attention away from his knotting heart down to the man before him.

"May the darkness meet you at your new beginning," Sam whispered.

The knife slid over Darion's throat, and Death took his victim.

Sam stood as Ana laid the man down and closed his eyes.

"Is it always like this?" she asked, straightening herself.

"No," he answered. "Sometimes it is a struggle... Others... other times it is no more than a blink."

"And you let them choose?"

Sam nodded.

As his shadows settled around the floor, he watched Ana. "I wanted you to see what a good death looks like," he admitted softly.

"What about those that you offer immortality to?" she asked. "You didn't offer it to him."

Sam shifted, closing his arms over his chest. "Becoming one of my demons is more than simply immortality," he said. "It's pledging yourself to a cause they may not see as worth it. It's surrendering yourself to a job for all those days, a job that you are paid for with immortal breath and abilities that most people won't see as *wholesome*."

He remembered the woman he'd mistakenly offered a demon life to. The words she spat at him, the hiss of her tongue as she called him unholy and monstrous, called his friends worse. It was one Millie had helped him with, and Millie had been devastated by the hurtful words.

He held up his hand, his talons extending from his nails. "My demons help me in other realms. They hear the call of death and take souls just as I do. Without them... without them, those existences can end up like the ones in the prison. Wandering aimlessly, becoming more vile with every day in limbo."

"You left them like that," she said, her head tilting.

Sam avoided her gaze. "I left them like that thinking that they would fester their anger and madness into something more dangerous than what they already were. And I was right."

"And the ghosts that guard this place?"

His lips lifted slightly at that. "Soldiers that Millie and Rolfe decided didn't deserve any sort of reprieve or revenge," he said. "My demons cannot offer immortality, but they can leave souls without a bridge if they wish."

"Why not do that to more than you do?"

"Not exactly good manners," and the sight of the mild amusement in her eyes and the twitch of her lips lightened his heart for just a moment. He resisted letting it relax him too much, and he continued explaining.

"People deserve that reprieve," he said. "People—" he glanced back over his shoulder at the space that Darion had sat in "—people like Darion are good. People like him... they don't deserve to be left to their own scars and wander this place with no real way to go forward."

His eyes darted over her again, the air in the room intensifying with every sweep of their lashes over one another.

"That's the song you hum," he said with a jerk of his chin. "What is it?"

"My mother once sang it to put me to sleep," she replied. "And after she died, after my father and I fled to Icemyer, the witches sang it again to me sometimes. They told me to memorize it." Ana's finger dragged along the wooden table like she was checking for dust. "I was never told why."

With the last word, her eyes met his.

"It's the same song I used to hear in my dreams," he admitted. "Years... *centuries*... ago. When the sun still shone onto this kingdom and we lived under someone else's tyranny."

Ana settled her hips against the table. "You miss it," she said. "The sun."

A slow nod came from him in confirmation. "Sometimes I wonder if you're all I was ever waiting for to remind me of how much I miss it."

She held his stare, and Sam swallowed as he gathered his next words.

"Ana, you reminded me of everything I had nearly thrown away, nearly given up on. You remind me of everything I ever wished for and promised the people under my rule. You remind me of a life not in hiding." He hesitantly stepped forward, watching her the entire time.

"I need you to understand something," Sam said slowly. "There is more happening here than mercenaries coming after you. There is more than you and me." His hands creased on the edge of the table, bending the wood. "I have demons out there dying, and I... I need your help in understanding this."

Ana's eyes narrowed. "I don't know what I can offer."

"I think you know more than you realize," Sam said. He lifted up his shirt, and Ana caught a glimpse of the scar on his chest, cutting through his tattoos, from where she'd stabbed him. Her eyes narrowed.

"How do you still have a scar?" she asked.

"Whatever was on the knife you stabbed me with is also being used on my demons in Firemoor," he said. "I know you bought it from Cordelia on Third. But I wonder what else you know about it from your time in Icemyer."

Ana's gaze hardened. "Why should I help you?" she whispered. "You plan on locking me in this dungeon and letting men torture me. Why would I tell you anything?"

"Because you are my salvation, Ana, and I can't go on another day without you in my arms," he admitted, stepping closer to her. "I can't stand another moment without your forgiveness... and I... Ana, *I'm sorry.*"

Chapter Fifty-Two

Ana's heart skipped. She couldn't discern the look on his face or why he held such agony in his eyes. But as he drew closer, she rooted to the spot. Her gaze cast down to the moonlit tile floor and the dried rose petals dusted over it.

His fingers drifted over her hand, causing her breath to catch. Just that delicate touch... that whisper of intimacy... she couldn't meet his eyes as it continued up her bare arm, from her wrist, to her elbow, shoulder, collar, and finally to her throat. She began to tremble with every stroke of his finger, every whisper of what felt like a shadow on her skin.

"Ana..." he breathed as his knuckle landed beneath her chin, and he tipped her head back to reveal the wet silver glimmer lining the bottom of his eyes. And through the darkness, she held his devastating gaze and watched as Sam slid to his knees.

Death bowed before her, holding her hand in his, and he whispered, *"Forgive me."*

Two words that weighed the room and staggered her heart. A booming declaration that seemed to crack through time. Her knees nearly gave out at the caress of his thumb across her knuckles. That beautiful way his face shadowed in pain stretched over his features. His brows knitted as he swallowed, appearing to teeter between reality and dream in front of her, and both drawing him into an agony he wasn't prepared for.

"Forgive me for all that I am... For all that I have done... and for all that I will be," he continued.

The words rang in her ears. A tear spilled over her cheek, and she watched as one crawled down his own. She reached to wipe it away, and Sam kissed her palm.

"Forgive me, Ana," he said again.

Ana's heart nearly burst. Everything they'd shared together, everything he'd shared with her since discovering who he was... All the raw pain tore her extremities to restless shreds. This... she pondered if this was the devastation the witches had warned her of. Why they had always told her he was never to be trusted or admired. If they knew she would fall for him more than she already had.

Because she had. She was utterly fallen and broken and terrifyingly in love with him. With all that he was, with everything he had done, and everything he would be.

She watched another tear trickle over his beautiful skin, the moonlight glistening off the trail over his face, and she brushed it away too.

"I forgive you."

Breath left him as if he'd been holding it for days, *years*. His shoulders limped as he rose to his feet, his forehead coming to rest against hers, and she felt him trembling as his lips brushed her own.

Just the brief friction of it made her heart skip. She staggered forward to kiss him, but he pulled back slightly, dodging like he thought he might fall into a spell if he allowed himself to give in. He paused her, their breaths becoming heavy as both his hands wrapped beneath her jaw, and when he pressed his lips to hers, her knees buckled.

Sam was sheer devastation, and she willingly let herself be destroyed.

Every sweep of his tongue held her soul in it. This was worth every blip of her past, every darkened day when she'd asked for it to end. Everything had brought her to him.

He was kissing her like it was the last time he would ever see her, and she limped into his aggression and surrendered to him completely.

Their shirts were discarded to the ground. Sam pulled her leggings off one at a time, making sure to kiss her thighs, down her calves, to her feet as he crouched to undress her. She couldn't breathe as he leaned forward and hoisted one of her thighs over his shoulder, his tongue raking over her clit. But as perfect and as weak as her knees gave at the pleasure of his kiss, she needed him inside her more.

He was a tower over her when he stood, his hands wrapping beneath her jaw, lips pressing once more to hers. She worked the buckle on his jeans, freeing his hardened length and pushed herself up onto the edge of the table so he could claim her.

And he did. He pushed inside her, making her curse at the feel of him again. Different, somehow. Everything lay bared between them. They could finally be who they truly were, no holding back or secrets or lies.

But there was one thing she'd yet to hear from his lips.

"Will you say my name?" she whispered as she held his face in front of her, her jaw trembling with even mentioning it.

Sam's dark eyes met hers. He stilled fully inside her, their bodies flush, and his hand met her cheek. "Is that what you want?" he asked breathlessly. "Deianira."

He kissed her again, sending her heart fluttering, her thighs lifting and opening up more for him to drive deeper. Her ass was nearly off the table, but Sam held her steady, his pace deliberate and filling, hitting that spot inside her with every thrust. Her hips rocked into his as his mouth moved to her jaw. His hands splayed over her thick thighs, hiking them higher, and the whisper that brushed over her ear made her gasp.

"*My Deianira.*"

Hearing it ruined her.

She shattered beneath the weight of it. How it seemed to exhale from his lips as a poison, one he never thought he'd be addicted to. Thunder shook the glass as he said it again, and a tear slipped down her cheek.

"I love you," she breathed heavily into the crook of his neck.

Sam paused inside her and pulled back. That pain echoed in his furrowed gaze. Tears streaked the bottoms of his eyes. She could feel her own cheeks stained with the tears she couldn't stop, and she pressed her hands to his face.

"I love *all* of you," she continued. "And who you are never needs to be forgiven."

Sam didn't reply verbally. He stared at her, a tear spilling over his cheek. His response came in the form of a deep kiss. So deep it sent her backward with the wrap of his arms, and he buried himself deeper inside her.

With every deliberate thrust, her skin tingled, and she spiraled into the shadows that seemed to linger around them. They became a single obscurity of love and pain, their pasts entwining and becoming a threat they would not run from, but rather one they would embrace together.

She swore once, she felt a feather on her cheek.

The mere power of him consumed her to the point of no return. His need and lust and desire for her, for the moment they had just shared, for how he had revealed himself to her in its entirety. Everything he was and is had been laid before her, and she loved him more than she knew how to put into words.

Her orgasm crested like a wave. Building and building, and she tried to hold it back, to keep herself from spilling over as she wanted to feel him buried inside her until the sun decided to show its face again.

"Fuck, Deianira," he hissed as she tightened around him.

"Sam—"

They came apart with hitched gasps, her nails digging into his shoulder and neck, drawing blood as his hand on her ass left his mark. And for a few moments, they stilled. Everything that they were, everything that they would be, radiated between them in that quiet space, with only the noise of their breaths heaving between them. As he pulled out of her and turned away to fix himself, Ana swore she saw a smile dare to lift his lips, but it wasn't there when he turned back to her to help her dress.

Once they were both clothed, Ana found herself trapped once again between arms as his hands pressed into the edge of the table, his body hovering tall over hers, bangs mingling with her own wild curls. This was her favorite way to be engulfed in him. She loved the dominating and safe way he held there, his chest rising and falling against hers, foreheads nearly touching…

"I love you," came his breathless voice.

Hearing it from him almost caused her to lose her mind. Her jaw quivered, breath catching in her throat as Sam held her steady.

"You're so fucking beautiful," he rasped. "So fucking smart… cunning… *relentless*…" His gaze ran down her face, and he reached to tilt her head back and expose the soft space beneath her chin, thumb rubbing over her skin. His eyes met hers, cold fire blazing in them. "And you're all mine," he declared in a hoarse voice.

She didn't bother arguing, correcting, or otherwise.

Because he was right.

She had been his all along.

A smile flinched on his lips, nearly lighting up his eyes as he continued to stare at her and hold her cheek. "I have something to tell you," he whispered, and she wondered what it could possibly be. What had him smiling and holding her as he was.

315

"Something… something I want you to consider."

"Tell me," she begged.

The door burst open then, and Rolfe came barreling in.

"Boss, the—" He stopped short upon seeing both Sam and Ana on the other side of the table. A grin lit up his face. "Making up, I see," he teased gruffly.

Sam chuckled softly, Ana dipping her head slightly as she, too, chuckled into Sam's neck. Sam flipped Rolfe off.

"Something wrong?" he asked his friend.

"Ah…" Rolfe's expression went grim. "Something like that."

Sam balked and stepped back from Ana, panic suddenly stretching over his face. "What is it? Is it Millie? Is she—"

"She's fine. Got the green shit out," Rolfe said, and Sam's chest visibly caved with relief. "But there's something else." Rolfe's gaze darted to Ana, then to Sam. "I'll tell you on the way up."

Sam nodded to his friend, and the door closed behind Rolfe as Sam turned back to Ana.

"Time to go back in my cage?" she asked, only half-teasing.

Sam's fingers rubbed up and down her arms, that soft smile lingering on his lips. "Stay here," he told her. "I'll be back, and we can talk about what you want from this."

"I want you," she said without hesitation. "I'm yours."

"I will never grow tired of hearing you say that." He brushed a curl back off her face, that haunting beauty stretching over his features with a knit of his brows. "My Tower," he whispered. "There is so much more to this, everything you have ever wanted. We can do it together." His hand entwined with hers, and he turned her arm over to see the rose and raven tattoo there. "Mine," he breathed.

Ana reached up for his jaw then, her thumb brushing over the head of the snake on his trachea, and Sam shuddered. "Mine," she said back.

He pulled her hand into his to kiss her knuckles, his eyes never leaving hers. "Forever yours," he promised.

Ana moved beneath his grasp as he shifted, his lips brushing her forehead. "Stay here. I'll have Rolfe come get you soon," he said as he stepped away.

"Afraid to let me roam your castle on my own, Your Majesty?" she asked with a broad smile.

"Rather not lose any more demons," he winked. He laughed when she rolled her eyes, but continued heading to the door.

Shit, that fucking *laugh*.

"I'll give you the grand tour of your new home later. All the places I plan to fuck you until you no longer have control over your own body."

Chapter Fifty-Three

Rolfe had a shit-eating grin on his face when Sam reached him at the top of the stairs, and Sam shoved him to the side when the bastard hound began to make mocking gestures.

"What's wrong?" he asked, trying to get to the point.

"I'll let Mills tell you that, boss."

Millie was grunting about her wound when they reached her in the foyer, and she groaned at the bandage wrapped around her waist.

"Wait," Sam said before she could secure it tighter. "Let's see it," he said with a gesture of his hands.

"I'm not unrolling this fucking thing—"

Shadows picked her up by her wrists and sat her on the foyer table before she could say another word, and they strapped her down. Millie raised an annoyed brow as Sam hovered over her, his eyes turning scarlet, and her lips pursed.

"This is bringing out all your overprotective male instincts," she grunted. "And anger that I haven't seen in years. You're losing your shit."

"Was there ever a time when you doubted me being an overprotective ass?" he asked as he loosened the bandage and lifted the corner.

"Never said that that," she said, now staring at the ceiling. "I just wanted to make sure you knew it."

Sam ignored her as he poured over her wound, looking for any glimpses of green through his scarlet vision. It was just as nasty and black as it had been that morning, and Sam didn't like the look of it.

"She still isn't healing," he said to Rolfe.

Rolfe nodded and came to stand at his side. "I got out everything I could see, boss," he said.

Sam turned back to the wound. He squinted, ignoring the putrid smell coming out of it, and bent lower.

A glimmer of what looked like green glitter caught his eye. "Roll, can you grab the tweezers?" he asked his friend.

Rolfe ran off, and Sam blinked the red out of his eyes, the normal world coming to life around him as he settled his hips against the table.

"You really don't need to restrain me anymore," she said.

"I thought you were enjoying it," he replied.

Millie rolled her eyes. "Hard to enjoy something when your heart is breaking," she grunted.

Sam turned back to her, a lump rising in his throat at the way Millie was staring at the ceiling. It'd been at least a century since he'd seen such a look on her face. He reached out and squeezed her thigh.

"I'm sorry for the way I spoke to you about her," he said softly, and Millie swallowed whatever emotion laid in her eyes.

"It's fine," she said. "I should have listened to you."

"I could still be wrong—"

Millie laughed. "Samarius Cain... *wrong*." She shook her head. "I've been your Hand for centuries. Never once have you been wrong about anything, no matter how hard the truth was to swallow."

Sam looked over her, noticing how she continued to avoid his gaze, and he hated himself for making her feel this way.

"Bring her to the castle," he said. "We'll talk. Maybe we can all figure this out together. If her friends are being used as you suspect..."

His voice trailed, and Millie finally looked at him. Sam grasped her hand.

"We'll bring them home, too."

"Here you go, boss," Rolfe said as he came running from the kitchen, tweezers in his hand.

However, Sam didn't look away from Millie, and he kissed her knuckles before turning his attention to Rolfe. The shadows tightened back around her torso, Sam's eyes turning scarlet once more, and he bent over her to find the glitter again. He had to hold her wound open, grateful for the grip his shadows had over Millie as she began to squirm, though it wasn't grunts of anxiety that left her.

It was pain-filled laughter.

Sam fixated on the glimmer in the cut, steadying his hand as he pressed the tweezers inside. And when he grabbed it, Millie jerked her hips off the table, crying out.

"Try healing yourself," Sam said as he held the thing up to the light.

It looked like glass—the most minuscule piece of glass, wild green coloring. "Did all of it look like this?" he asked Rolfe.

"Some," Rolfe replied. "The rest I scraped out. Like sludge in her."

"It doesn't make any sense," Sam said, shaking his head. He looked back down to Millie and watched as he held her hand over the wound, still struggling to heal.

"Can you shift?" he asked.

"Fuck, I'd better be able to," she muttered.

His shadows evacuated from her, and she sat up. She ran her hands through her hair, neck cracking, and within a couple of seconds, his beautiful horned demon sat in front of him. Sam's lips lifted.

"There's my girl," he said, giving her chin a playful nudge.

Millie's tail flickered up and did the same to him as she hopped off the table, and with a shake of her entire body, she shifted back into her regular self.

"Thank fuck for that," Millie said, obviously feeling better.

Sam placed the green glitter on his finger, and he watched as it disintegrated into his flesh, leaving behind a tiny red scar as the knife Ana used on him had. His lashes lifted to Millie.

"Call your witch," he said before turning to go up the stairs. "What did you need me for?"

"Oh!" Millie snapped her fingers and clamored up the stairs after him. "Firemoor knows you have Ana."

Sam stopped so abruptly that Millie ran into the back of him. "What?"

Millie stared at him as he rounded over her. "They know she's in this realm."

"How would anyone know that? The only people who know are—" And he stopped speaking. Rage filled his chest and swelled his every muscle. "Get that fucking Council on the phone," he growled. "We'll deal with your witch after."

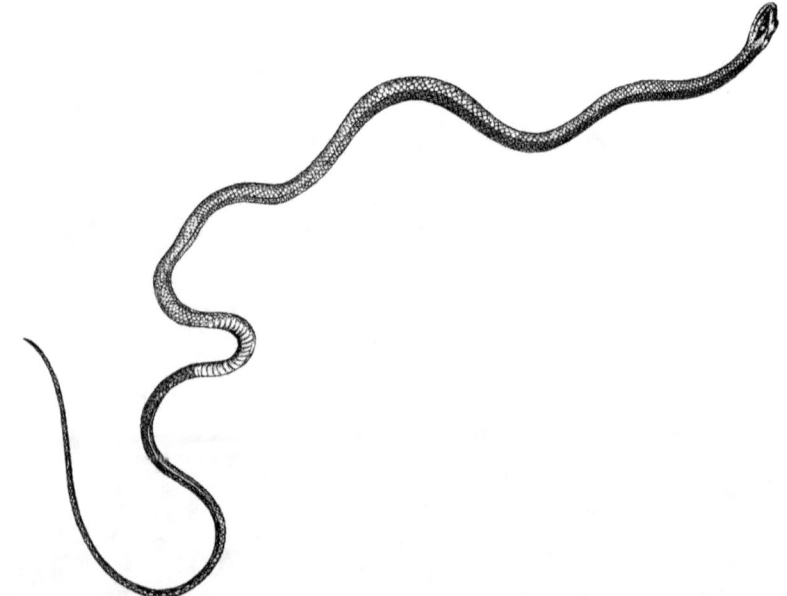

Chapter Fifty-Four

Home.

The word allayed in her mind as Sam disappeared through the door, locking it behind him. She didn't blame him for that. She knew she would have done the same were the tables turned. She was honestly surprised he left her there.

As she pulled back on her clothes, her attention turned to the three unconscious men hanging upside down from the rafters. She stepped closer, the dried rose petals crunching beneath her feet. There was something familiar about the one on the left. The ropes and wood creaked with the involuntary turns of the bodies, and as Ana approached, she realized all three were Firemoor soldiers, and one—

The one on the left was the one that had tried to kill her.

She clacked into the sink as she straightened, stepping back too quickly and knocking over a bottle of soap, the garden shears. She grabbed the porcelain edge as the man stirred, and when she went to pick up the soap, she saw a shadow pass by the window.

Not Sam's shadow. Not the kind of shadow that comforted her.

Something again moved outside, a flash of fire, and she squinted out the dirty windows. They were in the middle of a cemetery, so she wasn't entirely sure she should be spooked, but something...

Ana crept to the door, grabbing the shearing scissors on her way there.

A soft wind billowed her hair as she creaked open the door. She'd known there was a garden on the property, but this... she hadn't expected this.

In the soft light of the moon, the white roses seemed to glow back at her. Like they were soaking up moonlight in the place of sunlight and using it as their only nutrient. Beds upon beds, other flowers and bushes sprinkled in between. The garden was vast and jetted out far into the cemetery.

She held the shears tight as she crept through the winding rows, trying to keep her wits about her and not become too entranced by the flowers.

A limb snapped behind her, and Ana tensed. She took a step sideways, feeling the thorn of one of the roses jab into her arm, but she didn't wince away. She held her breath as the watered petals brushed her skin, and she heard another person's steady breaths not far away.

"I can hear you," Ana said, her voice cutting through the whispering wind. "If you're here for me, come on out. Let me kill you before the rain starts back."

"No, love—"

Lightning struck in the distance, the thunder rumbling in its wake, and Ana pivoted.

"—You'll be well on your way to the Spine before then."

Ana's insides froze as Jay emerged into the light, a loose rope around his slim shoulder, the stick end of a shovel in the other. Ana's thighs tightened in a ready stance.

"Jay?" Ana's gaze narrowed at him. At Jay. At her employer. At someone she thought was a friend. "What are you—"

"I really don't have time for this," he said, pulling the rope off his shoulder. "Bit a of a time crunch, you see."

But Ana's jaw was shaking. Her gaze darted to the door twenty yards back, looking for any route to it, keeping one eye on Jay the whole time. "You've been sending the assassins after me," she said. "That's the reason you let me stay upstairs. The reason you hired me. Why you kept watching me. So you could have me murdered."

Jay sighed, his lips twitching. "Keep your enemies close, love."

Ana ran.

She had no idea where she was going, just that no one would hear her, and she needed to somehow circle back to make it into the castle again. Thorns ripped through her arms and her hair, catching those curls every now and then and making her stumble. She made it all the way to an arbor of vine roses that crawled up and over, leaving little light to come in through the slats, and she turned to see if Jay was anywhere behind her.

Fucking… *Jay.*

Ana cursed the night she first spoke to him, cursed the day she went into his fucking gallery thinking he was a simple-minded fool who would pay her no attention. Cursed the day she'd thought him like her; someone seeking freedom from the other realms.

A rope threw around her throat.

Ana grabbed for it, kicked as Jay pulled her, tugging that thick rope tighter and tighter. She struggled, knocking into the arbor, scratching her face, but to no avail. It was so tight that she started to feel the darkness knocking in on her. And just as she felt her knees weakening, she thrust those garden shears back and into his thigh.

The rope was released, and Ana fell flat to the wet ground. Dirt buried beneath her fingertips as she coughed and coughed, trying to regain her breath. She needed to get up. She needed to get running.

Jay cursed behind her, but she knew that he was gaining his footing quicker than she was. Dizziness slammed into her as she pushed to her feet and staggered. Her hands grabbed the arbor, thorns pricking into her, and she let out a shriek but kept going. Gripping those thin white boards over and over, forcing her legs to work. She had to move. She had to run.

With a scream, she pushed out of the arbor, and just as her stumbling feet steadied, something struck the back of her head.

Ana crashed into the mud with the first drops of rain in the returning storm, and blackness swarmed around her.

Chapter Fifty-Five

"Everyone is at the tower," Millie announced.

She'd been on the phone since they'd made it up the stairs. Sam had sat behind his desk, staring at the blank screen and going over each council member in his head, trying to figure out which one of them was the spy responsible for this.

Firemoor had sent him a video directly—or General Prei had. Sam had watched it twice before throwing his own computer into the wall. Rolfe had gone downstairs and brought back food, telling Sam to sit the fuck down and eat something before he went completely feral.

Sam didn't argue, and he'd cleaned up his own mess before Millie had a chance to see it.

He stood from his chair as Millie closed the door, stretching his limbs to the dark sky, power rushing through his restless muscles. And as his eyes rolled from their scarlet blur, he looked to Rolfe.

"Do you mind checking on my Queen and getting her settled while we do this?" Sam asked him.

Rolfe smirked and rose to his feet. "Shall I give her the real Shadowmyer welcome?" he asked, baring his teeth.

Sam looked to Millie, who was grinning at him. "Maybe a bit," she said. "Scare her a little."

"Good luck with that," Sam muttered. "Fear makes her a bit... insatiable."

Rolfe's smile widened beneath his thick mustache. "This is going to be fun."

The grand television flickered on to the boardroom just as Sam cloaked himself in shadows, Rolfe left, and Milliscent sat on the front of the desk.

"Nice of you to join us," Millie said, her gaze skating over each person settled at the chamber table.

"What's this about?" Rogers asked.

Sam leaned back in his chair, his scarlet gaze seeping through the darkness as he drawled, "It's about which of you is a spy for Prei," his voice a low vibration in the air.

Deep in the middle of uptown, miles and miles away from Castle Corvus, thunder rumbled like a drum over SkyCor.

A few council members murmured between one another, some looking out the windowed walls as the wind seemed to whip so violently, papers and leaves swirled in the outside air.

"No one here is a spy for him," Fairland said, her eyes widening as another rumble of thunder sounded.

The lights in the tower flickered.

Others began to speak up as the clouds grew darker and darker, but there was one… just one… who remained silent.

"Sera," he called her name.

Sera looked directly into the camera as the rest of the room settled down. Thunder cracked again, this time so violent that the glass windows shook, and people on every floor of the building went to look outside.

"Sera, Sera…" Sam stood from his chair, slowly stepping around the desk, his shadows covering him, and then he sat beside Millie, his shadowed arms crossing over his chest. Wisps of black umbra curled in the air behind him, silhouetting the shape of his wings. He studied Sera's face a moment, watching her gaze dart to two people with whom he knew Sera trusted and was good friends with.

"Who is the spy?" he asked her.

Sera hesitated, swallowing hard, her eyes casting down to the table and then back to the camera. Shadows crawled up the sides of the tower as vines begging for the sun. They infiltrated every floor, seeping and spilling over the carpets and tile…

A couple of the Council members picked their feet up into their chairs as the umbra spread over the long conference room. And Sera began to visibly tremble when they tickled up her ankles to her thighs, around her waist, and to her wrists. Every inch up her body sent her lips quivering down, her jaw shaking with fear. A tear slipped down her cheek—

"Rogers," she spat, almost involuntarily. She shot to her feet, backing up against the wall. "Rogers—it was Rogers—"

Rogers bolted upright, cursing at Sera. "You little—"

Shadows sharpened into glass and cut across Rogers's throat. His blood spilled down his front, and Sam took that life without raising a finger. Other people screamed, jumping out of their chairs.

"Who else?" Sam interjected over the chaos.

"Evans," Sera stammered. "Evans and Rogers—no one—"

Screams cut through, overloading the speaker to the point sound began to cut out. Sam pushed off the desk, and Millie whipped around the back of it to thumb away on the keyboard, making sure their connection wasn't interrupted.

Sam was solely focused on the traitors in his midst. He stepped directly up to the screen and camera, only his scarlet eyes and silhouette pouring through the feed, and he tilted his head. Shadows sliced across Evans's ankles as he darted to the door. They pulled him down to the floor, surrounding him with their fog.

The only thing left of his body when the black receded was his blood on the carpet.

The room seemed to be motionless. Members of the council paused to watch their friend disappear, slowly moving off the table or out of the chairs, and every one of them slowly turned back to the camera and television.

Every darkened shadow deliberately evacuated from Sam's office except for the silhouette of his wings. And for the first time since the war, Death revealed his face.

Gasps sounded from the remaining Council members as he settled his hips back onto the desk, arms lazily hugging his chest. The shadows in the conference room continued to hover around the floor, a warning for any that might speak out, but none did. Apparently too stunned at the revelation that he'd been living among them all this time.

"Now," Sam sighed, looking at each of them directly for the first time. "The rest of you will be waiting on a phone call tomorrow from Milliscent with instructions. If I find out more of you are slipping information to any of these other realms, I'll pay you a personal visit," he said. "We'll get to know each other *very* well…" The tip of a shadow tickled a few of the women's cheeks with the words, making them tremble.

"Are we clear?" he asked.

Each person on the screen nodded, unable to manage anything else, and Sam finally released them.

The screen went black.

Millie stood from the desk and circled in front of him, a wide smile on her lips. "Your Majesty," she said with a flutter of her eyes. "I wish your girl had been here to see that. She'd be as bothered as I am right now."

"Down, kitty," he teased as he, too, pushed off the desk.

"You know… once she's settled…" Millie's brows wagged at him as he moved around to the other side and felt his smile heightening at the suggestion.

"Maybe if you're a good little demon," he said, voice dropping.

She leaned over the desk, palms pressing into the wood. "Ooo… Daddy, let me play," she pouted. "Pretty please."

And this time, Sam actually chuckled out loud. "Begging from your feet doesn't suit, Mills. You know I prefer you on your knees."

"So do I," she grinned. "You know, speaking of your lover… Rolfe has been gone a while now," Millie said. "Think he skipped off with her?"

"Or perhaps had his head snapped," Sam grunted, thinking of anything that Ana might do.

"That's one of the reasons I like her so much," she said. "Ready to strike at any moment. Did you find out how she killed the guards?"

Sam smiled fondly. "I'll let her tell you."

The door opened slowly, the creak of it like an awaiting pin to drop. A grim-faced Rolfe appeared in the door, and Sam shot to his feet, his stomach plummeting to the ground.

"Fucking—Roll—" Millie was out of the chair and helping him in the room.

Sam hardly moved. He couldn't. Something was wrong. *Ana…*

"Where is she?" Sam demanded.

"Boss, I—"

The shadowed fog trickled over the floor, filling up every square inch of the ground as it traveled to Rolfe. Rolfe swallowed, his hands running through his hair. "Boss…"

Sam took one step around the desk. "Where… is she…"

And finally, Rolfe found the courage to look Sam in the eyes. "She's gone."

Sam tried to stifle his rising rage. He tried to stop himself from sending shadows around his friend's throat and strangling him until he couldn't shift anymore. The tried not to snap the entire castle in half with a lightning strike.

"Where is she?" he asked, his voice coming out like the rattle of Death himself.

"Someone snatched her in the garden," Rolfe said fast. "There's—"

Sam lost it.

Shadows dove around Rolfe's wrists and ankles, and before Sam could stop, his hand was around Rolfe's throat, teeth bared, and he threw him into the wall.

"How could someone get to her?!" Sam shouted. "How—*How*—"

Rolfe struggled, his body stretching and flashing between himself and his hound form. He writhed beneath Sam's grip, but Sam only grew more enraged as images of Ana going out into that garden, someone snatching her away, filled his mind. Rolfe's claws scratched his arms, his torso, his face.

Sam didn't care. Rolfe could rip his flesh to shreds.

His hand tightened on Rolfe's throat. *"Where is she?"*

"Sam, stop!" Millie shouted, hitting Sam's arms.

Shadows swirled around Millie and threw her back. But Millie didn't stop, and neither did Sam.

"I followed—" Rolfe couldn't breathe.

"Samarius, let him go so he can tell you!" Millie shouted. *"He can't breathe!"*

"I followed the scent—"

Sam couldn't see. His vision was red. He couldn't take his hand down. Even with Millie beating on his arms, he was slipping. Slipping into a feral void that ended with nothing but pain and death around him.

The sound of a cat screaming filled his ears, and Sam froze as Millie entered his peripherals.

"Release him," Millie seethed. She held a hissing Luna up by her scruff. "Or I eat the fucking cat."

And he knew she would.

Her promise sent him reeling. Sam stammered, blinking back into himself, falling away from the rage that had seeped his veins and flooded his mind. He hadn't gone that feral in years. He stumbled backwards, releasing Rolfe and evacuating every shadow from around the room.

Luna landed on the ground with a screech as Sam fell to the floor. He sat there, his chest heaving, the cat curling up behind him, and Rolfe staggered into the wall and coughed.

"I'm sorry," Sam breathed, looking up at Rolfe.

Rolfe clutched his throat and waved him off, shaking his head. "All good, Cain," he said.

"It's not. It's—" Luna crawled into Sam's arms and began to purr as Sam stammered on his words and the air in the room relaxed, until all the three heard were those purrs and their heavy breaths.

"How far did you trail them?" Sam managed, this time in a calm voice.

"To the highway," Rolfe replied. "I have someone tailing them further."

The look Rolfe and Millie exchanged made Sam sit up.

"That vulture you've been fucking?" Millie snapped.

"Yes, the vulture," Rolfe said. "What's wrong with her?"

"She's a vulture," Millie argued.

"Enough," came Sam's low growl. He pushed to his feet, Luna in his arms, and he took a deep breath before looking between them. "Did you smell anything else? Stench of Fire or Iron?"

"Both," Rolfe said.

Sam growled under his breath. "I'll fucking kill them," he swore. "I want a horde," he told them.

Millie and Rolfe's eyes widened. "What—really?"

"I'd like those fuckers to remember who they're dealing with when they cross my borders and take my things," he said. "Will you come with me?"

"To find her?" Millie asked.

"To bring her home," Sam said.

"Sam…" Millie shifted on her feet, arms crossing. "You realize the moment we go to her… the moment you defend her… they will declare war on us," she said.

"As far as I am concerned," Sam sneered, "they declared war on us the moment they strung my people up in the middle of a field and publicly tortured them."

"You had the chance to declare that war before you crossed two borders to get those demons," Millie said. "You didn't. But this… They've been hunting her for years. She is more important to them than any of our kind in their ranks. Aiding her, hiding her, taking her back, they will call all that treachery."

"What would you suggest I do?" he snapped. "Leave her to rot and be tortured by General Prei and his men?"

A sly smile wrapped itself on Millie's lips, and she laughed at the ground. "I believe I speak for Rolfe and me both when I say this: If war

329

is what it takes to keep Death's Queen, then we go to fucking war. We are simply asking if you are ready for this. I know we have dreamed and spoken of it, but... this is it. This will be the beginning."

Sam looked to Rolfe for confirmation, and his friend nodded. "Ready when you are, boss."

A knot twisted and wrapped around Sam's stomach, the snake on his throat shuddering, as he thought of all the things Ana might be going through right then. The thought of someone taking her from him and thinking she was theirs to manipulate and control... to torture and to break...

"Deianira Bronfell is the match," he declared in a voice so dangerous that even the lightning outside did not feel like a threat. He looked between his awaiting friends, seeing smiles curl on their lips.

"Everything burns."

Chapter Fifty-Six

As Millie and Rolfe made a few phone calls, Sam paced his office, Luna purring in his arms. He continued to replay everything that had happened that night. The deaths. The intruders. The Council. Ana in his arms. The declarations they'd made and the things he was ready to give her.

Every second that passed was a thorn in his heart. Anger rose with every crack of lightning outside. He couldn't control the shadows around his feet or how the roses on his desk wilted and came back to life every time a whisper of that fog ascended over them. Everything in that room rose and fell; it teetered at the balance of life and death. He held that power like a surge of electricity in the room, and when he heard the sound of a deathhound's paws clamoring up the stairs, Luna scattered out of his arms.

"Fuck it's cold in here," Millie said as she made it upstairs just after Rolfe.

Millie patted the top of Rolfe's gigantic wolf-like head, which stood as tall as her own. "Such a good boy," she said in a teasing voice, her fingers running through the shaggy black hair.

Rolfe snarled, baring his teeth, and Millie just laughed. "You want to play fetch?" she said, backing up and grabbing an apple from the bowl on the kitchen table. "Come on. Good boy. You want it? You want the apple?"

His tail flipped back and forth, anger seeping in those icy eyes as he warned Millie to stop. Sam chuckled under his breath. "Enough, Milliscent," he said. "He'll take out your throat again."

Millie straightened and tossed the apple back on the table, then blew a kiss at the great, sneering deathhound, to which Rolfe let out a low growl. "I have missed that thrill," she admitted as she looked at Sam.

Sam's phone rang, and he frowned between the pair as he held it to his ear.

"What?" he snapped into the receiver.

"Fuck of a way to answer your phone, love," Jay said on the other end.

Sam sighed heavily. "Jay," he managed. "You caught me at a bad time. What is it?"

The way Jay laughed made Sam stop in his tracks. His entire body went rigid, and he stared at the desk.

"You remember I called you the other day about our girl," Jay said. "About how I couldn't find her. Well, I found her," Jay said, and Sam could practically hear the smile in his voice.

Sam's fingers tightened around the phone.

"Good thing, too," Jay continued. "I can't wait to take her home. People will throw parades in my name. The one to bring the Tower back for trial... if we ever make it to trial. Something tells me they'll torture her for a few weeks before chopping off her head."

Lightning hit the window, and Sam began to shake.

"You're fucking dead," Sam hissed.

Jay laughed. "No, love. She is."

Sam nearly hurled his phone across the room. He pulled it away from his ear, entire body trembling, and stared at the now blank screen.

Fucking...

"Jay has her," he said before his friends could ask. "Fucking—"

The phone flew from his hand and crashed into the opposite wall. Lightbulbs in the chandelier blew. The entire castle shook beneath a crack of violent thunder.

"What—Jay? From the gallery?" Millie balked. "That idiot?"

"We'll find out more when we get to them." Sam turned to Rolfe. "You found where they are?"

Rolfe nodded.

"And backup?"

A roar sounded outside. A great muffled echo of humming motorcycles speeding up the long drive through the middle of the cemetery. Thunder rumbled with the declaration of demons answering their calls, and Sam saw Millie and Rolfe exchange a smile.

He stepped over to the circular window overlooking the front, and the sight of twenty or more people all driving maniacally up to the castle filled his vision. His heart knotted, that so many of them had answered the call without questioning why. Just that their king needed reinforcements, and the thrill had driven them to help.

"Ready, boss?" Rolfe asked.

Sam took another moment to watch the demons stepping off their bikes, stretching their arms and chatting with one another. A few he recognized immediately, flashes of how he'd once turned them filling his mind.

"They're here for you," Millie said, stepping up on the other side of him. "Did you think they had forgotten?"

"They owe me nothing," Sam said softly.

Millie reached to his chin and turned him toward her. "And that's why they come."

As the front door opened, Sam, Millie, and Rolfe made their way down the grand staircase. The horde all emerged inside, all staring up at the walls and the great foyer before them, taking note of their surroundings in a place no one had ever ventured.

And when their eyes landed on Sam, a few of them nudged the others, and one slowly stepped forward.

"Sam…" A dark-skinned man with his twisted hair pulled high away from his face approached, and Sam smiled at him as he extended a hand.

"Thorn…" Sam acknowledged him. "You don't remember my face," he continued. "But you remember the day you chose this."

Thorn's thick chest swelled with something akin to pride, a surge of memory filling his head and reminding him of who he once was and everything he'd been through.

"I do," Thorn replied. "I remember that trench and the fire around us. I remember this—" he pointed to the burnt skin up his arm. "And I remember the choice."

"A new beginning or a chance at revenge," Sam said. "All you had to do was trust me."

Thorn's chin lifted, and a woman stepped forward, her hand sliding onto Thorn's shoulder. Sam remembered her, too. As he did each of the people whom he'd sat with and given a choice.

"Is it time?" the light, brown-skinned woman, Vera, asked.

Sam looked between them, then to every other demon that had come at Millie and Rolfe's requests. No questions asked. No questioning loyalties or why they'd been sitting on their asses for centuries…

All of them were there for a unified reason: that it was time to take what had once been theirs.

The door flew open again, and a vulture flew inside. The beast twisted in the air, and when she landed, a woman had replaced her. She pulled her hood off her head, revealing her stark white curls, blindingly pale skin, and blue eyes lined with white lashes. She looked like she'd just stepped out of a painting, though Sam remembered well the day he'd turned her too. Her jagged stare landed on Sam, but she stalked to Rolfe.

Sam took a step back, his eyes washing over each person, and then he settled his hips against the foyer table, fingers creasing around its edge.

"Firemoor has decided they want something that is mine," Sam said slowly. "As has Ironmyer. The Spine. And Windmoor. Last week, one of Prei's assassins tried to take her. And last night, one of their spies succeeded."

A few of the people exchanged glances, confusion on their expressions.

"Her name… is Deianira Bronfell," Sam continued.

Murmurs broke out… murmurs that Sam knew he would hear, but as his eyes searched the men and women in front of him, he did not see disdain or wariness.

"I know most of you have heard her name and the destruction that happens in her wake," he said. "And I know some of you may be wondering why I would defend someone like her…" He reached behind him and picked up the small box of matches from his back, pulling one single match from the inside. "Deianira is my match," he declared. "She's here, and she wants the same revenge as we do. She wants to watch these undeserving leaders suffer for the pain they have caused not just people like you but the people you once were. The ones being cleansed and told you did not belong. Everything she has done has been to get here so she could use Death as her mercenary for revenge, without ever knowing the vengeance she craves is the same as ours." He took a long pause as he searched the changing expressions.

"Deianira Bronfell is your Queen," he declared. "Firemoor has taken her."

"Where is she?" Vera cut in, her weight shifting as a look of anger flashed in her eyes.

Sam looked to Rolfe, who stepped forward. "She's being held where sunlight broke the shadow border in the south, at the intersection of

Firemoor, Windmoor, and the Spine. It will take us a few hours to get there—"

"What are we waiting for?" Thorn asked.

Shadows swirled Sam's feet as he stared at the ground, feeling his chest swelling at the sight of the people in front of him already willing to go to battle.

"When we leave this castle, the war begins," Sam said slowly. "The moment any of us cuts one of their soldiers, the peace this realm has felt for centuries is over." His eyes rolled up to Thorn. "All of you have a choice in this. I will force no one to spill blood in my name if you do not want to."

Necks and knuckles cracked in the crowd, a few already shifting into demon forms. A ripple of growls and snaps pulsed the air. Sam's stomach twisted and twisted at the sight before him. People who had only used those forms during the last war called them into action after they'd waited for the perfect time.

And as the last few of them turned, Sam rocked forward onto his feet. Shadows and black fog swirled his legs, wrapping up his torso. Chills ran over Sam's flesh. He felt the shadows wrap inside his shoulder blades, and the extensions of his muscles made his body shudder. They merged with his bones, mending and breaking the skin on his back with crushed feathers and hollow limbs. His eyes fluttered with a reassuring twist of his bones, as his broken wings spread wide for the first time in centuries.

With a faint smile on his lips, his wing stretched and reached over to Millie's cheek, making the blonde seductress limp with the brush of it over her skin.

"Fuck," she whispered in a voice that he was sure was typically reserved for the bedroom. "There's the terror I've been dreaming to see," she said as she ran her hands through her blonde hair, curled horns appearing in the locks.

Sam turned back to the horde, and one by one, they dropped their heads. His shadows curled along the tile floor, entwining with every person's ankles, and a shudder swept the room.

"We raise the dead today."

Chapter Fifty-Seven

Ana woke to a sun-filled sky littered with reaching tree limbs. Her vision blurred, making her dizzy, and she started to grab her head as it throbbed.

Iron shackles stopped her.

And everything from the night before came crashing back.

Her time with Sam. His leaving her. The three bodies. The shadow outside. Jay—

Jay.

"Well, well," came that familiar voice. "Look who is finally awake."

Ana focused her gaze on his approaching figure, feeling anger rise from the pit of her stomach, but she didn't curse him.

"The Tower..." His tone was mocking, and he crouched down in front of her. "Not so scary without all your assets in control, are you, love?" He reached out and flicked a curl, though Ana didn't flinch.

"Come closer and find out for yourself," she replied.

"Ooo... snappy," he teased. "No wonder Death fell for you. Too bad he'll be too late to save you."

Ana laughed coyly, shaking her head. The thought of what Sam might do when he found out who exactly had taken her. Not to mention simply any person taking her, had her thighs squeezing at the thought of his rage.

"I don't need anyone to come after me," she said. "I can get myself out of this just fine. But when he does come..." She whistled in a mocking way. "I'll sit back and enjoy the show."

"You'll be dead before he gets here," Jay said.

"Will I?" Her head tilted as she looked around at the legion of men walking between tents. "And which of these lovely reapers will take

Death's Queen into the next life?" she asked.

Jay didn't find it as amusing as she did.

Ana laughed again. "Tell me, Jay... When did you figure out who I was?"

"Samarius isn't the only one who noticed you the night of the festival."

"Oh? So you know who he is," Ana realized.

"Of course, I do."

"And so you kidnapping me... this is revenge for who, exactly? Firemoor? The Spine King? Windmoor? A Father of some sort—"

"I was at the Ironmyer castle when you took control of Firemoor's missiles," Jay spat.

"Oh that..." Ana huffed a sadistic laugh. "That was a fun day. All those screams... I'll never forget the way those Nobles threw themselves from the windows as the missiles came raining in." Her eyes drifted to the sky, remembering that day, and she couldn't stop her delirious smile. "The Iron King was at least a little fun in the bedroom. He had an interesting way with his tongue before I cut it out." Her gaze flickered up to him. "What relation were you to him? Let me guess... Bastard son?"

Jay's lips pressed to a thin line, and Ana knew she'd struck a nerve.

She chuckled again. "If you grew up as his bastard, then you know all the ways his people struggled to eat and breathe in that gods-forsaken death hole. One inhale down by the mines and shards of metal attacked your lungs. I did your people a favor."

"You killed innocent people—"

"I destroyed a castle full of pious cravens who did nothing to earn the titles they bore," she snapped. "I gave those people a chance at revolution—"

"And look at them now," Jay interjected. "Rioting and killing each other in the streets."

"What's left of their oppressors are the ones pitting them against each other," she argued. "Look at who is controlling the well-equipped militias and tell me I'm wrong. Firemoor is behind that. They are funneling in weapons and money as they have always done, trying to keep the rest of us quiet and subdued."

"Do not try and convince me that what you did was righteous," Jay snapped. "You murdered innocent people in every quadrant on your way to power—"

"I'd love to know your definition of innocent," Ana muttered.

"—People were organized and happy before this. Kingdoms were prospering—"

"*Kings* were prospering," she nearly shouted. "Kings who care nothing of their people, kings whose fathers didn't give two fucks about their people. All they cared for was control."

"And that is different from what you want, how? From what Arius wants?"

Ana almost laughed. "I do not know what Samarius wants. Sorry, you took me from him before I could find that out."

Jay straightened to his feet over her, eyes hardened with rage as he took a step back. Ana chuckled at the sight of him so righteous and raging before her because of a father that never claimed him.

"Don't tell me you're angry about these places being destroyed. It's not my fault that every one of their rulers thought more about how good their cock would feel buried between my breasts or my thighs rather than realizing they were being played."

"Yes, you're a right little whore, aren't you?" Jay toyed.

Ana's smile widened. "A whore with a thirst for blood and vengeance. Some might call that a Queen."

Jay stared at her. "You've always been confident, Ana," he said. "I've admired that about you since we met. But you deserve everything that's about to come for you."

"Oh, is the little bastard boy sad that he promised Daddy revenge on the whore that fucked him senseless and drove a knife through his throat?" She tutted her tongue in a mocking manner, her lips curling upward. "He begged like a dog, too."

Jay's knife was at her throat in a second, and Ana couldn't stop laughing.

"Do it," she dared him. "Break my skin and bleed me. You'll only make him come faster."

"He'll never find this place," Jay said. "It's out of his reach."

Lightning caught her eye in the far east, and a smile lifted the corner of her lips at the sight of the darkening cloud threatening closer and closer.

"Samarius has a deathhound and a horned demon as his two closest allies," she said. "Not to mention legions of ghosted demons that he can raise from the cemetery outside his home and the ones that walk the streets that have waited centuries for revenge... And then, a weapon you've never heard of."

"What kind of weapon?" Jay asked.

Ana looked around the camp, surveying every reaper and demon in his legion, her heart swelling. She scratched her nails together, and then...

Ana began to sing.

The words were in the language of the ancient Moorian of Icemyer, where the witches had found their power in the old caves far north. The power of forbidden lyrics and texts and crystals and song...

The song hummed from deep within her as it had the night in the dungeons. When the ghosted demons Sam had stationed with her ripped themselves apart trying to get to her. One going so far as to go into the cell with her, and she'd watched his blood spill from his throat as he shredded his ears and pulled out his own dead heart.

It was no different from the scene about to happen in front of her.

Reapers and demons all froze as though the know-how to walk had suddenly evacuated their tiny minds. They shuddered with every word leaving her lips, and Ana smiled when a sweep of wind circled them.

The noise of motorcycles buzzed her ears. She heard a howl, a monstrous bellow echoing from tree to tree like it was staking claim to this territory. A vulture circled overhead. And she swore the ground began to shudder.

A thunderous clap cracked the sky and splintered the clouds.

Men surrounding them seemed to lose their footing. Ana didn't stop her quiet song, not even as a few of the reapers around her held their hands over their bleeding ears and began to fall to their knees.

"What are you—" Jay did a double-take in her direction and pulled a knife from his boot. He grabbed Ana up by the hair, exposing her neck, but Ana just laughed.

She laughed and laughed, and when the sinister noise echoed in the trees, she couldn't wipe the delirium off her face and started singing again.

"Stop!" Jay shouted. He shoved the knife in her face, just beneath her nose. "I'll cut out your tongue, you little bitch."

Ana licked the sharp edge of the blade, the blood trickling down her mouth when she dragged it over her top lip. "Don't be a tease. Call me a bitch again and cut my face like you mean it," she toyed. "Get me wet, little Iron boy."

Jay shouted like he was about to hurt her, but—

A deathhound jumped into the middle of the camp.

Men shouted, pulling guns from their holsters and shooting at the great beast. Jay staggered back, screaming at the legion around him while Rolfe howled like he was enjoying the spray.

His teeth bared, and he lunged at a soldier just as motorcycles roared into the clearing. Jumping through trees and flying in on one wheel. More gunfire sounded as people on the backs of bikes pulled two at a time and aimed for everything.

Chaos of blood and screaming bullets, only secondary to the screams, filled the air.

Ana watched the demons that had ridden in, the ones with the horns and those with forked tongues, the ones with burned limbs and yellow eyes, shifters and reapers and all manner of creatures thought to have been eradicated from their world five centuries earlier.

All of them.

Hiding in Shadowmyer.

Necks of Firemoor soldiers cracked, heads breaking as demons bit them off.

But even with the fear rippling through the camp, nothing compared to the way the air chilled and stiffened when the black fog came rolling over the now blood-stained ground. Clouds covered the sun as Death took back his territory. Lightning cracked into the tree behind her, sparking fire off the limbs.

Death appeared from within a shadowed cloud like he was greeting an old enemy.

Grand wings, tattered black, and missing feathers, broken on the left, rose high at his back. These were not the faint images of them she'd seen in flashes of lightning. These were the real things. Wings he'd not used since he was nearly stripped of them.

Eyes glowing scarlet, his stature seeming to be taller than he usually was… the fight parted for him as he stalked into the battlefield. She squinted, noticing something different about his face, and she realized parts of his skin were missing like the deathhound that had arrived moments earlier. The right edge of his mouth, exposing straight white teeth and muscle, curved upward like a smile. A patch on the left by his now red eyes. Beneath the collar of his jacket, she noticed more exposed skeleton and muscle, like his flesh had once been ripped off by savage fangs, and she remembered the skeleton makeup he'd been wearing that first night at the festival.

Someone turned their gun on him, one bullet striking his chest. Sam turned his head slowly in the man's direction, and with the next shot, shadows grabbed the bullet before it could hit him. His hands hadn't moved from his pockets, but the man with the gun was suddenly in the air. Heads turned in the direction as Sam lifted the man up and up, struggling body writhing against the bindings.

And ever so slowly... the shadows began to peel away his skin. People around cowered away, shrinking behind trees and some falling to their knees. Others couldn't look away, horrified by the display of an angered god bringing his wrath upon people who had taken something he loved.

Sam stood in the middle of the field and slowly stretched in a circle, his eyes pouring over every opposing being. "Now that I have your attention..." He pulled his hands from his pockets and started removing his gloves, one finger at a time, exposing long talons with the movement.

"Where is my Queen?"

The affirmation of him calling her his Queen rocked her. Not his plaything. Not just her name.

His Queen.

His voice rattled bones and whispered like the night on fire. As if his tone could break apart the earth and shatter it beneath the stars. It ripped and vibrated the thunderous swirling clouds in the sky. Death's broken wings flickered upwards at his back, a warning and threat that no mortal being not taking their last breath had seen in centuries. One man fell to his knees and began to beg into his clasped hands, and Sam moved to tower over him as the man prayed to the gods for salvation.

His thundering laughter splintered over the wheezing wind. "There are no gods here—" Shadows swept beneath the man and circled his throat, lifting him off the ground so that he was eye-level as the expression on Sam's face moved from vile amusement to eager evil. Sam wrapped those long fingers beneath the man's jaw, and breath ceased as he said in a violent whisper—

"*Only Death.*"

Lightning cracked with the soldier's neck, and Death took his next victims without ever hearing their final pleas.

Ana could only watch, could only try to understand and keep up with the carnage flying around her. The vulture had come down from the air and shifted. She fought alongside Rolfe's deathhound form. Ana tried to call out to Sam as he stripped soldiers of their lives with not only his shadows but his own bare hands.

"Sam!"

But through all the chaos, Sam didn't hear her.

He couldn't *hear* her.

Jay dragged Ana up to her knees, his hand at the roots of her scalp, the threat of a knife at her throat. Ana struggled, her skin shifting against the blade, and even though Jay may not have meant to, the blade cut through her.

Blood seeped from her throat, a dripping tap that couldn't be turned off. She coughed, lurching forward, but Jay hadn't realized what he'd done. Her eyes fluttered, heart beginning to pound in her ears. And just as Jay threw her on the ground and saw the blood, Ana began to plea.

Sam…

Calling to Death as she'd done before.

Samarius… Death… I'm here. Look for me. Find me.

She managed to sit up on her knees, and when she did, she found Sam's raging red eyes staring at her from across the field.

Jay grabbed her hair again and pulled her backward. She choked again, kicking and wishing she could scream.

Shadows swarmed the ground, diving in and out of the tree roots and leaving dead grasses in their wake. They whipped up Jay's feet, his legs, his hands, and his neck. He dropped Ana, making her slam into a great root, but those shadows swirled her like they meant to heal her.

Sunlight died behind grand wings.

And Death stood over her dying body.

Sam didn't speak to her at first. He was staring at Jay's now bound figure, his hands in his pockets. "Jay…" His head tilted as he finally looked down to Ana and gave her a wink. "Should have smelled the Ironmyer stench on you."

Millie dove to the ground at Ana's side when Sam moved past her. The demon pressed her hands to Ana's cheek, to her neck, and the blood pouring out of Ana stopped. Millie began to work Ana's shackles as Sam honed in on Jay.

"This place isn't yours," Jay said, struggling against the shadows. "It never was. It never will be."

"And who's going to stop me?" Sam asked. "The obsidian legions of Ironmyer? The fire legions? That fucking…" Sam shuddered, his fingers cringing close and opening at the next name he spoke through clenched teeth, *"General Prei."*

Ana had never heard him say any name with such poison. Like speaking it hurt him, damaged something within. Even Millie stilled at the sound of how he said it.

Sunlight flared at Sam's back, black clouds enclosing in, thunder rumbling the ground beneath. Every demon had stopped fighting, every mortal now dead on the ground, and they all watched their king.

"Death doesn't get to win," Jay said. "And neither does your precious girl."

A heinous smile wrapped itself on Sam's lips. "Death always wins," he hissed. "And as for my Queen…" he looked back over his shoulder to Ana on the ground. Those eyes struck her, held her still. To truly look at Death in his demonic form, without the restraints of power he usually placed upon himself. Beautiful and horrifying all at once.

A talon tickled over her cheek and under her chin, a loving gesture that skidded her heart.

"She gets everything she wants," Sam swore softly. He took one step back, revealing Ana heaving as Millie finally released her wrists. "Tell me what you want for this traitor," he asked of her.

Ana considered Jay. Considered everything he'd told her, and she gripped the dirt beneath her nails.

"I want him suffering longer than his father did," she hissed. "And I want to watch him beg just like his pathetic daddy."

Lust and greed flickered in Sam's eyes. Jay lifted further off the ground, his body struggling against the umbra. He took out his phone, opened the camera, and Millie stood as she took it from his hands.

"Are you sure—"

"It's time," Sam cut her off.

And little by little, those shadows squeezed.

They squeezed, and they squeezed, and the sound of Jay's whimpering and pleading became music to Ana's ears. The sickening sound of ripping flesh and breaking bones. She began to shake as she didn't dare turn away. Didn't dare look from the sight of his bulging eyes, his gasping mouth. Sam eased that tension and heightened it every couple of seconds, toying with the man who had taken his woman away from him.

And then Sam stepped up to the breaking body.

"Let this be a warning to anyone who tries to take her—to touch or even look— at Deianira Bronfell again," he said, his low voice thrumming into the camera as he looked back over his shoulder. His wings flickered up, red eyes raging into that video, and the true portrait of Death spoke to the entire world.

"I will rip this entire world apart just to see it free," he hissed. "We are no longer something you will persecute. We are no longer hiding who we are. To those in the other realms thought beneath the boot, we see you. We hear you. And to the worm that thinks he can take this world again—" Sam stepped directly in front of the camera, nearly trembling as he spoke his next words "—I'm coming for you, you fucking bastard."

Sam took one step back and snapped his finger.

Shadows ripped Jay's body into nothing more than dust on the wind.

Millie cut the camera and stared wide-eyed at her king. "Sam…"

"Send that to whomever you need to," he spat. "I'm no longer playing." His eyes went to Ana as they moved back to brown, the skin enclosing over his face again, his wings tucking in behind him, and he crossed the space between them.

Sam hauled Ana off the ground, and even before her feet were steady, he was kissing her. Ana grasped his arm and his waist to hold herself upright, staggering at the feeling of his hand on her head and her hips, pulling her closer. Publicly claiming her for all to see.

And when he finally pulled back, he held her face in his hand, those dark, pain-filled eyes searching her face.

"Are you hurt?" he asked.

Ana's palm flew into his cheek, and the slap cracked with lightning.

"You're an *idiot*, Samarius," she shrieked. "Do you know what you've just done?"

Sam rolled his neck, tongue darting out to lick the blood off his cracked lip, and his lashes lifted as he said, "That depends," with a restriction in the back of his throat, and she was ready to hit him again for whatever smart comment he was about to say.

"Do you mean to ask if I know about the war I just officially started or if I am aware of the heads Thorn and Damien will need to send Firemoor?"

"Thorn—" She blinked at the new names, the mention of it completely throwing her off, but she huffed and pulled herself back together fast. "You just started a war you will not be able to get out of!" she nearly shouted. "You should have let them take me—"

"No one is *ever* taking you from me again," he declared over the thunderous rumble. "No one is *ever* touching you again." He straightened then, fluffing the lapels of his jacket. "Every other realm is about to get a lesson in all the things I will do to make sure of that," he hissed.

Ana stepped back from him as she registered the words in her hazy mind. But Sam huffed an audible breath, like he was calming himself down, and he wrapped his hand around her cheek.

"I'm sorry I left you last night," he whispered. "I should have taken you with me."

"And your castle would have been targeted instead," she argued. "At least you still have a home to go back to. I can handle a few scratches."

"This hurts worse," he admitted, his voice cracking. "A home, I can rebuild. But you…" Rage seemed to teeter at the edge of existence, and he growled with a shudder that she had not heard before, his eyes flashing scarlet.

"Where are you injured?" he asked again.

She blinked at the way he looked at her, at the concern in his gaze. She didn't know if her heart rate was stumbling because of how enraged or aroused she was at all that had just happened.

"It's just a bunch of scrapes," she told him. "I'm fine."

"You're not—Ana, you were kidnapped—"

"It's nothing worse than what I've put myself through before—"

"But—"

"Samarius," and the way she said his full name seemed to snap his mouth closed. He stared down at her, jaw tight, nostrils flared… and finally, he took a deep breath and kissed her forehead.

"Milliscent," he began as he took a step back, still hanging onto Ana's hand. "Get on the phone with the Council and media outlets. The people need to start moving to the boats or underground before Firemoor finds out what happened here. I do not wish for them to be caught in the crossfire."

Ana looked between them, noticing how natural the statement seemed to be, the pair seeming to have planned for this for some time.

"Underground?" Ana repeated in confusion.

"Already texted a few people on the way here," Millie replied. "I'll make a list of everyone and call."

"Rolfe—"

"Clean up," Rolfe grunted. "Got it."

"No," Sam said. "Thorn and his legion here can clean up. I want you running ahead home to make sure no one has infiltrated while we've been gone. I imagine a few of Firemoor's spies might have seen us leave this morning. Or noticed the horde of demons on the highways."

A few of the men and women around them seemed to find the

statement funny, and for the first time, Ana actually looked at the people who had accompanied Sam to find her.

These were people she'd seen on the streets. Everyday people that she assumed were… well, human. And she realized then the extent of the people who had come with Sam after the last war. The number of people biding their time and waiting to take their revenge.

People that had been waiting for her.

Sam pulled Ana's hand to his lips, holding her gaze as he said, "Let's go home."

Chapter Fifty-Eight

Wind cursed and splintered over the scratches on Ana's skin as they rode away on his motorcycle. Even with Sam's leather jacket around her, she had to bury herself behind his body to keep the cuts from ripping her apart. Sam kept one hand on hers around his waist, his thumb brushing her knuckles, a reassuring gesture that he was there. That she was okay—that *they* were okay.

But even through her hazy state, all she could think about were the words Sam had just said, about how he would let no one hurt her and how she was his. About the line he always told her, of how he was terrified of the things he would do to keep her.

He was hiding things from her, and she wanted to know everything.

"Pull over," Ana yelled from his back as they looped over the oceanside ridge.

Sam stiffened. "What?"

"Pull over!"

"It's going to rain," he shouted back. "We need to—"

"Samarius, you pull over right now, or I'm jumping off."

Her warning made him bristle at her over his shoulder, and on the next turn, at the cliffside overlook, Sam slowed the bike in the awaiting dirt.

Ana nearly threw herself off before he'd balanced it and cut the engine. Her bare feet staggered in the cold soil, chilling wind circling, and she paused at the roadside railing.

That singular ray of sunlight stared back at her from far across the seas.

"Tell me how you would keep me," she said as the first drop of rain hit her cheek. She glanced back over her shoulder, seeing Sam staring at her from his leaned stance on the bike, arms wrapped over his elbows. He watched her with downcast eyes, something akin to rage slowly spreading in his gaze and his taut jaw. He looked right briefly and then back to her as he pushed off the bike.

"You're going to freeze, Ana," he said, his tone a warning as he ignored her statement. "We need to get you healed. Get back on the bike. We'll talk at the castle."

Rain stung her body, but Ana didn't care.

She wanted answers.

"No," she argued, stepping away as he approached. "You always said you are terrified of the things you would do to keep me. You just started war when you could have let me die to keep your family, your kingdom, your people... all of them could have been safe. All you had to do is let Firemoor take me. Instead, you've chosen to 'keep me' as you continue to say. So tell me why. Tell me *how*."

"It is not that simple," he replied.

"Try me," she snapped. "I have read the witch texts of Firemoor, studied the rituals from the wastelands of Icemyer. I have heard the ways Death claims his demons and slaves—"

"I do *not* have slaves." He was towering over her in a split, but Ana didn't back down.

"Then tell me, *Death*," and the word seethed from her lips. "Tell me what you would do to keep me."

Sam huffed in annoyance, then wiped the rain off his face as he stepped back in a circle. For a few moments, he didn't speak. Lightning struck in the distance, and just as Ana opened her mouth to speak again, Sam said,

"I would claim you, Deianira," in a haunting voice.

Ana swallowed beneath the conviction in his gaze when he met her eyes, and she held her knees steady as he continued.

"I would break every binding the witches tried to place upon me to keep you," he continued. "I would take your being into the next existence. Watch this mortal life fade from your eyes... And then I would recite the text never spoken aloud."

Ana's eyes widened. She knew the text, or she knew of it.

"I would make you *mine*." His voice quieted to barely a hover over a whisper, and he reached to move her wet curl from her face. "Your tether would tie to mine. You would become a part of me, an extension unlike the others. You would bear my mark on your skin and around your neck. You would have an immortal existence that would mean we are one."

Her heart skipped at the fantasy he told, and she knew he was imagining it by the look in his eyes.

"This is how I would keep you," he whispered. *"Forever."*

She didn't know what to say, how to respond. He was serious. If only she would ask, he would do it. She could go beyond what she'd only ever dreamed of. No crown would match becoming his. She could be his demon, free herself of the thing she was told she would have to be.

Sam released her face, apparently thinking he had scared her, and he took two steps back.

"Why would you do this?" she called out as he turned on his heel. "Answer me. Why would you bind me to you and break every rule you ever gave yourself. Why do you want me for all eternity?"

"Because I refuse to lose you," he growled, suddenly standing over her. "Because I love... I love you more than anything this world could ever give me. Everything you are, every part of you, every broken piece that makes up your whole... You are everything I have ever wanted, everything I did not know I was missing. You are a part of what is left of my existence. My other half. My match. And because you were right. I *will* have you as my Queen. I will not let you go, Ana. No matter what terrors or armies might come after you... May they pray for my mercy if they think they can take you from me."

Ana swallowed as she watched him start to step away.

"I thought you knew this the other night," he said. "I thought you were in this with me. That you were ready."

"Ready for what?"

"To take this world with me."

Lightning struck close, cracking over the water and sending a charge through the rain.

Ana didn't shift.

"This is what you meant to talk to me about," she realized.

Sam stepped closer. "Everything you said that day in the dungeon. Revenge against all those who have wronged you, wronged your family, ruled so ruthlessly and oppressed you... They're the same people that once tried to break me. I have lived beneath these shadows waiting for the right time to strike once more. You have crippled these armies and their kingdoms. You have paved the way for this... Everything you've ever worked for. All of it was leading you here to me." He paused before her, his hand over her cheek. "I know you

349

meant to use me, but I have a better proposition."

Anticipation swelled in her chest and knotted her muscles.

"Tell me," she found herself saying, almost desperate to hear him say it.

"Become my immortal half," and a dagger of lightning jolted the earth at his back, but Sam didn't flinch, and Ana... she couldn't look away from the hunger and determination in his eyes. From the need for her to say yes and become his as no other had become before.

"Let me take you into the next life and bring you back as my own. Match, Queen... *wife*... my Tower. Let me keep you."

Ana didn't respond. She was shaking with the thought of it.

Sam held her cheek in his hand.

"Take your time thinking about it," he told her softly. "Even if you never agree, I still wish for you to stand by my side as we take revenge and give this place back." He brought her knuckles to his lips, holding her gaze. "I love you, Ana. Let me give you the crown you deserve and the wings you didn't know you were destined for."

"Wings?" she repeated, unable to will the fantasy of such an honor from her mind.

Sam's lips twitched upward, delirious need swelling in his gaze. "*Wings*, my Temptress. Immortality. Vengeance. Your crown..."

"What's the downside?" she asked, almost smiling at him.

His arms settled around her waist, bringing her closer. "You would be stuck with me the rest of your life."

"I'd hardly call that a downside," she teased.

He nudged her nose with his before resting his forehead against hers. "Even if we had no one to fight, no kingdoms to overthrow, I would still want you as mine. We could sit on the ashes of this world as everyone tore each other apart, watch the chaos surround us, if only it meant I could have you at my side."

"We'll get rocking chairs and sit them on Firemoor's hill," she said.

"Watch the sun set over the world's remains," he added.

She held tight as he swayed with her slightly, and she grasped his shirt in her fists, chin jerking toward his. "The only ones left in existence."

Something shifted in his eyes then, and Sam's lips slammed to hers. Lightning snapped again as she threw her arms around his neck, drowning beneath his promises and desire. Beneath the fantasy of being wholly his and having all the things she'd planned for, but better.

She would be with him.

Sam pulled back and held her face in his hands. And for one brief moment...

Sunlight broke the clouds.

Ana let her head tilt back, basking in the warmth of it on her rain-covered cheeks, and she nearly started crying, but instead... a quiet laugh choked from her, and she opened her eyes to find Sam smiling in front of her. Golden light on his cheeks and glinting off the water droplets held hostage by his black hair.

Smiling.

She reached out to touch his face as she'd never seen it before. Beautiful and bright and so full of a barely recognizable haunting happiness that she had not seen on him since before the tattoo. On the days when he would smile at her while she prepared dinner, or he watched her laugh at whatever TV show they fell asleep to.

He swallowed as the clouds pushed back together. "Let's go home," he whispered. "I'd like my Queen cleaned up before the next idiot thinks he can try and take her from me," he added with a wink.

"Overprotective and capable of killing without moving a finger," she said as he took her hand. "The dream man."

He smirked at her over his shoulder. "Temptress... for you I would keep them at their edge until you told me they'd had enough."

She answered in a low groan and then pulled him back toward her, her mouth landing on his in a hungry kiss. Sam clenched her waist, dipping her slightly, and with a tug on her hair, he yanked her back. She moaned at the tingling sensation, of the push and pull, the bite on her lip, and the red glow in his eyes.

She could hardly wait to see him unleashed on her.

Chapter Fifty-Nine

Traffic was already beginning to back up.

Cars of humans fleeing to the boats awaiting them on the western shore, others packing bags to move into the underground bunkers they'd been building for years just in case this were to happen.

Sam had been preparing for this moment for centuries.

Anticipation was thick in the air. There was a rumble of predatory revenge rippled over the wind. Every demon. Every witch. They all answered the call of vengeance. No riots or fires. Everyone in Shadowmyer knew.

The world they would come back to would be free, and their king would make it so.

Rolfe and Millie made it back to the castle before Sam and Ana. Sam revved up to the front doors without bothering to cloak their ascent. The horned demon and deathhound were waiting on the pair at the front door. Sam cut the engine and pulled his helmet off.

"I see people are moving," Sam said to Millie.

"I called the local news places," Millie answered. "They've put out an emergency alert to all humans that invasion from Firemoor is imminent, and they should take shelter or get to the ships as soon as possible."

"And our army?"

Millie smiled coyly. "Helping people out of the city, then reporting for duty by the end of the week."

Sam nodded and looked at Rolfe. "We should clean a few more rooms," he said. "Find whatever supplies we have stashed in the underground cellars."

"You'll need more than weapons," Ana said as she came up behind him, her hand slipping into his. "Prei has caches of missiles all along the borders. The ones I sent to Ironmyer were barely a dent in his armory. But I can get us in."

Millie's lip quirked as she exchanged a proud glance with Sam, and then she held out her arm to Ana. "I'm so glad he decided not to kill you," she said. "You're going to make quite the asset. Come on," she said with a nod to the door. "I'm the best healer in this little menagerie. I'll get you cleaned up."

"Milliscent," Sam drawled in a warning tone.

But Millie just winked at him. "What's wrong? Is Daddy afraid I'll hurt my new Queen?" She laughed. "I'll be gentle."

"I certainly hope not," Ana chimed in.

Sam stared between them, unsure of if he was ready for these two to become the friends he knew they would more than likely be. Rolfe clapped him on the shoulder.

"We'll make dinner," he said with an upwards nod.

Rolfe attempted to speak with Sam as he put three whole chickens in the oven with lemon and rosemary, along with potatoes, stating that they deserved a hearty meal after the slaughter they'd just had. But Sam was so distracted that halfway through, he went to the bottom of the stairs and paced for the next hour.

"Fucking Death," Millie muttered when she finally sauntered down. "She's alive. She's home. What more do you want?"

"How is she?" he asked sharply.

Millie smiled softly. "Taking a nap," she said. "She passed out while I was stitching her. You forget mortals can grow so tired, Samarius." She reached the bottom of the steps then and gave his cheek a quick pat. "She's fine."

Though Sam wasn't keen on leaving her alone. Not after...

"Boss, no one is getting into the castle," Rolfe said from the edge of the hallway.

Sam's already tense body tightened more at the mention of it.

"Sam." Millie grabbed him by the shoulder, jerking him out of his protective daze. "She's okay," she assured him. "Come on. She won't wake up for at least an hour or so," she said, tugging his arm.

"She'll wake up somewhere she doesn't know," he argued. "I should wait on her."

"Sam, we have to talk business," Millie said, her voice growing snappy. "Rolfe—"

Rolfe stepped up and clapped a hand on Sam's shoulder. "I'll watch her, boss."

Mille wrapped her arm into Sam's. "Let's chat."

Despite the growing knot in Sam's stomach, he followed her back into the kitchen where she turned the kettle on. She didn't speak until she had a cup of green tea in front of him, as if she needed him to settle and be calm.

"I sent the video to my contacts in the Spine first," she said. "Then to the ones in Firemoor. They tell me Prei has been sitting in his makeshift office staring at the screen ever since." She turned to him, head tilting. "What did you mean?" she asked, and Sam finally looked up from his cup. "When you said 'to the worm who thinks he can take this world'? Who? Prei?"

Sam's fingers knotted around his cup, but he didn't answer.

"Sam?"

"I don't think he's who he says he is," Sam answered. "But until I know for sure, I don't want you worrying."

The answer didn't leave room for questioning, and Millie didn't push it.

For a while, he stirred his tea, replaying everything that had happened in the last few days, how tired he was. And with Ana upstairs, all he wanted was to go curl in that bed beside her. Hold her as he'd done so many times, and answer every question she had. Though, he knew he couldn't. He knew that would have to wait for another day.

Sam had to look twice down the hall as he saw movement in the corner of his eyes. Ana and Rolfe were coming down. Rolfe was smiling as he said something to her, and Ana eyed him sidelong.

Sam immediately pushed to his feet to meet them. He gave Rolfe a grateful nod, and Rolfe squeezed his shoulder as he walked on past into the kitchen where he pulled the food from the oven.

Ana's smile lifted into her tired eyes when she saw him coming toward her.

"Hey," she said, her voice soft.

Sam wrapped a hand around her cheek and took her fingers into his with the other. "Hey," he whispered.

It was the only word he could manage in that moment. After all that had happened in the last week… they could breathe and be themselves again. No secrets. No lies.

Sam swallowed as he stared in those bold green eyes and tucked one of her curls back. "Welcome home."

A jagged breath left her, the word catching her off guard, but she didn't let him go. The right corner of her lips lifted like she might smile, making Sam's heart skip, and he squeezed her fingers tighter.

"When I saw him dragging you, your neck bleeding, I went so cold," he said.

"It was the only way I knew to get your attention," she replied. "To bring myself near the brink of death so near, hoping I could reach you in my pleas."

Sam frowned. "I didn't hear you," he whispered, voice full of confusion. "I didn't... you asked for me?"

"I called you," she said. "I... I asked you to find me, and when I looked up, you were staring at me. I thought you heard me."

"Ana... I didn't," and the pain in his voice made her throat tighten. His hand swept across her cheek, holding tight. "Why can't I hear you?"

And she wasn't sure if she was supposed to know the answer.

Her stomach growled then, and all thought of the slight went amiss.

"Does home have any food?" she asked.

Sam's smile widened to his eyes and he leaned forward to kiss her forehead. "I have a deathhound," he replied. "The fridge is always stocked."

Rolfe gladly put out another plate, and Millie poured Ana a glass of wine. Sam let his gaze wander between the three, seeing how easy Ana spoke with Millie, with Rolfe, like she'd been part of it all for a long while.

"How many rooms are in this castle?" Ana asked as everyone settled into eating.

Sam slowly sat back in his chair, brows furrowed in thought as he chewed his chicken. "You know, I'm not sure," he admitted, and Ana started to chuckle.

"You don't know how many rooms are in here?"

Sam frowned in Rolfe's direction, who shrugged and merely took another bite of his food.

"Honestly, I've not used much more than the first two floors for a couple of centuries now. My office is at the top of the stairs here. I've no reason to go higher. We closed off some of the back ends, the chapel and the ballroom, a few years back." He adjusted himself, staring at the table. "Could be a legion of homeless in the high towers, I'd have no idea."

"Sam!" Ana laughed, her head throwing back. "How do you not

know?"

Sam shrugged. "Always trusted Roll to sniff it out if there were any intruders."

"Got it covered, boss," Rolfe said with his mouth full of sandwich.

"Yes, you're always patrolling between your seven meals a day," Millie said.

"Eight," Sam corrected. "You forgot the three AM snack," he added.

Millie and Rolfe began to argue across the table, but Sam turned all of his attention to Ana. He watched her smile at Millie, at Rolfe, and saw the softness in her eyes that he'd not seen in over a week. More relaxed, almost at home at his table and in his castle.

He caught her eye, his heart swelling at that moment. She was his. Everything was open between them, and they were in this together.

Ana's lip sucked behind her teeth, and Sam noted every rise and fall of her breasts, every swallow of her throat and sweep of her lashes as she watched him too. He wanted her alone, not just for... activities... but because he wanted to know how she was doing with all of this.

Sam's gaze flickered to Millie, who gave him a reassuring smile over her cup.

"Come on, Rolfie," Millie said, curling a hand on Rolfe's shoulder as she stood from the table. "Let's go play fetch in the gardens."

Rolfe's brows furrowed as he growled up at her. "I'm not done."

"We'll find a fresh rabbit for you to gnaw on," Millie said, her fingers digging into his collar even more. "Mommy and Daddy need some time alone," she drawled.

Sam and Ana didn't move as the two demons exited down the hall, Millie chasing after Rolfe and slapping his ass playfully, Rolfe growling but playing along. But even though Sam wanted to laugh and follow their antics, he couldn't take his eyes off Ana.

And once they were alone, Ana shifted slightly in her seat, elbows propping on the table. A beat of quiet silence rested around them, padding the chilly room as a rumble of thunder sounded in the far distance.

"Are you okay?" Sam asked her.

Ana took a long drink of the tea Millie had made her, and she seemed to contemplate the weighted question. "I'm not sure," she admitted. "This all feels... surreal."

Of course it did. Two days ago, she'd been sitting in his dungeon. Just hours earlier been tied to a tree. He looked up at the clock, barely 6pm.

And he hated himself for what he was about to ask her.

"Later tonight… I have something I need to ask you about," he said.

Ana's head tilted. "What's wrong?"

"The other night when I left you, I went to Firemoor to bring three demons home that had been publicly tortured in their capital," he said, watching the expression on her face. "I need to know if you recognize what was used since you spent some time in Icemyer."

Ana swallowed. "Was it green?"

Sam nodded.

"Take me to them," she said, standing.

Chapter Sixty

The pair didn't speak as he led her down the hall and into the room the demons were in. When they entered, Ana stilled at the threshold, though Sam went to the side of the first demon.

"Fucking Death," Ana whispered.

Trey was still barely conscious when they approached. The green ooze hadn't stopped its penetration, no matter how much the three had tried to get it out.

"How..." Ana was grim-faced as she reached for one.

"Do you know what it is?"

"Emerald death," she answered. "Or that's what they used to call it. Though I don't... I don't know how it is in this... paste."

"What is it exactly?"

"It's a crystal," she replied. "I don't know everything about it. I didn't even know it could be turned into... this..." She mushed some between her fingers, grimacing at the texture. "We used to burn it on solstice nights when the demons would get rowdy." She turned to him. "The witch in town, Cordelia. She can help you. She sold me the knife with it in the blade."

Sam gave her a nod before checking on the other two, making sure they were stable and seeing if he could get a little more out of the wounds of the last one. But when the demon began screaming in pain and his back arched off the table, Ana took Sam's hand.

"Let him rest," she said. "Call Cordelia."

Sam led her out of the room and into darkened, unfamiliar halls. He hadn't said much more. But the way he'd looked at his demons, the sorrow on his face and the pain in his eyes... She'd wanted to hold him and tell him they would get their revenge. That no one and nothing would touch any of the people he'd made promises to again. She would have meant it, too.

Seeing him raw and without any walls around him, had her falling for him all over again. She loved the man she'd come to know, but the ferocity he felt for his beings, for his realm, despite everything he'd been through and witnessed...

"Villainy is in the perspective," her father had told her when she'd *questioned their plans. "To the crown, you'll be their worst nightmare... to their servants, you'll be their salvation."*

She'd burned half of those servants alive, though she kept telling herself the new beginning they'd receive was better than continued starvation and slavery.

Looking at Sam, she realized he was the same. And that both of them would play their villainy cards. They would be the nightmares, the rage, the vengeance for as long as they needed to.

At the next hallway turn, lamps lit the walls, illuminating various paintings that stretched down the corridor. Ana's eyes adjusted to the light, and she felt Sam's grip on her hand loosen as she stepped forward to the first of the grand paintings.

A city on fire. The castle in the back, the people jumping from the walls. She'd stared at a similar painting nearly every afternoon for two years back in Ironmyer.

"I've seen this before," she said, her fingers tracing the edges of the lines. "I mean... something like it. It wasn't this exactly."

"In Ironmyer?" he asked.

Ana nodded and took a step back. "It was in the hall outside their Throne Room," she said. "Though I don't remember this—" She pointed to the dark shadowed area, of a man with great black wings standing atop a burning wall.

Sam stepped up beside her. "The Fall of Atrion," he said. "Ironmyer wouldn't have me in their painting. They've tried to pretend I don't exist. As though their previous king had never helped King Atrion punish me for speaking out against him."

Ana looked up at him. "Millie told me something."

"That doesn't surprise me," he muttered, his hair falling over his eyes. His gaze lifted to hers, a flash of the person she'd fallen in love with shining in that moment. The smile she'd missed.

"What did she say?"

"She said you were once enslaved by Atrion, when the Myers and Moors were unified."

Sam ran a hand through his hair and looked up at the painting again. "I was," he sighed. "The powers I possess… the things I can do…" Shadows curled around his fingers, the hallway darkening with a thunderous rumble. He stared at his hand as the umbra swirled and swirled as snakes slithering over his skin. "Men have always desired it," he continued.

He looked up at the painting, a haze casting over his features as the memory filled him. "I was once only a shadow," he said. "I existed between everything. Back when everyone worshipped the gods Firemoor continued to hang onto as a way to control the masses. I always heard the distresses of people. Always went to them to try and give them some sort of comfort in their grief. After a while, I began to help ease their pains. I comforted them in their final moments and helped them into the next life."

He paused, his eyes darkening as they moved to the next painting. One of his, she assumed, by the black canvas and white chalk line work—the abstract of men on their knees before a giant.

"I went to Atrion's wife, Queen Adaline, when she lost her first born. I was there to help her grief and take him. Though I only appeared in darkness, the king knew I was there. He blamed me for the death of his son and said I had taken him away."

Sam stopped at the next painting and stared at his hand again.

"He used witches to set a trap for me," he said solemnly. "I became ravenous with anger and betrayal. And from my cage, those witches gave me a body—a prison. Immortal still, but…" Sam opened and closed his fist, a twinge in his jaw, and she could see the rage in his eyes. "One witch thought if she gave me wings and a deadlier form to shift into that it would ease some of the pains of being trapped in this.

That I would still have the freedom of the wind and darkness, along with all the same powers I'd possessed."

Ana looked to the shadows of his wings against the firelight before them, seeing the missing feathers, the broken arch. She wanted to touch them, to reach out and feel the softness beneath her fingers. So much so that she lifted her hand into those shadows and let the cool umbra swarm her hand. A shudder ran over Sam's body at the simple touch, and he looked down at her like he might take her fingers into his.

"Can I see them?" she asked softly.

Sam shifted the weight in his shoulders, and she watched as he rolled his neck, the shadows swirling over his legs and up into his bones. His eyes fluttered once, and before he said another word, a black feather tickled her cheek.

She beheld them in the darkness, nearly weeping at the feeling around her. They blocked out the firelight as they rose higher, and though he made to extend one out, the tightness of the hall blocked him from doing so. And instead, he merely let it curl around her shoulder, a small smile lighting his eyes.

"They're not as grand as they once were," he said. "But they still make an entrance when I need them to."

"They're beautiful," she said as she stroked one of the feathers. A few were missing, showcasing bone beneath. She noted the burn marks on the membrane there, and she remembered Millie saying they'd once been burned.

"He tried to burn them," she said, eyes meeting his.

A tick rested in his jaw at the memory. "He tried to rip them out first," he told her. "And when that was too slow, he set fire beneath me."

"How did you escape?"

"I didn't," he said. "I burned and broke, my body healing over and over as fast as the flames licked my flesh. Seeing he couldn't kill me, Atrion grew bored. He ended my punishment and swore he'd do worse the next time I acted out." Sam shook his head. "Smug bastard," he grunted. "Hazel was the one that came to me that night to try and heal my wings, but... It wasn't long after that she was murdered."

Ana blinked. "How old was she?"

Sam stepped down the hall a few feet and stopped at a painting of a woman, old and fragile, with a dark hood over her head. She looked almost... comforting. Like she'd have made the best soup to mend any and all your ailments. A soft figure, and yet, she reminded Ana of one of the older witches she'd met in Icemyer. One that spoke few words but watched her relentlessly.

"Hazel was over two thousand years old when she died in my arms," he said softly. "After her High Priestess discovered what all she'd tried to do for me, and she tortured her in front of me until Atrion said enough, then he cut her heart out."

"Why did you go along with it for so long?" she asked. "With being Atrion's puppet when you could have gotten yourself out?"

Sam's head hung, those shadows trickling over his shoulders and fingers. "I was told if I helped, he would give me everything I wanted when the war was over. Territory to rule over. No more chains. No more cage." Sam sighed. "I realized one day that I would never be free unless I took it. Hazel found a way out of it for me."

A realization washed over her. How he'd begun making demons. The creature he had spoken about making her.

"She gave me a way to make my own immortal demons, an army of shifters and dangerous creatures capable of things the witches had only been rumored to have the power to do in the past, and then she wrote Death and the Corvids poem after the Myers and Moors split apart, in the midst of the war. The rest of her coven went ballistic when they found out," Sam continued. "After she was killed, the others began creating those texts against me. The same ones that they taught you in Icemyer. They started trying to find small ways to bind me."

Sam exhaled heavily as he turned toward her. "I once thought they were my enemies. I thought, after all these years, they still wanted to keep me contained in this realm, but I realize I could be wrong. I have been so wary of them these last centuries." He seemed to shake his head at his own prejudice, pain stretching across his eyes.

She felt for him. She felt how hard it must have been to need to trust a people who had done so much against him once. But these were different times.

"To win this, you'll need them," Ana said softly.

Sam faced her fully, and she turned her head to look at the sincere expression on his face. "I know," he said. "I need you, too. I need you to take Millie to Icemyer and speak with the covens that raised you."

The news settled in her. She hadn't expected this. To become his was one thing, but this... She realized that he trusted her. He was giving her power to help them take their revenge. To help his people and every person she'd done the things she did for.

His wings turned back shadows as she stepped closer to him, the darkness wreathing her body instead, and she sank into it.

"Do you ever miss it?" she chose to ask.

"Miss what?" he breathed.

"The pure shadow you once were," she replied.

Sam took her hand in his and brought it up, their elbows bending together as their splayed fingers met. "I did. For a long time," he answered. "I thought becoming only that again would settle the desire in my heart. That it would set me free from the thing I thought had broken me."

"And now?" She shifted slightly and met his eyes as their fingers entwined together.

His tongue darted out over his lips, head dipping closer. "Now, I can't imagine not being able to do this," he whispered, his lips brushing hers. "To kiss you and hold your beating heart against mine. To feel your skin—" his fingers trailed her bare arm to her collar, to her neck, and chills ran over her flesh. "—to be inside you and feel you surrender." He paused to tilt her head back, locking eyes.

"Would you love me if that's all I was?" he asked. "If I was nothing more than the darkened space around us and your last breath? If all you could see and feel of me was that whisper?"

His shadows moved around them, trickling up her skin. She sank into the feeling of its calm press comforting her.

"I have, and I would forevermore," she answered.

And she meant it.

She shifted on her feet, a smile growing on her lips as she moved her hands up his chest.

"Although… I am partial to this form…" she added suggestively, allowing her eyes to travel to his lips.

His hands tightened around her waist to the point of the most delicious pain, her flesh squeezing between his fingers. "Are you?" His lips lifted at the left corner, that beautiful smile she loved so much, licentious and poison all at once. "What do you like about this form?"

Her nail trailed over the bob of his throat, outlining his snake tattoo. It seemed to shiver at her touch, and Ana leaned in to lick the dip between his collarbones. "Everything."

He grasped the top of her ass and squeezed, causing a soft moan to leave her. She could feel when he curled a finger in her hair and tugged it slightly, his neck stretching longer.

"I think you might enjoy the umbra as well," he said, his voice a caress over her flesh. "Perhaps even the wings wrapped around you, tickling your skin."

Her knees went soft at the mention. At the recollection of how he'd looked on that battlefield. Broken wings. Talons on his fingertips. The scarlet eyes and the shadows all around him.

She wanted all of that. Unleashed and ravenous upon her. As Death and Samarius all at once. She wanted to fall into that place and drown beneath the shadows that clung so tightly to him. Feel everything and nothing and the final edge.

His soft smile widened, apparently having felt her shift in his arms, perhaps seen the dilation in her eyes at the mention. "Tell me what you want... *Deianira*," he whispered against her lips.

The softness of her name had her knees in a puddle, her core nearly throbbing.

"Death," she hissed.

A bolt of lightning struck outside the moment his lips crashed into hers. She wasn't expecting it. Wasn't expecting the hunger, the rage, and all the desire in between. Ana pushed, writhing in his grasp to fight, yet she found herself flush against him, her thigh hiked high around his waist, the dig of his nails in her flesh. But Ana finally pulled back, causing Sam's lips to latch to her throat, to her collar, down between her breasts. Her back arched as she let him in.

Grasping his hair at the base of his neck, she tugged him off, back up to her face, where his predatory eyes tore into her. Heavy breaths staggered between them. He leaned in, then tried to pull her back into him.

She dodged his kiss, the tip of her tongue licking his, her entire body lighting on fire at his touch, at his tease. His fingers tightened in her hair and yanked her head back, exposing her neck, making her smile wide-mouthed and chuckling. Sam towered over her, and just when she thought he might launch her into the next life, he spat in her mouth and pushed her away.

Ana staggered, her breaths fluttering as she caught her balance. But Sam just pushed his hands into his pockets and looked at her through his dark hair. That dominant aura crept into her and ran over every inch of her exposed body, down into the marrow of her bones and the rush of her blood.

He consumed the air, the light, the space.

"Run... *my Queen*," came his rasp.

Her heart skipped. She took two steps back down the unfamiliar corridor, and suddenly the darkness swept in on her. Shadows on her every side, sliding up her legs, whispering between her thighs, teasing her curls.

Ana took one more look at him, watched his eyes turn scarlet—

She bolted down the hallway.

Chapter Sixty-One

Ana running down his hall with no knowledge of where to go or what might be at her next turn made his muscles coil in desire. He contemplated how far to let his love go. If he should follow her with shadows and push her where he wanted.

Perhaps to the front of the castle.

Shadows swarmed after her, but Sam didn't move. He could feel where she was. Every turn she made. Feel her fleeing pulse hovering in the air like a beacon to his greed. He felt her dip into one of the great rooms, the door clicking behind her, and Sam finally moved off his spot.

As much as he wanted to scare her, to tease her slow with each click of his boots, he also wanted to hold her more. So, fleetingly, he played.

He knew Ana had hidden in the ballroom, could feel her beckoning him. He rattled the handle a couple of times, and then he opened the door.

Ana had a piece of glass in her palm, fisting it so tightly that it cut her skin. He could smell it, see it from the mirror on the other side of the room. Shadows curled around the floor, twisting and mending over the hardwood, seeping into the cracks. They trickled around Ana, toying with her hair and grazing between her thighs.

Sam whipped the door back, and Ana rose to her feet to strike.

The glass shard slammed high into his chest, nearly hitting his collar, and Sam laughed at the pain. His head threw back, delirious with delight at her play as the blood trickled down his skin.

"Wicked girl..." He leaned forward, his teeth baring with a snarl. "Do it again," he hissed.

Ana grasped him around the neck and brought his lips to hers. It was short-lived, and she shoved him after a moment, her nail scratching his skin, but he held on. Their tongues lashed every time they kissed—between every slap and scratch and shove. The piece of glass she'd had in her hand fell to the ground, and the blood from the open gash on her palm wet his cheek and his throat. The smell of it made him wild. The iron and the sour, mixing with her sweat and the sage and spiced vanilla from the shampoo she'd used upstairs.

He was yanking her hair back when he moved to kiss her throat, but she wasn't having the foreplay. She was unbuckling his pants and tripping on her own. He reached for the hem of her shirt and pulled, sending the stitching in shatters. One stroke of her hand, and he groaned into her mouth. Both his hands wrapped her cheeks as his lips never left hers.

They slammed into the wall, her wrists pinned beneath his tightened hand above her head, paintings knocking dust into the air around them. Her knee wrapped around his waist, and she arched into his chest. He bit her throat, tasted her blood where he'd scratched her, and she wriggled free from his hands enough to push her hands in his hair and claw his scalp. The pain tingled his body and melted a shiver down his spine.

He wanted her claw marks all over his flesh, embedded in the tattoo designs and claiming him as hers.

Because he was. Mind, body, and complete existence.

With the taste of her on his lips, he kissed her again and grasped her breasts, making her breath hitch and her moan into his mouth. He needed to be inside her. He wanted to feel her convulse around him as he fucked her until she couldn't walk. His shadow stirred, the tattered wings flickering, and he felt her shift.

She pulled back, scarlet lashed across her cheeks and her beautiful lips. Not even the last sunrise he'd seen was as beautiful as she was then. Disheveled, angry, and lustful, her bright eyes boring through him. She held his face in her hands, and every fiber of his body and shadow came alive when she whispered,

"Show me death, Samarius… *Keep me.*"

Chapter Sixty-Two

I hate you.

I hate you.

I love you.

"What?" he asked breathlessly.

"Keep me," she repeated. "Show me the edge of my existence and *keep* me."

"Ana…" he whispered. "Are you sure…"

"I am begging for *you*. As I have always done." Her bloodied hands stroked his lips. "Take me, Samarius. I want everything you want. I want revenge and love and power and a real home to fight for. And I want *you*… more than anything else. So keep me. Make me yours. *Completely*."

Her answer came in the form of an all-consuming kiss. His teeth raked her tongue as he yanked at the roots of her hair, feeding her body in desire and surrender all at once. He grabbed her by the waist and hauled her up onto his shoulder, her ass broadcasting to the shadows all around, and he carried her down the halls and into the sunroom.

Her ass hit the table, and she leaned forward to kiss him, her thighs tightening around his waist. Sam groaned like he might give in, like he might fuck her before taking her life, but in the next moment, the shadows tightened around her wrists, and Ana was forced into the center of the table, her arms and legs spread into an X on the surface.

She thought she might be bound there while he did his work, but he loosened the grip on her wrists as he climbed onto the table behind her, and held her back against his chest like he was cradling her into the next life.

"Last chance, Deianira," he said as the shadows tightened around her wrists.

Her chest rose and fell with a shaking breath, and she felt her eyes flutter at the tickle of his hair on her temple, the whisper of his words on her cheek…

"Bind me, Samarius," she whispered, and his shadows shivered. She turned so she could see his face, and her head tilted back to look into his eyes. "Bind me," she repeated, a plea in her voice. "Break me. *Bleed* me…"

A rattle shook him, as if those words had summoned a power of Death he'd been hiding. His throat bobbed, and she saw the scarlet seeping into his brown pupils that, for a moment, made her reconsider.

But she wanted this. She wanted him. She wanted to be *his*. And this meant she could have him forever.

"If I do this…" he began, "You will be bound to me in a way unlike the others. What you will become… You will be completely and utterly mine. Are you ready for that?"

"Bind me, Samarius," she whispered. "I am yours already."

Sam's eyes darted over her face again, and then he kissed her cheek, her forehead, and her lips. She noted a glint of silver as it ricocheted over a knife now in his hand, and when he looked at her again, the shadows of his grand broken wings curled around them, and he held up the glowing dagger.

"You know what I have to do," he whispered.

Ana swallowed, her heart picking up its pace. "I do," she managed.

Sam smiled against her cheek, his fingers curling around her throat. "I love when your heart flutters like that," he whispered. "Does this scare you, baby?"

"No," she breathed.

His smirk widened, the tip of his knife pressing into the pillow of her breast. "Liar," he accused. A single trickle of blood dripped down her skin, and his nose nuzzled into her hair as he whispered, "Be a good girl and scream for me, Deianira," and his voice was a chill on her flesh. "*Truly* scream," he rasped. "Let me feel your fear as you grow cold."

His lips pressed hard to her cheek, and before she could utter another word—take another breath—the knife ripped across her flesh.

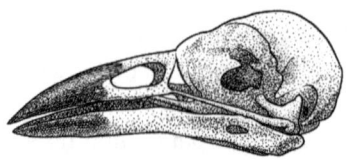

Ana choked. She flinched. She shuddered.

Sam cradled her body into his as her blood spilled over them, casting her body in a sheen of scarlet that glowed black in the moonlight pouring in through the window. Hand pressing to her cheek, he watched her eyes darken and plead for him. He could feel her mortal tether in his fingers, and one tug would have ended it, but he let her fall to that edge. Choking on her blood and shaking in his arms, her hands grasping his forearm as he rocked her and hummed that lullaby she'd sang when she'd helped him in that very room a few days before. He let her savor those final seconds, the final moment of her mortal life.

She stared at him with those pleading green eyes, a tear running down her cheek, and he wiped it away.

"I've got you, baby," he promised. His lips pressed to her forehead, and he cradled her cheek after. "To the things I am doing to keep you," he whispered upon feeling the chill of her last breaths run over his skin. "And to all the things you will become."

As the last of her breaths left her body, he began speaking the words he'd memorized so many years before.

"You'll use this when she finds you," Hazel told him as she ripped the page from her textbook and handed it to him.

Sam frowned at the witch, at the ritual on the parchment. "When who finds me?"

"The Ballad." Hazel reached up and cupped his cheek, her withering eyes once so bright, now stained with the age finally catching up with her. "I do not have much longer in this life. This binding spell... the one you use it on will become tethered to your immortal life. She will be yours, unconditionally. Do not use this lightly, Samarius. You must choose the one whom you cannot live without. She will be the one that makes this all worth it."

Sam looked down at the body he'd been imprisoned in, at the shadows that snaked between his fingers when he called upon them. "Even this prison?" he asked softly.

Hazel smiled. "It won't be a prison with her."

As his shadows consumed her existence, he watched her disappear from his arms.

And he waited.

He waited as the sky splintered in flashes of violent crimson light. He waited as the ground trembled outside and broke. He waited, leaned against the table, covered in her blood. Waited, and waited, and waited...

Thunder quaked the castle a few moments later. Sam sat up at the flicker of amber light before him. A tether appeared in midair. Bright as gold. The sun on a string. He reached up and wrapped the thread between his fingers, feeling a tug in his own abdomen, and he knew what it was.

It was the binding to Ana's new existence—

Her *immortal* one.

The creature that would haunt dreams with him and stalk the darkness...

And when she finally emerged, he swore his darkest desires had been answered.

Chapter Sixty-Three

She appeared in the wake of a dying shadow.

Bearing a wilting rose tattoo beneath her chin and his charcoal vine mark on her throat. Wearing nothing more than a blanket of blood across her bronze skin. A fog-like swirl settled in the bottom of her eyes, and her pupils flashed a deep shade of emerald as she came to.

And her wings... He had to stop himself from falling to his knees.

The sight of them spreading wide and mingling with the fog stroked his skin as a seducing whisper. Lightning seemed to linger in admiration of them appearing in her shadow. Full black feathers, not broken and tattered as his were. These were new. Encompassing. A look of evil and macabre that made his need for her nearly unbearable.

Her eyes cleared of the scarlet, and he recognized her coming back to him in the gaze she met him with. Scared, but powerful. Feeling an unfamiliar ache in her chest that he knew had her itching to spread those new wings and take flight.

She was an extension of him... Not merely another of his demons. Her existence was his. And together, they would rule the dominion of life itself. Power he'd never known before was at his fingertips.

She had brought him the other kingdoms through her own blood.

They would take the world with his.

Sam tugged on her tether as he pushed off the table, and as if he had awakened something in her, her eyes widened, and a shiver ran over her wings, making the tips flicker up towards the sky. His lips rose just so at the right corner as he stalked the space between them. Tension rising with every step. When he reached her, he wrapped that tether around his finger, tugging forward and letting the gold strand become visible around her throat, the tattoo under her chin now a glowing amber.

"How do you feel?" he asked, pride rising in his chest.

Ana lifted her hand to the moonlight, and as she stretched her fingers, a long talon grew from one of her nails. Her dilated gaze moved to his, and he saw the power and confidence shiver over her body.

"Like a goddess," she answered.

His lips met hers in a hungry kiss, one that surrendered his being and awoke his heart. This was a true force. Entwining through them and seeping into every crevice of their now immortal existences. His hand wrapped into the roots of her hair, and he tugged her head back to expose the dying rose mark on her skin. The sight of it and her deliriously smiling face made him insatiable for her.

"Mine," he growled, that restriction in his throat hanging in the balance of the room.

She reached up and wrapped a bloodied hand around his cheek, long nail scratching into his skin. "Yours," she promised.

He kissed her hard again, biting her lip and wrapping an arm around her waist, feeling the feathers of her soft wings brush his fingers. She was everything he had ever wanted. All-consuming and hungry, they had fallen for one another in the shadows of their own true selves.

When they parted, lightning cracked again, and with a kiss to her palm, Sam dropped to one knee. "Marry me," he asked of her.

Her chest visibly rose with a heavy breath. "What?"

"Tomorrow," he said, squeezing her hands. "In front of the entire kingdom. Become my Queen and my wife as you were always meant to be."

"I believe becoming your demon surpasses being your wife," she said.

Sam rose back to his feet. "You're not my demon," he countered, and she looked confused, so he went on. "You are my Ana. My *Deianira*. My siren. Temptress—"

A smile quirked on her lips at the words. "Witch..." she said, apparently recalling the names he had once called her.

He leaned down, lips pressing to her jaw. "My goddess of chaos and destruction..." His forehead pressed against hers as he whispered, "My *Tower*," in a rasping breath. "You are not another of my demons. You will not be bound and imprisoned in a singular realm to hover over like some reaper waiting for blood. You will have *every* realm.

Every being's existence. You, wicked girl, are Death's final lullaby."

Visible goosebumps rose on her flesh. "The song of monsters," she cooed, chin lifting.

"The *Ballad* of nightmares," he swore, and her lips lifted at the salutation.

He settled his fleeing heart and paused a moment to step back and admire her again. Imagining how she would wear the name as a cherished scar and honored medal. Imagining how soldiers and generals would fall to their knees in fear of her.

His temptress in a lightning strike. The thorned vine squeezing his bleeding heart.

He took her hands in his again and let his pride for her rock to his core. "I love you, Deianira. Will you be my wife?"

And he would have begged her for the chance to call her such.

A final promise that she was his.

"I love you," she said, voice barely above a whisper.

He nearly fell back to his knees upon hearing it.

"When they hear of our marriage and my being crowned Queen, especially after the slaying today, you know they will come. With more fire than they had originally planned to. Are you prepared for that?" she asked.

His maniacal laughter filled the room. His head threw back with it, eyes fluttering in a manner usually reserved for his release. It was a laugh that shook with thunder and made every raven and crow outside flutter into the sky.

And with it, came the howls of a deathhound. The caws of the crows. The roars of demons, shifters, and reapers alike. A chorus outside of an army rallying for the revenge they'd been promised centuries earlier, and for the king and queen that would lead them to it.

"Oh, my Temptress..." His deviously delighted grin lit up to his dark eyes—

He hauled her flush in a split, and suddenly the grin was gone. Replaced with a danger that rolled his shoulders high and masked his pupils in scarlet. His shadowed wings flickered in the flash of the lightning strike from the arched windows, her own wings rising with his...

And he said in a staggering voice—one that vibrated the depths of the earth and trembled the air into a vigorous quake, resonating as a warning to any who might dare to try and take his home, his crown, or, most especially, his Queen.

"Let them come."

THANK YOU
for reading

Ballad of Nightmares,
First book in the Nightmares Duology

If you enjoyed this story, please consider leaving a review on Amazon, social media sites, or your preferred review site. Reviews really mean a lot (even if it us just a couple lines) and help us as authors get our stories out there.

Acknowledgments

I never know just where to start with my acknowledgments. This time, I think I'll start with why this story meant so much to me.

I found Sam and Ana about a month after I lost my father. Their story was born out of a dark place that I fell into this last year trying to cope with his sickness and eventual death. Some of Ana's darkest places came from my own. I didn't expect to fall as in love with these two as I did, but now they are a part of me forever. Sam helped me look at death in a different way, from the perspective of death, and it helped to keep me floating above water. While writing Flames of Promise may have prepared me somewhat for the hurt I would feel, Ballad continues to help me get through it, even on my worst days.

Anyway. To my huge thank you's because I could not do this without any of you.

To my Street Team, my Nightmare of Ravens. You all are the most amazing people. I love being able to pop into our chat and discuss any and everything with all of you. Through this, I have made some lifelong friends, and you all have become family. Thank you all for being there and continuously hyping me up as well as each other. You are all so supportive. I love all of you!

To Kay, thank you for always keeping me on track and reminding me of all the things you know I will forget. I am so excited to crash—I mean go to Apollycon with you!

To Leighann, you have always been there, and I truly could not have dedicated this book to anyone but you. You read these darkest parts and let me know those stories needed to be told, no matter how scared I was that it might have been too raw. Thank you for being there and really helping me this year, always answering my questions, and more.

To Angie, thank you for dealing with my chaotic brain through this one when I was questioning EVERYTHING! You have truly been so inspiring working so hard when I pop in to your DMs asking if you can read something. Thank you for helping me take this book to where it needed to be! I hope I get to see you in a few weeks!

To Lex, thank you for pausing to read anytime I surprise you with a draft! Thank you for always inspiring me. I can't wait to see your career skyrocket and all your ideas come to life! You are going to kill it.

To Emily, thank you for taking what was basically a Pinterest board and my chaotic rambles and turning those vague words into the absolutely stunning cover on this book! It really encompasses everything about the book, and I am in awe every time I see it. You are amazing!

To my amazing family, I love y'all. Thank you for always being there no matter what. For always supporting, reading, and pushing me forward and giving me strength to continue moving through it. I can't wait to be closer so I can see you more.

To Zach,, you have never doubted my choice in making writing a career, and have supported it every day since I made it real. Thank you for always making me laugh and keeping me sane during my breakdowns. I am really looking forward to this new chapter for us, with moving and having our son in the fall. I know you're going to be the best dad, and I can't wait to see it.

Lastly, to all of you. To all the people reading ARCs right now. To everyone reading after its release. To anyone leaving reviews and telling your friends to go check out this book. To all the amazing content creators taking time out to read and make videos/posts about my books. You all are the real rockstars. Without you, I would not be able to make my dream of writing a career.

So, thank you all. Truly. For all the support and love you've given me to help me through these hard times. I appreciate all of you so, so much. There isn't enough words to say exactly how much I appreciate everything you do.

I'll see you all in a month with the next one.

Other Works by Jack Whitney

Now Available:

Dead Moons Rising
Book One in the Honest Scrolls Series

Flames of Promise
Book Two in the Honest Scrolls Series

The Gathering
An Honest Scrolls Novella

Sweet Girl
A Cupid Novella

Ballad of Nightmares
Book One in the Nightmares Duology

Coming Soon in 2022:

Anyone And You
An autumn erotica novella
August 30th, 2022

Title T.B.D.
A Halloween Novella
October 11th, 2022

Title T.B.D.
A Jack Frost Novella
December 6th, 2022

About the Author

Jack Whitney is an adult dark fantasy and romance author out of North Carolina, US.
You can usually find her playing in dark and strange worlds.
Her characters are always in charge.
She is fueled by coffee, whiskey, and shadow daydreams.
If you're reading her books, they probably came with a warning label.

Welcome to the Nightmare of Ravens.

Jack also feels very weird about writing bios because she's not sure what you want to know.
She is almost always stalking social media and procrastinating, so if you would like to find her to ask more questions, please feel free.

@Jack.Whitney.Writer